ON DANGEROUS GROUND

It's devastating enough when Pru's husband confesses to a long-term affair over what should have been a romantic dinner to celebrate their twentieth wedding anniversary. The, when her daughter, Molly, announces she's leaving for Vietnam on a Gap Year project, Pru knows her comfortable family life is over for good.

Just as she's picking up the pieces, an email brings news that Molly has become involved with a group of political activists and could be in serious danger. Pru embarks on a desperate search for her recalcitrant daughter. Totally out of her depth, she meets Ben, a veteran of the US war. He's intelligent, handsome, but damaged, and still haunted by the atrocities of that conflict. Together they tackle corrupt police, greedy property dealers and a ruthless local party cadre; and when eventually Pru finds her daughter, she also discovers an inner strength she never knew she had.

ON DANGEROUS GROUND

Sue Cook

WINDSOR
PARAGON

First published 2006
by
Headline Review
This Large Print edition published 2007
by
BBC Audiobooks Ltd by arrangement with
Headline Book Publishing

Hardcover ISBN: 978 1 405 61553 2
Softcover   ISBN: 978 1 405 61554 9

British Library Cataloguing in Publication Data available

Printed and bound in Great Britain by
Antony Rowe Ltd., Chippenham, Wiltshire

For my parents, Bill and Kay

I owe my very grateful thanks to:

Peter Rimmer for his contacts, introductions, feedback and inside information. Billy Kelly for his friendship and his insight into the character of Ben Coder and for introducing me to Phuong, Co Thanh, and Nga. Chuck Searcy, of the Vietnam Veterans Memorial Fund, Michael Liscio and Dennis Koselke for telling me some of their life history. Marty Bullard for his guided tours and insight into Vietnamese village life. Than and Kien for their tour of Hanoi. Father Chau Bui Van at the Sao Mai orphanage. Thanh and Cuong Dang. Stuart Craig and his wife Hoa for their help and wonderful hospitality in Hanoi. Anna Craven for the same in Ho Chi Minh City. Mr Tinh the driver. Liza Donoghue for accompanying me on my first trip to Vietnam in 1997 and for her encouragement and inspiration. For the germ of the original idea, Annie Flower. Dottie Flower and Kathy Panama for letting me borrow some of their own experiences in Vietnam. Wendy Oberman, Jenny Sharman, Brenda Mansour, Annabelle Lloyd, Chris Green. Binh at Thanh Binh restaurant in Chalk Farm, London.

For their expertise, thanks to:

Dr Duncan Dymond, consultant cardiologist at St Bartholomew's hospital, London. Pete Flynn for his invaluable contribution to the helicopter rescue described in Chapter 19.

Finally, thanks to so many friends whose encouragement and support has sustained me— they know who they are! To Charlie and Megan for putting up with Mum spending rather too much time locked in her study with her supply of 'writer's chocolate'. And last, but not in any way least, to my one-man support network, without whom this book would still be only half finished, my husband, Ian Sharp.

Chapter One

'Damn. Wrong knife.'

Pru had spread marmalade on David's toast with the knife she'd used to dole out the dog's Meaty Chunks a few moments before.

Well, what the eye doesn't see . . . she thought. It won't kill him.

'I don't believe it!' exploded David from the breakfast table. Pru looked round guiltily. So he'd seen her. But he was engrossed in the paper, nose six inches from the pages, too lazy to find his glasses.

He glanced up at her.

'Henman—he had it in the bag. Four-one up in the last set, and he just pisses it away. Can you believe that?'

Pru didn't seem required to comment. She placed his dogfood-impregnated toast and marmalade in front of him. Molly came thumping down the stairs.

'Somebody's taken my history folder. They must have done. It was here. On this table. Last night. Mum, where have you put it?'

She flounced about looking noisily under papers and opening and shutting cupboards and drawers.

'Bloody hell,' muttered David at the newspaper.

'Have you looked in the bathroom?' suggested Pru good-humouredly. 'I thought you took it with you when you went up to bed.'

'What would my history folder be doing in the bathroom? Mum, you're so sad.'

John Humphrys was continuing an argument of

1

his own with some politician on the *Today* programme.

'Just let him speak a moment, can't you?' Pru frowned at the radio on the windowsill. Still reading the paper, David's fingers groped across the table, found the plate of toast and shoved most of one piece into his mouth in one go.

She's right. You are *sad. Waiting on everyone hand and foot, Getting blamed for everything. Your trouble is, you have no charisma. No one takes the slightest bit of notice of you.*

Pru was used to the Voice and its constant criticism. It had been with her as long as she could remember. Sometimes, when things were going reasonably well, she was hardly aware of it at all. But the minute she was down and low on self-esteem, there it would be, putting the boot in. A psychiatrist would probably say it had taken the place of her mother.

She had never done anything quite well enough for her mother's liking. Other people had always done better. But then her mother's abiding aim had been to protect her from the world's most cardinal sin—Big-Headedness. Heaven forbid.

Mummy was ninety-three now; too old and powerless in her Sussex old people's home to protect her from anything. But the Voice was just as effective as her mother had been. And it was well on form this morning.

You let yourself be used. The best mission you can find for yourself is cleaning and washing and making meals for David and Molly—and Jack when he's home from university. And they don't appreciate you for it anyway. You like to think you've got a brain, but do you use it? Did you take in that last news

2

item? No, you didn't, did you? That discussion on the Euro was important. You don't concentrate on anything. And you're getting worse as you get older. You might as well not have bothered getting that university degree. Look at the job you've ended up with. Copy editing! Sad is the word.

'Oh, bugger off, can't you?' muttered Pru.

'Jesus,' grumbled David, looking at his watch.

'It *is* in the bathroom!' shouted Molly down the stairs. 'It can only have been you that put it there, Mum. I'm really late now.'

Molly grabbed her long brown hair, twisted it expertly at the nape of her neck and snapped on a clip. Pru found herself gazing at the curve of her daughter's smooth young face and neck with a mixture of envy and maternal pride.

'What time will you be home?' she called, following Molly into the hall.

'Oh, usual time. About five o'clock. Oh, I nearly forgot. I've got something for you to look at. Today preferably.' Molly fished some dog-eared papers out of her schoolbag and tossed them on to the hall table. 'It's my application to do six months in Vietnam teaching English.'

'Vietnam?' Pru felt a jolt in the pit of her stomach.

'Yes, Vietnam,' said Molly with sarcastic patience. 'You do know I'm doing a gap year before university.'

'Moll, you are not going to bloody Vietnam!'

'Don't be ridiculous, Mum. This project's really good. Read those papers. There's a website as well.'

'Why do you have to choose a third-world country? Why can't you find a placement

3

somewhere like Greece or Spain? Or Italy? You know a bit of Italian from all our holidays in Tuscany. Florence, for example. All that architecture and culture . . .'

'Mum, I want to go Vietnam *because* it's a third-world country. You only want me to go somewhere safe and boring because it's easier for *you*.'

'What about your heart problem? You might get some tropical illness and then what?'

'I won't get ill. I'll have all the vaccinations and I'll look after myself.'

'And it's very hot and humid there . . .'

'You didn't stop Jack going to Costa Rica, did you?'

'Yes, I know, but that was different.'

'Why? Because he's a boy!'

'Because there weren't any health worries.'

'Look, we'll have to talk about it later. I'm really late now.'

'Too right we'll talk about it later!' shouted Pru as the front door slammed over her words.

David was coming towards her on his way to the coat rack. She looked at him appealingly.

'Did you know about this?'

'First I've heard of it. Sounds like a good idea to me, though. Character-building. Give her a broader perspective on life.'

'But you know how risky it could be with her heart if she picked up an infection of some sort over there. There are so many safer places she could go, closer to home.'

'Well, she's eighteen, darling. She's got to start leading her own life sometime. And she can have her annual check up before she goes. Ring Dr Jewell and see what he says.' David unhooked his coat and headed towards the front door.

Out of habit she clenched her buttocks, ready for the inevitable passing pat. It was particularly irritating when she wasn't braced for it because her bottom would wobble, emphasising one of her body's growing number of little betrayals now that she'd passed forty.

She used to say, 'Please don't do that,' but he continued to do it, so she'd given up protesting. And anyway, there was little else by way of physical contact between them lately. When had they last made love? She couldn't remember.

'By the way,' he assumed a hard-done-by expression, 'don't bother about supper for me tonight. I'll be late again. There's a lot on at work at the moment. One client has just brought his deadline forward two weeks and another keeps coming up with one complaint after another. I don't know what time I'll be able to get away.'

He sighed theatrically, picked up his briefcase, opened the front door and hunched his shoulders against the rigours of the day ahead.

'As long as you don't have to work this weekend.' She brushed ineffectually at some dog hairs clinging to the back of his jacket. 'We've got a date, remember?'

'Of course. Yes. As if I'd forget our twentieth anniversary,' said David, stepping back into the hall to give her a perfunctory peck on the forehead. Lucky she'd reminded him. He made a mental note to remember to book a table at II Sorriso. Normally Lucy took care of things like that, being his secretary. She wouldn't take kindly, though, to booking an expensive restaurant for him and Pru to celebrate twenty years of wedded bliss. Lucy was beginning to get difficult lately. He sighed again.

' 'Bye. See you later.'

Pru watched him trudge down the path. She noticed his right shoe was badly worn down at the heel. Accelerator foot.

You should get him to buy some new shoes.

For once, Pru hardly listened to the Voice. She was still reeling from Molly's announcement. She picked up the sheaf of papers and brochures and took them back to the kitchen. She couldn't face reading them yet. Anyway, the gap year expedition was still several months away. There were plenty of other projects around the world to take Molly's fancy. She was more than likely to change her mind.

*   *   *

The dog lifted his ears as Pru walked back from the hallway and looked at his mistress devotedly. She ruffled his frizzy head.

'Where's the fun gone, Freddy?' The spaniel aimed a lick at Pru's nose. She felt empty suddenly. Purposeless. A sense of running out of road. Perhaps the Voice was right. She should have done her education more justice. Pru found herself wondering if she'd somehow lived the wrong life. She hadn't been the most dedicated of students; she'd been far too busy having a good time. But she had got a decent degree in French and fairly soon settled into a promising career as a translator when she left university.

She'd been with David for two years by then and he'd pestered her relentlessly to get married. He

6

was good company; intelligent, left-wing, funny, good-looking, and he loved her. What more could a girl want? True, the stomach-churning, heart-skipping excitement had subsided a little, but after two years together that was surely par for the course. Why not get married?

Her mother still pursed her lips and took every possible opportunity to make barbed remarks about them 'living in sin'. David was never allowed to share Pru's bedroom back at home, even though they were both well into their twenties by then. Mum always insisted he slept on the old camp bed in the sitting room.

'While you're under my roof, you'll go by my rules and do the proper thing,' she had always said. And of course Pru's father went along with what Mum wanted. He hated conflict. Marriage seemed the logical next step.

So there was the white wedding with relatives in attendance, the idyllic honeymoon in Corfu, their first little terraced house in Wandsworth, and then the two children, nicely spaced, two and a half years apart, one of each.

Holding her first baby in her arms, just minutes after his birth, Pru experienced the euphoric shock of knowing real, unconditional love for the first time in her life. Pru the career woman simply evaporated like smoke.

Family clinics and mother's helps, food processors and school runs had taken over. Occasionally, she would gaze out of the window at the orderly little street they lived in and wonder what had happened to the Pru she used to be. The stubborn, rebellious teenager, the outspoken vice-president of the Students' Union; the singer in a rock band, campaigner for civil liberties and marcher against nuclear arms.

I have measured out my life with Calpol spoons, she'd think to herself.

But she didn't regret a moment of it. Bringing up Jack and Molly had been the most fulfilling experience of her life. Ordinary as it sounded, that had been the simple truth of it.

Now her job as a parent was nearly over. She was about to be made redundant. She'd always known, intellectually, that this moment would come; but it still hurt like hell, now that it had. Fred gazed into Pru's face and twitched his ears understandingly. Freddy could always make her smile.

She fetched him a bone-shaped biscuit from a jar in the kitchen. Jack had been six and Molly just four years old when they'd got him from the breeder. He and the children had grown up together. Now aged fourteen, his muzzle had gone grey and the arthritis in his hips made getting about a slow and painful business. More than anything these days, he liked to lie on the sofa, his chin resting on his favourite cushion, watching everything going on around him. His feathery tail would flap with pleasure whenever he was addressed directly.

He hadn't gone out into the garden yet for his morning ablutions and ritual spat with next door's cat.

'Walkies?' said Pru.

His eyes still fixed on hers, Fred twitched his long, orange ears and sighed.

'OK. Maybe later then.'

Pru ruffled the furry head once more and got up

to begin the business of clearing the breakfast detritus.

I'd respect you more if you really got off on doing housework. Here we go. The Voice was back. *But you can't stand it. What a mug! You spend half your life doing things you hate.*

For God's sake, lighten up, will you?

On the radio the talk had turned to the weather. An environmental campaigner was drawing attention to unprecedented global weather changes that had been manifesting themselves over the past five years.

'There's been a heatwave in Moscow, the worst floods in living memory in Brisbane, a spate of hurricanes across the United States, thousands killed in an earthquake in Turkey . . . We've even had a tornado in Birmingham.'

Pru folded down the tops of the cereal packets, put milk and fruit-juice cartons back in the fridge and loaded crockery and cutlery into the dishwasher.

'The implications are frankly frightening,' the lobbyist continued. 'But it's never discussed. Did you know that the forecasters at the Met Office have to sign the Official Secrets Act? Makes you wonder, doesn't it?'

You're way behind with editing that book, interrupted the Voice again. *And,* getting into its stride, *there's a whole load of shopping to do before you get stuck in front of that computer—not to mention all that washing.*

Oh, sod the shopping and the washing, thought Pru.

Three years ago, with Molly and Jack well into their teens, she'd started doing some freelance

9

editorial work for a publishing firm David had put her in touch with. It specialised in books on sport. Not a subject Pru knew much about. And she had fallen well behind with her current project: a book on the history of golf.

She walked into the front room which she still referred to as her 'office' though for several years now it had been open to everyone in the family as it housed the computer. First Jack and then Molly used it for their school projects and brought their friends in to play games and find dodgy-sounding forums on the internet. Even David sat hunched over it some evenings 'looking things up on the Web'. Pru had to make sure she kept her notes and papers out of the way or she'd find them with web addresses and phone numbers scrawled all over them.

She switched the machine on and opened the chapter she'd been working on in *Golfing Through The Ages*:

The number of holes on a golf course varied right up until the year 1842. The first courses are thought only to have had four or five holes. The size of the available plot of land was the crucial factor...

The man in the illustration was leaning smugly on his number-whatever iron, wearing a yellow and grey diamond patterned sweater and appalling checked trousers. Half-heartedly she dragged a few images around the screen and clicked on Save. 'Bong,' said the computer. Pru repeated the process, got bonged again and growled in exasperation.

She stared at the screen for a few seconds, then called up a menu, moved the mouse until she found what she wanted . . . and clicked. The screen filled with playing cards. Her shoulders relaxed.

Chapter Two

The restaurant proprietor was sweating slightly as he tried to settle the half-dozen diners who had all arrived at once. This was one of Fulham's most popular restaurants and he was proud of the personal service he gave his clientele.

'I'm sorry we're late, Franco,' David apologised, handing over their coats.

'I have saved your table, sir, don't worry. It's nice to see you and the Signora here again. It's been quite a while.'

'I know.' Pru smiled. 'Life seems to get more and more hectic.'

'Well, you look as young and beautiful as ever, signora.' Franco's eyes sparkled as they met hers. 'What would you like to drink?'

Why did a simple, glib compliment from a paunchy restaurant manager make her want to cry?

'Campari and soda for me,' said David at once.

'Actually I'll wait for the wine,' said Pru. 'I'll just have some fizzy water for the moment.'

Another waiter arrived to hand them a menu each.

'Wine list, sir?' A third waiter joined the attending throng.

'Er, yes, thank you,' said David distractedly.

11

'We ought to have champagne, with twenty years to celebrate,' ventured Pru as the waiters retreated.

'Oh. Yes, yes good idea. Um ... the house bubbly should be pretty good here. OK?'

'Fine, lovely.'

Pru looked across at him expectantly. She'd actually been looking forward to this. Family life had been a matter of basic logistics management for so long now, it would be good for David to be able to relax away from the pressures of work, and they'd be able to talk like the old friends they used to be.

'Isn't it great to have a night out, just the two of us, for a change?' she began brightly. 'I always thought, once the children were older and we didn't need babysitters any more, we'd be going out all over the place: theatre, cinema, dinner parties, restaurants ... But we seem busier than ever, 'Specially you at Fraser's. They don't ease up on you as you move up the company, do they?'

'Look,' said David irritably, 'don't start getting at me again for working long hours. I've told you, we've got a lot of new clients and they all want the personal touch. They don't like to be handed over to a junior manager. I'm sorry, but that's the way it is.'

He looked up as Franco returned, beaming attentively.

'We're ready to order, I think. What are you having, Pru?'

'I think I'll have the terrine to start and then I'd like the sea bass, please, with spinach and ... um ... dauphinoise potatoes.' Pru smiled up at him, glad of the interruption.

12

'I'll have the scallops in Pernod,' said David, putting on his glasses and peering at the menu. 'And the steak. Medium.'

Pru watched the tense set of his jaw. The tiny muscle just in front of his ear was twitching as it always did when he was worrying about something. The little mannerism was one of the few things that still linked him with the young university student she'd met all those years ago. She'd loved his slim, athletic body and thick, dark unruly hair. Over the last few years the body had gradually thickened while the hair had steadily thinned. He wore it close-cropped now, almost shaven, flecked with grey. A neat, anonymous, business-like style.

'And we'll have a bottle of the house champagne.'

'With pleasure, sir. Celebrating?' Franco turned to address his question to Pru.

'Um ... yes. It's our ...' she glanced across at David, 'wedding anniversary.'

'My congratulations to you both.' He smiled from one to the other benignly. 'May I ask how long?'

This time it was David he addressed, but he didn't seem to hear. Pru had to fill the silence.

'Twenty years, believe it or not.'

'Not! Definitely not! Twenty years! I can only say you must have been a very young bride, signora.'

'Well ...' Pru looked down at her napkin. She had never been good at fielding compliments.

Gauche as ever, commented the Voice.

'The champagne will be my gift to you. On the house. I hope you have a very ... special evening.'

'Ah, thank you,' said Pru, smiling politely.

13

'Yes. Thanks,' said David. He looked suddenly depressed. Surprised, Pru watched his face, waiting for him to look up and at least make eye contact. When he did glance up, almost furtively, he seemed shocked to find himself meeting her gaze and looked quickly down at his plate again.

Suddenly, blindingly, it hit Pru that something was wrong. And she knew what it was. She'd probably known for months but hadn't let herself face it. He was having an affair! Her heart started beating so hard that the noise almost deafened her. She wasn't sure her voice would work.

'David,' she leant across the table towards him, 'who is she? I've got a right to know.'

He groaned softly and buried his head in his hands.

'Oh, God . . . you know then.'

'Congratulations to a very special couple!' announced Franco, advancing towards their table, holding aloft a bottle of champagne and apparently addressing the restaurant at large. 'Happy Anniversary!'

The cork flew from the bottle with a loud pop, hit the ceiling and landed in Pru's lap.

*　　　　*　　　　*

So, said the Voice, *that's it then. You couldn't even hang on to your husband.*

Pru sat dully in front of her computer, half listening to the radio, her hand on the mouse absentmindedly moving playing cards from place to place on the screen. The game seemed to help impose a semblance of normality on a life that otherwise had fallen apart.

Her eyes were too swollen and tired to focus properly, but she didn't have the strength of will to concentrate on the game anyway. She'd never felt so exhausted. Drained of all feeling. She thought of phoning her closest friend, Stella, but couldn't face the emotional effort it would take to explain, even to her, what had happened or how she felt about it.

'Hi, how are things? Me? My marriage just broke up actually.'

What *did* she feel anyway?

Even the Voice could find little to say.

Heartbroken. What a simple word to sum up the collapse of a human being. Radio and TV reporters were always asking people how they felt. It was the first question they'd put to someone whose child had been abducted, or whose home and possessions had been destroyed in a fire, or who had seen their family wiped out in a traffic accident. Pru was always surprised the unfortunate victims didn't come back with, 'How do you think it feels, you bloody idiot?'

David hadn't come home that night.

She tried to block the excruciating scene in the restaurant from her mind. The abandoned champagne, the shock on Franco's face, how the conversations at the other tables had petered out in fascination and all eyes had followed them as she beat a stumbling, tear-streaked exit followed by David, ludicrously trying to saunter out behind her as though people often rush out of restaurants at the pop of a champagne cork.

You made a proper spectacle of yourself. What must people have thought?

Out on the pavement she'd screamed at him.

15

She couldn't remember exactly what she'd said now. Something about how could he have betrayed her trust after twenty years of marriage. That he'd wasted the whole of her adult life. She'd asked him how long the affair had been going on. He'd said he thought about two years. Two years! How could he have been so dishonest for so long? And with Lucy of all people. The boss and the secretary. What a cliché.

She'd met Lucy once or twice. Quite ordinary-looking. Much shorter than Pru; always wore figure-hugging clothes. Ears rather too large, protruding through straight, pale hair; the perfect fingernails of a woman who does no housework. She'd always been super-polite whenever Pru rang David at the office, politely asking after the family. She'd even commiserated with her on David's long working hours. How hypocritical can you get!

Well, if they're not happy, men just go for the nearest available comfort don't they?

I wasn't a bad wife surely. Was I? I did try to take an interest in him and his life, but I suppose I gave up in the end. He was always so secretive.

As she'd raved and ranted out there on the street for all to hear, throwing her dignity to the winds, Pru had half hoped he would say it had all been a terrible mistake and she was the one he'd always really loved and wanted. But he hadn't tried to lie. He just stood there looking utterly miserable, weakly repeating how sorry he was. He hadn't meant this to happen.

'Well, just fuck off!' she'd yelled at him finally. 'I'm better off on my own anyway. I don't want to see you or touch you ever again. Go and live with

16

your little floozy and good luck to you both. You deserve each other.'

You might have thought of something a little more original to say, commented the Voice. *Sounds like a script from a bad movie.*

She'd stood facing him on the street, tears streaming, nose running, all screamed out and not sure what to do next. A cab with its light on came round the corner. She flung out her arm, sobbed her address to the driver and got in. It clattered away, leaving the figure of David, ever diminishing, framed in its rear window.

Alone in the big double bed, desperate for sleep but unable to stop her mind running riot, the bedside radio had kept her company, its banal phone-ins and snippets of news going into battle for her, fighting gamely against the destructive thoughts that were doing their best to tear her into a million useless pieces.

Finally, at around six in the morning, she'd sunk into a coma-like sleep, only to be woken by Molly bursting into the room an hour later, demanding to know what had happened to breakfast. And where was Dad?

Pru knew her own swollen eyes and puffy face would give the lie to any attempt at explaining David's absence by an early meeting at the office or an unexpected business trip.

'We had a row. He'll be back later. I'd rather not talk about it now,' she'd said.

Molly had started to protest her right to more details, but seeing the state her mother was in, thought better of it. Instead she put her arms round Pru and said, 'I'll make breakfast for you this morning, Mum. What do you want on your

17

toast?'

Pru had made a valiant effort to eat the toast and make polite conversation before Molly left the house to start her last week as a schoolgirl.

'I thought I'd be in floods of tears, saying goodbye to all my friends, but now the time has come, I can't wait to finish at that place,' said Molly. 'I'll always have my good friends anyway. Big Wide World, here I come!'

'I just hope it's ready for you, Moll.' She reached out to squeeze her daughter's arm across the table. The Vietnam discussion would have to wait. She didn't feel up to it now.

*   *   *

Somehow the next few weeks passed. Pru threw herself into the business of finishing the golfing book. She just wanted to get the tedious thing over and done with. Then, she promised herself, she'd find something more challenging. Go back to full-time working maybe.

Molly slept in till midday most days and then went straight out to her waitressing job at Mungo's Brasserie. Pru had half hoped her daughter wouldn't have the determination to stick at a boring, menial job to earn the two thousand pounds she needed to fund the trip to Vietnam. But she was amassing a small fortune. The battered Peter Rabbit cash box she'd kept her money in since she was seven was crammed with five- and ten-pound notes. Pru was faintly surprised she'd extracted so many tips from the strait-laced clientele at Mungo's, given the way she'd been looking lately.

18

Since leaving the discipline of school, Molly's hair had been through the whole rainbow of colours. Just last week her mass of dark purple braids had metamorphosed into a vivid orange, shoulder-length mane, shaped into points and tipped with black.

It looks like a bloody Hallowe'en wig. Other people's daughters don't feel the need to make these conspicuous, attention-seeking fashion statements. Why does yours?

Working on the theory that Molly rather enjoyed trying to shock her, Pru had simply stopped voicing her disapproval. And she'd been congratulating herself on her self-restraint—until her daughter came home one afternoon with a red and black daisy-chain design tattooed around her upper arm.

'Molly, how could you!' It was the health aspect that concerned Pru most. 'What about your heart? You could have got an infection from the needle. Shouldn't you have some antibiotic cover?'

'Chill, Mum, I'm not stupid, you know. I rang Dr Jewell and he said it was OK as long as I went to a reputable place. Which I did. Anyway, he's never heard of anyone getting endocarditis from having a tattoo.'

'What's the point of taking the risk, though, Moll? And it's so unattractive.'

'That's what you're really bothered about, isn't it, Mum? What it looks like. Well, it's my body, not yours.' She headed for the stairs. 'Anyway,' she called down over her shoulder, 'it's just a temporary one. It'll be gone in three years.' Adding wickedly, 'So they say anyway.'

* * *

19

Pru and David agreed to be civilised 'for the sake of the children'. Pru would live in the house until Molly had finished her education. Then they'd sell it and work out a settlement. Criticising each other in front of Molly and Jack would be taboo, as was putting pressure on friends and family members to 'take sides'.

She dialled friends' phone numbers, but more often than not, hung up before the first ring. She'd call them some other time, when she felt more cheerful. When she—and they—could think of something to talk about other than David's duplicity. For so long she'd been David's wife, Jack's mum, Molly's mum. Now those roles were nearly gone, she wasn't sure who she was.

Do you have an identity of your own at all?

The two people she loved most in the world, Jack and Molly, were the most difficult of all to confide in. Molly was reluctant to be drawn into any conversation that might involve criticism, however implicit, of her dad. Jack, on the other hand, was furious with his father. He had taken to ringing Pru from his student flat in Newcastle once or twice a week, ostensibly to ask for recipe ideas when he had a girlfriend to entertain, or to talk through one of his politics essays. She was touched and flattered, but the conversation invariably turned into a loyal tirade about how selfish his dad was and how she didn't deserve to have been treated this way. His angry sympathy was well-meant, but it made her feel like a victim.

'It does take two, you know,' she tried to tell Jack. 'We weren't enhancing each other's lives any more. It just took me longer to realise it perhaps.'

20

Jack wouldn't hear of it.

'You've been a great mum and wife, and he's a self-centred shit. I hope he doesn't expect me to be nice to this Lucy woman. He can forget that!'

He had been keen to come home, 'to make sure you're OK'. With some difficulty, she managed to persuade him to stay in Newcastle and continue with his summer van-driving job. She needed to come to terms with things at her own pace.

What really surprised Pru was that she hardly missed David, now that he'd finally packed up his clothes and books and his treasured CD collection and moved in with Lucy. He'd spent so much time 'at work' in the last couple of years that she'd got used to seeing very little of him during the week anyway. What she did miss somehow was the fact of being married; part of a couple; a unit. Holidays together, occasional weekends with friends ... they'd have been in the car side by side, taking it in turns to do the driving; companions even if they hadn't had much to say to each other. All they seemed to have in common now were Jack and Molly. Perhaps it had always been that way.

After sharing each other's lives for more than two decades, bringing up two children together, they had become strangers almost overnight. Contact between them had been reduced to the occasional brief conversation over the phone which was invariably something to do with one of the children. What did that say about the quality of their relationship? she wondered. Why hadn't she seen it? Perhaps they should have split up years ago.

Molly was becoming increasingly uncommunicative too. Late home night after

21

night, sometimes not coming home at all, she'd taken to ignoring Pru's calls to her mobile phone, just sending enigmatic texts with the information that she was staying with 'friends'. She knew her mother couldn't argue with a text message. At least Pru knew she was safe. Thank the Lord for mobile phones. But she felt bereft. Her relationship with Molly may have been volatile, but she missed it terribly.

She loved her two children equally intensely, but the feelings were different. Her love for Molly made her ache, physically, inside sometimes. The history with the heart defect had perhaps honed her maternal instincts more sharply, but it was more than that. It was her daughter's unswerving, artless idealism; her concern for other people's lives and feelings. Molly always met the world head on, no matter how hard the knocks. And Pru could see how much those knocks hurt sometimes, suffering quietly along with her, trying to pretend she hadn't noticed. Physically and emotionally, her daughter seemed so much more vulnerable than the charming, open, easygoing Jack.

*   *   *

'Did you know Molly just got sacked from Mungo's?' David's tone was almost accusatory.

'No!'

'Tim just called me. That's the last time I pull strings with a mate to get her a job.'

'Why?'

'She's been nicking food from the kitchen. He found her taking burgers and chips out in her bag.'

'She doesn't like burgers!'

'Well, she seems to now.'

'Are you sure? It doesn't make sense. I don't know what's got into her. She seems to have changed in the last few weeks. Ever since we split up.'

'Yes, well, maybe you should make a point of talking to her, Pru. She may be eighteen but she still needs active parenting.'

'Hold on a moment! Why don't *you* talk to her! You're the one who walked out and left us!'

'OK. I know, I know.' He backed down readily enough.

Nice try, thought Pru. Cheeky bastard.

'When did you last spend any time with her?' she persisted.

'It's finding the time . . .'

'Well, *find* the time. She couldn't even tell you her A-level results last week. You had disappeared off the face of the earth.'

'I had to go to Brussels.'

'Had to? I thought it was one of those Eurostar Citybreaks?'

'Yes, well. It was. But she did well, didn't she? Molly. The A-levels?'

'Yes, she did. I'm really proud of her. Needed a bit of reassurance about getting a B for English but they've accepted her at Durham anyway.'

'Is that for the History and Politics course?'

'Look, why don't you ask her yourself? Take her out somewhere. Show some interest in her life. And see if you can find out what this business with Mungo's is about. It seems to me like attention-seeking behaviour. And it's your attention she wants. She's had plenty of mine, I can assure you, David.'

'OK, I'll try and see her tonight. If I can get hold of her.'

*   *   *

David phoned back next day.

'I've had a long chat with Molly and I've found out what's been going on. She's befriended this chap called . . . er . . . Duncan, I think she said. Apparently she's been spending a lot of her time with him and his mates down on Wandsworth Common, where those benches are, by the pub.'

'You mean, where those down-and-outs hang out in tents?'

'She's been giving him leftovers from Mungo's and . . . probably other things as well.'

'I don't believe it. She's got half the boys in the neighbourhood queuing up at the door for her. Her mobile never stops ringing. And what does she do? She goes out with a tramp!'

'I don't think they go out, exactly.'

'So what the hell do we do? Keep quiet, I suppose, and just hope she sees sense.'

'She's over the age of consent,' agreed David. 'She could marry the bloke if she wanted to. Anyway, you know what Molly's like. She loves to be needed. Show her one of life's victims and she's in there with her Florence Nightingale outfit on.'

'Don't,' Pru groaned.

'Incidentally, you'll be pleased to know I've got the restaurant to keep her on—on condition she stops pinching stuff.'

'I always thought being a parent would get easier as they got older.'

'She'll be off to Vietnam soon. That'll sort her

24

out.'

'Bloody hell. It's the devil and the deep blue sea, isn't it?'

'Gotta go,' said David. She could hear Lucy's voice in the background saying something about 'supper tonight'.

*   *   *

Pru gave up all hope of talking Molly out of the Vietnam visit. Her objections were mainly on medical grounds, but Molly had anticipated that. She'd gone to see her consultant cardiologist at Bart's.

'Dr Jewell says it's fine for me to go to Vietnam. You needn't have any worries,' she announced on her way out to Mungo's one afternoon.

'I didn't know you had a hospital appointment?'

'You're always telling me I should take care of my own responsibilities now I've left school. So I did.'

'But I always come with you for your check ups with Dr Jewell.'

'Well, you don't need to any more. I'm eighteen.'

'What did he say, exactly?'

'As long as I'm careful with hygiene and stuff— which I am anyway—and take a supply of penicillin with me, just in case of problems, he says I'll be fine. He thinks it's a good idea, in fact. He said it would give me more confidence.'

'How do I know you're not making him sound more positive than he actually was? He must have had some concerns.'

'No.'

'What if you pick up some kind of skin

25

infection? Or you need dental treatment?'

'Well, then I'll have the antibiotics, won't I?'

'I can't believe he was so blasé about it.'

'You can ask Dad if you don't believe me.'

'Ah. So Dad went with you?'

'Yes. So, you see, there's no need to worry. I'm late now.' Checking her lower half in the mirror in the hall, Molly tugged at her black trousers so that they just skimmed her narrow hips, allowing a casual glimpse of midriff beneath the skimpy black T-shirt with *Mungo's* printed in white across the front. 'See you later.'

*   *   *

As Pru sat down to wait in the thickly carpeted reception area at David's office in the City, she began to regret being so impulsive. The girl on the reception desk obviously knew all about David and Lucy. When Pru had asked her to let Mr Taylor know his wife was in reception, her thickly charcoaled eyes had widened with barely disguised fascination. With any luck, a good bit of gossip was about to unfold in front of her very eyes.

She waited until Pru had retired to the sofa before picking up the phone and murmuring into it.

'We're just locating him for you,' she called over, a moment later.

Presumably it was Lucy who had fielded the receptionist's call. Pru felt her heart rate quicken. What would she say to the woman if she came to escort her to David's office like she always used to? Stay cool and dignified. See what opportunities arise, she told herself. She wasn't sure if she was relieved or disappointed when David emerged through the swing doors himself.

'Pru! What a surprise.' He took her elbow, steering her back towards the lift. 'We're just popping out for a coffee,' he called over his shoulder to the crestfallen receptionist.

*   *   *

'I feel thoroughly undermined and betrayed.' Pru finally managed to get down to business after five minutes of queuing and complicated decision-making over their order in a nearby coffee bar. They sat perched on stools at a narrow counter overlooking the street. Besuited City types scurried to and fro on the other side of the plate glass. 'Why the secrecy, David? I'm gobsmacked.'

For a second or two he tried affecting a look of injured puzzlement. 'Secrecy? What do you mean?'

But he knew exactly what she meant. And shrinking under her steady gaze, he knew she knew he did.

'Dr Jewell.'

'Well, Molly was worried you'd . . . you know, fuss.'

'Too bloody right I'd fuss. Has it occurred to you that fussing is the right thing to do? You know as well as I do, if she gets any sort of infection it could settle on her heart. With serious consequences. What if that happens while she's in Vietnam?'

'*If*. That's why we went to the doctor, to find out how big an "if" it is. And, it turns out, it's not that big. Which is great.'

27

'The truth is, it's more important to you that she thinks you're cool, isn't it? Going along with what she wants, while I'm demonised as neurotic and overprotective.'

'Pru, she's going to Vietnam, whatever either of us says. I thought it was better for at least one of us to keep onside, you know?'

'It still feels like a real betrayal, cutting me out like that. After all we've been through together with Moll.'

'Look, Pru. One minute you're telling me to spend more time with her, then you're annoyed because you feel excluded. You can't have it both ways.'

'You're twisting things now. Worrying about Molly's health is something we've always shared, right from the start. And that's how it should be still. No matter what happens between us.'

She tore open a sachet of sugar and watched the brown grains sink slowly beneath the foam on her cappuccino. David drew patterns on his with his plastic stirrer.

They were both back in their twenties again, keeping vigil beside a Perspex pod in the Charing Cross hospital. Inside, a tiny, blue-tinged baby, sleeping. All around them, tubes, cables, surgical tape, sensors, digital read-outs, flashing lights and electronic alarms; David's fingers and Pru's unconsciously entwined for comfort.

'We shared so much once,' continued Pru more gently. 'We couldn't have got through it without each other.'

Molly had been born blue and fighting for breath. The heart valve that directed blood flow to the lungs wasn't properly formed. Two days later,

28

they'd wept in each other's arms from sheer relief when the corrective surgery was over and their baby had survived, her colour a fresh, healthy pink at last. But their worries still weren't over. The prospect of open-heart surgery in four years' time to insert a second bypass hung over them like the Sword of Damocles.

The anxiety had been all-consuming back then. Pru had thought of little else. She'd had Molly sleeping next to her in a cot beside the bed. Several times a night, every night for four years, Pru would wake up and slip her hand through the wooden bars to make sure the baby was still warm and breathing.

After the second operation, Molly at last began to thrive. She grew in size and strength until she looked as strong and healthy as all the other children of her age. But the anxiety had never disappeared completely. There were regular reminders; the annual routine check up at the hospital; the need for a course of antibiotics for dental treatment, even just a routine check and polish. Any bacteria entering her bloodstream could head straight for the weak spot in her heart and settle there, making heart failure a real possibility. And then there was the scar itself, almost nine inches long, running down the centre of Molly's chest from collarbone to sternum. She'd been through a painfully self-conscious phase with it about the time she started secondary school. Just recently, though, and much to her relief, Pru had noticed Molly going out sometimes in the kind of trendy, skimpy tops her girlfriends had been wearing all summer.

'I'm really sorry, Pru.' David's voice brought her

back to the present. 'For everything.' That little muscular twitch again.

'Well, that's something then.' She took a sip of her coffee. Amidst the anger she felt almost sorry for him. A long time ago he'd seemed so strong. She saw now that he'd been slowly shrinking, fading from her sight. How long had that been happening? Five years? Ten? More perhaps. Was it that he was actually diminishing, or was it her perception of him that had changed? Perhaps to Lucy now he was as strong as he had once seemed to her.

'As long as you understand.' She finished her coffee and reached for her handbag. 'You're moving on now with your new relationship and I'm getting used to that. I'm finding I'm quite enjoying my freedom, in fact. I wish you and Lucy happiness together, I really do. But whether we like it or not, whatever happens, we're linked for the rest of our lives. There will be times ahead which involve us both: graduation ceremonies, marriages, births, family funerals, and . . .' she took the plastic stirrer he'd been fiddling with out of his hands and rapped him lightly on the knuckles with it '. . . anything and everything to do with Molly's health. OK?'

'Sure. Message understood. That it?' He looked like a naughty schoolboy who'd been let off a detention.

*   *   *

'I hear you gave Dad a bollocking,' said Molly later that night.

30

Chapter Three

The wedge between mother and daughter seemed to be driving itself deeper. Pru turned to her old friend Stella as she always did when she needed a sense of perspective. Stella was one of those people who kept her ear to the ground. If she didn't know something herself, she knew someone who did. She carried a notebook in her handbag, so wherever she went, if someone recommended a book to read, or an alternative health practice, a good swimming coach for the children, or she saw a plant she liked in someone's garden, she'd whip out the little book and scribble down the details. She was also a documentary film editor. As a result, she was a walking mine of information.

They'd met at the Wednesday baby clinic at the doctor's surgery. Jack was nearly one and Stella's son, Ollie, just a few weeks older. There'd been a Wendy house in the waiting room and when Pru arrived at the surgery with Jack, young Ollie had already taken up residence inside. Liberated from his buggy straps, Jack had crawled in to join him— only to be welcomed with a solid clout on the head from Ollie's trainer cup, the lid of which came off, drenching Jack in sticky red blackcurrant juice. As Jack let out a wail like an air-raid siren, Stella had leapt to her feet, mortified, and rushed to the Wendy house. Getting down on all fours, she'd pushed her head and shoulders in through the doorway to grab her child by his dungaree straps, treating the rest of the waiting patients to a view of her tightly trousered and generously proportioned bottom.

As she'd tried to drag Ollie out and stand up, the house had come with her, stuck round her waist. She sank back down to her knees again while Pru struggled vainly to disentangle her, both women giggling uncontrollably as the two children bawled in competition and the other patients tutted over their out-of-date *Country Life* magazines, exchanging disapproving glances. Eventually a young man had got up from his chair and ignominiously extricated her by placing a trainered foot on Stella's coccyx and hauling the house upwards and off her by its roof.

Still giggling, the two mothers had gone back to Pru's place for coffee and had been firm friends ever since, as had their two boys.

The women sat now in Pru's kitchen, finishing a chicken korma, Stella pouring out the last of the bottle of red wine they'd just shared.

'Let's face it,' she said, 'Molly's going to Vietnam. With or without your support. If you keep disapproving, she'll just stop telling you anything and you won't know what's going on at all.'

Pru sighed heavily and stood up to put the kettle on.

'Maybe David's right about keeping "onside" with her, as he so irritatingly puts it.'

'You want to know what I think?' Stella continued.

'You're going to tell me anyway,' Pru smiled.

'I think you should stop raising objections and make yourself part of her adventure. No matter what you feel inside. Get involved. Help her buy the equipment she needs, find out a bit more about

Vietnam, help her sort out flights and all that kind of thing. Try to make her feel you're in this together. That way she'll include you in her plans. Keep the channels of communication open. And throw her a wonderful farewell party before she goes.'

*   *   *

Somewhat warily, Molly accepted Pru's suggestion that the two of them go to a well-known outdoor shop in Covent Garden and get her kitted out for the trip. GapKo, the company hosting Molly's teaching project, had sent a daunting list of things to bring with her: sleeping bag, mosquito net, waterproofs ('I wouldn't be seen dead in those,' muttered Molly), walking boots ('You'll need them high at the ankles, there are snakes over there,' warned Pru), torch, first-aid kit, heavy-duty insect repellent, sunscreen, a universal bath plug, a peg-free washing line (whatever that was) and an enormous rucksack.

'It's got to be big. The GapKo people said at least seventy litres,' declared Molly. A somewhat theatrical store assistant insisted on taking the two of them under his well-toned muscular wing, selecting a backpack with the right sort of support and then showing Molly exactly how to pack it, loading each of their purchases into it, one by one.

'Roll everything up so that it stays flat and put hard, lumpy things on the outside so they don't dig into your back,' he advised with earnest enthusiasm. 'And make sure the straps are exactly the right tension to distribute the weight evenly.' He helped Molly thread her arms awkwardly into the harness. 'You don't want to go getting back problems, do you, darling?' He gave a yank on one of the waist straps and Pru and Molly squealed with laughter as she fell dramatically backwards and lay on the shop floor, waving her arms and legs in the air like a dying insect.

*   *   *

The weekend before Molly was due to leave for Vietnam, Pru spent Saturday morning at Marmalade in Mount Street having her shoulder-length brown hair trimmed, blow-dried and highlighted. Then she took a cab to Knightsbridge and spent the next three hours in Sloane Street, coming home with a beautifully cut, cyclamen crêpe-de-Chine dress, a Wonderbra, and the most gorgeous—and the most expensive—shoes she'd ever bought in her life. Soft red leather, strappy, three-inch high heels. She'd cashed in an ISA. Stella had persuaded her.

'We all spend far too much time planning for the future instead of enjoying the present,' she'd said. 'You've had a rough time. Give yourself a makeover. Treat yourself. What does that advert say? You know you're worth it!'

'Wow! Go for it, Mum,' laughed Molly, walking into Pru's bedroom and catching her trying everything on. 'You look great. And happier somehow, with your tits up higher like that!'

And, studying herself critically in the wardrobe mirror, Pru decided she didn't look too bad for a woman in her late forties.

Getting on for fifty the Voice preferred to call it.

'Wait there a minute, Mum. Don't move.'

34

Molly dived into her bedroom and re-emerged almost immediately holding a tiny, pale blue carrier bag.

'Here. This is for you.'

Inside, under some silver tissue paper, was a little oval box.

'It's an early birthday present,' continued Molly. 'I was going to give it to you at the airport. But they'd go so well with that dress, I think you ought to have them now.'

'Molly!' Pru hugged her. 'How lovely of you.'

'I didn't have time to wrap it properly.'

'The shop's packaging is pretty enough anyway,' Pru reassured her, fumbling to open the box. Nestling inside was a pair of earrings, two little cascades of red and pink stones.

'Oh, Moll.' She held one up to her ear lobe and looked in the mirror. 'They're beautiful! Just perfect. Oh, God, I'm going to cry.' She threw her arms round her daughter again. 'Thank you so much, Moll. I'll wear them to remind me of you while you're gone.'

'You shouldn't need reminding.' Molly was trying to hide a broad grin of pride at the success of her present.

'I'll wear them tomorrow for your farewell party.'

'Can Duncan come?'

Pru sighed. 'Oh, Molly. I thought you'd finished with him?'

'Well, I have, sort of . . . It's difficult. He's so hopeless at looking after himself.'

Pru stopped herself from voicing what she really thought: What will our friends and family make of you having a grubby-looking *Big Issue* seller ten years older than you for a boyfriend? It was what her own mother would certainly have said. But Molly had got the message anyway.

'All right. Forget I asked.' She marched out of Pru's bedroom and down the stairs, calling over her shoulder, 'I should have realised you're far too snobby to see beyond physical appearances to the value of the person inside!'

The front door slammed, making the house shake.

*   *   *

Pru had bought two cases of best-quality Australian fizz—the *Independent* had recommended it as their Wine Buy of the Week, 'almost as good as real French champagne'—and raided Marks and Spencer for a trolley-load of canapés and party food. Summer was tipping into autumn. The leaves on the horse-chestnut tree beyond the fence at the end of the narrow little garden were already turning orange round the edges, but the Saturday of the party dawned bright and warm.

After blowing up three pink balloons and tying them to the front gate, Pru mowed the lawn—the brown patches weren't so evident when the grass was freshly cut—while Stella spread a blue-and-white checked cloth over the rickety teak table outside the kitchen door and laid out plates, cutlery and glasses. Molly was doing her last lunchtime shift at the restaurant and expected back at three for the start of the party.

As the guests filtered across the kitchen threshold out into the watery sunshine, politely

36

finding plants to admire, Pru tiptoed among them, making small talk and topping up glasses, trying to stop her ridiculously high heels from sinking into the lawn. Glancing through the open kitchen door towards the front of the house, over the shoulder of Molly's oldest friend's mother, she saw her daughter arriving home, untying the pink balloons from the gate with a look of pure disdain and throwing them into the front garden.

Following Pru's gaze, Stella rolled her eyes skywards and winked at her across the lawn. Pru winced and smiled in return. Several trays of canapés later, it occurred to her that her daughter had yet to make an appearance in the garden.

She slipped back into the house and ran up to Molly's bedroom, following the thump of music and smell of cigarette smoke. There she found her daughter, lounging on the bed with half a dozen tousle-haired mates, a few six-packs of beer, a couple of bottles of Coca-Cola and two catering-size packs of crisps.

'Hey, come on. This is your party,' Pru reproached her. 'Everyone's here because they love you and want to wish you well before you go off to the other side of the world. The least you can do is come down and talk to them for a while.'

'It's *your* party, you mean,' hissed Molly. 'I didn't ask for this. Why must you always try and hijack everything I do?'

Don't crumble now. Even the Voice seemed to take pity on her for once.

Hang on. Just hang on.

*   *   *

37

Pru lay on her back on one of the garden loungers, her shoes discarded on the grass, disconsolately watching the tiny glow of a satellite cruising its predestined path across the night sky beneath the pale and distant stars. She shivered. There wouldn't be many more evenings this year warm enough to sit outside after dark. It was hard to believe that this time next week she'd be entirely on her own in the house.

She wished, in a way, that Molly were leaving tomorrow. Get it over with. She'd wanted so much to maintain a positive sense of connection with her daughter while she was away in Vietnam. The party had been intended to cement that. It turned out to have achieved just the opposite. She was trying to understand Molly's perspective on things. Her daughter needed to break the umbilical cord now, Pru could see that. There she was at eighteen, desperate to start out on her own path in life but not yet mature enough to handle the situation with sensitivity and understanding. It was bound to be a painful process for both of them.

The last of the guests had departed more than an hour ago. Stella had helped with the clearing up before she left but, looking around her, Pru could see a few more stray dirty plates and glasses skulking under bushes and garden chairs. She got up, gathered a trayful and padded wearily back towards the kitchen.

'Mum! You still up?'

Molly stood in the kitchen doorway, silhouetted against the light inside. In the long, baggy Bart Simpson T-shirt she liked to sleep in; hair in a ponytail and face cleansed of the usual make-up, she could have been thirteen again.

'I know. I'm just waiting for the dishwasher to finish its cycle so I can put the last lot of glasses in before bed.'

'I thought Stella was still here.' Gently, her daughter took the tray out of Pru's hands. 'I'll sort this lot out. Sit down and I'll make us a cup of tea.'

Pru pulled out a chair and sat down heavily at the kitchen table. Molly filled the kettle, dropped teabags into a couple of china mugs and came to sit down opposite her.

'Um . . . do you think it went well then? The party?'

'I think people enjoyed themselves, yes,' said Pru carefully, prising some stray bread crumbs out of a gap in the table's wood grain with her fingernail.

'I'm sorry, Mum.'

'It's OK.'

'I was out of order.'

'I wasn't trying to interfere, Moll. I was just trying to embrace the fact that you're going . . . away.'

'I know. I'm really sorry.'

The kettle came to the boil and switched itself off.

'I do understand how difficult it must be for you, me going off to Vietnam, Dad . . . you know . . . not here . . . and Jack up in Newcastle.'

'Well, I've got to get used to it. It was always going to happen. You leaving home, I mean.'

'The real truth is, Mum, a lot of me doesn't want to go away either. It's all a bit scary. I won't know anyone there. I don't understand Vietnamese. I don't even like kids that much. But I can't let myself wimp out. It's just something I know I've got to do.'

'A rite of passage,' affirmed Pru.

Molly got up, reboiled the kettle and came back to the table with two mugs of tea. 'I need to grow up. And I'll never manage it, all safe and cosy here with you. Do you see what I'm trying to say?'

'Yes, of course I do, Moll. I know I can be a bit overprotective sometimes. There's that song, isn't there? The hardest part of love is letting go, or something like that.' Pru cupped her mug in her hands. 'I just hadn't realised quite how hard.'

'Mum—I love you to bits, I always will. You're the best mum anyone could have. Kind, generous, thoughtful. You still look great too . . . for your age.'

'Thanks!' Pru laughed.

'Hey, you're going to have a great time for the next six months without having me to cook and clean and tidy up for.'

'I know. I can go out clubbing till all hours. Watch what I like on the telly. It'll be terrific, I can't wait.' She reached out to caress Molly's cheek. 'I love you too, Moll. I'll be fine. Just try to keep in touch, that's all I ask.'

' 'Course I will. I'll really miss you, Mum.'

'OK, let's leave this lot and go to bed. We'll both be knackered in the morning.'

Molly stood and kissed her mother on the forehead. Pru got to her feet too. They hugged each other tightly.

' 'Night, Mum.'

*   *   *

All the way to Heathrow in the car, they bickered.

Pru couldn't stop herself from running through a

40

few last reminders.

'Now you've got your tickets and passport . . . and you did pack your malaria pills, didn't you? I last saw them on the kitchen table. And what about insect repellent?'

Molly put up with this for a minute or two and then snapped.

'Mum! Stop fussing.'

She leaned forward, tuned the radio to a rock station and turned the volume up. Pru turned it down again.

'Where have you packed your emergency antibiotics? You must try to keep them somewhere cool.'

'Mum . . . you worry about *your* life and I'll worry about mine.'

Before they left home Pru had put on new jeans and a nicely cut olive green top that Molly had often admired, and had taken some trouble with her make-up. She'd wanted Molly to go away with a memory of happy, attractive, loving, loveable Mum.

So much for that. Now they were both scowling. Both trying not to cry.

Failed again, called the Voice smugly.

Shuffling slowly forward in the check-in queue, Pru just switched off altogether. It all seemed too painful to bear. Neither of them wanted to sit in the coffee lounge trying to find jolly things to say, so they wandered round the Body Shop and W.H. Smith until the screens told them the flight was boarding.

'Will you miss me, Mum?' Molly asked finally at the gates of passport control.

'No, I bloody won't!' Pru was trying to smile, but

41

in a way she really meant it. She could stop having to worry about getting things wrong all the time.

'Well, thanks a lot, Mum.' They hugged restrainedly.

Molly swung her rucksack on to her back and, with a last limp wave, lumbered towards the X-ray conveyors and her new adult life.

'Molly!' Pru couldn't let this be the moment of separation. 'Wait!'

Molly turned. Pru lunged past the protesting passport officer and threw her arms round her daughter.

'Just remember I love you, that's all.' Her voice was muffled, buried in Molly's hair. 'Always have. Always will.'

'I know, Mum,' said Molly. 'I love you too.'

And then she was gone.

Chapter Four

So Pru was on her own. The house that had once been so full of noise and mess was painfully quiet and still.

It was when she went shopping in Tesco a couple of days after Molly left for Vietnam that the fact of her aloneness really hit her. She started at the fruit and veg aisle as usual and got as far as the dairy section before she realised she wasn't going to get anywhere near filling the trolley. She abandoned it with its pathetic contents—two apples, a loaf of bread, a mushroom in a brown paper bag and half a pound of butter—and left the store.

She tried to take refuge in work, but *Golfing*

Through The Ages was still far from finished. She found it so hard to concentrate. In a grand gesture one day she deleted all the card games from her computer, but found herself making endless cups of tea instead. A week later, she reinstalled them.

To Pru's surprise, Molly phoned twice in the first fortnight. She said she was settling into the GapKo hostel . . . that she'd met several people her own age there—a German girl she liked and a couple of backpackers from New Zealand . . . that the countryside was spectacular, the language impossible . . . and that she was 'quite enjoying' the teaching job she was doing at a school in a village called Tra Binh, about fifty miles north-west of Ho Chi Minh City, where the children were cute and affectionate and keen to learn English. She'd made friends with one particular family, Quang and Linh, who grew rice and kept pigs and had two little boys of about six and eight years old. The elder of the two, Thanh, was one of her pupils.

'The Vietnamese are lovely people, Mum. They'd give you their last crust. And life is so tough for most of them. Do you know, they're trying to kick a whole load of families off their land near here! It's insane.'

'Who are "they"?' enquired Pru.

'The authorities—the bastards on the local People's Committee.'

'Are you sure it's as simple as that?' Pru was sceptical. 'Maybe they owe rent or something.'

'No, they don't,' Molly persisted. 'They work really hard and now they'll lose their livelihood. Everyone just gets ripped off all the time. And the police are heavy shit, too. My friend Giles runs this bar in the city and he's always having to pay bribes

43

to the cops. They'd close him down if he didn't. Sometimes he has to pay two lots of police in the same week.'

'Well, just be careful you don't get on the wrong side of them yourself, Moll,' said Pru anxiously. 'Don't meddle with things you don't understand. You could get yourself into real trouble. Remember that girl who got arrested last year doing her gap year? Burma, I think it was? She was protesting over something and they put her in jail. She was there for months.'

'Give me a break, Mum,' sighed Molly. 'I know what I'm doing.'

'Who's this Giles, by the way?'

'He comes from Kent but he's lived here a few years now. He's been showing me around Saigon. It's a great place. Really buzzy.'

'And he runs a bar?'

'Yes, he runs a *bar*,' teased Molly.

'And he's a nice . . . boy, is he?' As the question left her lips, she knew it sounded naff. Molly, of course, was on to it at once.

'Yes, Mum, he's a very nice boy. And he's just a friend, so nothing you have to concern yourself with.'

You blew that one, didn't you?

Molly changed the subject and went on to say how humid it was, how she hated seeing birds kept in cages everywhere you went, and that she had decided to go vegetarian.

'That way I'm not expected to eat dog or boiled sparrow or anything gross like that.'

'Yuk. Is that what they eat?'

'They eat all sorts of things, Mum. Turtles, snakes, rats . . . you'd hate it.'

44

'You are looking after yourself, though, aren't you, Moll? Being extra careful about your health?'

'Yes, Mum.' With a sigh of exaggerated tolerance, 'I eat loads. Noodles and vegetables. And fruit. Really healthy stuff.'

'Have you got a number there I can call you on?'

'No, not really,' said Molly vaguely. 'Actually, Mum, I wouldn't want you ringing up all the time. I don't want to sound mean, but it makes me feel homesick. Anyway, we can email each other now.'

'Oh, OK. That's good. You've got access to a computer then?'

'Just at weekends, at the GapKo office. If I can get into town. And if Roger lets me borrow his laptop.'

'Who's Roger?'

'God, Mum! Roger Griffiths. He's the GapKo man over here. The group leader.'

How was she supposed to know that? And why did conversations with Molly so often end up sounding like interrogation sessions?

'Well, it'll be brilliant to get your news,' Pru ploughed on. 'You know, keep track of what you're doing. I can't picture you over there somehow. I'd love to know silly things like what the bed you sleep in is like, what your typical day consists of, what your friends are like . . . that sort of thing. At the moment it feels like you're on another planet.'

Molly was silent on the other end of the line. Beginning to feel pressured.

'So maybe I'll hear from you in a couple of weeks,' Pru finished lamely. 'It's been good to hear your voice, darling.'

'You too. Better go now, Mum. Love to Jack when you talk to him next. Tell him I'll send him a

45

long email soon. Love you loads.'

'OK. Love you loads too, darling. Big hug.'

' 'Bye.'

Pru stared miserably at the phone for a few seconds then pulled herself together. The book was supposed to be finished by next week. She turned back to the computer; the slogan she'd made into her screensaver floated around the screen reminding her to 'always be bigger than your task'.

Today it only made her feel mutinous.

Just grow up and get on with it.

She pushed the mouse and *Golfing Through The Ages*, Chapter Fifteen, took its place on the screen. She stared at it unseeingly, sighed, and gazed out of the window in the hope of inspiration.

The catalpa tree next door had been shedding its dinner plate-sized leaves on the lawn as it did every September. No point bagging them up now, there'd only be more. She'd leave it a couple of days. She ought to cut the rose bush back too. And the hypericum.

You could do so much more with that garden, if you bothered to take the trouble.

'Well, at least I'm not out there snipping away resentfully while you tell me how much better other people's husbands are around the house and garden than mine, and that it was all my fault because I didn't manage David properly. He's not around to do it now anyway.'

You've spent so many years living through the kids and David, you frankly haven't got a life of your own, have you?

'That's a bit hard,' said Pru. 'What else could I do? Anyway, I wasn't living *through* them. *With*

46

them, and *for* them a lot of the time, maybe, but not *through* them.'

What have you got now then?

'I'm waiting,' said Pru. 'I just need a little time to adapt. There have been so many changes in the last few weeks.'

She clicked the mouse and the Freecell game appeared on the screen.

'Just a couple of games while I think.'

Pathetic, muttered the Voice.

```
Hi Mum
How u doing? Just wanted to tell
you I won't be contactable for
the next couple of weeks. I'm
taking a break from the teaching
project to try and help out some
Vietnamese friends of mine. I
think I told you on the phone,
the police are trying to move
them off their land in order to
build a stupid tourist complex or
something. It's dreadful for
them. Not even any compensation.
They need the land, they can't
survive if they can't grow their
crops to sell. Don't worry—we
shall not be moved!!!!!!! I'll
keep you posted. Love you. Big
hug, hope all is well in London
XOXOXOXOXOXOXOXOXOX
```

'Oh, for God's sake, Molly!'

She phoned Stella.

'It's just so typical of Molly,' sighed Pru. 'Taking

up the cudgels for people she thinks are being unfairly treated.'

'I know, but you've got to admire her, haven't you? She's got spunk.'

'Yes, but it's naïve as well, Stella. She's in a communist country. They don't like people who buck the system. I'm genuinely scared she'll get herself into trouble.'

'I'm sure she won't. Molly's a bright girl.'

'I just wish I'd been stronger. I knew in my bones she shouldn't go over there. I should have put my foot down.'

'She'd have gone anyway,' said Stella. 'No use beating yourself up. I'm quite sure she'll be all right. I know it's difficult, but try not to worry.'

Reluctantly, Pru dialled David's number.

'Oh, she'll be OK,' he said breezily. 'She's out there with a reputable organisation, isn't she?'

'Yes, but she says she's left it for a couple of weeks. I just wondered if I should go out there . . .'

'For Christ's sake, Pru! You're overreacting.'

'Maybe I am, but she went there specifically to work for this teaching project. She signed an agreement. She can't just up and do something else. Who's going to be responsible for her? Where will she be staying?'

'Look, Pru, just remember how you were with Jack when he was guarding turtles' eggs in Costa Rica. You nearly had kittens when you found out the poachers carried guns. You were convinced he was going to get shot! He came home all right, didn't he? That sounded much more dangerous.'

'It *was* dangerous. And this could be dangerous too.'

'I'm sure it's not dangerous in Vietnam. People

48

go there on package holidays.'

'It's off the beaten track, though . . . there are different kinds of dangers.'

'Pru, I can only advise you to try and curb that active imagination of yours and wait and see how things go. *I'm* not worried, I trust Molly. And so should you.'

Well, bully for you, Smuggy Chops, she thought as she put the phone down.

She'd take old Fred for a walk on the common— if she could persuade him. He hadn't had his breakfast yet. Usually when she forgot to feed him, he'd nose his way into the study and place a heavy paw on her knee to remind her. She switched off the computer and went to get his lead. As she entered the living room, she saw that he'd got down from his place on the sofa, but then his legs seemed to have given way beneath him. He was lying on the floor on his side, panting slightly.

Pru knelt down next to him and put her arms around his warm, brown body, her cheek brushing his soft fur.

'Oh, Freddy, you poor, dear thing. What's the matter?'

He raised his brown eyes to look up at her.

'Don't go,' she whispered. 'Don't leave me.'

The spaniel tried to lick Pru's face, but the effort was too much. He breathed out; a long, long sigh. And didn't breathe in again.

'Oh, no! Oh, God. No . . . Fred.'

In that moment, it seemed to Pru that the comfortable life she had taken for granted for so long, shattered finally and irrevocably apart. Clasping Fred's body to her own, with deep, black, silent sobs, she grieved for all that had once been so dear to her and was no more.

*   *   *

The prospect of freedom was staring Pru in the face. In some ways she was beginning to like it. No one rang at half-past midnight asking her to come and collect them from a party somewhere; her mascara and jewellery could be found exactly where she'd last left them. The washing basket was less than half-full. She wasn't required to produce meals at particular times or get out of bed early to iron a shirt. When she opened the fridge now, food that had been there the day before, and the day before that, was still there. She'd never in her life thrown so much in the bin. Intellectually, she realised she had to find a new framework for her life. Emotionally, it wasn't so easy. Taking only herself into account didn't feel right somehow.

She sat at the kitchen table with a glass of wine, wrapped in her dressing gown, poring over the *Guardian* crossword. It was nearly midnight. She'd taken to going to bed later and later. It was the fear of not being able to sleep. There were five clues she just couldn't fathom.

After ten more minutes, she gave up trying and extracted the 'Guardian Jobs' supplement from the main paper. Now that the golf book was nearly finished, she needed what her mother would have called 'a proper job'. It was time for a new beginning. There'd been too many endings lately. She needed to start earning some sensible money too. David had said he'd continue paying the mortgage until they got round to selling the house, but she didn't want to lean on him. It was a matter of pride.

All the more interesting jobs on offer, it seemed, required years of experience. Glasses perched on the end of her nose, Pru turned the pages with a growing sense of despondency. She scrawled an asterisk alongside one of the smaller ads: 'Assistant Conference Organiser, Glorietta Cosmetics plc. Based Kensington. Flexible hours. Call our recruitment line now.' It shouldn't be too difficult organising conferences. And there might be free samples.

The Voice tutted. *Sounds a bit shallow. Won't a cosmetics company want someone younger, more glamorous?*

She turned another page. Of all the hundreds of jobs on offer, there was only one other she could even contemplate applying for. 'Information Co-ordinator, Mental Health Charity. You will be required to develop working relationships with professionals in the field, assisting them in the presentation of all aspects of their work to the press and public.' She knew nothing about mental health, but she could maybe put her editorial skills to good use . . .

I suppose you might manage that, dear, with a bit of bluffing.

She'd apply for both; see if she at least got an interview. She'd been putting this off long enough. Picking up the remains of her drink and tucking the paper under her arm, Pru shuffled into her office, turned on the desk lamp and jolted the computer out of its slumber. She was sure she had an old *curriculum vitae* on file which she could update. First, as always, a quick email check. Pru was only really interested in messages from Molly

51

or Jack. Anything else could wait till tomorrow. Tonight there was one from each of them. They'd be replying to the short message she'd sent to them on Sunday after Fred died.

Hi Mum
Got your email. I'm so sad about my gorgeous darling Fred. I cried all Monday night. All through my life he's been around and it is weird to think he is not there any more. I so wish I could have been there to say goodbye. I'm starting to cry again now, thinking about it. At least you were with him and he didn't suffer. Oh God I'll have to change the subject. I'm writing this in an internet café and this Dutch girl came over to me just now and asked if I was OK!!

Just to warn you, you might be hearing from Roger Griffiths. He's a bit pissed off with me. We had an argument about me helping my Vietnamese friends fight their eviction. Just because he's happy to turn a blind eye to injustice, he thinks I should too. I don't know how he can work in a country where he's supposedly helping the people and yet not do anything about the terrible things going on right in front of him. People like him could really make a difference, it's so infuriating. I've got to do what I believe is right. He might mention me having some trouble with the police but don't take any notice. It's not really true, he's just hoping you'll persuade me to stay at the school. He's got ginger hair. I hate men with ginger hair. They all have vile tempers don't they!

Will you warn Dad as well? About Roger complaining about me I mean. I can't remember now if I put Dad's email address on the form.

Am sending this from the Kim Café in Saigon. Will try to get back here again next week or so to send you another one. Don't worry if I can't though. I can't use Roger's laptop anymore for obvious reasons. Will you put some flowers on Fred's burial spot for me. How could we forget our floppy-eared little thing eh Mum? Thanks Mum. Lotsa love from your lovely daughter Moll xoxoxoxoxoxoxoxo

'Pissed off with her? I bet he is!'

It wasn't simply Molly's decision to leave the GapKo project that worried Pru. It was the phrase 'trouble with the police...' It kept bouncing around in her brain like the slogan on her computer screen. Trouble with the police...in a communist country . . . thousands of miles away.

If she'd hoped Jack's message would restore her peace of mind, she was disappointed.

Dear Mum,

I'm so very sorry about Fred. It must have been tough for you going through that on your own. I wish I'd been there to help out. You should have called me. I might have been able to come back down to London for a few days. Molly will be devastated.

Have you spoken to her lately Mum? I'm worried about her. Do you know what she's doing over in Vietnam? She sent me an email with a story about a corrupt government official who is turning people off their land so that he can sell it to some property developers. She said she was organising a protest! She makes it sound like she's taking on the whole Vietnamese government single-handed! I can't tell from her email whether she's being a heroine or out of her depth. Probably both! I'm not sure what the police are like in Vietnam but they had better be nicer than the two who arrested me in San Jose for not having my visa on me. British policemen are like social workers in compar-

```
ison! The trouble with Moll as we
all know is that her heart rules
her head sometimes. Maybe you or
Dad should have a word with her.
I would go over there and check
up on my Lil Sis myself but I've
got this dissertation to finish.
Anyway I'm sure everything will
be fine but keep me informed!
Hope you're well and not too
stressed.
    Love you! Jack xxx
```

If even Jack was worried . . . !

Forgetting the plan to write her *curriculum vitae*, Pru typed the words 'Vietnam' and 'travel' into the Google search box. As, almost idly, she browsed the various websites, taking in the picturesque views, offers on hotels, articles about the country's climate, food, history and culture, she made a conscious effort to think logically. Trying so hard not to be overprotective was getting in the way of her natural instincts.

Should she go to Vietnam herself? She didn't want to overreact, but if Jack was right, and his sister really had got out of her depth with the police over there, she'd never forgive herself for failing to see the seriousness of the situation.

Was she trying to find reasons to go? Or reasons not to go? Certainly she could think of nothing she'd rather do than escape the grey prospect of November skies of London in favour of discovering a country she'd up to now only associated with a war. There was also something comforting about giving herself permission to slot back into the old familiar maternal role and defer the prickly business of trying to find a new definition for her life a little longer.

On the other hand, the idea of going alone was somewhat daunting. Pru had done a fair amount of travelling in her life, but always with company. She reminded herself of some of the foolhardy trips she'd undertaken without a second thought while she was at university. Gap years were an undiscovered concept back then so it was during her first long summer vacation that the joyous freedom of travelling had revealed itself, hitchhiking across Europe with various friends. It had taken them a couple of leisurely weeks; sleeping rough in parks, cemeteries, building sites—wherever seemed a good place to lay out their bedrolls—and ending up in the elysian Greek islands where the inhabitants fed them on tomatoes, fresh figs and homemade bread. Images flickered randomly across her memory: guitars round campfires on the sand, counting shooting stars as she drifted off to sleep and, in the morning, plunging into the then unpolluted, sapphire-blue Mediterranean sea to wash.

But she also remembered some of the close calls. The two Turkish lorry drivers who had given her and her friend Maggie a lift in what had then been Yugoslavia. As night began to fall, the men had feigned concern for the girls' welfare and offered to put them up in a cheap hotel they knew of in Skopje. The girls had accepted their kindness at face value—naïve in the extreme, looking back—and they'd duly arrived at a small guest house.

Thankfully, they had locked themselves into

their bedroom. Later that night the terrified girls had been awakened by a hammering on the door. The two men wanted payment for their 'kindness'.

Pru couldn't remember how long the knocking had continued, nor if they'd managed to sleep all the rest of that night. What she did remember was that in the morning, the receptionist informed them the men had checked out. And had left Pru and her friend with the bill.

She'd been so childlike and trusting. There had been several occasions when she could have been seriously hurt, even killed.

She came close to being shot one night in Germany as they'd settled down to sleep in a half-built house in a residential street. Alerted by a barking dog, an elderly local man in a pair of striped pyjamas had appeared, the moonlight glinting on the barrel of a pistol which he was pointing straight at them, his finger trembling on the trigger. It was Pru's A-level German that had saved them on that occasion.

On another occasion, in Morocco, she'd been suffering from laryngitis. It was almost funny now. She had wriggled out of her sleeping bag early one morning in Tangiers, nursing a sore throat. As she sat on a bollard watching the sun rise over the still water, a uniformed policeman had strolled up offering tea.

A policeman, thought the eighteen-year-old English girl, what safer company could there be? Inside his guard hut, he'd poured them each a cup of tea from his thermos, then kicked the door shut and pounced on her. He was far stronger than she was and Pru was only too aware of the gun at his belt. If he shot her, who would question whatever

57

story he came up with? Unable to scream because of the laryngitis, a silent but desperate struggle ensued in which she managed, eventually, to grab one of the cups and throw the scalding hot contents in his face. While he clutched at his eyes, yelling with pain, Pru wrested the door open and made her escape.

What amazed her now was that her parents had let her face such dangers at such a young age. But Mum seemed to have been blissfully unaware. She and Dad simply hadn't asked any questions. Perhaps they didn't care. But they must have done. Or perhaps they'd simply trusted her. Pru was a bright, sensible girl. Of course she wouldn't get herself into difficulties. Exactly what both Stella and David had said about Molly.

In any case, what else could her parents have done? Back then, there had been no email and only very basic telecommunications. Making an international phonecall was a complicated palaver involving the search for a telegraph centre in a reasonable-sized town. She had phoned her mother just twice in the whole three months away. Having been a controlling, authoritarian parent, Mum had finally had no alternative but to let go. Now, with modern technology, there were more choices.

She remembered Stella describing a TV documentary she'd been editing for the BBC about a tribe of Iroquois Indians and their rites of passage from adolescence to adulthood. They'd send a young boy into the forest full of dangerous wild animals and hostile rival tribes, and see how he fared. When he returned safely, having successfully fended off and fought the dangers, he was welcomed back to the tribe as a full-grown man. What the boy didn't know as he made his journey, was that the elders of the tribe would track him all the way, keeping a secret watchful eye from among the trees, but only if he was in real mortal danger would they intervene to help him.

Figuratively speaking, modern communications meant Pru could track her daughter's rite of passage through the forest. Her own mother hadn't had that option. Pru's job now was to decide when to keep a low profile and when to rush out from the bushes and intervene.

Tomorrow, she promised herself, she'd take charge of the situation. She'd get in touch with GapKo herself, find Roger Griffiths' email address, or a phone number preferably, and find out exactly what was going on.

She climbed into bed, but anxieties about Molly kept intermingling in her dreams with the exploits from her own past. Waking for the third time, drenched in perspiration, Pru got up to make herself some tea. She'd have to divert herself with something; those job applications perhaps. Standing at her desk, she nudged the computer mouse. There was a new message. Failing to find her glasses, she screwed up her eyes to peer at the screen.

```
I'm sorry to tell you that Molly
seems to have abandoned her work
here for the moment. It was made
clear to her before we took her
on that this was to be a full-
time, twenty-six week commitment.
However, she has broken that
```

agreement and left the village in
pursuit of some venture of her
own. I'm not able to bring anyone
over to take her place for the
next three weeks at least, so if
she contacts you, would you
please try to persuade her to
resume her post with us? This is
a perfectly safe country for
foreigners as long as they don't
get on the wrong side of the
authorities here. However, Molly
is in danger of doing just that.
I do not wish to worry you, but I
must inform you that GapKo cannot
be held responsible for her while
she remains away from our
protection and authority.

   Best wishes,
   Yours sincerely,
   Roger F. Griffiths, Co-
ordinator

Chapter Five

Weary and sluggish after spending the best part of
seventeen hours shaped like a question mark, Pru
walked stiffly down the airplane steps into 103
degrees of implacable, pulsating heat. There was
no doubting the country she'd landed in was a
communist one. The arrivals hall was a long, bare
barn of a place, lit by fluorescent tubes and
furnished with half a dozen wooden booths,

ranged in a row at the far end. In each booth sat a khaki-clad immigration official. In the queue she'd been assigned to, Pru shuffled forward a foot at a time, sweating already, her clothes sticking to her body.

Finally at the front of her line, she dumped her heavy shoulder bag at her feet and shoved her passport and immigration form into the booth. With a brief but intense glance at her face, the official swept her papers out of sight on to a worktop beneath and studied them with dispassionate concentration. Looking idly beyond the uniform, Pru saw a smooth-faced young man, probably about the same age as Jack, with hair that straggled around his collar under his hat. He snapped his head up, making her jump. Fixing her with a disdainful stare, he thrust the papers back towards her and jerked his head in the direction she'd just come from. Pru looked as she felt, utterly blank. Wordlessly, he jabbed a long-nailed index finger at the top corner of the yellow immigration form. She found her glasses and peered at it. She'd forgotten to fill in her passport number.

'Can't I write it in now?'

He jerked his head again back towards the end of the queue. Too jaded to argue, Pru shouldered her bag again and dragged herself to an unoccupied wooden trestle table to rectify the omission.

She was overtaken quite suddenly by a powerful impulse to get on the next plane back to London. What on earth was she doing coming all this way by herself to a country she knew nothing about and where the only person she knew was her own daughter—who was probably not going to be best pleased to see her anyway? This was madness. Why hadn't she realised before? If only Stella were with her. Together, they would have turned all this into a bit of a laugh. Her friend had been raring to join her, but she was in the middle of cutting a documentary on teenage drinking and, although she'd tried to re-schedule, simply hadn't been able to get away at such short notice. Pru had even tentatively suggested to David that he might join her but had been heartily relieved when he'd said he had too much work on. He had never been the most stimulating of travelling companions, even at the best of times. Exploring other countries or cultures held no interest at all for him. All he wanted from a trip abroad was some guaranteed sunshine and a swimming pool to 'veg out' by.

Finally through passport control, there was another queue and another form to fill in—under the watchful eye of a female official this time—demanding the itemisation of every article of value she was wearing or carrying. Fortunately, Pru hadn't brought much with her; just a cheap watch she had bought for the trip and a hundred pounds sterling. Her left hand, of course, was ringless now. Having claimed her suitcase from the conveyor, there was more queuing to have her possessions X-rayed again, and yet another wait at the exchange bureau to buy some dollars. At last she was heading for the Way Out sign, a full hour and twenty minutes after the plane had touched the tarmac.

*   *   *

Outside she blinked in the remorseless glare of the Asian sun. Everywhere was seething activity: shouting, arguing, hooting, two-stroke engines revving, car doors slamming. Pru shut down her overloaded senses, narrowing her attention down to the middle-aged Vietnamese man who had appeared in front of her. 'Taxi?' He was already taking the suitcase from her hand. 'Where you go?'

Forgetting to pre-arrange the price, she settled gratefully into the back seat. The driver attached his right thumb to the car horn, where it remained throughout the rest of the journey, and the cab shot out of the airport car park, narrowly missing a pedestrian. Less than a minute later, they just missed a young man on a moped with a small brown dog peeping out from a cage strapped on behind him. The driver stamped hard on the brake and Pru's bag scudded off the seat and on to the floor. She retrieved it, scooping her passport, purse, half a tube of mints and lipstick back into it. Two minutes later and it was on the floor again; a young woman in pale pink silk pyjamas this time, pedalling indifferently in front of them on a bike. Pru left the bag where it lay. There seemed to be no speed limits, no highway code, no traffic lights and no pedestrian crossings. Everyone just wove in and out and around each other in a bizarre mixture of madness and serenity.

Most of them wore headgear of some kind—baseball caps, beanie hats, the occasional traditional conical straw hat—but not a crash helmet in sight. Too hot perhaps.

Nearing the city centre, Pru's overwhelming impression was of shambolic untidiness. Heavy-duty electricity cables criss-crossed the streets and festooned the sides of buildings. TV aerials jutted starkly into the sky. Parked motorbikes and scooters cluttered the pavements, and most of the remaining space was taken up by people squatting in small groups under tattered awnings or make-shift parasols. Some were hunched over portable cooking rings; some were eating, bowls held close to their chins, shovelling food into their mouths with chopsticks, while others were washing up in plastic bowls before tipping the dirty water into the gutter. Was this late lunchtime, early suppertime, or did people cook and eat all day? Pru looked at her watch. Just gone three o'clock.

*   *   *

'Imperial Hotel.' Her driver coasted to a halt outside a shabby glass and concrete building and yanked on the handbrake. 'Twelve dollar.' *The Lonely Planet Guide* said eight dollars was the right price to pay from the airport to the city but on balance, Pru decided, twelve US dollars seemed a fair price to pay in return for still being in one piece.

The driver had swung her case out of the boot and was back in the driving seat and moving off almost before she'd slammed the door. Pru found herself standing on the pavement in the torpid, mid-afternoon heat. Most of the traffic was on two wheels, and carrying an unbelievable variety of cargo for such low-powered vehicles: crates of fizzy drink, sheets of hardboard, stacked cabbages, cartons of fruit, livestock. Scooters zipped by, the cotton shirts of their riders billowing behind them. Some were driven by young girls, straight-backed and elegant in white silk tunics, often wearing long silk gloves reaching beyond their elbows. Handkerchiefs covered mouths and noses to mitigate the pollution; there was no breeze in the hot, dense air to disperse the dust and fumes. Several motorcycles puttered precariously by with whole families on board. A small boy waved at her from one of them. He was standing, like a mascot, between the arms of his father who was driving. His mother perched side-saddle behind, one arm around her husband's waist, the other holding tight to a toddler on her lap. Two pairs of live chickens, trussed together by their feet, dangled from the handlebars, flapping feebly, only half-conscious.

Pru waved back, then turned towards the grimy double-glazed doors of the Imperial Hotel. Cheap metallic stick-on lettering boasted 'AIR CO DITIO ING IN EVER OOM'. She pulled the aluminium handle on the right-hand door. It didn't open. She tried the left-hand door. That didn't open either. She pushed it. It rattled but remained shut. Moving her hand back to the door on the right, she pushed, hard. It flew open with an alarming metallic grinding noise and she almost fell into the concrete-floored lobby where the concierge, a sallow man with limp, dishevelled hair, had been watching her with detached interest from behind a plastic-upholstered desk. There was a strong smell of old socks and stale cooking. A black-and-white television screen aimed subtitled entertainment at no one in particular from a shelf high above his head.

'Do you speak English?' asked Pru. The man inclined his head diagonally in what could have been a yes or a no.

'*Parlez-vous Francais?*' she persisted. '*J'ai reservé en Angleterre. Je m'appelle Madame Taylor.*'

'Passport, please,' said the man impassively. She produced it from her bag. He studied the document—first the front cover and then the back page—looking exaggeratedly from Pru's photo to the real thing and back again. Finally, he unlocked a drawer under the counter, dropped the passport into it and slammed it shut.

Her feet were aching. Her head was hurting. She yearned for a shower and a sleep. Probably in reverse order.

He turned to the rows of wooden pigeon holes behind him and selected a key with a huge yellow plastic tag dangling from it. Number 8.

'Second floor.' He waved vaguely towards a wide, uncarpeted stone staircase.

No sign of an offer of assistance with her baggage. Trying not to acknowledge a growing sense of loneliness, Pru lugged her suitcase up the stairs.

*　　　*　　　*

A flimsy wooden door opened on to a small, cheaply furnished room. In one corner a wardrobe of plywood and Formica leaned forward at an alarming angle, its door hanging open. A mosquito net sagged from a frame above a plain single bed on which was spread, despite the heat, a nylon blanket in nursery shades of pastel blues, lime greens and yellows. Woven into the centre of it was a moon-eyed cartoon puppy with a bonnet on its head. Around the edges assorted words were embroidered in capital letters. Pru took a step

66

closer to read some of them: 'LOVE', 'DOGS', 'CUTE', 'HAPPY', and, bizarrely, 'IMPETUS'.

As Molly might have said, 'Random or what!'

The only natural light came from a casement window with a metal grid across it and curtained in thin, bottle-green netting. It overlooked not the world outside but the stairwell. Anyone going up or down could see directly into the room.

Pru looked in the bathroom. Bathroom actually wasn't the right word. There wasn't a bath and it wasn't a room. It was a square cubicle, shoddily constructed in the same wood as the wardrobe. The brown-stained basin was fixed to the wall on rusty brackets. Next to it, the toilet had a flimsy white plastic seat which had been cracked at some time and stitched together with nylon twine in a criss-cross shoelace pattern. Attached to the taps in the basin was a length of pale pink rubber hose with a shower head on the end of it. Presumably you were supposed to hold it above your body with one hand as you stood in the middle of the floor and soaped yourself with the other. A drainage hole underfoot confirmed her suspicions.

Next to the 'bathroom' doorway, installed for some reason halfway up the wall, was a single electric socket into which was plugged an adapter, loaded on all sides with plugs and cables. One cable trailed across the room to a small fridge which whirred and clicked at irregular intervals and which, on inspection, turned out to contain one bottle of mineral water and a plastic jug, very similar to the one her doctor back in London kept in the loo for patients to provide samples in. Another cable led to a cheap lamp on a homemade plywood box beside the bed. A third ended at an old electric kettle on the floor, and a fourth went directly upwards to a contraption with a dust-clogged grille and two control knobs. The 'air conditioning'! Reaching up, Pru turned one of the dials to the 'on' position. Nothing happened. Perhaps the plug wasn't in properly. Gingerly she pushed it. A blue flash sizzled out of the overburdened socket. With an involuntary squeal, she threw herself backwards.

Suddenly she was all out of resources. She lay down on the Puppy blanket, too tired and hot even to weep with any real energy.

* * *

She awoke abruptly. What time was it? How long had she been asleep? The room had become quite dark. It took a moment to remember where she was. She lay still, feeling uneasy. Somehow she felt she wasn't alone. She kept her eyes shut, listening. Then she heard a faint movement; a rustle of clothing. Someone *was* there! Adrenaline flooded her body. She scrambled off the bed.

Standing stock still in the centre of her room was the concierge. How long had he been standing watching her as she slept? She looked round for her handbag. It was still beside the bed where she'd left it.

'What do you want?' she demanded. He assumed an affronted look.

'Visitor for lady,' he said sulkily, not attempting to move.

Pru stared at him. Did he mean himself?

'Why do you not knock before coming into my room?'

'Visitor downstair,' repeated her intruder implacably.

How could she have a visitor? She'd only just arrived. Molly didn't know she was here. It must be Roger, the GapKo man. She'd emailed him with her hotel details just before she left. He hadn't wasted any time then.

Pru walked to the door and opened it wide, standing pointedly aside to let the concierge pass.

'I come down in a moment,' she enunciated slowly.

She held his gaze for a moment or two, facing him down. He shrugged, turned slowly and slouched out. Pru shut the door firmly after him.

Her pulse rate returning to normal, she examined her face in the discoloured mirror above the washbasin. Her left cheek was red and blotchy from the itchy Puppy blanket. She splashed her face, neck and wrists with cold water, quickly combed her hair and then, having carefully locked her door with a clatter of the hotel's unwieldy key tag, she headed back downstairs.

As she reached the first-floor landing, she could see through the banisters a chunky man in green combat trousers and light khaki shirt, pacing around the reception area below. Faded ginger collar-length hair and matching wispy beard framed a pale and rather pudgy face. In his early-thirties probably. Hearing her footsteps, he looked up.

'Mrs Taylor!' It wasn't a question. There wouldn't be many European women staying at a hotel like this off season—or any season come to that. He extended a predictably moist hand. No doubt her own hand was clammy too, in this

69

humidity.

'Roger Griffiths. From GapKo.'

'Hello.'

'I thought I should see you as soon as possible.'

The concierge was back at his station behind the reception desk, watching them. Roger glanced at him: 'Could we have some tea here, please?'

The man disappeared reluctantly through a doorway behind him, curtained with multicoloured plastic streamers.

By mutual consent they walked towards a scuffed brown leatherette sofa and armchair set at right angles to each other across from the reception desk. Pru made for the chair. Roger lowered himself awkwardly on to the sofa, knocking the lightweight wooden coffee table sideways with his knees. Absentmindedly, she realigned it.

'Well, welcome to Vietnam, Mrs Taylor.' There was a barely detectable Welsh cadence.

'Thank you . . . I think.' She smiled. 'Please, call me Pru.'

'Hmm.' His eyes swept round the unprepossessing hotel foyer. 'I'm sorry you couldn't reach me on the phone before you left, Mrs . . . er . . . Pru. I was in Singapore. NGO seminar.'

'So tell me about Molly. What's been happening? Where is she?'

'That is a very good question.'

'You have some idea where she is, though, don't you?'

The concierge sidled up with a huge green thermos flask and two tiny decorated ceramic cups on a tray which he placed on the table in front of them.

'Well, she hasn't exactly kept us in the loop, I'm afraid,' continued Roger. 'I have to say, I'm very disappointed with Molly. Hundreds of kids apply for these jobs every year. We have to turn so many of them down. I really thought she had what it took for this project.'

'I'm very sorry about that. I can only say in her defence that she's a very idealistic sort of person and I'm sure whatever she's done has been for a good reason.'

You hope.

'Well, I'm hoping you can get her to see some sense, Pru. I really appreciate your coming out here.'

'Can't you get someone else to take her place?'

Roger reached across the table and pulled the thermos towards him. Lining up the two tiny cups beneath it, he pressed down on the lid with a freckled paw, dispensing pale brown liquid into first one and then the other. He pushed her cup towards her across the table.

'It's too late for that now, more's the pity. The kids we had on the shortlist will all be doing other things.'

'So when did you last see Molly?'

'That would have been, I think, about ten days ago.' He leaned backwards and sideways on the sofa to rummage in one of his trouser pockets, didn't find whatever it was he was looking for and began scrabbling around in another one.

Pru waited patiently.

'She'd been pestering me to help this family she's got involved with. Their young boy is one of the kids she was teaching. Molly's a good little

71

teacher actually.' His pocket-searching had finally yielded a blue-and-white checked handkerchief which he spread out on his knee, folded carefully into a pad, then used to dab at the sweat on his forehead and neck before opening it out again, blowing his nose in it and shoving it back in the pocket he'd found it in. 'Apparently the family is being kicked off their land. Something being built there. A golf course, I think she said.'

'Yes, she mentioned something about that to me too,' murmured Pru.

'Well, of course, these things happen all the time. Land ownership can be quite a vague concept over here. I pointed out to her that we're guests in somebody else's country and it's not our business to try to effect social change. But she accused me of copping out and flounced off. Packed her bags, left the hostel, and I haven't seen her since.'

'Didn't you try to stop her? Didn't you ask her where she was going?' queried Pru.

'I knew where she was going.' He assumed a pained expression.

'Well, in that case, why didn't you just go and talk to her yourself, get her back on track?'

'She was going,' continued Roger deliberately, 'where she goes most weekends. To stay with her boyfriend here in Saigon.'

A trickle of sweat meandered down from Pru's left armpit and tracked a few inches along the front of her bra before continuing down her abdomen and losing itself in the waistband of her trousers.

'Boyfriend?'

'Oh. I was hoping she may have confided in you.'

72

'Well . . . sometimes she does and sometimes she doesn't. She's a teenager. Sometimes you get too much information and sometimes nothing at all.' Pru ran her mind back over her last phone conversation with Molly. 'It's not someone called Giles, is it?'

'That's the one.'

So her instincts had been right.

'What's he like?'

'Well, how can I put this? I wouldn't be too happy if my teenage daughter went out with someone like that.'

'Have you got a daughter?' He was too young, surely.

'No. But *if* I had . . .'

'What's wrong with him?'

'Words like smug, self-satisfied, and arrogant spring to mind, for starters,' said Roger emphatically. His face was beginning to flush. The scourge of the redhead. 'A hustler. An operator. All in all, a downright dodgy piece of work.'

Perhaps there was more to this than mere practical concern for her daughter's welfare.

'Did he do something particular to upset you?' Pru enquired.

'Well . . .' he was groping for the handkerchief again '. . . for another thing, he's a womaniser. The minute he hears a good-looking girl has arrived in town, there he is, hanging around like some tom cat with offers of free cocktails at his club, champagne dinners, jaunts up the Saigon River on his mate's speedboat and all the rest of it. I tried to warn Molly . . .'

The blush was spreading down his neck now, creeping under the collar of his shirt. Pru

73

wondered vaguely how far down it would travel.

'Molly does attract attention, I know. It's a bit of a worry sometimes.'

'I tried to take her under my wing, you know, when I saw the danger signs. But I'm afraid there was nothing I could do. The charming Giles Fitzbollocks wins again.'

'I'm sorry?'

'Well, whatever his fancy name is . . . Fitz-something or other. Means bastard, doesn't it?'

'So he's British?'

'English,' he corrected her. 'Through and through. Public-school type. All floppy hair and posh accent.'

Pru risked her tongue on another sip of the tea.

'He's the kind of guy who reckons he's a cut above everyone else, you know. Thinks he can push the boundaries and get away with it. But you don't do that for long over here. They watch you. They bide their time. They wait till you've taken enough rope and then . . . they make their move.' He banged his tea cup on the table by way of punctuation.

Hell hath no fury . . . thought Pru. 'And who do you mean by "they"?' she asked.

'The police, the People's Committee, the military . . .'

'The military? Forgive me, but this is all sounding a bit overdramatic.'

'Mrs Taylor, we're not talking about good old Blighty here. This is Vietnam. It is a beautiful country. The people are fabulous. But it is a totally different system. Totally different. Underestimate it at your peril.'

'So why exactly do you think Molly is in danger?

Because she's involved with this Giles Fitz . . . um . . . thing?'

'I'm pretty sure he's been encouraging her to get involved with this family up in Tra Binh. It's bloody irresponsible. He knows what the consequences could be.'

'What could they be, exactly?'

'If she starts acting as militant as she talks, your Molly could find herself in jail.'

'So what can I do that you can't? I don't know this country. I can't speak the language . . .'

'She's your daughter, not mine. I've said my piece and she's not taken the slightest bit of notice. And Giles certainly isn't going to listen to me, is he? He probably sees me as his—you know—rival.'

Pru tried not to smile.

'It might give him a bit of a turn, though, when he finds out Molly's mum has come over to sort him out.'

'I came to sort Molly out, not Giles.'

'But Giles knows what she's up to in that village. In any case, I've got to carry on living here and I don't want my name linked with that idiot. Or with your daughter's exploits, to be honest.'

'Well, that's not very supportive . . .' began Pru.

'Seriously, I've worked hard to get GapKo accepted over here. Molly could jeopardise everything. If she gets into trouble with the authorities, I have to dissociate myself. You can understand that, can't you?'

Pru wiped a drop of sweat from under her chin with the back of her hand.

'I'm not sure I understand anything. Frankly I'm more baffled now than I was half an hour ago.' She dispensed some more green tea into the little cup.

75

She needed time to think. It was just as hot but tasted more bitter now.

'I tell you one thing . . .' Roger leaned towards her '. . . I wouldn't waste time, if I were you. I don't think Molly understands. She is playing with fire. She's a good kid, I can see that. Her heart's in the right place. But she's been misguided.'

He lifted an elbow to unbutton his shirt pocket, revealing a dark patch of sweat under his right armpit, and took out first a biro, then a creased business card.

'This is where you can reach me if, or when, you get her to see sense. And . . .' he turned it face down on the table between them and scribbled something on the back '. . . I'll write down the address of the bar here.'

He finished writing with a dot and a flourish and pushed the card towards her, smearing it through some spilled tea.

'Oops, sorry.'

He withdrew it quickly, wiped both sides on his trousers and handed it back again. She took the dampened card from his pale, chubby fingers.

'It's in District Four, near the river. Not too far from here.'

'And will Molly be there?'

'If she's down in the City she will, but as far as I know she's out at the village during the week, doing her Joan of Arc bit.'

'And how far is the village?'

'Fifty kilometres or so. Bit more maybe.'

'What about Giles? He'll be at the bar, will he?'

'Oh, he'll be there all right. He's always there. Holding court.'

Roger looked at his watch.

76

'I'm sorry to have been the bringer of bad news. Let's hope that this time next week, Molly's back at her job in our school, all safe and sound.'

'You do want her back then?'

'Of course I want her back! She's a great asset to the project. I'm having to do some of her stints in the classroom myself. I *need* her back. I miss her. The children, I mean . . . we all, miss her.'

He was flushing up again. Sweat trickled down both sides of his face from his temples.

'I'm sorry, I really have to be going now Mrs . . . er, Pru. I've got a meeting back at the office.' He stood up awkwardly and waited for her to stand too. 'You will keep me in the loop, won't you?'

'Of course.'

At the hotel doorway, he hesitated a moment as if about to add something important, then seemed to think better of it. He yanked at the door, managing to get it open a couple of feet before it jarred on the stone floor.

'Good luck.'

Negotiating the narrow aperture, Roger blended into the greying evening light outside.

Studiously avoiding eye contact with the concierge as she passed his desk, Pru went back up the dingy stone staircase to her room. She held the tea-stained business card at arm's length and peered at it. In tiny print on one side were GapKo's addresses in Ho Chi Minh City and Hanoi with Roger's name at the top. She turned it over. 'Nautical Club,' he had scrawled in biro, 'Le Than Ton Street. District 4 HCMC'. Then underneath, as if an afterthought, 'Proprietor—G. Fitzpatrick'.

It was nearly six o'clock. It felt like days rather than just a few hours since Pru had arrived at Ho Chi Minh airport. What she'd have loved more than anything was a long cool bath. She looked despondently at the piece of hosing attached to the taps in the basin.

Half an hour later, she'd had what her mother used to call a 'strip wash' and had unpacked her case, draping her clothes on the four plastic hangers provided in the wardrobe. In case of passers-by outside the staircase window, she'd got dressed prudishly under a towel, like a little girl changing on a crowded beach after a family day at the seaside. Now, wearing the pink shirt-dress she'd bought for Molly's farewell party and with her hair brushed and tied back, she felt fresher and stronger. More in control. Ready to face the consequences of landing unannounced in Molly's new, mysterious, secret life.

Chapter Six

Pru squeezed out through the gap the hotel's front door allowed her and found herself once again back in the teeming madness of Ho Chi Minh City's streets. The hot, steamy air was almost suffocating.

She'd decided to walk to the Nautical Club to give herself a better feel for the place. She opened her *Lonely Planet Guide* at the page she'd marked and peered at the simplified map of Saigon. She knew she needed to start by walking through the market place called Benh Thanh, just across the road. Then what? She'd forgotten the names of the streets already. It was difficult to memorise such alien words. Lung Hong Tow or something. Where was that card? The light was beginning to fade. She rummaged in her bag for her glasses.

Like a scrap of bread thrown into a lake, she was surrounded within seconds by predators, pushing and jostling for a little piece of her. A woman in a conical straw hat, her face streaked with tears and dirt, clutched a limp, glazed-eyed baby to her chest with one hand and reached out pleadingly to Pru with the other. 'Money for food . . . need food for child.'

Pru shook her head and turned back to her map. There was a tap on her back and she looked round into the toothless grin of a gaunt old man holding out his left arm which was festooned from hand to shoulder with Day-glo coloured furry nylon animals on strings. His other arm was a stump, finishing just above where his elbow should have been, and he was rotating it wildly to indicate his wares. 'Two dollar. Cheap. Very nice.' Pru shook her head and tried to assume a detached, polite smile.

'You take cyclo?' A flock of pedal-powered passenger vehicles had appeared from nowhere.

'Where you go?'

'You want see shops?'

'See city? I show you.'

'Two dollar. Very cheap.'

Five or six sinewy, weather-beaten Vietnamese men aged between thirty and sixty, all smiling and beckoning, sat like languid birds of prey, high on the saddles of their customised push bikes above what seemed to be old pram seats welded between

79

two wheels at the front.

'No, thank you. I walk.' She'd better get out of here. Now a grubby little girl with enormous black eyes was tugging at her dress. On a strap around her neck she wore a tray on which was ranged an assortment of goods and trinkets. Maybe if she bought something they'd all go away and leave her alone.

She peered down at the tray, searching for something that might be even vaguely useful. The child had been watching Pru's face keenly and noticed her gaze fall on a cheaply printed copy of Graham Greene's *The Quiet American*. She snatched it up and thrust it at Pru.

'Good English book. You buy!'

'No, thank you. I've read that,' said Pru.

'Postcards?' wheedled the child, pointing to a wad of cards held together with a rubber band.

'I'll take this,' said Pru, bending to pick up a little yellow book with a pen-and-ink drawing of a woman in a conical hat on the front. A Vietnamese phrasebook. Might come in handy. Pru had rather prided herself on her aptitude for languages, but her French degree had been precious little use here so far.

'Three dollar,' said the girl.

'One dollar,' returned Pru.

'Two dollar.' The girl's ear almost brushed her bare shoulder in her attempt to look coyly appealing.

'One dollar,' said Pru firmly.

She fished out her purse and took out a five-dollar bill. The smallest she had, dammit. Now she'd have to hope the girl would admit to having change.

'One dollar,' she repeated firmly. The child fidgeted in a cardboard box at the back of the tray and came out with four crumpled dollar bills. As she handed Pru her change, however, the chorus of voices vying for her attention rose to a new crescendo. Those four dollars were probably a week's average wage.

A boy of ten or eleven wearing a similarly loaded tray around his neck presented himself in front of her, barring her way.

'You buy from her, why you no buy from me?' he demanded, half reproachful, half coaxing. 'I hungry. I need eat. Please!'

More cyclo riders had arrived to watch and try their luck with this lost-looking European woman.

'Lady take cyclo?'

'You want see War Museum?'

The woman with the babe-in-arms tugged at her arm, apparently near to tears again. The man with the toys was still waving his stump. The small boy was walking backwards in front of her picking out items from his tray, one by one, and waving them in front of her face. Enough was enough. Fixing her gaze above their heads she turned and walked purposefully to the kerb. Just across the street was Benh Thanh market. She could lose them in there.

But there was no gap in the steady stream of traffic. And no prospect of one either. She took a tentative step off the pavement but leaped back, nearly bowled over by a moped whose rider was almost hidden from view by five rattan armchairs precariously balanced and tied on around him. The sellers and beggars closed in more insistently.

'No!' she shouted to all of them in general. 'Go away!'

81

She tried again to leave the kerbside. This time she got a full two yards out before a tidal wave of motorcycles, seemingly moving as one, bore down on her and she scampered back to the safety of the pavement again.

Pull yourself together! Everyone else is managing to get across without looking like a terrified rabbit.

She felt a touch at her elbow. A very old and wrinkled woman, half Pru's size, was looking up at her, nodding and smiling gappily.

'Look. No, thank you. Please go away!'

'*Zi!* . . . *Zi!* . . . Come!' Bony fingers clasped Pru's upper arm and she felt herself being propelled forcefully into the maelstrom.

'Oh, my God! I'm going to die,' she squeaked as the traffic swarmed and swirled around them. Seconds later, she was standing on the pavement on the other side of the street, unscathed. Still smiling, her diminutive guiding angel released Pru's arm. 'Thank you,' Pru called out after her, but she had disappeared into the crowd.

Her relief was short-lived. The motley band of mendicants had followed her across the street. She was beginning to regret the decision to wear this conspicuous pink dress. She plunged into the crowded marketplace. Hurrying through the aisles and passageways, she had vague impressions of fabrics and clothing, bedlinen and tableware, heaped baskets of fruits and vegetables she'd never seen before in her life. Unmentionable insects and reptiles stared out angrily from jars of liquor; there were live birds for sale in cages; baskets of oozy-looking sweets. The smells that assailed her senses were an ever-changing pungent blend of herbs, spices, cheese, dried animal blood, exhaust fumes and warm tar. The stall holders added their own exhortations to those of her entourage. 'Madame, you buy from me? You like? Look. *Look, Madame! Very good.*'

She was approaching the other side of the market now, but there were several exits and entrances to the place, and she had no idea where she'd emerge and how near to or far from District 4 she would be.

'You want cyclo?' Two or three cyclo riders, pedalling lazily past, slowed almost to a standstill, keeping pace alongside her as she walked, lolling back on their high saddles, arms loosely swinging at their sides.

'Where you want to go?'

'Where you from?'

'English? American?'

More cyclo riders were arriving as if by telepathy. Some were young, all impudence and bravado; the older ones were more taciturn. It seemed the only way now to shake off her marauding coterie. Pru ran over to the rider who looked the least intimidating; in his late fifties, she guessed, and not as rakish as the rest.

She took out Roger's piece of card. 'Nautical Club, please. Le Tanh Ton Street.'

He smiled encouragingly but looked blank. She held the card out in front of him. He peered at it, head on one side.

'Ah, Nautical Club. Yes, lady. I know. Lee Tang Toh.' That's what she thought she'd said. Pru fell inelegantly into the plastic seat, planting her feet on the footplate welded to the bottom of it, and off they wobbled, leaving the disappointed faces behind at the roadside. She felt culpable for every

83

ounce of her nine stone ten pounds as her driver pedalled laboriously away from the kerb and into the teeming traffic. Gradually he got some momentum going and they became part of the shifting shoals of vehicles. She lifted her face to a welcome, cooling breeze.

'English?' he called. Pru swivelled her head to look up at him.

'Yes.'

'English people good people. Me like English.'

'Thank you.'

'Me Hien. You name?'

'Pru.'

'Pooh.'

'Um, yes. More or less.'

'You first time in Vietnam?'

'Yes.' She struggled for something else to say. 'Holiday.'

'You like?'

'Oh, yes,' she lied. 'Very nice. Very . . . hot.'

How feeble!

But turning back to talk to him was preferable to looking ahead. The seat she sat in, being mounted below and in front of the driver, put her first in line in the damage stakes if there should be a collision. It amazed her that there hadn't been one already. When he wanted to turn right, her driver did just that; no hesitation, no indication, simply pedalling straight across the oncoming traffic. Her eyes searched his face for signs of madness but it remained impassive under the peak of his red baseball cap.

Turning frontwards again, she watched nervously as they meandered into the middle of a busy crossroads. A lorry was heading straight for them, its klaxon deafening. How would Molly feel when she found out that her mother had followed her out to Vietnam only to die ignominiously in the twisted wreckage of a converted butcher's bike, a ten-ton truck and a couple of Honda 50s? Pru shut her eyes. Astonishingly, when she opened them again, the lorry had passed without incident and the junction was already receding behind them. There was nothing for it but to consign her fate to the gods and enjoy the ride.

The cyclo pottered creakily into a narrower, quieter side street. In the space of less than twenty minutes, night had fallen.

'Not far now, lady. Not far.'

He swung their chariot left into another murky street and then, without warning, stopped pedalling. They came to an almost immediate halt. Something brown scurried noiselessly along the gutter, away into the gloom.

'Here, Miss Pooh.' Her driver pointed triumphantly towards a pale blue-painted doorway set in between what looked like two deserted concrete shops.

She scrambled out of her seat, losing a sandal in the process.

'Is this the Nautical Club?'

Hopping on one leg to avoid putting her shoeless foot on the ground, she looked about her. All she could see was what looked like a closed-down restaurant, blue-painted doors and shuttered windows. Blue neon letters draped in sagging electric cables spelled 'Nautical Club'.

The man nodded, smiling expectantly as, still teetering on one foot, she looked for her purse.

Now she could just discern distant talking and

85

laughter; the odd shout or guffaw rising momentarily before blending back into the general hubbub. A woman's voice was crooning something Stan Getzy in tones rather more shrill than the composer probably had in mind. She could just make out the sound of a piano.

'How much?'

'Two dollar, lady.'

She ought to barter, but then two dollars for half an hour's hard pedalling through the streets of Saigon seemed fair enough. Not that he seemed the least bit exhausted. Looking at him properly for the first time she could see what a strong, lean, weathered body he had. Should she give him a tip?

She took out two dollar bills.

'Hard work!' She smiled, proffering the notes.

He took them swiftly with oil-blackened fingers, tucked them into the top pocket of his shirt and began to move away.

'Wait!' She took another dollar bill from her purse and handed it to him. He looked astonished.

'Miss Pooh very nice lady.'

'Thank you.'

Grinning toothlessly, he leaned forward on his handlebars to watch her as she retrieved her sandal from the gutter, wriggled her foot back into it and walked uncertainly towards the bar's entrance.

*   *   *

The unpromising street door opened into a small, square entrance lobby with just a pair of Western saloon-style doors between Pru and the bar which, she was surprised to see, was jam-packed. Most of the front part of the bar was taken up by a scratched and battered black grand piano and customers were standing or sitting on stools around it, heads close together to hear themselves speak above the music.

Strutting among them, the singer had made a determined effort to be a Vietnamese version of Tina Turner. Her long black hair had been energetically backcombed to make it look thicker and she was encased in a strapless, thigh-length, velour and Lycra number which matched the colour of her generously applied scarlet lipstick. Legs that couldn't in all fairness be described as shapely ended in preposterously high-heeled silver court shoes. As far as the singing voice was concerned, the middle register was fine, but the higher notes were letting her down badly.

Cool and elegant by contrast, a young woman with a sheet of long, shining black hair, enviably slim in pale grey damask trousers and top, slipped serenely among the customers, carrying a tray of drinks.

Taking a deep breath, Pru straightened her back, sucked in her tummy and pushed open both doors—to a chorus of whistles and a round of raucous applause. Horror-struck, she stopped in her tracks, then realised the approbation was for the singer who had just finished her set. Composing herself again, she stepped forward into the mêlée.

* * *

Giles Fitzpatrick looked up as the doors swung open. He liked to keep a check on everyone who came and went; partly for security reasons, partly because he prided himself on being the best and most attentive bar manager in Saigon, and partly from sheer curiosity—especially where his female clientele was concerned.

Nice-looking woman, he thought. And alone if I'm not mistaken. She was English, he was pretty sure of that. Most of his customers were regulars; expats from the UK or the States, working over here on long-term contracts with international corporations; insurance companies, law firms, or the construction industry. This woman didn't fit any of the usual categories. She seemed to be looking round for someone. Intrigued, he lit a cigarette and watched her through the tendrils of his exhaled smoke as she pushed her way diffidently round the piano towards the bar.

Pru had hardly eaten or drunk anything since she got off the plane—and that was beginning to feel like days ago.

'Excuse me, please.' She squirmed behind the backs of two Englishmen, engaged in some spiritedly elaborate story.

'Well,' broke off a stripe-shirted, thirty-something business type, turning round to look at her, 'darling! I didn't know you cared.'

Bloodshot eyes, in a face too flushed and fleshy for its age, scanned her blatantly from head to foot and back again.

'I just need to get to the bar.'

'Just make sure you pass this way on your way back, love,' he joked.

'Face the other way next time, though,' brayed his companion, 'it's my turn next.'

Ignoring the hand that brushed across her

bottom, Pru forced herself to push on through. At the bar, the next hurdle was deciding what to drink, assuming the bar staff spoke English. Everyone else here seemed to. Actually, something to eat was what she really wanted.

'Good evening, lovely lady, what can we offer you?'

'Hi,' said Pru warily.

A tanned young man in a loose silk Hawaiian shirt and chinos had appeared at her side.

'Oh, trust Giles to get first bite of the cherry!' someone called out.

'That one lost her cherry yonks ago,' laughed someone else.

'That'll do, thank you, guys,' Giles called across at them over her head.

'Yeah, yeah.'

They turned back to their original conversations with affected nonchalance. So this was the undesirable 'Fitzbollocks'. Molly's lover.

'It seems to me that what you need is a drink and somewhere to sit down. Where can we put you?' Absentmindedly rumpling his already untidy blond hair, Giles looked thoughtfully around his bar— the little booth opposite the piano would be perfect. He knew the young couple sitting there well enough to get them to move.

'Come with me.'

Whatever Giles murmured as he stooped briefly over the couple's table, it was effective. Glancing at Pru with a momentary flicker of interest, the man stood up and retreated towards the piano, pulling his girlfriend with him by the hand.

'Tam!' The pretty Vietnamese waitress glided towards them. 'Drinks on the house for Robin and

Kate. And . . . what can we get for our mysterious new customer?'

'Half a gallon of water and a gin and tonic, please.' She smiled at Tam.

'And mine's on the bar, if you wouldn't mind . . . Thanks, my angel.'

Tam melted away.

'Please.' Giles gestured Pru to sit down in the vacated booth and perched himself on the edge of the bench-seat next to her.

'Well,' he began, his eyes searching her face with intimate interest, 'usually I like to find out a lady's name before I buy her a drink.'

'It's Pru. And you're Giles.'

'How do you know?'

'The chap over there referred to you by name just now.'

'Ah, yes, sorry about them.'

'That's OK.'

'So, what brings you to Saigon—and to my bar in particular?'

His pale grey eyes held hers with a warmth and interest that seemed genuine.

'I've come from London,' began Pru guardedly. 'Just arrived this afternoon . . .'

Tam arrived with a tray and deftly set before them Pru's gin and tonic, decorated with a slice of lemon impaled, sail-like, on a plastic swizzle stick, a large glass of iced water, a squat, chunky glass of what Pru assumed was whisky on the rocks, and two little dishes of salted nuts and olives.

'So are you here on holiday? Or is it business?'

Not an easy question actually.

'I suppose a bit of both.'

He smiled. 'Enigmatic.'

Giles picked up his whisky and raised it towards her in salute. More than anything she wanted to gulp down the water, but dutifully took up the gin and tonic and chinked his glass.

'Cheers.'

Never had gin and tonic tasted so good. Quite suddenly, Pru began to relax. Here she was, far from home, in a Saigon bar, and—for tonight at any rate—not as someone's wife or mother, sister or daughter, but as herself, in her own right. She had a vague but liberating sense that a whole lot of shackles and chains were, for the first time in years, beginning to loosen their grip on her spirit.

Prudence, you need to eat something. That drink is going straight to your head.

She plunged her hand into the bowl of nuts.

Giles was watching her, smiling expectantly. 'And?'

'And what?'

'Well, there's obviously a story to tell. A business trip would be one thing, but a woman like you doesn't travel alone to a country like this for a holiday. Vietnam is too beautiful a place not to share with someone.' He was studying her, frankly flirtatious now. 'Unless you're a backpacker, which obviously you're not.'

Another gin and tonic appeared in front of her.

They chinked glasses again.

'So, Mystery Lady?'

The singer began crooning into the microphone again. Giles moved a little closer.

'"*I never can say goodbye . . .*"' chortled the imitation diva.

Shame, thought Pru.

Time to bite the bullet.

'I'm looking for my daughter.'

'Really?' Giles waited.

'She's been here a few weeks now, working for a charity in a village somewhere.'

'We get a lot of English girls here doing that now. Gap-year kids. I might even know her.'

'You might indeed.'

'What does she look like? What's her name?'

'Molly.'

The grey eyes blinked twice involuntarily.

'Molly Taylor?'

'That's right.'

'The gorgeous Molly! Yes, indeed. I know her very well.'

'So I gather.'

'Bloody hell!' Involuntarily he shifted a few inches back on the seat, to a rather less intimate distance. 'So you're Molly's mum! I can see the likeness now . . . the long legs . . . the green eyes. Well . . . it's good to meet you, Mrs Taylor.'

'It's OK, Giles. You can stick with Pru. So where can I find her?'

'Does she know you're here?'

Pru ignored that. 'I know she's left the hostel. Where is she staying now?'

'She's up in a village in the hills, a couple of hours' drive away. Out towards the Cambodian border.'

'Cambodia!'

'She comes back to stay with me most weekends.'

'And what's she doing there?'

'Good question. I'm not too sure myself. Looking after some children, basically.'

'You must know more than that.'

92

'Not really, no. We don't talk much about her work when she's with me. All I know is that she left the job she started off doing because she found some kids vegetating in an orphanage outside the village somewhere.'

'An orphanage?'

'Yes. I think she felt they needed her help more than the community school did. But don't ask me. Molly's a law unto herself!'

'So she's all right then? There's nothing to worry about?'

'Yes. I mean—no. No, there's nothing to worry about and yes, she's all right.'

'It's so hard to judge things when you're hundreds of miles away and your imagination's working overtime.'

'And she doesn't know you're here?'

'No, she doesn't. I thought I'd surprise her.' Pru injected as much airy confidence into her voice as she could.

Giles raised an eyebrow.

'She'll be surprised all right. Hey,' he got to his feet, 'what am I thinking of? Have you eaten anything? I don't suppose you have. Can I get you a little steak and chips? Or we do a wonderful seared tuna salad. My cook's the best French chef in Saigon.'

'Actually, I'm starving. The tuna sounds great. I haven't eaten in . . . God knows how many hours. Thank you.'

'Stay right where you are.'

Giles picked up his glass and she watched him saunter towards the bar at the side of the room, dispensing pecks on cheeks, pats on backs, and 'How're you doings?' She felt awkward now that he had left her there alone. She didn't have much in common with the rest of the clientele, most of whom looked to be in their twenties or thirties and were probably still thrusting their way up whatever greasy pole destiny had chosen for them.

Behind the bar, Giles was engaged in earnest conversation with the young waitress. Catching Pru's eye over Tam's shoulder, he stepped closer to murmur something in the girl's ear. She turned away and, with a quick, furtive glance in Pru's direction, vanished into the kitchen.

Giles picked up a pack of cigarettes off the bar, tapped one out against the palm of his hand and lit it. He looked entirely at home in his smoky, artificial, night-time world. There was a touch of the Hugh Grant about him. Rakishly handsome. A bit of a smoothie. Not Molly's usual type at all. A far cry from Duncan the down-and-out. Thank God for that at least.

A moment later, he was back beside her with a knife and fork, wrapped in a serviette. 'Sustenance for the weary traveller coming right up. Two minutes.'

'Thank you. Now what can you tell me about this family Molly's apparently got herself involved with? She said they were being evicted from their property or something. Is she living with them? Is she going to get herself into trouble?'

'I really can't tell you all that much, I'm sorry, Pru. I think it's best if she tells you herself. It's her story not mine.' He was going to leave it at that, but added as an afterthought, 'She'll be all right. Molly's a great kid. I love her to bits.'

'I want to go and see her at the village tomorrow.'

94

'You could do that.' He shrugged. 'Or you could wait a couple of days and see her when she's back in town. She usually comes down here for the weekend. I can look after you till she gets here. Show you round a bit.'

The waif-like Tam arrived carrying a plate of glistening salad leaves with a delicate piece of grilled tuna on top.

'This looks wonderful. Thank you.'

'How long are you here for?'

'It's a ten-day trip.' Pru attacked her tuna steak.

'Well, we'll have to make the most of your company while we have you, won't we?'

'How long does it take to get to Molly's village?'

'About two hours . . .'

'What's the place called again?'

'Tra Binh.'

'And is there a train or a bus?'

'There's a bus that goes some of the way. But after that you'd be stuck.'

'Perhaps I could hire a car?'

'Tourists don't hire cars over here.'

'Why not?'

'Not to drive themselves.' Giles pulled the ashtray towards him and stubbed his cigarette out, half smoked. 'You can hire a car with a driver for about fifty dollars a day. Plus the guy's meals and drinks. It has to be done through the proper channels; one of the hotels or a travel agency. That way the authorities can keep tabs on you.'

'So they're still quite paranoid over here then?'

'They just like to know what everyone's up to. And make sure people see the best side of Vietnam.'

Pru had been rummaging in her bag, looking for

95

her map of Vietnam. But she only had the simplified Ho Chi Minh City guide with her.

'I've got a map back at my hotel. Perhaps tomorrow morning you could show me where this place is exactly, and then I can work out how to get there. Unless you've got a map here?'

'I tell you what.' Giles stood up, 'I'll do better than that. I'll take you. On the bike. Tam and Kien can look after things here for the day.'

'Oh, that would be wonderful. Are you sure?'

She hadn't at all relished the idea of finding her way to this remote village on her own.

'It'll be good to have an excuse to get out of town. And see the adorable Molly, of course.'

'Well, it's kind of you. Thank you.'

'And you, dear Pru, should go now and get some beauty sleep. I'll get my cook to run you back. He's finished here for the night.'

Pru was too tired to even pretend to protest. She finished the last of her gin and tonic.

'Wait there a minute, I'll go and get Kien. Where are you staying, by the way?'

'The Imperial Hotel. Near Benh Tanh Market.'

Giles looked surprised. 'Not the cosiest of hotels.'

A minute later he was back accompanied by a slim young man with neat, centre-parted hair, blinking nervously behind thick round spectacles. He looked more like a student than a chef.

'You know where you're going then, Kien.' The three of them walked towards the door, Giles plucking a set of keys from a hook near the bar on the way and handing them to him.

'Look after her.'

He took Pru's hand and kissed it. Over his

96

shoulder, she saw two young women smirk at each other. She pulled her hand away.

'Shall we say eleven-ish tomorrow morning? Here?'

Pru would have preferred an earlier start. She could hardly wait now to see Molly.

'We won't get there till about lunchtime then.'

'Absolutely.' He smiled, either not noticing or deliberately ignoring her disappointed tone. 'Sweet dreams, Mrs Taylor.'

Kien pushed open the door and Pru walked obediently through. Parked just outside on the pavement was a powerful motorbike, gleaming in the dark. Kien sat astride it, kicked the stand up and fired the engine. Rather gingerly Pru got on behind, yanking at her dress in a vain attempt to stop it riding up. She hadn't ridden pillion since her late-teens when she'd had a succession of boyfriends with motorbikes or scooters, and had prided herself on her skill in leaning into corners, keeping the balance right, loving the speed and the excitement. She slung her bag round her neck, leaned back a little and clasped the chrome rack behind her with both hands.

'To the manner born.' Giles grinned, making no attempt to disguise a lingering look at rather more thigh than Pru would have chosen to reveal.

He lifted a hand in farewell, winked exaggeratedly and turned to go back inside. Kien scooted the heavy machine on to the road. As he revved up to move off, the bar door opened to let in some more customers. In that moment, she had a glimpse of Giles seizing a busty brunette around the waist, swinging her round to face him and kissing her lightly on the mouth. The woman pressed against him, laughing. The door swung shut.

Oh, Molly, thought Pru.

Chapter Seven

Pru woke feeling hot and groggy after a shallow sleep. She flailed her way out of the mosquito net and headed for the basin and a cold splash. Her watch told her it was seven o'clock. Even this early in the morning, the heat was almost unbearably oppressive. She wiped beads of perspiration from under her eyes and along each side of her nose.

You're probably getting the menopause

'Thanks a lot,' rejoined Pru.

She cleaned her teeth, making sure she didn't swallow any of the water, brushed and tied her hair back, then applied smudgy grey eye pencil and some lip colour, ducking her head around to find gaps between the black patches on the mirror.

Trying to keep cool, she dressed slowly, selecting beige cotton trousers, white cap-sleeved T-shirt and a navy cardigan to tie round her waist, just in case. Bending to pick up her canvas trainers, something caught her eye under the bed. She peered for a moment or two in revolted disbelief before confirming beyond any doubt the presence of a squashed cockroach almost as big as a sparrow.

She tucked the shoes under her arm, grabbed her bag and *Lonely Planet Guide* from the bedside table and made for the door, pushing aside the chair she'd wedged under the handle overnight to deter any more unwelcome intruders. And there she was, out on the concrete stairs, ready to start her first full day in Vietnam. An oily cooking smell wafted up towards her. At the bottom of the stairwell she stopped to put her shoes on. A woman in loose yellow pants and matching top was squatting there, washing plates and cutlery in a plastic bowl on the floor. They exchanged polite smiles.

Well, better face whatever was on offer for breakfast. She'd have given it a miss, but she had to eat something with her malaria pill.

Following the kitchen smells, Pru turned back on herself underneath the staircase and away from the direction of the foyer, into a murky passageway. There was one door on the right-hand side. She put her ear against it. No human voices, but the chirrup of birdsong. She pushed the door open and stepped into a room furnished with four square tables covered with red-and-white checked oilcloths. Each was set with a carafe of water, a small bottle of soy sauce, a bunch of chopsticks in a pot and a plastic ashtray. The birdsong came from a medium-sized brown bird in a cage in one corner of the room. Health and Safety would never allow such a thing back home.

'Hi there, Bird.'

It cocked its head on one side, looking at her with one eye, as caged birds do, adopting a wary silence.

There was no one around. Perhaps there wasn't anyone else daft enough to be staying here. Pru lifted the lid of a large saucepan on a narrow sideboard. It was full to the top with sticky boiled rice. She put the lid back. Three steel containers were plugged into wall sockets, so presumably had heating elements. The first one was full of noodles and mostly unidentifiable mixed vegetables. The second contained paper-thin strips of crisp—well, crispish—bacon; the third, fried potatoes.

Pru put four or five bacon rashers and half a dozen pieces of potato in a bowl, stuck a couple of bread slices into the toaster and decanted some tea from the thermos into one of the mugs. It was rather a relief to be on her own here. Now she could look at her map and think about the day ahead.

'Hey there, good morning,' said a breezy voice with an Australian accent.

Bugger, thought Pru.

Looking up, she saw a tall, lean figure, unshaven, baggy-eyed, with a halo of bushy brown hair, and wearing an unironed, faded blue T-shirt and knee-length, dark green shorts covered in pockets. He began festooning the back of one of the chairs with a battered camera, a medium-sized rucksack and a shabby canvas hat. Not a backpacker; a good twenty years beyond that stage. A photographer perhaps.

He picked up a plate and began helping himself to food, systematically opening and closing the containers on the sideboard. Plate loaded to its fullest capacity, he sat down opposite his gear and stripped the paper off a pair of wooden chopsticks. He waited until he'd filled his mouth with rice and vegetables before addressing her thickly,

'You just arrived?'

'Well, yesterday. Yes.'

He swallowed. 'Like it?'

Pru carried her mug and modestly filled bowl to the table next to the one he'd laid claim to.

'To be honest, no. Not really.'

'Not really? You must be joking!' He got up, filled a glass to the brim with orange juice at the sideboard, knocked it back in one hit and refilled it before taking it back to his seat. 'Saigon's a great place. The whole country is. Beautiful landscape, good grub, really cheap, and lovely people. I'm always wangling my way over here, finding stories to cover.'

'Is it Saigon or Ho Chi Minh City? People seem to call it both.'

'Ah, well, it's supposed to be Ho Chi Minh, but people are going back to calling it Saigon these days. It'll always be Saigon to me.'

'You're a journalist, are you?'

'Yeah. *Sydney Daily News.* South East Asia correspondent. Freelance.' He looked round the dingy dining room. 'Sure, *this* place is a bit of a dump. A lot of a dump. But I save on the exxes staying here. A bed is a bed, basically, isn't it?'

'Up to a point, I suppose so.' She arranged her bacon rashers on one slice of toast and placed the other slice neatly on top. 'Could do without massive great dead cockroaches for company, mind you.'

He shovelled in another mouthful of food, then half stood, bending across from his table towards her, reaching out a hand to be shaken.

'I'm Kenny, by the way. Kenny McKinnon.'

'Pru Taylor.'

He was back at the sideboard again, going for seconds. The bird chirruped from its cage, probably in amazement at the amount of food one living creature could put away.

'And you're doing a piece over here now, for your paper?' she asked.

'Yeh.'

'What about?'

'It's about this American guy—a war vet—who's trying to raise funds for a kids' charity over here.' Kenny paused to mop his mouth with one of the paper napkins.

'The Vietnamese people don't object to American veterans coming over here then, after all the appalling damage they did?'

He raised an eyebrow. 'The war finished nearly thirty years ago, you know. And some of the vets do great stuff over here.'

Pru picked a piece of fried potato out of her bowl with her fingers and ate it. 'You wouldn't have thought they'd want to come back after what they went through.'

'Nah. It's the opposite. They come back in their hundreds. It's therapy.'

'For holidays?'

'A lot of them come over in groups for a couple of weeks to lay a few ghosts, yes. And then some of them get hooked and come back again and again. Stay for months on end sometimes. They start setting up orphanages, land mine projects, helping disabled people . . . that kind of stuff. Like this guy I'm seeing today with his limbs for kids, you know. Trying to put something back.'

'I can understand that. A need to make amends somehow.' Pru took a last bite of her bacon sandwich, leaving a couple of nibbled crusts on the plate. 'It must have been tough fighting a war while the rest of the world was going all peace and love. Especially such an unpopular war.'

She remembered the anti-Vietnam War protests in the late-sixties. Her mother still had a picture of Pru's elder brother, Brian, on a march in London, holding out two fingers in the peace sign and wearing a horrendous kaftan and flared trousers.

She'd been struggling to open her map of Vietnam. 'I can never manage bloody maps.'

Finally having tamed it, she put her glasses on and peered at it.

'What are you looking for?'

'The village I'm going to visit today. My daughter's there.' She scanned the villages along the Cambodian border. 'It's called Tra Binh. I can see Loc Ninh, Tra Vinh . . . Tay Binh . . . but not Tra Binh.'

'Wait a sec and I'll have a look for you.' Kenny was taking a little silver tin out of his rucksack. 'But what I need before anything else . . .' he put the tin on the table and opened it carefully '. . . is a nice little spliff.'

Using the inside of the lid as a work surface, he deftly crumbled a thin line of dried brown vegetation on to a cigarette paper. 'Good stuff this,' he stated earnestly. Then, looking up at her, 'You don't mind, do you?'

Kenny held the battered roll-up horizontally in front of his face to inspect his handiwork before putting it between his lips and lighting up.

'I thought they were really strict on drugs over here?'

He breathed in deeply, waited a few seconds and exhaled a stream of aromatic smoke with his reply.

'They are. Trafficking's a capital offence. Firing squad. But I don't deal. I just smoke the stuff.

103

Anyway, no one's going to suss me here.' He took another pull. 'Unless you dob on me, of course.'

'They don't dish out the death penalty too often these days, do they?'

'Like hell they don't! There's something like twenty-seven different offences you can be executed for.'

'Like what?'

'I can tell you most of them. I did a piece with Amnesty back in January. There's treason, espionage, sabotage, hijacking . . .' he counted them off on his fingers, 'banditry—whatever that means—terrorism, undermining peace, crimes against humanity . . .' He took another toke on his joint, hissing loudly through his teeth. Pru waited. 'Anything to do with the manufacture or selling of drugs. And obviously murder, rape and robbery.' He exhaled again, slowly. 'Oh, and fraud. I think that broadly covers it.'

'So how many people are executed, say, in a year?'

'This year, so far, fifty-three. About forty of them for drugs. They don't publicise the others if they can help it. One of them was a Canadian geezer, back in April. First Westerner they've shot since the war. You don't mess with these guys. Want a puff?'

His eyes were those of a hard-core pot smoker, dark-ringed and red-rimmed.

'No. No, thanks.' Pru sipped her tea. She was getting used to the astringent, bitter taste.

'This hotel could be done for crimes against humanity,' she observed. 'The electrics in my room are lethal.'

Kenny stretched out on his chair, elbows behind

his head, looking up at the ceiling, holding his breath, welcoming the narcotic into his bloodstream.

'Have you heard of Tra Binh?' she asked.

He got up and lumbered over to where she was sitting.

'This is the Cambodian border running down here . . .' she murmured.

'That's right. And Tra Binh is . . . somewhere over . . .'

They pored over the map.

'There!' they said together, each stabbing a finger at the same place.

'That's four or five inches north-west of Ho Chi Minh City on Highway Thirteen . . . which is,' she checked the scale at the bottom, 'about eighty kilometres, by the look of it.'

'Bit less maybe,' said Kenny. 'In point of fact, I think I have heard of Tra Binh.' A lump of ash fell on to the map. Pru blew it on to the floor. 'I might be wrong but I think there were some demos there a few weeks back. Protests about something. Land probably. Or health issues. Education maybe. It's usually land, though.'

'What happened?' Pru urged him. 'Can you remember?'

'I just seem to remember seeing the name on the wires a few times.' He sucked on the last of his joint, holding the soggy brown stub between thumb and forefinger and whistling out the last few sacred wisps of smoke through his teeth. 'I can try and find out for you, if you like? If it's the place I think it is, the head honcho's a real hard bastard. Maybe I'm wrong. Just rings a bell.'

He opened his little tin again, crushed what was

105

left of the roach into the lid and snapped it shut.

'Well, time to get my arse into gear.' He began slinging the straps of his various bits and pieces over his shoulders. 'How are you getting to this place today?'

'A friend of my daughter is taking me.'

'Does he know his way around?'

'I think so. He runs a place called the Nautical Club here.'

'Ah—that'll be Giles!'

'You know him then?'

'Everybody knows Giles. That's good he's taking you. He's resident here, not a tourist. They don't like tourists going off the beaten track. Makes 'em kind of edgy.' He shambled inelegantly towards the door. 'Nice to meet you anyway. Enjoy your trip. Catch you later.'

'Yes. Hope so.'

He clattered out of sight.

Pru sat in her chair, staring at the little words in italics on the map. *Tra Binh*. Where Molly was.

'And good luck!'

Kenny's curly head had reappeared for a moment round the door for this final valediction and then was gone again.

'Thanks,' she called weakly after him. She became aware that the concierge had crept into the room. Had he been listening? How much English did he understand? Instinct told her she didn't want him knowing where she was going, with whom or why. She left him collecting the plates. A brief backward glance as she left the room caught him fingering her rejected toast crusts, his eyes fixed on her in a look that seemed to Pru both menacing and insultingly intimate.

106

Despite the enervating heat, she found the energy to run back up the stairs to her room.

*   *   *

It was getting on for ten o'clock. It would take about twenty minutes to get to the Nautical Club. She'd be earlier than Giles had suggested but that was too bad. Perhaps she should take a taxi. She didn't feel like facing hawkers and beggars this morning. She made a quick check in her shoulder bag to make sure she'd packed everything she could possibly need for the trip. The map was the most important, then her purple leather zip purse containing a little under three hundred dollars, digital camera, bottle of water, tissues, sun cream, mosquito repellent, malaria pills, some mints and a foldable floppy hat she looked ridiculous in and was hoping to avoid wearing if she could possibly help it. Before leaving the room, she took a ten-dollar note out of the purse and stuffed it in her pocket. That way she could pay the cab without having to flash too much money in a public place.

Down in the lobby, she thrust her key at the concierge, meeting his eye with a new directness.

'I'd like a taxi straight away, please.'

'You go where?'

Mind your own business, she thought, but better give him some information.

'Le Than Ton Street.'

He screwed up his face in puzzlement. She tried again, remembering the cyclo driver's pronunciation the day before.

'Lee Tang Toh.'

Slowly, without breaking eye contact with her,

107

he picked up the phone, waited, gabbled a few sentences into it and hung up.

'Another thing,' said Pru loudly. 'There is a dead cockroach under my bed. I should like it to be removed by the time I get back tonight.'

He looked back at her expressionlessly. All right. What about trying French again. People here must surely understand that language, after so many years of French occupation.

'Il y a un . . .' what the hell was the word for cockroach? *'. . . un grand insecte sous mon lit. C'est affreux. Je demande que vous le nettoyer toute de suite, ou je ne paye pas l'addition.'*

He shrugged. He obviously didn't know what she was saying. He got the message she was complaining about something, though.

'And,' she continued, raising her voice a little more. He might not understand her but it was surprisingly enjoyable to get some of her aversion to this little man off her chest, 'the air conditioning doesn't work. And the electrics up there are bloody dangerous. The socket in my room nearly killed me.'

His eyes hardened with dislike. Pru hoped hers returned the look in kind. In fact, she found herself staring him out. And winning. He turned on his heel and flounced out through the nylon curtain behind the desk.

The taxi arrived almost at once. It drew up at the kerbside and, seeing her waiting there, the driver beckoned through his open window. She wrenched open the recalcitrant hotel door and strode towards the car.

Ten more minutes through the hooting, weaving, throbbing Saigon traffic and they were outside the

Nautical Club. She paid the driver the three dollars he asked for and got out.

The light of day revealed the blue paintwork on the wooden doors and shutters to be faded and peeling off in places. In the silence of the empty bar, the doors creaked as she pushed them open. A rotating fan in the ceiling provided some small respite from the heavy, inescapable heat outside. There was no one around. Just that distinctive morning bar smell of stale cigarettes and beer. Pru stood uncertainly by the piano, wondering what to do.

'Hello?' She took another step forward into the gloom.

There was a rustle out at the back somewhere and Tam came through. Dressed in jeans and T-shirt, she looked only a little less fragile than she had done in the silk *ao-dai* she'd been wearing last night.

'Is Giles about?' enquired Pru.

The girl inclined her head with a small smile and turned back the way she had come. Presumably she was going to tell Giles she'd arrived. Pru wandered around. It was easier to take in her environment without all the noise and people. There were oil paintings on the wall . . . a nautical theme . . . galleons in full sail, fishing vessels battling with ocean breakers, a holiday beach scene that looked like somewhere on the Costa Brava—nothing that had an obvious connection with Indochina. Fishing nets, glass floats and polished oars adorned the walls and ceilings.

'Giles with you soon.' The girl had returned.

'OK, thank you,' said Pru.

109

'You like a coffee?'

'Er . . . no, I'm fine, thank you. Some water would be good.'

Tam inclined her head again and disappeared.

Pru sat down at the piano and diffidently touched one of the keys. It was a long time since she'd played. When she was pregnant with Jack, bored, unemployed and at home on her own most of the day, she'd spent a lot of time at the piano in the living room. Her father had been a boogie fanatic in his spare time, and when he died, shortly after she and David got married, he left her his piano and the stool to go with it, packed full of old sheet music—a book of Oscar Peterson exercises, old Duke Ellington scores, Ramsey Lewis . . . she'd begun to teach herself some of the easier numbers. She'd revelled, not so much in learning whole pieces, but just in the spine-tingling sound of some of the chord sequences.

She tried to remember her favourite exercise—a lovely series of chords working down the keyboard, stretching the fingers of her left hand to the full octave.

'Nice.' Giles had appeared in the doorway, wearing only a towel round his middle. 'You're booked!'

Pru laughed self-consciously and stood up, trying not to look at the well-nourished, tanned upper torso of her daughter's boyfriend.

'Sorry I'm a bit early.'

You're not sorry at all; you're annoyed he's not ready! Why don't you say what you really feel?

'That's OK. You're honoured actually. I don't normally get up before midday. And last night was a bit of a late one as it turned out.'

He came towards her.

'So how are you this morning, sweetheart? How was your first night in Vietnam?' He stretched out his arm and wrapped it round her neck, pulling her towards him.

My daughter's boyfriend, nearly naked and just out of bed, is going to kiss me.

'Not too bad, thanks,' she managed, between receiving a peck on each cheek, hoping her face wasn't unpleasantly damp with perspiration.

Giles, on the other hand, smelled faintly of soap, sandalwood perhaps, fresh from the shower.

'I promise not to keep you waiting too long. Tam will make you a cappuccino with my brilliant new machine. I must have tried out at least eight of them before I found this one. Cost a fortune, mind you. Had to import it from the States in the end. 'Course, when the bastard thing goes wrong, I'm on the phone long-distance to some technician trying to follow all these complicated instructions. Worth it, though. Best cappuccinos in Saigon. Enjoy! Back in a sec.'

Pru had been desperate to cut in and impress on him how anxious she felt to get to the village and make sure Molly was all right. But it probably wouldn't have made much difference. Giles would take as long as he took and that was that.

The girl came back, threw Pru a 'you changed your mind then' sort of glance and busied herself in front of the chrome knobs and dials on the coffee machine. She had evidently forgotten Pru's water request.

Giles reappeared in the doorway.

'One for me too, please, darling,' he said quietly to the waitress, winked over at Pru and retreated again.

*   *   *

It was past 11.30 by the time Giles hauled his Honda Shadow on to the road. 'We don't need to pack any supplies,' he said. 'There'll be fresh produce for sale along the route and plenty of places to stop for a drink.'

'What about crash helmets?' enquired Pru.

'No one wears them here. To be honest, they limit your vision and your hearing—the two faculties you need most to survive on the roads in this country. For me, it's a choice between keeping all my wits about me to avoid an accident or protecting my head in case I do hit the deck. I prefer the first option.' He put the key in the ignition. The bike started up with a roar, then settled into a pulsing growl.

Pru settled herself behind him on the bike, leaning back against the luggage rack.

'Don't worry, sweetheart, I'll make sure we stay on the road.'

A moment or two later and they had become part of the chaotic ebb and flow of Saigon's traffic. The breeze rippled through her shirt. She lifted her face to it, feeling cool for the first time since she'd left London.

'This is just great!' she yelled at Giles's shoulder blades.

'I'd rather you put your arms round me,' he called back. 'The road surface is terrible. Potholes everywhere.'

'A bit like London then, but it's speed bumps there.'

112

She put her arms round Giles's waist, her knees clamped close to his thighs, her chest pressed into his back, her hands under his ribcage. It was a long time since she'd had her arms round a man like this. Resting her cheek against his back, she could feel the muscles in his shoulders moving as he changed up through the gears.

Don't enjoy this too much, Prudence. This guy is your daughter's boyfriend, remember.

She stiffened again and sat up straighter. Ten minutes later, the mad, mercenary city was receding behind them.

'When do we start seeing the real Vietnam?' she shouted.

'Five or six kilometres,' he shouted. 'You're lucky, you're seeing it on a good clear day. We're still in the rainy season.'

Already the closely packed city shops and tenements were giving way to crumbling suburbs. They were out on the open road now, but it was a narrow one. The ancient Russian buses and overloaded lorries could pass each other from opposite directions, but with no room to spare for any other road users. Pru lost count of the times they had to swerve off the tarmac and take to the dusty verge. How everyone maintained an air of complete serenity and the roads weren't littered with casualties, was beyond her understanding.

She stopped looking ahead, put her trust in Giles and concentrated on what was going on to either side of her. It was less stressful that way.

The concrete buildings were still cheek-by-jowl, but mostly single-storey now. Still the main preoccupation was selling, but now it was heavier goods and effectively divided into sectors. There was half a mile of wrought-iron works—everything from gates to lamp stands—then a series of coffin-makers, then several huge, haloed Virgin Marys in stone stood outside their makers' workshops, presiding benignly over passing humanity; after that were stacks of lorry tyres. Finally the buildings began petering out altogether and there ensued a good two miles of diggers, tractors, and other heavy plant for sale. Construction and road building were evidently the current growth industry.

Superimposed on all of it, though, along the sandy, stony verges, individuals squatted placidly in front of whatever they had to offer for sale. It looked more like something to do than a serious occupation. Some hunkered down in front of baskets containing various fruits and vegetables, presumably harvested earlier that morning. Others sat on low, plastic stools alongside racks of assorted hats and baseball caps, or woven baskets, or plastic toys. Some presided over a few cans of fizzy drink stacked up in pyramids, sheltered ineffectually by tattered umbrellas planted in the dust.

Giles slowed down and swung the bike to the left, off the main thoroughfare and on to a rutted red-dirt road. Pru hung on tighter as he changed back up the gears. This was more like it. A patchwork of paddy fields opened up on either side of them; acre after watery acre, criss-crossed with narrow green pathways and stretching almost to the horizon. In the distance on her left Pru could make out a range of mountains. Here and there, isolated figures in conical hats were bent double, black cotton trousers rolled up to the knee, hands thrust into the mire, presumably teasing and separating the green rice shoots.

Pru didn't hear the roar of another motorbike until it overtook them. Veering in front of them it came to an abrupt halt, forcing Giles to brake hard and stop too. The two engines throbbed in the rural silence while Giles and Pru gazed in surprise at the pair of uniformed officials who sat staring back at them. They didn't look friendly.

Pru couldn't tell whether the uniform was police or military: olive green with long brown leather boots and those upswept hats. The pillion rider dismounted while the driver stayed astride his bike, presumably ready to thwart any attempt they might make to escape. He was short and fleshy-faced. He extended an open palm towards Giles but his hooded eyes lingered on Pru.

'Papers.'

Giles shut down the engine. 'You'll have to get off,' he murmured.

They both dismounted so that Giles could access a small compartment under the seat in which were some dog-eared maps, grubby bits of paper and a couple of spanners. He sorted out a flimsy yellow form that looked more like the receipts Pru got from her local hardware store for batteries and light bulbs than an important legal document. The official took it without removing his gaze from Pru.

'This not main road. Where you go?'

As Pru opened her mouth to answer, he deliberately switched his gaze to Giles.

'Tra Binh,' said Giles.

The soldier, or whatever he was, turned his attention to the bike, strutting slowly and theatrically round it like a flamenco dancer. Pru realised she was smirking and straightened her face. With a contemptuous kick at the back wheel, he arrived back at his starting position.

'Where you come from today?'

'Ho Chi Minh City, officer.'

Pru was surprised at Giles's deferential attitude. He'd been talking with such apparent bravado in his bar the previous evening.

'Why you go Tra Binh?'

'Because my friend here has a daughter who is working there.'

The soldier flicked his eyes back to Pru.

'Passport, please'

'My hotel has it, in Saigon. Ho Chi Minh City.' He scrutinised the very backs of her eyes for a moment and then turned to face Giles—stepping so close to him that the polished toecaps of his army boots were almost touching the scuffed fronts of Giles's trainers.

'How long you stay?'

'It's just a short visit. Two hours, three perhaps.'

'You know you are in military area. You should not be here.'

'But this is a mother who needs to see her daughter.'

Unfolding Giles's yellow driving licence, their interrogator walked over to his waiting colleague and they held an animated conversation in Vietnamese, inspecting it together. Pru and Giles waited.

'Do you speak Vietnamese?' whispered Pru to Giles.

'Not enough to understand that lot.'

'We're not doing anything wrong, are we?'

'They don't like foreigners wandering about

without an authorised guide.'

'Mister Fisterpick.' He was back. 'You have two hours.' He thrust Giles's licence back at him. 'If we see you after two hours . . . you under arrest.'

'We might need more time than that,' protested Pru. She resented being so steadfastly ignored. 'How far away is it?'

And you wonder where Molly gets it from!

'Maybe twenty minutes. You go now. Bye-bye.'

He watched them steadily as Giles got back on to the bike and Pru slid on behind. As they accelerated away up the road, she swivelled in her seat to look back. The two men were still staring after them.

Chapter Eight

Ten minutes or so further on, they arrived at a settlement of small houses. The centre of the village was a wide muddy crossroads lined with several shops—open-air shacks of concrete and wood and corrugated iron. Some had fresh produce and household goods on display: sacks of grain and nuts, baskets of oranges, French-style bread rolls and packets of snacks and biscuits. Most of the others seemed to specialise in motorcycle parts. There was hardly anyone around. Giles slowed down and parked near a grocer's shop with a low wooden table and bench outside.

'You want a beer?'

'Is this Tra Binh?'

'Yup.'

A young man in a black and grey striped jumper

117

put down the magazine he'd been reading behind a stack of Omo packets and came towards them, cautiously polite.

'I haven't seen Omo in years!' said Pru.

'Two beers, please,' said Giles.

'Coca-Cola for me, actually.'

'One beer and one Coca,' he corrected.

Two glasses full of ice were produced together with a can of beer for Giles and an opened bottle of Coca-Cola for Pru. She swigged straight from the bottle, remembering all the travellers' advice about bacteria in ice. Giles ignored his glass too.

'So is Molly nearby somewhere?'

'Patience is a virtue, Prudence,' teased Giles. 'Or should it be the other way round?'

A man in grey cotton bomber jacket and blue slacks walked past them into the back of the shop to talk to the proprietor.

'Police,' said Giles.

'How can you tell? He's not wearing uniform.'

'Most of them don't. He'll be checking us out.'

'What for?'

'Seeing what we're up to. As I said, foreigners aren't encouraged up in the villages.'

'Molly's here, though.'

'Yes, and they'll be keeping a careful watch on her activities, I can assure you. She's had a few hassles, but she doesn't like being bullied. Brings out her stubborn streak. I don't suppose you need me to tell you that.' He laughed.

'What are they so wary about?'

'Oh, I don't know really. It's a communist country and maybe they don't want these overdressed Americans and Europeans wandering about corrupting people's expectations and interfering with the natural order of things.'

Another man, weatherbeaten and wiry, rode up on a bicycle and began inspecting some sacks of potatoes.

'That'll be another one,' said Giles.

The proprietor bustled over to him and they held an exaggeratedly casual conversation by the vegetables before both men wandered off without having bought anything.

'So who were the guys who stopped us on the road? Police or army?'

'Military of some kind. They're all basically police, though, really.'

'Why didn't he ask you for your passport?'

'Because I had a licence for the bike, which means I'm an expat. Tourists aren't allowed to hire transport.'

A boy of about ten or eleven peeped cheekily round one of the concrete posts supporting the shop's awning.

'Halloo . . . Mr Gile.'

Giles turned.

'Hey there! How are you, Little Fish? He's one of the kids from the orphanage,' explained Giles.

'You come to see Molly?' asked the boy.

'That's right. This is Molly's mother. Can you take us to her?'

The boy examined Pru with wary interest, then his face cleared. 'Sure.' She must have passed muster.

'You want a drink first?'

'OK. I take Coca-Cola for later.'

Giles summoned the proprietor, ordered an extra bottle of Coke and paid the bill. 'Let's go. We'll leave the bike here.'

'Hello,' said Pru, solemnly holding out a hand. 'My name is Pru.'

'I am Bong. It mean Little Fish.' Not sure what to do with the hand, he grinned shyly for a minute and then grabbed it, pulling her away from the drinks shop and up the road. 'You like see my home?'

'I like very much to see your home.' Pru smiled. 'You speak very good English'

'Molly is my teacher,' he asserted proudly. 'I show you.'

Round the corner from the drinks shop, they turned up a narrow red mud lane which rose quite steeply between some low, fenced concrete houses. The stucco was peeling in places, revealing dusty breeze blocks beneath. Occasionally someone would stop, mid-chores, to stare at the sight of two foreigners walking past and Pru would smile and wave. A curious dog barked half-heartedly from one yard, three hens retreated fussily from their pecking outside another, waiting for them to pass.

Five minutes later there was nothing on either side of them but acres of open fields, distant figures in conical hats bent double, pulling up green leaves and piling them into baskets by their sides, absorbed in their work. Nearer the road, two teenage girls, trousers rolled up to their calves, were swinging a bucket slung on ropes backwards and forwards, rhythmically scooping water from an irrigation ditch and then, on the backswing, jettisoning it skilfully across the crops. Not missing a beat, they watched the three passers-by with detached curiosity.

Up ahead on their left a little copse consisted

mostly of what looked like young birch trees. Through the slender trunks Pru could see a concrete house with a woven bamboo roof, peeling whitewashed walls and a ramshackle corrugated-iron lean-to clinging to the front of it. As they drew closer, there was the sound of singing. Pru stopped in amazement. Politely, Giles and the child stopped too.

There in the shade of the lean-to was a low wooden table with ten or so children, from toddlers to late-teens, sitting on child-sized plastic chairs around it. One girl, too disabled to use a chair, sat on the floor, a misshapen leg curled beneath her. Molly was standing on a wooden crate, her hair in a loose ponytail, wearing a baggy shirt and jeans and holding aloft an animal picture book, conducting them in a rendition of 'Old MacDonald'. Each child had been allocated an animal noise and waited for Molly's cue to oink or moo or cluck. They were giggling infectiously. An old woman squatted nearby spreading out what looked like nuts on rush matting in the sun. Bong ran forward.

'Me play too!'

Molly looked up, putting the book down on the table, and held her arms out to Bong. 'Where've you been again, you naughty . . . ?' The words died on her lips. What was Giles doing here? And was that . . . ?

'Mum?'

'Hi, Molly.'

Pru stepped forward hesitantly.

'Mum!' Molly ran forward and flung her arms round her mother. 'What on earth are you doing here? I mean, it's lovely to see you, but how did you know? Why are you . . . ?'

She pulled away, looking at Giles.

'Hi, precious.' They kissed quickly.

'What are you doing here with my mum?'

'She just walked into the bar last night—amazing, isn't it? She's come over 'specially to see you.'

'I feel quite choked up.' Pru managed to find her voice, just. 'You looked so in your element there, Moll.'

'I know. I love them to bits—aren't they gorgeous? Hey,' she turned towards the children, 'look everyone—this is my mum. Say hello.'

'Hello,' three or four of the children piped up dutifully; the others stared at this stranger with placid interest, sucking fingers or fiddling with T-shirt hems.

'Hello,' responded Pru, enchanted. 'You've always had a way with children, Moll.'

'I still don't understand, though . . .' Molly looked back at Giles.

'We thought of waiting until you next came down into town but your mum was rather keen to come up and see you here. She was a bit . . . you know, concerned about you.'

'Concerned?' Molly's face clouded. 'About what?'

'Well, you'd gone AWOL and GapKo want you to go back and complete your contract.'

'So you don't trust me. You still think I'm a stupid little girl who needs looking after!'

'Roger's worried about you. You said yourself you'd had some trouble with the police. Even Jack's worried.'

'Look. I've got to be allowed to manage my own

life now, Mum. I know what I'm doing. I'm not a child any more.'

'Come on, Moll. Reneging on your contract, disappearing off without telling Roger why or where you were going. Doesn't sound particularly responsible adult behaviour to me.'

'Well, you can go back and tell dear, pretty Roger that I'm doing something much more worthwhile than his pathetic little set-up. He knows that anyway. And you can have a nice discussion together about what a hopeless, wayward child I am.'

'Molly, this isn't fair. I get an email at home from the man who is employing you. Or was. He says you've gone AWOL. You're in danger of getting on the wrong side of the authorities over here. He can't be responsible for what might happen to you. I send you *two* urgent emails asking you to ring me. I hear nothing. What am I supposed to do?'

The children began to look anxious. Giles shrugged self-consciously, wishing he wasn't there.

Molly had turned away, back towards the orphanage, but she wheeled round, ponytail flying out behind her. 'Try and get a life of your own instead of living through everyone else! We're all sick of the responsibility.'

No one in the world could hurt Pru like Molly could. She always knew exactly where to plunge the knife to maximum effect and when to twist it. She began striding towards the orphanage again. Pru followed her.

'All I wanted to do was to make sure you're safe and well. I'm your mother, for goodness' sake. That's what mothers do!'

123

Molly plumped herself down on one of the little plastic chairs, staring moodily at the ground. Pru sat on another one next to her and took hold of her daughter's hand. Molly didn't look up, but she didn't pull her hand away. Encouraged, Pru continued.

'It's not a matter of whether or not I trust you. I know your heart's in the right place. You're a wonderful person. But you can be a bit . . . impulsive.' She was about to mention Duncan the Down-and-out, but thought better of it. 'And life has a habit of doing the unexpected. You've got to recognise it's hard for *me* having to second guess and wonder what's happening. I'm not here to criticise. Talk to me. Tell me about what you're doing. Then I can understand. You looked so happy a moment ago.'

Molly stood up again, undoing and re-tying her hair, still not looking at her mother.

'Yes, I was. And now I'm angry. You make me say things I don't mean. And then I hate myself. It's not fair. I'm trying to do good things here, Mum. All these kids are here, buried alive, because they've got no parents or because they've got disabilities. Or both. They've got nothing. No books, no toys, hardly any human contact, just old Hanh over there. I'm bringing something into their lives. I really am. How can that be wrong?'

'It's not wrong. Of course it's not, Moll. It's a great thing to be doing. But bear in mind you're in a communist country now. It's a totally different system. It's not up to you to change the way things are.'

'I know that. But if you really believe we should just lie down and accept the status quo all our lives, we might as well all go and top ourselves.'

'Tell me about this family being evicted from their home.'

'There's no point telling you about that. You'll just have the same prissy, you-can't-change-anything attitude.'

'But, Molly, you could be putting yourself in danger. Can't you see that? Roger's really concerned. You could end up in jail here. It happens.'

'Mum, I'm not going to do anything that will get me into trouble. There was an unfair property deal going on, but it's pretty much blown over now anyway. All I'm doing is working out my next few weeks here doing something I care about. Roger Griffiths can find more teachers. It's a nice enough little school but I wasn't making a difference there. I am here.'

'Well, you must go and talk to Roger and explain how you feel. And if you're going to stay up here, you must promise me you won't flout the authorities.'

'I'm not going to flout the authorities. Whatever that means. There's nothing for you to worry about. Now please, in the nicest possible way, go home. Other people's parents don't go chasing after their kids doing their gap years.'

'Oh, God, that's not what I wanted to do, Moll. OK. If you promise me there isn't anything to worry about, I can go and do a bit of exploring. I've been reading about some lovely beaches around Nha Trang. I think I'll find myself a hotel around there. I have to say, I don't like Saigon at all.'

'That's a great idea, Mum. You'd love that. They

do massages on the beach and everything. You'll have a much better time than sticking around here. I do love you, Mum. But this is *my* thing, you know? I have to start living my own life.'

'Give me a hug. And then will you show me round before I go?'

'Sure.' Molly put her arms round Pru and squeezed her.

A boy in an oversized red and white striped T-shirt ran up and clutched at Molly's knees, peering up at Pru with big wary, brown eyes. One side of his face and his bare legs and feet were covered in disfiguring, raised dark brown marks.

'Molly not sad?' he asked anxiously.

'No, my angel.' She stroked his hair tenderly. 'Molly not sad at all.' She looked at Pru. 'See his face? It's because of the chemicals still hanging around after the war. A lot of kids have these black birthmark things, and nobody wants to know about them. They hide them away in places like this.'

Pru looked around at the other children. 'Some of these kids need quite a lot of care . . .'

'Yup.' Molly indicated the disabled girl on the floor. 'Nhung over there gets sores because she can't change position on her own. They need constant bathing and she's in pain all the time. She's so sweet-natured, though. Always singing to the younger ones and telling them stories.'

Pru peeped inside the gloomy room. Three of the children were settling down to sleep, just some grass matting between them and the concrete floor. The old woman was placing the two youngest head to toe in a steel cot. Pru realised she

126

hadn't once heard any of them cry. Not even the babies.

'I think you're amazing. I don't think I could do what you're doing here. Does everyone sleep in this one room?'

'Yup.'

'And what about you? Where do you sleep?'

Molly indicated a loosely woven bamboo screen. 'I've got some cushions on the floor behind there. I can't sleep on the concrete. I've tried, but my hip bones hurt.'

Nhung shuffled painfully across the floor on one buttock, holding a bowl of rice. She reached the cot and began spooning the food through the bars to the two little girls.

Giles looked at his watch. 'We'd better be getting back if we don't want to incur the wrath of the local cadres.'

He took Molly's face in his hands and kissed her lightly on the lips.

'We'll leave you to it then, babes. Maybe see you Saturday.'

Awkwardly Molly held her arms out towards Pru.

'I appreciate your coming all this way, Mum,' she said simply. 'I know it's because you care. And I love you too. It's just . . .'

'I know. I understand. It's been great for me to see what you're doing.'

' 'Bye, Mum. Have a good time on the coast.'

'And you will be careful here, won't you, Moll? Promise me?'

'Of course I will.' Molly lifted a hand in acknowledgement, then put it to her lips and blew her mother a kiss.

Fighting with her emotions, Pru followed Giles down the path through the copse, back towards the village.

*   *   *

Once on the back of the bike, Pru allowed herself the luxury of letting hot tears flow freely down her cheeks. Anyone seeing it would assume her eyes were watering from the wind in her face. She regretted coming here now, pursuing Molly to this beautiful but intimidating country. And yet she felt proud. She'd seen a new side to her daughter's character. The self-centred, stroppy teenager had evolved into a self-possessed, feisty young woman with a sense of perspective beyond her own needs and feelings. It was like cutting the umbilical cord for a second time. She could actually feel the physical tug of it in the centre of her gut.

By the time Giles's bike pulled up outside the bar in Le Than Ton Street in Saigon, she'd got her emotions under control. She needed a drink, though. The willowy Tam was opening the shutters ready for the evening's business. Kien had a precarious two-foot stack of ashtrays in one hand and was nonchalantly setting them out on the tables. Intuitively, Giles told him to get Pru a large gin and tonic.

'You can come and chill in my sitting room, if you want.'

Pru nodded. She didn't feel like speaking at the moment. She just wanted to curl up in a ball and sleep. She certainly didn't feel like going back to that dingy hotel room. She followed Giles round behind the bar and through to a small but

128

comfortable living room. He moved a few items of clothing strewn over a squashy two-seater sofa and plumped up the cushions. She sat down gratefully. Kien came in, put her drink on a little lacquerware table and retired.

Opposite Pru, behind a huge television set, was another doorway. Unbuttoning his shirt, Giles walked towards it,

'Excuse me for a minute while I go and change.' As he pushed open the door, Pru recognised with a pang Molly's blue silk dressing gown hanging on a hook. She'd bought Molly that for her fourteenth birthday. She'd been a child then, just a couple of summers ago. How fast things change.

Pru must have fallen asleep on the sofa. She awoke to the murmur of bar chat, distant background music, the sound of pans being brought out of cupboards in the kitchen, the sharp smell of cigarette smoke. She was in darkness. Giles must have crept past her and left her to sleep. She still felt exhausted, but more emotionally than physically. Back in her early-twenties, she remembered, she'd had a strong sense of something very special waiting for her—a purpose to her life which would eventually, somehow, be made clear. Suddenly it struck her forcibly that perhaps that purpose had been fulfilled now. She'd brought two human beings into the world, seen them through childhood and set them on their way. What more worthwhile job could there be? But . . . that was it. Her role was over.

She reached for her drink, now tepid, the ice long melted, and drained the glass. Might as well have another one. How else was she going to

129

spend the evening? She'd decide where to go next in the morning. She pushed open the door and emerged behind the bar, nearly knocking a tray of drinks out of Tam's hands.

'Ah, Pru!' She suspected Giles had forgotten she was there. 'What can I get you? Another one of those?'

'Thanks. Yes, please.'

It was still early in the evening and the bar was less than half full. She perched herself on a stool at the end of the bar and surveyed the clientele. In the alcove where she'd sat with Giles the previous night, a young couple sat locked in intimate conversation, touching noses, stroking cheeks and entwining fingers. Six business-suited gentlemen, Asian, but probably not from Vietnam (Indonesia maybe, thought Pru), black shiny briefcases at their feet, conversed excitedly, presumably about the day's transactions. A champagne cork popped and four young women giggled delightedly as Tam filled their glasses for a rowdy toast: 'Happy Birthday, Lizzie!'

A man sitting alone in another alcove frowned in abstract irritation. It was his hair Pru noticed first. There was a lot of it. Light brown, silvery at the sides and brushed away from his face. A likeable face despite the furrowed brow. Boyish almost, as though middle age had crept up on it unawares. She liked his clothes too; plain, soft white shirt, cuffs turned back, slightly crumpled chinos. In front of him was an open laptop—the cause, it seemed, of the frown. A cigarette burned in an ashtray beside it. He stabbed at the keyboard with alternate index fingers, pausing every so often to drag on the cigarette or take a mouthful of beer.

On his tanned left wrist, next to a wide leather watch band, she noticed a bracelet of wooden beads, and on his finger a silver ring with a mauve-coloured stone. Normally Pru disliked the idea of men wearing jewellery, but on him it looked utterly unselfconscious and natural.

He paused and stared intently at the screen for a moment or two. Then, muttering to himself, he pressed a key repeatedly with one finger. Delete probably. Whatever he was writing, it evidently wasn't coming easy. As she sat there watching he suddenly looked up, straight at her. His eyes were a startling deep blue, almost violet, and despite his obvious frustration there was a hint of detached amusement behind them. She looked away quickly and picked up her drink, sipping at it self-consciously.

Giles's packet of cigarettes was sitting on the bar. Marlboro Lights. Idly she moved it towards her, reading the message on the side. 'Be careful not to smoke too much, because it is harmful for your health,' it warned mildly. None of the shock tactics you got back home in the UK with the threat 'Smoking Kills' in bold, black letters. It was years since she'd smoked. In her student days, she'd got through a pack of twenty a day. Cheap nasty ones at that. She'd stopped eventually when she fell pregnant with Jack.

Pru picked up the packet thoughtfully and slid one out between finger and thumb. She put it to her nose and sniffed. The smell of fresh tobacco. So evocative. Days of immortality and discovery; deep conversations lasting far into the night; ideals and ideas; politics and philosophy. They'd thought they had such insight; that they could change the

131

world. Perhaps they really could have, but the day-to-day business of material living gradually, imperceptibly, pushed all the high-flown ideals into oblivion; packed them away in an old trunk like the photos and letters she still kept on top of the wardrobe at home.

Feeling herself being watched, she glanced up to catch the man with the laptop studying her thoughtfully. It was his turn to look quickly away. Trying to appear nonchalant, Pru put the cigarette to her lips. Damn. There was no lighter on the bar. Giles was flirting with the champagne girls and Kien and Tam must have been in the kitchen. The man looked up again. He'd think she was pretty odd if she held this cigarette in her fingers unlit for much longer. She got to her feet and walked over to him.

*　　　*　　　*

Ben Coder's powers of concentration were deserting him. Damn. It had been a long day and writing wasn't his forte. Instead of trying to construct all this persuasive prose for a group of overfed businessmen, how much easier and more effective it would be if he could stride into one of their board meetings and talk to them personally, from the heart. Just a few thousand pounds was all he needed and so many lives could be transformed. If he could just tell them face-to-face about the numbers of babies born with disabilities even now, three decades after the end of the war, because Agent Orange still lurked in the soil and in the very genes of the Vietnamese people; about the children killed or maimed by land mines every

132

year because no one was clearing them effectively, and about the desperate and continuing need for prosthetic limbs to help them live as normal a life as possible as they grew from toddlers to children, from children to teenagers, and on into full-grown adults.

He read through what he had written so far. It fell so far short of what he wanted to say. Angrily, he deleted the last half-page. That woman was putting him off too, watching him from the bar. Nice-looking. Seemed appealingly unaware of the fact, too.

Don't even think about it, he admonished himself. There had been too many women in his life. He'd just ended his relationship with Alanna back in Cleveland after five years of being made to feel guilty because he didn't want to marry her. It wasn't that he didn't like the company of women. Quite the opposite. He just wanted to give relationships a rest for a while. They were too much responsibility. If he needed a bit of sexual healing he knew where to go. Here in Saigon the gentle Kim-Ly was always there for him when he needed her.

Ben had never had a problem attracting female company. He was always amazed when women didn't see beyond the conventional good looks he'd been blessed with to the flawed, insecure character he truly believed himself to be. The war had damaged him. He knew that. The nightmares would plague him for the rest of his life. Faces. Always faces. Faces of children, faces of women, of old men, of fellow soldiers, of friends, of enemies ... faces distorted in pain and fear ... dead faces ... faces smeared with dirt and

133

blood.

Until the Vietnam War, his future had been clear and bright. He was a pilot. Like his father. Flying had been the love of his life. Now he wouldn't go within yards of a helicopter if he could help it, let alone fly one. He lit another cigarette. As so often happened, he found himself transported against his will, back into the midst of it all.

A bunch of Army boys on the ground had radioed for back-up at a village near the Saigon River where they'd been hunting out suspected Viet Cong supporters. He was at the controls of his Huey, swooping down towards the fighting. Looking down between his feet, sheer carnage spread out beneath him: smouldering craters, burning hootches, human bodies . . . Suddenly, ten or fifteen Viet Cong made a break for it out of the village. At the open door behind him, the gunner opened fire. As if in a dream, he watched the M60 gun-rounds spattering through the paddy fields towards the running men, reaching them, ripping into them, halting them, writhing, in their tracks. Then no more movement. Crumpled, broken bodies; red blood spreading out amidst the green shoots and the brown water.

It was as if one part of him was watching another part of him doing something he'd never have believed he was capable of. Most sickening of all, though, he'd caught himself almost enjoying the sport of it. In that moment he'd promised himself that once he got home—if he got home—he'd never fly again. He was glad his father hadn't been alive. How disappointed he'd have been in his only son.

Back home in a little town called Mount Vernon in Knox County, Ben's father, Al Coder, had lived for flying—and died for it. He was a crop-duster pilot, and a good one. Neighbours for miles around depended on him. Ben remembered watching proudly as his father's Piper Pawnee roared low and fast across fields of grain or soya crops, mere inches above the ground—the closer the better to avoid the pesticide drifting where it shouldn't. Al kept his plane at Wynkoop Airport, half a mile from where they lived, and in the summer he'd earn extra money at weekends towing gliders high up into the blue Ohio sky. From an early age, Ben would go with him whenever his school work allowed and hang around the airfield doing odd jobs. When he got a little older, Dad would let him squash up beside him in the single-seater and take over the controls. When they had the land and the sky safely to themselves, Al had taught him simple tricks and stunts. They'd been the happiest times of Ben's life.

*   *   *

'Excuse me.' He looked up to see the woman from the bar standing in front of him, an unlit cigarette held rather awkwardly in her hand. 'Sorry to interrupt. Could I borrow your lighter?'

He looked her full in the eyes for a second or two. Kind eyes, he thought. Slightly wary maybe. 'Sure.' He pushed a green plastic lighter towards her across the table and watched her pick it up, light her cigarette, inhale, exhale self-consciously, and replace it beside his packet of Winstons.

135

'Thanks.'

'No problem.'

He returned to his work and Pru went back to her bar stool. An Englishman might have lit the cigarette for her. But he was an American. Although they spoke the same language they came from separate continents, thousands of miles apart.

It struck her suddenly that she was still wearing the linen trousers and T-shirt she'd put on this morning for the motorbike trip. A bath and a change of clothes wouldn't go amiss.

*   *   *

Coming over and asking for a light like that. Couldn't she see he was trying to work? English accent. What was she doing here on her own? She didn't look like one of those power-suited businesswomen who passed through town from time to time.

He slammed the laptop shut and stood up. He'd made a decision. He would go tomorrow morning to the General Motors office and do what he'd just been thinking about doing. He'd tell them face to face about his delightfully simple idea. All they had to do was combine test-driving their new cars with delivering artificial limbs to the kids who needed them out in the villages and bringing families down to the city for fittings when they needed them at the hospital in Saigon. It would cost them almost nothing and they'd get a lot of kudos out of it. Screw the painstaking diplomatic letter-writing. He walked over to the bar, feeling liberated.

'Giles—another beer over here!'

Ben circled his head once clockwise and once anticlockwise. He'd been hunched over that damned screen for too long. In the middle of a *sotto voce* mobile-phone conversation, Giles went to one of the refrigerators behind the bar, manoeuvred the door open and plonked a bottle on the counter.

Ben glanced at the woman with the long legs and rumpled, chestnut-coloured hair sitting a yard or so away. What the hell.

'Get you a drink, ma'am?'

She looked surprised.

'Well, um, I think I'd better be going pretty soon.'

'Help me out here. Does that translate as a yes or a no?'

Pru laughed.

'OK. Yes! Thank you very much.'

'Giles . . . ?'

Giles finished his phone call, scooped some more ice into Pru's near-empty glass from a silver bucket on the counter, then snatched it away for replenishment at one of the optics.

'You've got to be nice to my girlfriend's mother, Ben,' he called over his shoulder.

'Yeah?'

'She's had a bit of a rough day.' Giles set Pru's glass in front of her with a wink and ducked down beneath the counter to forage in one of the fridges. 'She's come all the way over from London to see her beautiful, strong-willed teenage daughter only to find . . .' he reappeared with a bottle of tonic water and opened it with a flourish '. . . well, let's just say she wasn't exactly thrilled to

137

see Mummy.'

'Ah. Teenage daughters. I sure know about *those* delightful creatures.' Ben gestured his beer glass in her direction. 'To teenage daughters!'

Pru lifted her gin and tonic. 'Teenage daughters,' she echoed. They drank. 'So I take it you've got one too . . . a daughter?'

'Kathy May. Just turned thirty. I don't get to see her as much as I'd like but we get on pretty good these days.'

'So it gets better then?'

'Yes, I'd say so. Leastways, it did for me.'

'Molly and I used to be really close, but it's been a bit bumpy the last year or so. Didn't help when her father and I split up.'

'At least you've had her living with you. Kathy's mom moved interstate after we broke up. She was only four so we never got that close. Not until she left home and went to college and she kinda reviewed the situation for herself. I stopped being the big bad ogre who'd ruined everyone's lives—not that her mom badmouthed me that much. She was pretty good about that. But, you know, I wasn't there for Kathy. Some other guy was.'

'So she felt rejected.'

'I guess. So what's the story with this rough day of yours then? Is your daughter here in Saigon?'

'She's about fifty miles north of here, working in a ramshackle orphanage and getting tangled up in the problems of one of the families living in the village.'

'And what's so wrong with that?'

'I don't think she should meddle with things she doesn't understand. And in any case she's just

138

walked out on a four-month contract as an English teacher. Do you have the concept of gap year in the States?'

He frowned. 'A few kids do it but it's not the norm. Kathy May never did one and I sure wouldn't have encouraged it. It's hard to pick up the threads again after a year out. Most American kids want to keep going until they've got all the qualifications they need and then maybe take a break after that—if they want to.'

'Well, I think a gap year is a great idea—teaches them things they don't learn in school like confidence, independence, how to look after themselves. And shows a lot of them what a privileged life they've been leading; what it's like getting by every day without the things we take for granted, like hot and cold water on tap and labour-saving devices and technology.'

'Back in the States we try and teach our kids that at home, without sending them off on expensive jaunts to other countries.'

Pru flushed.

'Well, maybe that explains why so many Americans never go further than their own backyard and only about ten per cent of them even have passports!'

'Maybe we've got more interesting backyards than you.'

Just in time, Pru noticed a twinkle in his eye. He was winding her up. She smiled.

'In that case, what are you doing here, so far from your fascinating homeland?'

'Well, ma'am, I've dragged myself away to get a little charity project off the ground here.'

'What sort of charity project?'

'Basically it's helping kids to get artificial limbs.'

'Have you been interviewed for an Australian newspaper today?'

'How did you know?'

'I met the journalist at my hotel over breakfast this morning.'

'Oh, sure—Kenny McKinnon. A bit chaotic but he's a good straight guy and I need all the publicity I can get.'

'Is that what you were writing about over there?'

'That's right. Want another drink?'

'My turn. What beer are you drinking?'

'Oh, another San Miguel then, thank you, ma'am.'

'Do you always call women "ma'am"?'

'Only when I'm trying to show what a well brought up, all-American boy I am.'

'Call me Pru. And forget the well brought up bit!'

'And are you? Prudent, I mean?'

'Sometimes. I try.'

'I wouldn't try too hard if I were you. Usually means pleasing everyone else but yourself.'

Pru attracted Tam's attention. There was no sign of Giles.

'Same again please, Tam—a San Miguel and a gin and tonic.'

Tam inclined her head gracefully and took Pru's glass for refilling. Pru fidgeted on her bar stool. Ben must have noticed.

'Shall we go and sit over there where it's more comfortable? I need to watch over my gear anyway.'

The bar was beginning to fill up. She'd been too absorbed to notice. Standing up to follow Ben over

140

to his table, she stumbled and would have crumpled to her knees had he not turned just in time to reach out a strong, brown arm.

'You OK?'

'It's just ... I think it's ... I haven't eaten anything since breakfast.'

'Tell you what, forget the drinks, Tam. I'll take the lady for something to eat. Might catch you later. Sit down there, Pru, just for two seconds.'

She sat down obediently at the table, perching on the edge of the chair, resting her head in her hands. She watched him pull on a faded green jacket and drop his laptop into a scuffed brown leather satchel which he slung over his shoulder. Then in three easy strides he crossed back to the bar counter to retrieve Pru's forgotten navy cardigan.

He put it round her shoulders and she got gratefully to her feet. He hesitated a moment, then put his arm round her waist.

'OK, let's go.'

Chapter Nine

They were shown to a wooden table for two in a crowded, noisy restaurant. A middle-aged waiter, probably the proprietor, handed them each a two-page laminated menu.

'Hello, Mr Ben, how are you?'

Pru tried to study the extensive menu—the English translations were hard to follow. 'I'm not sure I want "pork with fresh garbage",' she laughed. 'What do you recommend?'

141

'Nearly everything here is wonderful—all fresh ingredients. There's *pho*—you'll see that word all over the place outside restaurants—it's basically meat and noodle soup, or fish and noodles.'

'Will I like it?'

'Are you a faddy eater?'

'No, not at all, but you do hear stories of people eating dog and snake and monkey brains . . . and, call me a wimp, but I'm happy to give anything like that a miss.'

'They do eat dog here quite a bit. You'll see them in cages by the roadside—or bigger establishments might keep several of them corralled out the back. There are certain days in the calendar which are dog-eating days—you'll see signs saying *"Thit Cho"* which means dog meat. But Vietnamese food is always fresh because most restaurants don't have fridges so it's wholesome and incredibly cheap. You'll love it. Guaranteed.'

'Let's go for it then. I'm starving.'

'Mr Tinh!'

The waiter hardly paused as he bustled past them. Ben murmured a few words in Vietnamese. Mr Tinh nodded and continued on his way to the kitchen.

A few minutes later a burner containing glowing cinders was brought to their table and a heavy iron skillet full of boiling meat stock placed on top of it. That was swiftly followed by a huge platter heaped with sliced greens, spring onions, pieces of squid, prawns, finely sliced beef and a mountain of transparent white noodles.

Pru watched the American deftly grasp a great sheaf of greenery with the chopsticks and plunge

142

them into the boiling stock. Some of the beef, squid and prawns went in after it. It smelled wonderful. Disentangling some noodles, he placed them on her plate, then fished out the already cooked greens and some meat and laid them on top.

She watched him admiringly. David would just have let her get on with it.

'And,' Ben tapped a chopstick on the rim of a little ceramic bowl, 'you have to have some of this. *Nuoc mam*—fish sauce. Made from fermented fish. No Vietnamese meal is complete without it.'

Pru tweezed some of the greens and a piece of squid from her plate and dipped it into the brownish-coloured sauce. He was right.

'Fabulous!' she managed, her mouth full of crisp, fresh tastes and textures. While they ate, she told him about her visit to the orphanage.

'Now I feel I've only succeeded in looking like an anxious, overprotective mother. I suppose I shouldn't have come.'

'Sounds like a strong-minded kid.'

'That she certainly is.'

'So a credit to you then.'

'How do you work that out?'

He smiled into her eyes. He had a heart-melting smile. Pru's stomach fluttered. It must be eating suddenly after all those hours without food.

'You've produced a daughter who has strong principles of her own, which she'll stick with no matter how uncomfortable it gets. Takes guts.'

'It was pretty uncomfortable for me too. I got a severe tongue lashing and told to go home and get a life.'

Ben held her gaze thoughtfully.

143

'Maybe it's good that she feels secure enough in her relationship with you to be able to do that?'

'That's one way of putting it. Another way is that she's pig-headed, thinks she knows everything, and discounts all my feelings and opinions as a matter of principle. What's more, I'm the only person in the world she feels she has absolute *carte blanche* to be truly vile to.'

'She knows you love her, however vile she is.' He looked down, not wanting her to read too much in his eyes, twisting the ring on his left hand. 'Sounds like an enviably close relationship to me.'

She changed the subject.

'I like your ring. Is it . . . significant?' Was she being too personal? There was something about him that made you feel you should keep a respectful distance.

'It's my graduation ring.'

'May I see?'

She unhooked her glasses from the neck of her T-shirt and Ben extended his hand across the table. She took it in both of hers. It felt dry and warm even in Saigon's sticky evening heat. She angled his fingers towards her for the best view of the ring.

'It's chunky. Lots of symbols carved into it. What's the stone?'

'An amethyst.'

'It's the same colour as your eyes.'

'Is it? Maybe.'

'What does it say? Cornell University . . . 1973 . . . Law?'

'Yup.'

'Where's Cornell University?'

'New York. Ivy League.'

144

'Remind me what Ivy League means.'

'Well, ma'am, it means it's one of the top eight universities in the States along with Harvard and Princeton and Yale. Maybe Cornell isn't quite so well known.'

'You're "ma'aming" me again.'

Ben smiled in mock deference.

'My apologies, ma'am.'

'I thought the Ivy League was something to do with sports.'

'It's both. Sports and academics.'

'So were you a football player, with all that padding and a cage round your face?'

'I was a wrestler. Guess I'm not a team player.'

'Oh!' She laughed. 'That explains what looks like a couple embracing here. It's two wrestlers. You must have been good then?'

'Yeah, not too bad. I was an all-star champion.'

'I'm impressed.' To the other side of the stone was the head of a rather endearing-looking bull. 'You weren't a bullfighter as well, were you?'

'Very amusing. I was born in the Chinese Year of the Ox. And I like the characteristics it stands for.'

'Which are . . . what?'

'Oh, things like determination, patience, actions speaking louder than words kind of thing. Dogged, I guess.'

'You mean, stubborn?'

'You could say that. And, of course, unbelievably charming.'

'Oh, really?' She laughed.

For the first time in years, she felt seen for who she really was. Looking into those eyes, she felt pulled towards him almost physically.

Be careful, Prudence. You're behaving like a love-

145

struck teenager.

She made herself break the moment, looking back at the ring.

'It's a lovely thing. Half your life history.'

'I don't know about half. It was four years of my life a long time ago.'

'What would you have on a ring to represent the last twenty years then?'

'There's a question.' He withdrew his hand gently. 'A peace sign, I think.'

'But you're a war veteran.'

'And that's why I care about peace.'

He lit a cigarette, exhaled a stream of smoke then, raising a questioning eyebrow, offered it to her. She took it. It was a gesture of unspoken intimacy, which she wanted him to know she was open to. Anyway, two cigarettes wouldn't turn her into an addict. He lit another one for himself.

Pru drew on her cigarette, not too deeply. 'What did you do in the war? I mean, were you very involved or were you more on the fringes?'

'I flew helicopters.'

She waited, hoping for more information. There were so many questions she wanted to ask. But how do you not sound crass saying, 'So did you kill people? Were you injured? Did you see any friends killed? Do you still think about it?'

Not ideal small talk over the dinner table.

'Do you still fly?'

'Nope.'

'So what do you do now?'

'I'm a lawyer. I specialise in personal injury and negligence cases—or I did. Worked my ass off for more than twenty years. But I've pretty much wound it all down now. Life's too short.'

'You don't look old enough to be retired.'

'I wouldn't call myself retired. I just stopped conforming to expectations. Got tired of pretending to sympathise with wimps and whingers: like a woman who gets her finger crushed in an exercise machine, putting an end to a brilliant—or so she says—artistic future. Or a guy who swears he was walking innocently along the sidewalk when up jumps a loose paving stone and breaks his ankle, ruining his career prospects. I used to get thousands of dollars in compensation for these people. Millions sometimes. And there were some tough stories. Bad things happen to people. But, I don't know, my heart went out of it, I guess. I wanted to do something for people who really do deserve a break, you know? Need someone to fight for them.'

He stared unseeingly out of the restaurant window at the teeming evening streetlife.

'Maybe I should have been more tolerant, but I couldn't carry on with any integrity once that feeling started taking me over. Now the only cases I'll take on are things like corporate negligence or medical malpractice, tragedies that shouldn't have been allowed to happen; cases where the small guy needs help to take on the big guys.'

'Like what sort of cases?'

'Oh, a baby born with brain damage after a botched delivery. Or a factory worker who's terminally ill, poisoned by his employer's careless use of chemicals, his family unprovided for—that kind of thing. I'll take those on. And I'm good. I'm tough. People ask for me specifically. And I don't charge megabucks. I just do enough to make sure I've got enough to live on and let me spend three or four months every year over here in Vietnam doing what I really want to do, making a difference to the lives of people here. So, I guess a new ring might have a peace sign and a paddy field on one side and a big guy and a little guy on the other.'

'Do you have an apartment here then?'

'No, I keep a permanent room on at the Continental. It's cheap but comfortable. They know me. That's all I need.'

'Isn't that where Graham Greene wrote *The Quiet American*?'

'It's where the Fowler character stayed in the story. Where all the journos stayed during the war. Greene actually stayed at the Majestic.'

He took out another cigarette and gestured the packet towards her in a way that showed he knew she'd refuse.

'And . . . you mentioned your first wife and daughter. Did you marry again?'

He put the cigarette in his mouth unlit and stood up.

She'd gone too far. She'd blown it.

Taking two twenty-dollar bills from his wallet, Ben intercepted the manic Mr Tinh, forestalling any offer of change with an airy wave—a gesture he repeated in Pru's direction as she tried to give him twenty dollars from her purse.

'I'll let you return the favour sometime.'

*   *   *

Outside in the heavy, night-time heat of the city street, he lit his cigarette and they stood looking at each other awkwardly.

148

'Well, a painful day ended with a lovely evening. Thank you, Ben.'

'My pleasure. I enjoyed it too.'

Neither of them quite knew what to do next. Hormones she'd thought gone forever had woken from a long sleep, making her tingle with self-awareness and half-remembered desires.

'I'm planning to travel up to the beaches near Nha Trang sometime in the next couple of days,' she ventured, 'but it would be good to see you again before I go . . . if you're free?'

'I'd like that. Meanwhile, can I do the gentlemanly thing and see you back to your hotel?'

'OK, why not?'

'We'll find a cab. Where is it you're staying?'

'The Imperial in Truong Dinh Street.'

'You mean Frum Zing Street!' he laughed.

'Do I?'

'It's a hard language to get used to. I'm still learning myself.'

'It's strange to be in a place where you can't work out the most basic signs. And the buildings all look the same—plain concrete boxes. I wouldn't be able to tell a bakery from a brothel.'

'Actually you probably would spot a brothel. They're all called karaoke bars.'

'How bizarre.'

Ben flagged down a passing cab and they scrambled in. Sitting on the torn black vinyl seats, Pru was acutely aware of the warmth of his thigh next to hers.

Ben issued some instructions to the driver in Vietnamese. If the words 'Frum Zing Street' were included, Pru couldn't distinguish them.

'What's the Imperial like?' he asked. 'I don't

149

think I've heard of it.'

'Not great. I asked the travel agent for a one-star hotel, thinking I wouldn't need anything too luxurious, but this is really basic. And the concierge gives me the creeps. If I wasn't planning on leaving so soon, I'd move somewhere else.'

'Why don't you do that anyway? You don't have to rush off immediately.'

Pru suppressed a hopeful stab of pleasure. He was probably just being practical. 'Oh, I don't think it's worth it just for another night or two.'

'Do you dislike it over here that much?'

'Well, I suppose I haven't seen it at its best. One day perhaps . . .'

The cab coasted to a halt outside the Imperial Hotel.

Ben knew he should let this woman disappear into the gloom and carry on with his life. But then, she was going back to the UK soon. There'd be no harm in prolonging their acquaintance a little longer. He sensed danger, though. Pru was having an effect on him. He realised he was beginning to imagine what she'd be like as a lover. She had a great body. He could take her to some of the coastal resorts himself, perhaps. Allow himself a few days' break. He stopped his thoughts in their tracks. He'd promised himself he wouldn't . . .

Pru was gathering up her things. 'Well, this is it. Salubrious, isn't it?'

He leaned forward to peer round her through the cab window and made a face. 'It does look a bit seedy.'

'Thanks for seeing me back—and for a lovely evening.'

'Listen, Pru, you haven't had much of an

impression of Saigon so far. I think you should book into the Continental tomorrow. It's about fifty dollars a night—not much more expensive than this, and a hundred per cent nicer. Tell you what, I could book you a room when I go back there tonight and you can bring your things over in the morning or whenever you're ready. What do you think? It's your call.'

'That's a great idea. Thanks, I'd really like that.'

'OK then. I've got a meeting first thing in the morning, but after that I'm free so I can show you around a bit, if you like? See if I can change your mind. I'd like to show you what a wonderful place Saigon really is.'

She struggled out of the car and slammed the door. To her surprise, Ben had already got out on his side and bounded to the entrance before her.

'Goodnight.' He bent and kissed her gently on the forehead. 'See you tomorrow. Lunch, then a guided tour.'

' 'Night.' She tried to sound light and breezy.

Aware of his eyes on her, she pushed hard against the hotel's knackered door, using all her body weight. For the first time, it hardly seemed to resist her at all, flying open with an ear-splitting screech, Pru flying in after it. The concierge, who'd been sleeping, head down on the desk, woke with a cry of alarm. Wincing at Ben in mock dismay, she tried to close it. It wouldn't budge. It was jammed fast on the tiled floor. Ben came to the rescue, lifting it slightly and heaving it shut.

'Goodnight,' he mouthed through the murky glass, struggling to keep a straight face.

Trying to stifle her own giggles, Pru turned towards the reception desk, just managing to raise

151

a limp farewell hand behind her in an unconsciously Molly-like gesture.

*   *   *

She unlocked her door and switched on the light, hardly noticing the drabness of the room. So much had happened since she'd left it. She felt clear-eyed and alive.

Suddenly Saigon didn't seem such a bad place after all. She propped the chair under the door handle and threw off her clothes, not caring whether someone came up the stairs or not. Deciding not to look under the bed to see if anyone had removed the cockroach, on the grounds that they almost certainly wouldn't have, she switched off the light, groped her way across the room and crawled under the mosquito net. Tomorrow she was out of here. Then she'd play it by ear and decide whether or not to head for Nha Trang.

Chapter Ten

Kenny didn't make an appearance in the breakfast room next morning and Pru ate her bacon and toast in grateful solitude. She smiled to herself, remembering the look of alarm on the concierge's face as she'd catapulted through the door last night—and Ben's face creased in amusement. Her stomach was churning a little. Maybe it was the change of diet, or the malaria pills. But she knew the real reason.

You've gone all aflutter over this American, haven't you? I sincerely hope you're not entertaining thoughts of a little holiday dalliance. Not at your age.

The question was, should she go to Nha Trang later today, or should she stay here in Saigon another day or two? Pru could actually think of nothing she'd rather do than spend the next few days travelling around Vietnam with Ben as her guide. It occurred to her that she might make herself useful on his charity project. She was a good driver and she had her licence with her. She could offer herself as one of his test drivers maybe. She decided she'd leave booking her flight for the coast for another twenty-four hours and see how things went.

After breakfast she packed quickly and within twenty minutes was downstairs, impatient to check out. Insouciant as ever, the concierge scribbled some figures on a cheap, lined accounting pad, tore off the top sheet and pushed it towards her. At the bottom of the page, beneath a lot of undecipherable hieroglyphics, he'd scrawled

'886.500 VND'.

Eight hundred and eighty-six thousand! thought Pru. I bet he's overcharged me.

'What is that in US dollars?' she asked

He sighed, took a calculator from beneath the counter, stabbed at it a few times with a bony finger and turned it round for her to see the total.

'Fifty-two,' read out Pru. Was that all? He must have got it wrong. 'For two nights?'

He rapped the end of his biro impatiently against the calculator as if to say, Just pay it! Pru pulled three twenty-dollar bills from her purse. Maybe he'd given her a reduction for the faulty wiring and the broken lavatory seat—not to mention the dead cockroach. She put the money down on the counter, scooped up her passport and turned away to do battle one last time with the wonky door.

Out in the commotion of another day in Ho Chi Minh City, Pru felt immeasurably stronger and more confident than she had ... was it only yesterday? Even the humidity seemed more manageable. Avoiding eye contact with one or two street vendors she sensed moving towards her, she selected a driver from a swarm of eager cyclos. This time she'd do things properly and fix the price in advance.

'How much to the Continental Hotel?'

The lean young driver in baseball cap and faded blue T-shirt with the words 'Ask me about Jesus' barely legible across his chest, had no trouble understanding that. Presumably everyone knew the Continental Hotel. He stretched his mouth into a cheeky grin around the cocktail stick he was chewing.

154

'Two dollar.'

'One dollar,' said Pru firmly, looking around theatrically as if considering taking her custom to another driver.

'OK. One dollar.' She'd obviously played the right game. He shrugged good-humouredly and gestured her to take her seat in front of him. Smiling back, she swung her case up on to the footplate, clambered in after it and they lurched off into the traffic.

This time she sat back and marvelled at the streets and pavements all thronged with people. The pavements, broad as they were, were almost entirely taken up with parked mopeds, bikes, cyclos and scooters. Pedestrians had to use the gutters and kerbs. Everyone, it seemed, was out of doors. There were men in 1950s chrome and leather adjustable barber's chairs having shaves and hair cuts; shoe wearers, mostly Caucasian tourists, were having shoe-shines; cyclo riders lolled under the awnings of their passenger seats and people squatted almost shoulder to shoulder at the kerbside, eating or cooking or washing their cookware or selling. Everywhere you looked people were selling things—food and produce of all sorts, clothing, shoes, toys, caged birds, caged dogs, newborn chicks, cold drinks, slices of pineapple on sticks . . .

Women wove in and out of the traffic with their wares in baskets suspended from springy bamboo poles, carried yoke-like across their shoulders. One young woman, who shuffled alongside Pru's cyclo for a while, carried a pyramid of what looked like sweet potatoes in one basket while her toddler sat stoically in the other. A gaunt-faced elderly

155

woman on a street corner selling T-shirts and beanie hats from her two baskets suddenly picked up her wares, slung her yoke across her shoulders and scuttled away, crablike, with her burden into the crowd. Other street vendors began melting away too, packed and gone in seconds, lost among the crowds. Looking round to see what was spooking them all, Pru saw two khaki-clad police officers strolling importantly along the kerbside.

Some fifteen minutes later, Pru and her luggage were decanted into the road beside a grassy square. She knew it was the Continental Hotel straight away; she recognised the French architecture and long terrace with its rattan furniture from the film of *The Quiet American* she'd seen starring Michael Caine.

There was a moment of misgiving at the reception desk. She hadn't told Ben her surname, she realised. They found her listed under 'Miss Prudence'. Smiles of relief all round. The staff were polite and smartly dressed—the women svelte and petite in *ao-dais*, the men in dark red uniforms. Pru's room was huge, filled with heavy, dark wood furniture: two sofas, a table and an enormous, ornately carved bed. There was a phone, the bathroom was clean and modern with a decent-sized bath, and the air conditioning worked. Things were definitely looking up.

She unpacked and hung her clothes in the wardrobe then leaned over her balcony, watching the city going about its frenetic, cacophonous business. Ben had said he'd call her in her room around eleven o'clock when his meeting had finished.

By half-past eleven, doubts were beginning to creep into Pru's mind. Perhaps she'd misread the signs the previous night. Perhaps the arrangement to meet hadn't been as definite as she'd thought. Or the business meeting had turned out to be more complicated than he'd expected. Perhaps he'd just changed his mind about the whole idea.

By midday, she'd convinced herself. He wasn't going to call. She went downstairs to the hotel's richly carpeted, chandeliered foyer and asked to use the internet. In the business centre, she sat in front of a computer screen and logged in to her Hotmail account. There were two messages from the publisher of *Golfing Through The Ages,* the usual junk offers of cheap house insurance and miracle vitamins, but nothing worth bothering to read or reply to. She sent an email to Jack, briefly describing the highs and lows of her trip so far, her meeting with Molly at the orphanage and how she'd seemed so much in her element there. She didn't mention that his sister's welcome had been a little less than wholehearted, nor that she'd met a good-looking American war veteran. She probably wouldn't see Ben again anyway. Then, having established there were several seats available on tomorrow's midday flight north to Nha Trang, she logged out.

The receptionist at the desk said he could book her flight for her whenever she liked, as long as he had twelve hours' notice. He also recommended a restaurant nearby for something to eat. It was nearly one o'clock now. Pru returned to her room to collect her bag. The phone by the bed rang loudly just as she opened the door.

Ben was full of apologies.

'Oh, Pru. I'm glad you're still there.'

He sounded so pleased to hear her voice that the defensive shield she'd been constructing around her heart instantly crumbled away.

'Hi. How was your meeting?'

'Great. Real good. I'll tell you all about it. Pru, can you get to the Nautical Club right now?'

'Er, yes. Yes, all right then.'

'Pick up a cab outside the Continental. I'll see you there.'

*   *   *

The Nautical Club was two-thirds empty. Lunchtime was never the busiest time for a Saigon bar. As Pru walked in, Ben looked up from the conversation he'd been engaged in at a table towards the back and came quickly towards her.

'I'm sorry,' he said quietly, 'this isn't quite what I'd planned. Giles has been trying to get hold of you. There's been some news.'

She looked beyond him to the table where he'd been sitting. There was Kenny McKinnon, the Australian journalist she'd met at breakfast yesterday, head bent earnestly over his spliff-making kit. He looked up warily as she approached. Then, remembering who she was, he smiled broadly and with a 'Hi there, how you going?' returned to his task.

Giles was perched on the edge of the table next to Kenny. He jumped to his feet.

'Pru! You've checked out of the Imperial then.

158

Wise move.' His glance passed almost imperceptibly across to Ben and back to Pru. The conclusion he'd come to was obvious.

'Now, what can I get you, sweetheart? Coffee? Gin and tonic? Or I've just got some wine in if you fancy that. Red. French.'

'OK, I'll have a glass of wine, please.'

Tam, who'd been hovering nearby, went behind the counter. She looked tense. 'And more beer for the guys,' Giles called after her.

'I'm getting a bad feeling about this,' said Pru. 'Is Molly in some kind of trouble?'

Ben spoke first. 'Tam got word from Tra Binh a couple of hours ago. Her uncle Quang has been arrested up there along with some other villagers. We think Molly might have been with them.'

'But you're not sure?'

'We're pretty sure. They were staging a protest. This land dispute thing. The demo was kind of Molly's idea . . .'

'Oh, for Christ's sake! She told me that was all over and done with.'

'Tam was simply told there was a skirmish between the villagers and the police early this morning and fifty or so people were arrested. That's all we know at the moment.'

'Fifty? That must be nearly half the village.'

'Nearly *all* the village,' said Giles.

Pru glanced over at Tam, but she seemed to be in a world of her own, stacking drinks on a tray at the bar.

Pru turned to Ben. 'What are they like, these local police? Are they violent?'

'Depends what you call violent, I guess. They're not pussycats, but they only get real nasty if people

159

get violent with them first.'

Tam distributed more bottles of beer to the men and put a chunky glass tumbler of red wine in front of Pru. It tasted like cobwebs.

'I don't think we need to get too worried,' said Giles. 'These things happen from time to time over here.'

'As soon as Giles called me, I got Kenny to come and meet us all here,' Ben continued in his warm, reassuring drawl. 'He's been checking things out through a buddy of his at the *Vietnam Review* who has some pretty good connections around these parts. The guy's promised to call us back in the next half-hour or so.'

Pru glanced at Kenny, hunched over the ashtray, wreathed in aromatic smoke. She wasn't at all sure how much trust she could put in his efforts.

'How can they arrest a whole village?'

'They just bundle them into trucks and take them to headquarters.'

'And where's headquarters?'

'The local People's Committee. Equivalent of the Town Hall.'

'Surely the best thing to do is go up to Tra Binh ourselves and find out what's been happening? If Molly *has* been arrested, I'll have to go to this People's Committee place, find out what charge they're holding her on and contact the British Consul. Find a lawyer.'

Ben, Giles and Kenny exchanged looks.

'Where angels fear to tread, eh?' said Kenny, exhaling the last of his joint as he spoke.

'I'm British,' said Pru, logically. 'They're not going to want a diplomatic incident, are they?'

Ben sighed inwardly. He'd been looking forward

160

to a fun, flirty day. Why did his involvements with women so often end in trouble?

'They don't like foreigners in the villages,' said Kenny.

'I know. I kind of found that out yesterday,' said Pru, looking at Giles.

'You might find yourself under arrest as well. And that won't help your daughter.'

'That might not be so bad. At least I might end up in the same cell.'

Pru finished her wine in two swallows. She was losing patience with sitting around, secondarily inhaling Kenny's dope.

'Look, why don't we just wait for Kenny's guy to call back before we do anything?' said Giles. 'Let's all have another drink.' To her irritation, she noticed Tam had silently refilled her glass.

'I'm sorry, but I can't just sit here and fidget,' said Pru. She looked hard at Giles. 'Aren't you worried? Molly's your girlfriend.'

'I'm concerned, of course.' Giles smiled sympathetically. 'But not that worried. The People's Committee up there will want to avoid trouble at all costs. I'm sure they'll be getting a nice juicy backhander out of this property deal. The last thing they'll want is central government getting to hear about it. What do you think, Kenny?'

'Sure. Hanoi's been issuing statements all over the place this last couple of months, boasting about stamping out local corruption. Le Van Sinh's head is on the block if he gets found out doing dodgy deals, that's for sure.'

'If I know Moll, she'll revel in the whole experience anyway,' added Giles.

'Well, I can't be as phlegmatic as you. She's my daughter and she's not as strong as you might think she is. I'm sorry but I have to go and see what's going on. Could you take me there on the bike again or shall I hire a driver?'

'I'm really sorry, sweetheart, but I've got to be here today. I've got a delivery coming sometime after lunch.'

'If you hire a driver, he'll be in touch with the authorities the whole time,' said Kenny into his tobacco tin. 'You'll never get there. He'll misinterpret all your instructions with a smile on his face. You'll be taken to a couple of tourist attractions and then brought back to Saigon.'

Giles chimed in. 'It's true, I'm afraid. He'll accidentally-on-purpose get lost, or the police will stop the car and decide you haven't got the right papers and send you back.'

Pru turned her attention to Ben. 'You must know a lot of the villages. Does your charity help any disabled children around there?'

'Yes, quite a few. I know that district quite well,' Ben had to admit.

'Could you take me then? We could take some artificial arms and legs with us so we can say we're on legitimate business if we're stopped.'

He hesitated just for a second. He tried to imagine how he'd feel if his own daughter got into a situation like this.

'OK, let's take the bull by the horns,' he declared, fishing some keys out of the breast pocket of his shirt. 'The guy from General Motors has just given me a brand-new car to test drive for the charity. We'll pick up some prosthetics from the hospital—I was going to do that anyway—then

162

we'll head out for Tra Binh. With any luck the whole situation will be sorted out by the time we get there.'

'Right, let's go.' Pru took a last swig of musty wine and stood up.

'Well, good luck, guys. And when my mate calls, I'll give you a shout on the mobie,' said Kenny.

A few more impatient moments while the three men checked they all had each other's phone numbers, and then she and Ben were outside in the stifling heat of the afternoon, opening the doors of a shiny silver Saab saloon to the smell of baking vinyl upholstery.

*   *   *

Ten minutes later, cooler now with the air conditioning running, Pru was waiting in the parked car beside a pair of pale green-painted iron gates and a large sign bearing the name 'Cho Ray Hospital'. Ben emerged after a while, accompanied by a slight, kind-faced man in a white coat who Pru assumed to be a doctor. The two of them were sharing the weight of a huge cardboard box. Their unwieldy burden safely deposited in the boot, the doctor pumped Ben's hand warmly and stood waving and smiling broadly until they had pulled out into the traffic once more.

'That was Dr Chuong. He's very pleased,' said Ben, swerving to avoid a man sitting bolt upright on a moped, encased almost up to the armpits in brightly coloured children's hula hoops.

'I've persuaded General Motors to back this project for a year—with the option of continuing their support if it goes well. It means a lot to the

163

guys at the hospital, who've got more than enough to do just making the limbs, without trying to find ways of getting the kids fitted with them and then monitoring their progress as they grow.'

'I'm really impressed,' said Pru.

'Yeah, well, now I've got to make sure it happens.'

'How many limbs have you got in that box?'

'About a hundred, I think—hands, forearms, feet and lower legs.'

'Why are there so many disabilities? How do they happen?'

'It's a mixture. Some kids—a lot of kids—are born with deformities. There's no doubt in my mind what the reason for that is.'

'What?' Pru prompted him.

'You know about Agent Orange?'

'Of course I do. The defoliant the Americans sprayed on the jungle so that the Viet Cong had nowhere to hide.'

'That's right. Millions of gallons of it. One of the most pernicious poisons known to man. And do you know, the Red Cross reckons there are one hundred and fifty thousand children in Vietnam right now with congenital defects as a direct result of this stuff, but the US government still won't acknowledge any responsibility for it. Can you believe that?'

'Sadly, yes, I can.'

'I guess they know they'd have to put a whole lot of money where their mouth is if they did. There are land-mine injuries as well. A couple of thousand a year.'

An ambulance overtook them, its klaxon whining.

164

'Are there land mines up where Molly is?'

'Yeah, there will be some. She's quite near the Cambodian border. But the most dangerous area is a couple of hundred clicks further north around the dee-em-zee.'

'Diem Sie?'

'The old demilitarised zone or DMZ. In the central highlands between North and South.'

'Why the hell couldn't she have stayed in the city instead of heading for the hills? I wish I'd never let her come here now.'

You've always let yourself be walked over.

'I thought you said foreign travel was character-building and something all young girls should do?'

Pru was trying to think of a suitably cutting reply when, without warning, Ben pulled off the road and stopped the car on some stony ground in front of a concrete aircraft hangar of a restaurant. Two tan-coloured dogs attached to the wall outside on long chains barked unwelcomingly.

'Time for something to eat. I've seen what happens to you when you haven't eaten properly.'

Pru looked dubiously out of the car window. A dozen or so customers were sitting at long Formica tables, heads bent over bowls and chopsticks. They looked like local farmers. It was three o'clock, but not too late for lunch evidently. Vietnamese people seemed to eat at all times of day.

'Come on.' Ben was out of the car, slamming the door. She hesitated. All she wanted to do was to get nearer to Tra Binh.

'I don't feel hungry.' That sounded rude. She tried to adjust her tone. 'Honestly, I'd rather stop at a shop somewhere and get a packet of crisps and some water or something'

165

'Potato chips!' Ben looked heavenwards. 'What's the matter with this woman!' He came round and opened her door. 'Prudence, I know you're keen to get there. I do understand. But we've got to wait until we get some concrete information from Kenny. And anyway, you'll be no use to anyone if you're weak from hunger.'

She dragged herself reluctantly out of the car. Ben took her arm with an air of resolute good cheer and steered her inside.

'I've been here a couple of times. The food's always good.'

Approaching the only free table, he pulled a chair out for her and walked round to sit opposite. He lit a cigarette, inhaled gratefully, then offered it to her across the table. Pru shook her head. She was still smarting after that 'character-building' remark.

The restaurant's walls had once been painted pale blue. Now they were streaked with brown stains from cooking grease, dust from the main road and grime from people leaning against them. Half the right-hand wall was taken up by a shallow concrete trough filled with water in which swam several black eels and four smallish turtles, haunted by hundreds of flies. In the middle of the place, set on a table, was an enormous rectangular glass tank containing various species of sea life, all presumably doomed, a few rough boulders their only landscape.

Risking a glance across the table, Pru found him watching her with that look of gentle amusement again. She couldn't stop herself from smiling. He was so damned attractive. Her irritation dissolved.

A harassed-looking woman in a loose floral

trouser suit, long black hair in a tapering plait down her back, appeared beside them, looking expectantly from one to the other.

'I don't know about you, but I'm going to have some *pho* and a cold beer,' Ben announced.

'And I'll have exactly the same please,' said Pru.

The waitress flip-flopped off to the kitchen, returning with a large plastic plate on which were two sausage-shaped damp towels in plastic wrappers and a couple of pairs of chopsticks.

They snatched up the towels at once, Ben popping his sachet open loudly between the palms of his hands, and gratefully dabbed their faces and necks.

'So, how far from Tra Binh are we?'

'Just under an hour's drive now, I'd say.'

'Can we phone Kenny and see if he's heard anything?'

'He's phoning us, remember.'

'I just hate this waiting. Not knowing what's going on.'

There was a sound of vigorous splashing behind Pru. She looked over her shoulder to see a fair-sized fish flapping frantically in what looked like a child's seaside fishing net on a bamboo pole. The waitress hauled the dripping net from the tank, splashing several diners in the process, tipped the writhing creature out on to the restaurant floor and stamped hard on its head.

Pru looked away quickly. 'Glad I didn't order fish.' She grimaced.

'Well, you can't say it's not fresh.'

The waitress couldn't have wasted much time delivering the newly murdered victim to the kitchen because she was back at their table within

167

seconds, offloading two bottles of beer and some glasses. Their food followed smartly behind: glossy rice noodles mixed with thin slices of beef, mushrooms and various green vegetables in a white plastic bowl of steaming, almost clear broth.

'Good?'

'Very good. Delicious. I guess I was hungry after all.'

They fell silent while they ate. More skilled in the art of noodle management, Ben finished well before Pru did.

As she put down her chopsticks there was a shriek and a commotion at the far end of the restaurant. All the customers near the turtle trough were leaping to their feet. A few of them jumped on to their chairs; others ran out of the restaurant, chattering like terrified monkeys. The dogs joined in the din, barking and pulling at their chains.

Ben and Pru shot to their feet too, chairs scraping on the floor behind their knees. A snake, some five feet long, was slithering like a jagged streak of lightning towards the bead-curtained kitchen doorway. Pru couldn't tell an adder from a grass snake, but judging by the reaction all around, this one was bad news.

Ben looked towards the front of the restaurant, where the dogs were snapping and snarling furiously. A pair of gardening shears was propped up against the wall. Perhaps frightened by the kitchen staff, who were stamping and shouting, banging pots and pans together, the snake had turned back towards the diners. In one swift movement, Ben snatched the shears, reached out and hoisted the snake between the blades. Giving it no time to squirm free, he snapped them shut. Two segments of snake lay wriggling on the floor, the mouth still opening and shutting as if it hadn't yet realised the game was up. Everyone resumed their normal seated positions, laughing to each other in complicit embarrassment.

'You were so cool and calm,' marvelled Pru.

Ben laughed. 'Got plenty of practice immobilising snakes during the war. Lucky those shears were sharp, though.'

'Was that one poisonous?'

'Sure was. Deadly. An adder. Elliptical pupils, triangular head. I remember before I came out here, our drill sergeant used to say, "There are a hundred species of snake in 'Nam. Ninety-nine of them are poisonous. The one that isn't, crushes you to death."'

Behind them, a man who seemed to be their waitress's husband had picked up the head end of the snake in one hand and was approaching their table. In the other hand he carried an empty glass tumbler and a large kitchen knife. He banged the glass down triumphantly in front of Ben and then, holding the snake head downwards, cut a deft four-inch slit in the underbelly. Thin red blood dribbled into the glass.

The man was wielding the knife again, this time scooping out the snake's heart which he placed ceremoniously in the centre of a little enamelled saucer his wife had brought out to him. Picking it up with both hands, he held it out to Ben, who accepted it solemnly, also with both hands. The little bloody sacrifice was still pulsating. The woman was back again with a grubby, unlabelled clear-glass bottle. She added a shot of whatever

169

lethal alcohol it contained and gave the mixture a swirl with the end of a chopstick.

Ben knew what he had to do. He put the saucer to his lips and sucked the heart off it like an oyster from its shell. Then, with an appreciative nod, he tossed back the contents of the tumbler.

The onlookers all whooped and cheered, winking gleefully at Pru.

Ben gestured the glass towards her, mopping his mouth with his paper napkin. 'Snake blood and rice wine. There's a bit left. Would you like to taste? It's good. A bit salty.'

She shook her head, trying to smile. Actually, she felt close to throwing up.

'It's the men who are supposed to benefit from this anyway. Said to be mighty good for male sexual stamina.' Mischievously he added, 'That's why these guys are offering you their congratulations.'

She blushed, dammit.

Ben drained the last of the thin red liquid from the glass and smiled in exaggerated courtesy at his coterie of admirers. Several of them clapped him on the back or shook his hand—although whether applauding the slaying of the snake or the imbibing of its insides, Pru wasn't sure. The ritual over, they drifted back to their tables.

'I can't believe what you just did,' she murmured.

'It would have been a grave insult to them if I hadn't.'

'Perhaps we should quit while we're ahead,' suggested Pru. 'You might have to kill a cockroach next.'

He laughed. 'Those evil critters don't have a

heart. I know that for a fact.'

They stood up and Pru reached for her purse.

'It's my turn to pay.'

But the woman in the flowery outfit wouldn't hear of accepting any payment at all.

'I think you've got hero status here for life.' Pru smiled. Privately she thought, I think I'm in love.

Chapter Eleven

'Now what?' asked Pru as they settled themselves back in the car.

Ben looked at his watch. 'It's nearly four o'clock. Kenny must have found something out by now.'

'Can't we phone him? He won't mind. He's probably lost track of time, smoking all that dope.'

'He's a sharp cookie, though, Pru. Don't underestimate him.' When they'd arrived they'd parked under a mimosa tree, but now the shade had moved. Pru mopped her brow with the damp towel she'd brought from the restaurant.

'I'll start the engine running before we melt. Test out this fancy climate-control system.'

Ben let the handbrake off and cruised the car a little way along the dusty road to take advantage of the shadow cast by a narrow four-storey pink-stuccoed house standing incongruously alone. The air conditioning kicked in almost at once. Pru watched the figure on the instrument panel drop degree by degree, from an almost unbearable 36 down to 27, where it stopped.

Ben took his mobile phone from the breast

pocket of his shirt.

'OK. Let's see what he's got for us.' He keyed in a number and waited.

'Hi, Kenny . . . Ben. Has anyone got back to you yet?' Pru could hear the faint insect-like buzz of Kenny's voice in reply.

'Really? Maybe tomorrow then,' he said. Pru's face was a picture of frustration. 'Wait a minute, I'll put you on loudspeaker so Pru can hear.' He slotted the phone into the cradle on the dashboard.

'Can you still hear us?'

'Sure can, pal. Loud and clear.'

'So what have you found out so far?'

'It's difficult. There's a veil of silence over the place at the moment, but it is definitely a dispute over some farmland. The whole village has been edgy for weeks. There's some kind of property deal going down—a real big one. People have been served with eviction notices and threatened with various unpleasant consequences if they refuse to go. The villain of the piece has got to be this fella Le Van Sinh. He's the head of the commune's People's Committee. Cunning as a shithouse rat, by the sound of it.'

'And what about these arrests?'

'As far as I can gather, people turned up in the fields for work this morning to find two American geezers with fat cigars and Le Sinh and a couple of henchmen with clipboards and tape measures, pegging out this humungous plot of land. The workers chuck a stone or two and before you know it there's a pitched bloody battle going on. Reinforcements turn up on both sides with poles and sickles, rusty old bits of hardware left over

172

from the American War and goodness knows what else. Eventually two military trucks arrive and soldiers round up every protester they can get their hands on. They'll be in the cells at Committee headquarters, I'd guess.'

'Was anyone hurt?'

'I don't know. But they do this over here from time to time. Half a village gets arrested. It's a way of reminding the peasants who's boss. They never hold them for long, though. Mostly because the buggers are too mean to feed them.'

'So you do reckon they'll let them go tomorrow?'

'That'd be my bet. Anyway, fellas, I'll get off the line now and if I hear anything new I'll get back to you.'

'You do that. Thanks, Kenny. Appreciate it.' Ben unhooked the phone and dropped it back into his shirt pocket.

*   *   *

Pru was trying to fend off the pictures crowding into her head: Molly being manhandled into a truck . . . bleeding perhaps from a head wound. Knowing Molly, she'd be protesting like mad, of course. That certainly wouldn't endear her to the authorities.

'Ben, I really want to go there, right now. Until I know exactly what's happening, my imagination's going to be working overtime.'

'Let's just think about this rationally for a moment,' he said. He slid the window down and lit a cigarette, switching off the air conditioning. Pru took it out of his hand, took a long drag then handed it back to him, trying to suppress a cough

173

and letting out an undignified splutter instead.

Ben smiled benignly. 'You OK?'

She nodded.

'So,' he continued, 'if they're keeping these people in overnight, there's nothing we can do about it till the morning. It'll be dark by the time we get there. The People's Committee headquarters will be shut, and all we'll do is attract unwanted attention to ourselves.'

'I must admit, just one night in the cells might teach Molly a bit of a lesson,' said Pru slowly. 'I did warn her about interfering in local politics. As long as they really do let them out tomorrow and as long as you're sure she won't be getting any rough treatment . . .'

'I think that's absolutely the right attitude to take. It won't be comfortable sleeping on the floor with fifty villagers. She probably won't get fed. But as Kenny said, because they won't want the expense of providing rice for so many people, they'll very likely let them go in the morning.'

'And yet, until I know for sure she's all right, I can't help worrying. What do you suggest we do then?'

'We've got two options, I reckon. Drive back to Saigon and then get up real early in the morning and come back. Or get as near as we sensibly can now. I think I know where we could stay. There's a little family at a hamlet called Loc Hien about half an hour from here and twenty minutes max from Tra Binh. I've been helping them get their eleven-year-old daughter fitted with a special surgical shoe. They'd put us up for sure. It's your call. What do you think?'

Pru hesitated. Ben opened the door, unfolded

174

himself from the car and swivelled his foot on his cigarette end in the dirt. Stretching his arms above his head, he took a long, deep breath, held it for a second or two and then breathed out, bringing his arms slowly back down to his sides. There wasn't a spare ounce of flesh on his body.

'I didn't bring my toothbrush,' she called.

*   *   *

It was dark as they arrived at the village of Loc Hien. So dark that Pru didn't know it was a village at all until Ben stopped the car and turned off the engine with a final-sounding, 'Well, here we are.'

'I can't see anything. It's pitch black.'

'The only lighting up here is kerosene lamps or bulbs wired up to car batteries in individual houses. There's no street lighting. This is as close as I want to get with the car. I don't want anyone reporting our arrival. We're in the same district as Tra Binh and there are eyes and ears everywhere.'

'Will we get this family into trouble then?'

'I don't reckon so. I can give little Hong's new foot as my reason for being here.'

'And what about me?'

'Well,' he drawled, 'I guess they'll just think you're my lover.'

'You should be so lucky!' retorted Pru.

You mean, you should.

'I should indeed!'

Pru turned to search his face in the greenish light from the car's instrument panel, but he was getting out of the car.

'Now, I'm hoping this smart new automobile has a flashlight in the trunk.' She sat still in the

175

passenger seat, waiting. The silence was so intense she could hear the rhythmic swishing of her own blood in her ears as her heart pumped it dutifully round her body.

It made her think of Molly's heart; the surgery she'd had to endure as a tiny baby and the angst she and David had shared in those early days of their daughter's life. Her anxiety level rose. Pru knew she had to get to Tra Binh absolutely first thing in the morning.

'Ah, here we go.' Ben's voice was muffled but reassuring as he leaned into the open car boot, scrabbling under the boxful of arms and legs. 'A flashlight, a rug and a breakdown triangle. What else could we possibly want?'

He came round to Pru's door and held it open, waiting for her to get out.

'We're right above Hai's house,' he said quietly. He shone the torch in the direction of a sparsely wooded embankment sloping down from the road into blackness a few feet away. 'Do you think you can scramble down there?'

As Pru stood up, he swung the beam in her direction, sweeping it down her body from the white sleeveless cheesecloth shirt, navy jumper tied loosely around her waist, along the legs of her chinos and ending with her feet in a pair of blue-patterned canvas trainers.

'Good shoes.' He put a foot beside hers in the beam. His light brown shoe bore the same star-shaped logo. 'Snap. Converse All-Stars.'

She smiled. 'Well, of course.'

'Got everything you need?'

'No. But I've got everything I've got.' Pru patted her shoulder bag.

176

Ben picked up his own battered leather satchel, slung the rug over his shoulder and quietly closed the doors. The car winked its sidelights conspiratorially to assure them it was locked.

'Give me your hand.'

'Are there snakes around here?'

'We'll have to stomp on the ground as we go. They won't attack unless they're taken by surprise.'

His hand closed round hers.

'I'm so glad I met you,' whispered Pru.

'Me too. Real glad.'

He squeezed her hand a little tighter and tugged her gently towards the top of the slope. They plunged down, ankle-deep in undergrowth, making slow, wary progress, following the wavering patch of light the torch projected a few inches ahead of them. Whenever she could, Pru touched a tree branch or a trunk as she passed. It made her feel less alienated from the mysterious dark vegetation that surrounded them. She could hear creatures flittering through the undergrowth. She hoped fervently that Ben was right and that anything life-threatening would be running away rather than towards them.

'There's their roof,' whispered Ben. He shone the beam ahead of them. She could see a flash of metal, probably corrugated iron, and some thatched bamboo. 'If we keep to the left of that, we'll come out in their garden, I think.'

A moment later he stumbled, nearly taking both of them headfirst over the top of a pyramid of stacked firewood. The torchlight revealed they were standing on the top of a low, roughly constructed stone wall. Beneath them was a small yard. Ben jumped down and held out a hand to her. As Pru landed beside him, there was a snorting, rooting noise close by, and a loud grunt.

'Pigs,' came Ben's whispered explanation.

At that moment, silhouetted by the dim light from inside, a figure brandishing a pickaxe rushed from the house, looking wildly round in all directions and jabbering furiously. A young woman appeared behind him carrying an iron cooking pan.

Ben grabbed Pru's arm and pulled her with him away from the side of the house and into the open so that the couple could see them clearly. Pru was amazed how calm and confident his voice sounded.

'Mr Hai. *Chau!* It's Mr Ben. I am so sorry to frighten you.'

'Mr Ben?' The man peered at them, his expression changing from fear to pleasure.

Pru's emotions followed much the same arc.

'Mr Ben. Is good to see you. What you doing here?'

Ben walked forward extending his hand which was seized and shaken warmly. Lowering the iron pan, the woman stepped forward too, smiling uncertainly. Then two children emerged from the shadows. One had a noticeable dip in her gait. She must be the little girl Ben had been helping. They all shook hands.

'This is my friend Pru,' Ben put a hand on her shoulder, 'and Pru, this is Mr Hai and his wife Thuy—and there's young Hong, who I've told you about already, and her little brother Canh.'

Pru smiled warmly at each of them in turn. There was an awkward silence. Somewhere nearby, the unseen pigs fidgeted in their pen.

Thuy spoke. 'You come inside? Take food with

178

us?'

'We'd love to,' said Ben. 'If it's not too much trouble. Thank you.'

He untied his shoelaces and left his trainers at the entrance. Pru duly did the same. Hai motioned them to a cushionless wooden bench beside a low makeshift table. Everyone sat. Pru, Ben and Thuy on the bench, Hai and the two children on the floor, and in the flickering yellow light of two kerosene lamps, Pru found herself the object of four curious pairs of eyes. The most inquisitive belonged to Thuy, who Pru could see now was probably in her early-thirties. Hastily twisting her shoulder-length hair neatly out of the way around a little wooden stick, she sat herself next to Pru, absently smoothing the soft, rosebud-scattered fabric of her tunic across her knees.

'You have children?' she asked.

'Yes, I have a boy and a girl. Like you. But they are older.'

Hong and Canh, cross-legged side by side on the stone floor, jostled each other, stifling giggles. Hong wore a sleeveless cream dress with red polka dots on it and a frilled yoke around the neckline. It seemed a little too big for her, like a borrowed party dress. She had earnest brown eyes and a black shiny fringe as did her younger brother, Canh, who wore a pair of loose navy shorts and a grimy orange polo shirt with an un-recognisable cartoon bear on the front. They were both barefoot. Pru could see now that Hong's left foot was badly deformed. She looked away casually, not wanting to make the girl feel self-conscious.

'Do your children go to school nearby?'

179

Thuy wasn't sure she understood the question. She looked at her husband for help.

'Canh goes to school in the morning two hours. Hong works here with us.' He smiled gently.

Thuy turned back to Pru.

'How old are your children?' she asked.

The question was prosaic, but behind it, both women understood, was a dialogue on a deeper, more instinctive level which simply said: We are from very different worlds but we are women and we are mothers . . . and that transcends all barriers of language, geography, creed or culture.

'Jack, my son, is twenty and my daughter Molly is eighteen,' Pru supplied politely, adding, 'your children are very beautiful.'

'Like their mother,' interposed Ben. Thuy smiled shyly, then suddenly remembered her duties as hostess and put her hand to her mouth in embarrassment.

'You hungry. Need food. Tea? Drink?'

She issued instructions to the two children and Canh followed her into the kitchen which was an adjunct to the house as far as Pru could see, a lean-to off the main room. The child returned with an enormous enamel steamer filled to the brim with boiled rice, his thin little legs buckling under the weight. Hong meanwhile was busying herself at an enormous glass-fronted, mahogany display cabinet. So large was it, looming from floor to ceiling, Pru wondered if the house had been built around it. Perhaps it had been; and yet it seemed an incongruous piece of furniture in this simple village house. From one of the higher shelves Hong took out two decorated black lacquerware plates and matching chopsticks and set them on the table by Ben and Pru's knees. Then she fumbled at the back of the cupboard to bring out three very small assorted glasses. Hai emerged from the kitchen with a plate of some kind of green vegetable cut into slices. There was an aromatic smell of cooking oil and burning wood.

'They're cooking 'specially for us,' murmured Pru, indicating just the two plates. 'I feel bad, putting them to this trouble.'

'They want to do it. They are just the greatest, aren't they?'

'Especially as we turned up in their backyard, literally out of nowhere.'

'That won't have fazed them, don't worry. Nobody up here expects people to make appointments—they don't have phones.'

'You like?' Hong had taken the stopper out of a bottle of clear liquid.

'Yes, please,' said Ben. Then to Pru, 'It's rice wine. They brew their own and it's pretty strong, so treat it with respect.'

Pru held her glass up in salutation. 'What's Vietnamese for "cheers"?'

Hai and Ben raised theirs in return.

'*Tram phan tram!*' beamed Hai.

Ben translated. 'It means one hundred per cent, or something pretty much like that.'

'*Tram phan tram!*' she and Ben chorused to Hai.

The children giggled again.

'Thuy—no drink?' asked Pru.

Thuy gently shook her head.

'Vietnamese women don't drink. Don't smoke either,' explained Ben. 'Not that you'll ever see anyway.'

The liquor tasted high-octane, but not

181

unpleasant.

Hai and Thuy went back to the kitchen. Pru studied the display cabinet. There was the odd little collection of plates, bowls and glasses in the top part. The contents of the lower cupboard nearest her included an ashtray with '333' embossed on it in red, a tiny green plastic elephant, a toy soldier, a yellow duck that was almost certainly a bath toy, two disposable cigarette lighters and a carved turtle turning its head to look at its baby on its back. None of these items was displayed with any particular pride, looking as though they just happened to have ended up there. The cupboard on the right-hand side was entirely taken up by a simple altar, consisting of an inlaid wooden box with a rice cake and a fresh pear placed on top of it.

Beyond the cabinet, at the end of the room, hung a thin red curtain partitioning off what was presumably the bedroom.

For a mixture of reasons—partly privacy, but mostly to do with proximity to Ben—Pru was beginning to feel slightly apprehensive about the sleeping arrangements. Perhaps they'd all be sleeping in the same room. Go with the flow, she decided. In less than half an hour the table was covered with plates of food and the family were sitting themselves on the floor opposite. Mr Hai seized Pru's bowl and ladled two big spoonfuls of the sticky rice into it, motioning Ben to do the same, then edged their chopsticks a few inches closer towards them in encouragement. Obediently, they made a start on the crisp green bamboo shoots, cubes of fried tofu and neatly wrapped spring rolls, garnished with fresh green salad leaves, and a dish of *nuoc mam* sauce to dip them into.

'I've watched Thuy making these. It's like watching a skilled craftsman at work,' said Ben. The last dish to arrive contained chunks of something meaty. Ben noticed Pru's quizzical look.

'Pig's feet. Have one.'

Cautiously, Pru picked one up and laid it on top of her rice. Evidently thinking she was holding back, Hai whipped the chopsticks out of her hand and expertly transferred another one into her bowl. She nibbled one hesitantly. To her relief, it was delicious.

The family placed a little rice and some greens in their own bowls but seemed to eat very little.

'They'll have had their supper already,' explained Ben, 'but it's not polite to offer guests food and not eat along with them.'

Finally they'd finished the meal. It took a while because Thuy and Hai were full of questions about Pru and her children, what they were studying and what life in England was like, all the while pressing more food on them.

Relieved of the need to make conversation as the empty plates and bowls were cleared away, Pru realised she was feeling utterly shattered. She must have looked it. Ben said something to Thuy in Vietnamese. Throwing Pru a kindly glance, she picked up one of the hurricane lamps and beckoned them to the other side of the room where she stood, holding the curtain aside. They picked up their gear and followed her. The bedroom, like the kitchen, was an add-on to the main house. It was about ten feet square with walls of newly mortared red brick to waist level and, above that, woven bamboo matting.

'Hai and Canh finish building last year,' said Thuy proudly. On the floor to the left was a large square sleeping mat. Pru concluded this was where the children slept because on the other side of the room, screened by another thin curtain, was a better quality bed—a low wooden platform, about five feet square, again covered with rush mats. Between the two sleeping areas was a steep step up to a narrow doorway which presumably opened on to the blackness of the night outside.

'Is OK you sleep here?' asked Thuy.

'But it is your bed,' protested Pru.

'We sleep in other room. No problem. You sleep here.'

'*Cam An*. Thank you, Thuy,' said Ben.

'Have good sleep.' Thuy smiled into Pru's eyes, set the lamp on the floor and was gone, leaving the two of them standing looking at each other.

'Where's the toilet?' asked Pru.

'Outside—wherever you feel drawn to.'

She negotiated the step and found herself standing outside in total darkness.

'You might find this useful,' said Ben's voice behind her. His arm appeared round the door holding the torch.

With small shuffling and scrabbling noises all around her, Pru squatted on the ground under the stars, feeling more at one with the world than she had for years.

While Ben went outside, she got ready for bed—not that there was much to do. He had already spread the rug out on top of the matting. Should she take her trousers off? It was hot. It seemed a little forward to remove them and yet prudish not

184

to. She took them off, wishing she'd put on a rather more exciting pair of knickers this morning. These were plain white department store jobs—three in a packet. He came back as she was settling down on the blanket, and extinguished the lamp. She heard him removing his trousers. Then he lay down next to her, pulling the mosquito net down over them both.

'Quite a day,' he said gently.

'It's all a bit unreal,' she answered in the darkness.

'Sleep well, Pru.'

'You too.'

Acutely aware of Ben's presence next to her, she lay still, her senses too heightened now for sleep despite her tiredness. There was little or no breeze outside, so any sounds to be heard came from some form of animal or bird life. Twenty or so minutes later, she heard the children go to bed on the other side of the curtain; a little whispering, a muffled giggle and then silence.

Was he asleep? She sensed that he was as awake as she was.

Ben lay on his back, forcing himself to think mundane thoughts. He wanted to take her in his arms, if only to make her feel safe and protected, but he didn't want her to think him insensitive. She had her daughter to worry about. She was so quiet lying there next to him. Too quiet to be asleep.

'You OK?' he whispered.

'Yes. Just . . . my mind's buzzing,' she whispered back.

'Your daughter will be fine, I'd bet money on it.'

'I'm so glad you happened to be at Giles's bar last night.'

'I'm glad too.'

'And they tell you smoking and drinking are bad for you!'

His hand found hers in the darkness and within minutes both of them were asleep, fingers still entwined.

*   *   *

The daylight woke them, creeping in dappled patterns across their eyelids through the woven bamboo walls. Pru lay for a few minutes, mentally filing the events of the previous day and trying to prepare herself for whatever the day ahead might bring. She turned quietly to see if Ben was still asleep—to be confronted with a golden-haired bare thigh where his head should have been. He'd folded away the mosquito net and was sitting in the lotus position, wearing only his boxer shorts, back against the wall, eyes closed. Without moving a muscle—and there were plenty of them in evidence—the blue eyes opened abruptly.

'Good morning.'

'What time is it, yogi?'

'Early, Boo Boo. But that's good. A lot to do.' He unfolded his legs and stood up, stretched his arms above his head, then bent to touch his toes.

'All in working order?' smiled Pru.

'So far so good.' He smiled back.

Pru slid off the bed and went outside. Half a dozen hens and some white ducks were scuffing about idly in the dirt.

Backed up against the house in a third lean-to were the pigs' quarters; concrete and brick compartments housing seven young and surprisingly docile pigs. Above them, suspended along the length of the house beneath the low roof, sagged a long, reinforced plastic bag with a pipe at the far end, leading into the kitchen through the wall.

'Ingenious, isn't it?' Ben had appeared behind her. 'They collect methane from the pig shit in that bag and use it for cooking. That pipe leads into the kitchen and feeds a gas ring.'

'Wow. They don't waste a thing over here, do they?'

'They sure don't. Can't afford to. You feeling OK this morning?'

'I am.' She turned to smile at him. 'I slept surprisingly well.'

'Well, to make you feel even better, Kenny just called. Everyone's been released. Like we expected. Threw them out at five o'clock this morning.'

'Oh, fantastic!' Impulsively, she threw her arms round him. 'What a relief!'

He kissed the top of her head and then held her away at arm's length to enjoy the pleasure on her face. 'So what do you want to do now?'

Pru looked at her watch. It was shortly after seven.

'I would just like to go back to the orphanage quickly. If Molly thinks I'm checking up on her, that's too bad. I just need to make sure she's all right. Then I'm yours for the day. If you haven't made any plans?'

'There's nothing in this world I'd like more. We'll head for Tra Binh right after breakfast—which awaits us on the terrace.'

The 'terrace' was on the side of the house where

Ben and Pru had arrived unceremoniously the night before. Chairs of varying sizes were scattered around an old wooden table on which a large pot of *pho* was keeping warm on a charcoal burner. Bowls, cups, chopsticks, a big cooking pot and a teapot, its lid tied on with string, were laid out for them.

'Where's the family?'

'Oh, they'll have gone a long time ago. They get up with the sun. Hai has some building work somewhere, I think. Thuy will be in the paddy field, Canh will be at school for the morning and Hong will be around here somewhere doing what she can.'

'How can we thank them?'

'No need. They know.'

Chapter Twelve

Just about an hour later, Ben was parking the Saab in almost the same spot where Pru and Giles had arrived on the motorbike on her first visit to Tra Binh. Walking up to the orphanage, everything seemed much the same as it had before. The same dog barked from one of the houses; a woman in a lilac blouse and red cropped trousers, bent double weeding her greens crop, looked up and smiled. Further away, figures laboured quietly in the fields.

They reached the little copse.

'There's the orphanage, Ben. You can just see it through the trees.' Pru quickened her step then slowed again, looking back at him anxiously. 'It's very quiet. When I came before, I could hear laughter and singing by the time I got here.'

'They wouldn't be indoors,' mused Ben as they drew closer. 'Not in the daytime.'

'It's too early for naps,' said Pru. 'Maybe they're on an expedition, harvesting cashew nuts or something. She broke into a run. 'Hello! Molly? Anyone here?'

There was a faint answering call from behind the house. She ran round to the back. All the children were there, as far as she could tell, sitting or lying around the bare yard. Most of them looked half-asleep. Nhung was sitting against the trunk of a gnarled old olive tree, her wasted leg twisted up underneath her as usual, braiding the hair of one of the little girls. The small boy in the red and white T-shirt was dangling a gecko by the tail, watching it wriggle. As she looked, the tail broke off and the gecko dropped to the ground and scuttled off. The child examined the tail curiously and then put it in his mouth.

Seeing Pru, their faces brightened for a brief moment. Perhaps they were expecting Molly. Disappointed, their eyes dulled with lethargy again. Hanh, the old lady, had been spreading peppercorns across some matting to dry. She straightened up, making a helpless gesture with her hands.

'Where is Molly?' Pru asked her.

'Thoi khong hieu.'

Ben had arrived at her side.

'What is she saying?'

'She says she doesn't know.'

'Ask her what's happened to Molly.'

He spoke to Hanh again in Vietnamese, but the

189

old woman's body language was plain enough. She probably didn't know anything. And if she did, she wasn't going to admit it.

Leaving Ben to his fruitless questioning, Pru hurried inside the house. Molly had always liked sleeping late when she could get away with it. She approached the little screened off bedroom but it was deserted. Molly's bed was two flat cushions placed on a sleeping mat. Draped across it, tangled up with the un-stowed mosquito net, was the bottle-green silk sleeping bag they'd bought together in the camping shop—'cool in the heat, warm in the cold'. On the floor lay a pair of trainers and two grubby white socks, half inside out, lying where she'd dropped them. A sawn-off section of tree trunk served as an ingenious clothes horse on whose branches hung the loose cotton shirt Molly had been wearing the day before yesterday, a pair of cotton trousers Pru hadn't seen before, a purple bra and the woven Peruvian shoulder bag Molly insisted on taking everywhere.

Pru picked it up and looked inside. There was a little packet of tissues, a pot of lip balm, a cheap pair of sunglasses, a red hair scrunchie, an insect-repellent stick, her plastic tub of antibiotics, an almost empty pack of chewing gum and a pendant she suspected Duncan the Dropout had given her—a tiny silver moon, threaded on a leather thong. Pru took the lid off the lip balm. There wasn't much left. She put her finger in and applied some to her lips. It was as close to Molly as she could get just now. With a sharp pang of misgiving, Pru dropped the tub of antibiotics into her own shoulder bag.

Ben was studying her face. Perhaps, like Pru

190

herself, he was surprised by how calm she was. Survival instinct probably. She wouldn't sort things out by going to pieces.

'Maybe she's gone down to Saigon to see Giles. I bet that's what she's done.'

'How would she get there?'

'However she gets there for her usual weekend visits, I suppose. He told me she usually gets a lift with someone on a scooter.'

Ben looked at his watch. 'She might not be there yet.'

'It's nearly four hours since they were released, if Kenny got it right. And Saigon's a couple of hours' drive away, isn't it? If she left straight away she'll be there by now. But why would she leave her bag behind? Ben, I'm worried.'

Ben took his phone out of his pocket and went outside to perch on one of the plastic kindergarten chairs the kids had been sitting on making their animal noises for 'Old MacDonald'. Pru followed him.

It was two or three minutes before someone picked up the phone at the Nautical Club.

'At last! Tam, this is Ben . . . Ben Coder. Tam, everyone's been released up here, we gather. We're looking for Molly. Could you put Giles on, please? Really? . . . I see . . . Nothing at all . . .'

Pru tugged at Ben's arm. 'Who are you talking to? Let me speak to Giles.'

'Hang on a moment . . . don't go away, Tam.' He held the phone away from his ear. 'Pru, Giles is still in bed apparently. Tam doesn't want to disturb him. But she says Molly's not there.'

'Tell her to look in Giles's bedroom. She might be there without Tam realising.'

'Tam, can you just check in Giles's room for us . . . I know . . . yes, I realise that . . .' He smiled at Pru sympathetically, shaking his head. 'Not there. She's absolutely certain.' He reached for Pru's hand and squeezed it.

'OK, good idea, Tam. We'll check there right now . . . Sure . . . And please will you ask Giles to call me as soon as the lazy sonofabitch wakes up? I'll call back in an hour. If Molly turns up before then, would you call me straight away? Thank you, Tam. 'Bye.'

'Where did she suggest we check?'

'The people Molly's been supporting in this fight against the eviction order—it's Tam's uncle's family. Their house is quite near the orphanage. Just down the hill a way, she said.'

'Of course! I should have thought of that myself. That's where she'll be, I'm sure.'

They started back down the hill.

'We're looking for a house with a big banana palm in front of it,' said Ben. 'And a goat. Her uncle's name is Quang. His wife is Linh. There are a couple of kids too, I think.'

The woman they'd seen earlier was now sweeping the weeds she'd pulled into a pile with a bunch of long twigs tied together with string.

'Excuse me. Where is Quang's house?' asked Pru, smiling broadly to make up for her inability to form a complete, polite sentence.

The woman smiled back, her teeth stained dark red, lifting her broom to point out a dusty single-storey stuccoed house thirty or so yards away on the other side of the dirt lane.

Pru ran ahead of Ben and up to the entrance to the little front yard which was marked by two

192

roughly made brick pillars with no gate between them. Apart from a skinny brown goat tethered to a stake in the ground, there was no sign of life.

'Molly?' called Pru. Silence. 'Quang?'

Ben walked past her to peer into the house itself. 'Nobody here.'

A small figure darted out from behind the house, heading for the gateway. Ben shot out a strong arm and lifted the boy off his feet.

'Hi there, little guy.'

'It's Bong!' exclaimed Pru. 'Hey, Little Fish, it's me. Molly's mother. Remember?'

Bong was wriggling ineffectually in Ben's easy, powerful grasp.

'He's one of the kids from the orphanage,' explained Pru. 'Where's Molly, Little Fish?'

'I look for her. I don't know. She not here.'

'Was she arrested?'

He nodded. 'Many people here arrested. But free again now.'

'Where is Quang?' asked Ben.

'My husband at market,' said a quiet voice. A tiny, slim woman had appeared silently from round the back of the house and was watching them warily. Ben set Little Fish back on the ground and he scuttled off in the direction of the orphanage.

'You are Linh?' asked Ben.

She dipped her head.

'Do you know Molly?' asked Pru.

The woman studied Pru's face. Her expression softened. 'Yes.'

'She is my daughter. I am trying to find her.'

'Molly is lovely girl. She teach me English.' The woman was smiling graciously now. 'You like some tea?'

193

'No, thank you,' said Pru. She was anxious to keep searching.

'Yes, please,' said Ben. He glanced at Pru. 'We won't stay long. It's the polite thing to do. And she might be able to give us some clues.'

In the humid gloom of the little living room they sat on low wooden chairs sipping tea from small white china cups.

'Some people were arrested yesterday,' began Pru.

Linh looked away, toying with the hem of her skirt. She looked uncomfortable.

'Was Quang arrested?'

'He stay at People's Committee last night but he come home this morning.'

'And Molly was there too?'

Linh said something in Vietnamese.

'What?' Pru turned to Ben.

'She doesn't know about Molly. She hasn't seen her for a few days.'

Pru tried again. 'Were Quang and Molly both at the People's Committee yesterday?'

'Soon we have no fields. No home. We try to fight but no good.'

'Molly is helping you to fight?'

Linh nodded.

'And was she also released this morning with Quang?' persisted Pru.

'Quang not bad man. Not want trouble with police.'

She seemed not to have understood the question. Pru turned back to Ben for help. He addressed Linh in Vietnamese again. Pru waited as patiently as she could for the woman to finish her reply.

'She says she hasn't seen Quang this morning. He went straight to market after being released. She hasn't seen Molly either but she is sure she is safe and well. She will get word to Tam if they hear any news.'

The woman turned to Pru and held out her hand. 'Sorry because no help. Molly is very lovely girl. I like very much.'

Pru took the proffered hand politely. 'You tell Tam if you see her, yes?'

The woman dipped her head again. 'I tell Tam. For sure.'

As they walked back to the car, they called the Nautical Club again. Kien answered this time. Giles had got up and gone out, but still there'd been no sign of Molly.

*   *   *

'Ah, mate, how're you going?' Kenny's voice sounded muffled and distant coming from Ben's mobile in its cradle under the dashboard. 'You found her?'

'Drawn a blank so far, I'm afraid,' said Ben.

Pru leaned forward to speak into the phone, carefully enunciating her words to compensate for the bad line.

'There's no sign of her up here at the village. And she hasn't turned up at the Nautical Club. Where else could she be? Maybe she's still under arrest? Or maybe she wasn't arrested at all?'

'All I know is what I told Ben earlier. Three or four dozen villagers spent the night at the People's Committee and they let them out at dawn this morning. And it's definitely to do with a property

195

deal.'

'Have you found out any more about that?' asked Ben.

'It's serious shit, I can tell you that. A Californian company called Merrilands is right on the point of closing a deal on a big piece of land. They're going to turn it into a fuck-off leisure park—golf course, swimming pool, health spa, chi-chi little wooden chalets among the trees . . . you get the picture.'

'Who told you all this, Kenny?'

'This mate of mine on the *Review* has gotten drinking buddies with a guy from Merrilands who was seconded here a couple of months back. He's over on a nine-month contract to see the transaction through. And my mate says he's real edgy at the moment on account of the big boss being over to clinch the deal. If it all goes tits up, so does this guy's job.'

'So how does all this tie up?' Pru tried to organise her thoughts. 'This is a big property deal. Worth a lot of money to this American company and to the People's Committee chief who we reckon is taking a fat rake-off. The villagers are trying to fight it. They're not getting anywhere. The question is, how does Molly fit into all this?'

'Maybe she doesn't. Perhaps she never was arrested in the first place and she's just chosen this week to go off somewhere.'

'I'd give anything for that to be right, Ben, but all my instincts tell me it isn't. She'd have told Giles if she was going off anywhere. And the kids. She loves those children. Anyway, all her belongings are still at the orphanage.'

'Maybe they didn't let everyone go then; she's

196

still under arrest.'

'But why would they do that?'

'God knows,' said Ben. 'We're just going to go round in circles until we get some concrete information. Next stop, the People's Committee, I reckon.'

'There's a twenty-four-hour emergency phone number for the British Consul,' said Kenny's voice from the cradle. 'I'll find out what it is, if you want, and text it to you. If she is in jail, they can give you a list of English-speaking lawyers.'

'And can they get her released on diplomatic grounds, Kenny?'

'Probably not, Pru. If she's accused of breaking the law, she'll have to go through the due process. The Consul can't get people out of jail. I know this because I did a story once on a couple of kids who got done for drugs.'

For a second or two, Pru felt sick. 'She could be there for weeks then. Months.'

'Let's not jump to conclusions yet, Pru.' Ben put a consoling hand on her knee. 'Kenny, you mentioned this character before, the head of the People's Committee. What's his name again?'

'Sinh, funnily enough. S-i-n-h. Evil by name, evil by nature. Pronounced "Sing" though. Le Van Sinh.'

'Right.' Ben reached towards the hang-up button. 'We're off to introduce ourselves. Meantime, Kenny, you gotta promise us you'll call the moment you get wind of anything else, you hear?'

'Sure thing. Will do. Good luck with Doctor Sin!'

*   *   *

Ben and Pru sat in silence for a while, Pru struggling to absorb the full implications of what they'd been discussing, Ben trying to empathise with her—and, if he were honest, thinking some self-centred thoughts too. If it weren't for this mess with her daughter, he and Pru could be having some fun together. He really liked this gutsy, sexy lady. But then, he reasoned, if it hadn't been for this whole situation, they wouldn't have got together at all.

'So, next stop the People's Committee.' He forced himself to sound upbeat.

Pru sat looking through the windscreen, clenching her teeth. She couldn't crumble now. Gently, Ben reached out a hand and turned her face towards him and kissed her on the lips. She would have kissed him back but she'd been taken by surprise and the moment was over.

'We'll find her, Pru. Whatever mess she's in, we'll sort it out. She'll be OK.'

There was a timid knock at the car window on Pru's side. She looked up into the cheeky face of Bong.

'Hello again, Little Fish.'

'Hello, Molly Mum.'

'Do you know where the People's Committee office is?'

'Of course. You want I show you?'

'Yes please. Is it far?'

With Bong pulling Pru by the hand again, the three of them set off on foot up the road. Instead of turning left towards the orphanage at the crossroads by the Omo shop, they turned right, past a pile of what looked like the contents of a dozen or more family rubbish bins randomly

198

dumped at the roadside ('Sign of poor management by the People's Committee,' commented Ben) and into the equivalent of the village High Street, where ramshackle shops displayed everything from groceries to sundry bits of ironmongery. At the end of the street, set back from the road, was a low, double-fronted yellow stucco building with dark green-painted wooden-shuttered windows, two on the left-hand side of the main entrance, one on the right. A twenty-foot-long red banner with a party slogan in Vietnamese was strung across almost the full width of the building. The Vietnamese flag, red with a yellow star in the centre, hung listlessly from a pole in the dusty courtyard.

As they drew nearer, they could see that something of a fuss was going on. About a dozen people were gathered by a shallow flight of steps at the building's entrance. At the front of the group was a thin young man dressed in light grey trousers and a loose white shirt. On the ground at his feet lay a tiny coffin, little more than two feet long. He was shouting at the open door, his voice cracking with grief and anger.

Pru, Ben and Bong edged nearer.

'What's he saying?' whispered Pru, moved almost to tears herself by the sheer rawness of the man's emotion.

'It's something like, "Because of you my baby is dead. You could have let my son live." '

Behind the man, a young woman stood with bowed head, weeping softly. A tiny and very wizened old woman clung to her arm. The other members of the group—men, women and three children under the age of ten—stood close around

199

them in mute, protective support.

There was no sign of a response from inside the building. Presumably its occupants were keeping out of sight.

The man shouted out again.

'He's saying, "You bleed us dry. You take everything we have. Heaven knows, we have little enough," ' said Ben.

The man's voice broke. He couldn't go on. A movement caught Pru's eye at the window on the left of the building. A sallow, fleshy-faced man wearing an ill-fitting dark business suit over an orange shirt sauntered arrogantly into view. He stood for a moment, looking down at the little knot of people beneath him. He took a long pull on his cigarette, exhaled the smoke slowly and disdainfully down his nostrils, then turned his back and merged again into the shadowy recesses of the room.

Helped by one of the other men, the father picked up the casket and hoisted it on to his shoulder. The sad little vigil was over.

The others falling in behind him, they shuffled towards the open gate. As they reached the road, the mother stopped, calling out a parting shot of her own, before the dejected procession moved slowly away along the street, presumably to carry out the burial.

Pru stood trying to blink away her tears. 'What did she say?'

' "May you be damned forever," ' said Ben. His own eyes looked moist.

'What was all that about, do you think?'

'Do you know those people, Bong?' asked Ben.

He nodded. 'Their baby very sick but they have

200

no money for medicine. The chief take too much taxes. Nothing left to buy pills. Father and mother ask chief for help. He say no. So baby is dead now.'

'And was that the chief at the window?'

Bong nodded again. 'Mr Sinh. Nobody like. Greedy man. Take money for everything. Tax for garden, tax for house, tax for animals, tax for salt, tax for breathing!'

They stood in silence for a minute or two, too affected to speak. Ben drew a long breath.

'Well, I guess it's our turn to beg an audience now. Bong, you go and wait for us under that big tree across the street, OK?'

'I think I should do the talking,' said Pru. 'This is about my daughter.'

'Sure. Absolutely. I'll only butt in if I can help with interpreting something. But remember, I'm not that brilliant at Vietnamese myself.'

'We could take Bong in with us?'

'No, I don't think so. I think we're stronger on our own. We can't look as if we're getting ourselves involved with Sinh's village. We're two foreign visitors asking for information.'

'OK, let's go then.'

'One more thing.' Ben snatched at her arm. 'It is real bad form in Vietnam to lose your temper. Whatever happens, we have to stay cool.'

'That poor bereaved father wasn't exactly restrained, was he?'

'No, but he'd lost his battle already. His child had died. He had nothing more to lose.'

They walked purposefully across the yard. Bong stayed at the roadside behind the railings. As they reached the third and last step up to the building's entrance, a man materialised in front of them,

201

blocking their way. He looked to be in his late-forties, or early-fifties. Despite the heat, he wore a black shirt tucked into smart black trousers, cuffs buttoned neatly at the wrist. Lank black hair flopped forward from a side parting. His lips were smiling. His eyes were not. He didn't seem to feel the need to speak.

Pru turned on her friendliest, most charming smile—the one she always relied on to show people how honest and open, likeable and unthreatening she was.

'We've come to see Mr Sinh, please.'

For a second or two the henchman appraised them both, moving only his eyes from Ben to Pru and back again.

'You have appointment?'

'No, I'm from England,' replied Pru, somewhat illogically.

'Not possible today. Mr Sinh very busy.' He moved towards them as if to escort them back down the steps.

Despite herself, Pru felt her winning smile beginning to freeze.

'I'm sorry but we cannot go until we have spoken to Mr Sinh. It is very important.'

'We have come on very urgent business,' added Ben. 'We will not detain him long.'

'Wait one moment, please.' The official stood to one side, indicating them to step through the doorway, but carefully blocking the corridor leading to Sinh's office as he did so. The passageway was dark and dingy, painted in dull versions of the party colours—the woodwork in dull red, the walls dirty yellow. He ushered them towards the first door on the right of the building's hallway, opened it, waited for them to walk through and closed it quickly behind them, leaving them alone. Pru half expected to hear a key turn in the lock.

It was a small square cell of a room and completely bare. Not a chair, not a rug on the grey stone floor. What light there was came from a long slatted ventilation brick two or three feet above head height. Pru jumped to see if she could see what was on the other side, but wasn't anywhere near tall enough. She started pacing up and down instead.

'Right, I give them five minutes, and then I think we should simply walk into the guy's office.' She tried the door handle. 'It's not locked.'

'It won't be that easy, you know. They can just throw us out. They'll make you go through the motions of applying in writing for an appointment which, of course, they can delay for weeks.'

'I know. I've met these kind of petty officials before, back in my travelling days. You think they're small beer but they're actually really dangerous. In fact, I think the smaller guys are more dangerous than the big, important ones because they don't carry the same amount of responsibility.'

'And all the more so in Vietnam because of the geography. We're more than fifteen hundred clicks away from central government up in Hanoi. They try to keep a check on their party officials but it's damn near impossible from that distance.'

'Is it really fifteen hundred kilometres from Saigon to Hanoi?'

'About that.'

'What power has Sinh got, though, really? He's

just a jumped up little village councillor.'

'A hell of a lot of power when you think about it. He's in charge of a lot of land here. Several hundred acres of it. And it's land that is suddenly getting very valuable. It used to be just simple farmland, passed down from generation to generation. But all that's changing. Now, land means real big money. We're close enough to Saigon to be a prime target for investors. Tourism, big business, manufacturing . . . The capitalists are moving in.'

'Bit ironic, isn't it, after the communists won the war?'

'Absolutely. It's getting to be a stock saying: The capitalists may have lost the war in 1975, but they're sure as hell winning it now. The difference is that now their armies wear business suits and they're armed with briefcases.'

'But surely people can't just be kicked off their property after hundreds of years there?'

'That's the problem. They can. Sure, they should get some compensation, but I'd be surprised if they actually get very much.'

'So Mr Le Van Sinh is Lord of All He Surveys?'

'Totally. "The King's Law stops at the village gate." It's an old Vietnamese saying.'

The door opened. The henchman jerked his head to indicate that they should come out.

'I think he thinks he's got a starring role in some gangster movie,' muttered Pru.

He waited for them both to pass in front of him so that he could shepherd them along the corridor into Sinh's office.

Le Van Sinh had his back to them when they walked in, staring out into the courtyard, his head wreathed in cigarette smoke. The room reminded Pru of the mini-cab office in Wandsworth High Street. Shabby, dilapidated furniture; the smell of stale cigarettes. In the corner to the right of the window was, extraordinarily enough, a cheap wooden wardrobe similar to the one in her room at the Imperial Hotel, with a mirror inset in one of the doors. A portrait of Ho Chi Minh hung next to it, crooked, under an unlit fluorescent strip. To the left, against the drab yellow wall, was a brown leatherette bench seat and on a low table alongside it were set a flower-patterned china teapot and some matching cups on a tray. An electric fan groaned intermittently from a ramshackle fitting on the wall.

The man in black took his place at a desk near the wardrobe, first turning his chair to face outwards into the centre of the room for a better view of the imminent encounter.

Another cadre, white-haired, slightly paunchy, looked the two intruders up and down. Like his colleague, he evidently saw no need to respond to Pru's smile in kind. Without taking his eyes off them, he walked across the room to sit down opposite his colleague. There was a bigger, more substantial desk in front of the window, the only objects on which were an old-fashioned black telephone and a large and overflowing glass ashtray.

Outside, the mid-morning sun edged higher in a bleached, glaring sky. In here, the atmosphere felt dim and heavy; claustrophobically hot, despite the fan.

With the air of someone mustering his last shred of patience, Sinh turned to face them. Pru disliked him intensely on sight. Black hair, receding slightly

205

from his forehead, was swept back with some kind of pomade. His eyes were small and set deep in their sockets, almost lost between high, plump cheekbones and heavy, overhanging brows; his lips were full and fleshy. Spattered across his sallow complexion, like ink flicked from a fountain pen, was a constellation of black moles, from one of which, just at his jawline, four or five long black hairs trailed down to his collar. Pru wondered if the black suit and orange shirt he wore reflected the style of the Western moneymen he'd been doing business with.

He addressed Ben. 'You like tea?' But the tone was unmistakably, 'You don't want tea, do you?'

Ben duly shook his head. 'No, thank you.'

'You have no appointment. What can I do for you?'

Pru took over. 'I am looking for my daughter.'

Sinh's eyes switched coldly to her. Other than that, not a muscle moved.

'She was arrested yesterday morning.'

Still no attempt to reply.

'Along with some other people from the village. I need to know where she is now.'

'Who arrest your daughter? Why?'

'That's what I am hoping you will tell me.'

'Your daughter English? American?'

'We're English,'

'If she was arrested, it is because she has done something illegal.'

This wasn't going well. Pru could feel perspiration beginning to prickle on her nose and upper lip. Her shirt was clinging to her back and shoulders.

'Perhaps you are doing something illegal too,'

206

she countered. Ben nudged her as imperceptibly as he could. She took a deep breath. 'Mr Sinh, my daughter doesn't understand things here in your country. If she has done something wrong, I am sure it was a mistake and she is very sorry. It won't happen again, I can promise you.'

Again, the oppressive, menacing silence.

'She is just a young English girl who is working here for a charity for a few weeks. She's only eighteen.'

There was the merest hint of a flicker behind the cold eyes.

'I am not responsible for behaviour of foreign girls. I cannot help you.'

Ben interposed, in a reassuring, conversational tone, 'Could you just tell us where she might be? Her mother is understandably worried about her.'

'I do not know about your daughter. I can tell you nothing. Our meeting must now come to an end. I have an appointment.' With the smallest movement of his head, Sinh signalled the younger of the henchmen. 'Our visitors are leaving.'

Pru couldn't just walk meekly down the steps and out of the door. They wouldn't be granted access to this man's office a second time. She tried to keep her voice calm and rational.

'Now, look, Mr Sinh. You arrested a lot of people yesterday. People who are losing their land so that you can build this golf course or whatever it is. My daughter Molly was one of them. She has now disappeared. I need to know if you have released her or if she is still here.'

'Don't get confrontational,' warned Ben from the side of his mouth.

Sinh turned to the man in black and said

something in Vietnamese that was quite obviously along the lines of 'Get these people out of here'.

'I have a right to know where my daughter is. I'm not even asking you to release her, necessarily. I just need to know where she is.'

Both henchmen got to their feet and stood in front of Sinh, effectively cutting off any further conversation. Pru ducked her head round the paunchy one to resume eye contact.

'My daughter is not a criminal. If anyone is a criminal it is you, taking people's land to make money for yourself.'

'Oh, Pru,' groaned Ben.

'All right. I will leave, of course. But only after I have made sure that my daughter isn't here.'

Her heart thumping high in her chest, Pru turned and strode from the office, calling out her daughter's name.

'Molly! Molly . . . are you here? Can you hear me?'

She braced herself for running footsteps, arms angrily pulling her back. She opened the first door she came to along the passageway and pushed it wide open against the wall. The room was empty and bare of furniture. Leaving it open, she glanced behind her. The three party officials stood watching from the office doorway. A barely detectable smirk twitched around the lips of the man in black. Ben was standing uncertainly between her and them, not sure now whether to continue his hopeless efforts at international diplomacy or join Pru in her search. She seemed to be doing all right on her own. There were three more rooms to check, apart from the one she and Ben had been required to wait in. The next two were also empty. There was one remaining door at the end. It was this one or nothing. Pru pushed it open. Inside it was pitch black. The shutters were closed.

'Molly?' As her eyes accommodated to the gloom she could see it was an empty meeting room—half a dozen wooden chairs, an electric fan, a cheap trestle table and a picture of Ho Chi Minh fixed to the wall with ageing yellow sticky tape. In her heart now, she knew Molly wasn't here. They wouldn't be letting her do this otherwise.

Feeling like a rat in an experiment, but determined to maintain her dignity, Pru turned down a second passageway leading outside, to the back of the building. She found herself in a small quadrangle, shaded by a citrus tree. Most of the ground was covered with bamboo matting. Maybe this was where last night's captives had slept. An elderly man with a mop and bucket, slop-full of grey soapy water, shuffled across towards her. His fleeting glance at her face seemed to be full of meaning. She only wished she could read it. There was no one else in sight. And no other buildings; nowhere else Molly could be. Pru called her name again, just in case. A cricket stopped its sawing for a moment, waited, then hearing nothing more, resumed.

Deflated, she walked slowly back to the main corridor where Ben stood waiting. She realised her whole body was dripping with perspiration. The white-haired cadre came towards them to see them off the premises. Sinh had vanished, presumably back into his lair. His office door was shut now.

'It is most impolite that you come here without proper procedure.' The official's tone was one of smug tolerance maintained in the face of disgraceful behaviour. 'Please to visit us again some time. But only after you make appointment.'

He stood looking down on their retreating backs as they descended the steps back out into the courtyard.

'Self-righteous, disingenuous, arrogant, two-faced . . .' Pru was in tears of fury and frustration. Ben took her arm. As they crossed the street, Bong ran out from the shade of his tree and took hold of her other arm, looking anxiously up into her face.

'Not find Molly?'

Pru shook her head. Ben lit a cigarette and offered it to her. She took it gratefully. He lit another one for himself before putting in another call to the Nautical Club.

'No joy? . . . No, us neither. Keep us posted then . . . Thank you, Tam.'

'Now what do we do?'

They sat dejectedly on the dusty ground, backs against the tree trunk. It hadn't occurred to Pru that common sense and normality wouldn't prevail. Molly had got herself into a bit of a scrape but she'd done nothing really wrong. Surely, if you were a reasonable and honest person, you were treated reasonably and honestly in return. Suddenly, shockingly, the truth dawned. She wasn't in control of things at all. Not in any way. She didn't know where Molly was; she didn't know who was holding her, or where, or how she was being treated. What was certain was that if this big property transaction was worth as much money as Kenny seemed to think it was, then there was obviously a lot at stake for this ruthless Sinh character. And he was the one calling the shots.

She'd been so accustomed to life going the way

210

she wanted it to. There was nearly always a way of getting round things. Even throughout the split with David, she'd known somewhere in her heart that she'd bounce back; that she would survive. Today she had hit a brick wall. Her best efforts to charm Sinh and his cronies had cut no ice whatsoever.

A gust of wind rattled the seed pods in the branches above their heads. Seconds later, huge raindrops cratered the dusty earth around them.

'I've been expecting this,' said Ben. 'It's been so humid.'

The clattering pitter-patter became an insistent drumming. The ground changed colour from powdery terracotta to shining brick red. The tree afforded them shelter for a minute or two but quickly became saturated and enormous drops began to filter through the leaves.

Ben put his jacket over Pru's head. 'It shouldn't last long.'

Across the street, a gold-coloured Range Rover was pulling up in front of the People's Committee. Intent only on dodging the streaming rain, two burly, middle-aged men in chinos and short-sleeved check shirts jumped out from the rear doors. The older of the two wore a straw fedora; the other covered his head with a portfolio case. They ran up the steps and into the building.

'*They* don't seem to need an invitation,' remarked Pru dryly.

'Looks like a couple of my fellow countrymen,' added Ben.

'I see those men another time,' cried Bong excitedly. 'Hanh say they make big place for tourism in our pepper fields.'

211

Chapter Thirteen

If Molly's disappearance was linked with this leisure complex development—and it was looking increasingly likely to be—the key to finding her might lie in establishing more details, such as how much money was changing hands, whose hands they were and how near the deal was to completion.

Pru had suggested waiting for the Americans to emerge from their meeting with Le Sinh and asking those questions there and then. Ben wasn't so keen.

'They won't want to discuss confidential business affairs with us—especially not on the People's Committee doorstep.'

'We don't know that until we try. Don't be so defeatist.'

She had to raise her voice over the roar of the rain. Bong looked up at them anxiously but relaxed when he could see by their faces that they were not having an argument.

'Would it be such a bad idea,' continued Pru, 'to tell them we suspect Le Sinh of corruption and that he's holding a British girl in jail because he wants to stop her making a fuss about it? They might be horrified.'

'On the other hand, they might not give a damn,' said Ben. 'Why should any of that worry them, as long as they're getting the deal they want?'

'I'll tell you what might worry them: the media getting the story that Merrilands is involved in a corrupt property deal, destroying the livelihoods of

212

innocent, hardworking farmers for their own profit.'

'But, Pru, all that is speculation. It's highly likely, I grant you, but we don't have a shred of evidence. We'll just look ridiculous and hysterical.'

'Is that what you think I'm being?' Pru bridled. 'I prefer to say I'm trying all avenues. Not waiting around doing nothing and hoping things will come right on their own.'

'Listen. Say you were a big-shot American businessman—would you jeopardise a major business deal because some woman—no matter how beautiful she was—ambushed you from nowhere, soaked to the skin, ranting on about her missing student offspring?'

'You keep doing that,' she observed.

'Doing what?'

'Flattering me and making me feel foolish at the same time.'

'Sorry.' He ran his hands through his hair. 'I think.'

'I guess you're right,' admitted Pru. 'We need to be a bit cleverer than that.'

As suddenly as it had started, the rain stopped.

'I don't think there's anything more we can do up here,' said Ben. 'There must be another way of finding out what this company Merrilands is up to. We need to get at Kenny. Make him milk that contact of his a bit more.'

By mutual consent they scrambled to their feet and splashed back down the street to the car.

*   *   *

It was three o'clock by the time they arrived back

213

in Saigon. Bong had scurried back to the orphanage with a scrap of paper bearing Ben's mobile phone number, charged with the mission to get word down to them at once if Molly showed up. As they drove out of the village and away, Pru tried not to feel she was abandoning her daughter. There was nothing else she could logically do.

They made just one quick stop at a roadside stand to buy *banh mi*—baguette sandwiches filled with sliced cold meat and pickled vegetables. The bread was crisp and newly baked. As they sat and munched in the shade of the car's raised boot lid, a diminutive young woman approached them balancing mangoes heaped in two baskets on a springy bamboo yoke across her shoulders. Ben bought four. In the midst of her anxiety, they were nevertheless the most delicious mangoes Pru had ever eaten.

Back in her room at the Continental, she lowered herself into the first bath she'd had since leaving London. Lying almost completely submerged in refreshing, cool, fragrant water, she gave herself a talking to. She had to stay rational. Molly might be in a local Vietnamese jail somewhere because she'd taken part in an illegal demonstration; or being held hostage by a bent official trying to keep his corrupt intentions a secret. Either way, she wouldn't be subjected to torture or cruelty. This wasn't wartime. The worst she'd have to suffer would be a lack of creature comforts and a surfeit of boiled rice. She hadn't exactly been living in the lap of luxury at the orphanage anyway.

No doubt she'd be wondering where she was and how long she'd be held there. She might even be wishing she'd listened to her mother's warning about precisely this situation, though admitting she was wrong wasn't one of Molly's strong points. They wouldn't hold her for more than a day or two, surely. If the deal was on the point of completion, she'd be freed any minute now. There'd only be something to be really concerned about if she were to become ill.

She sat up abruptly in the bath. Those antibiotics!

'For God's sake, Moll!' she said out loud. 'Just don't get ill. Please don't get ill.'

She had to know what Kenny had found out. Until she did, there were too many uncertainties.

Fifteen minutes later, Pru was downstairs in the hotel lobby, clean and refreshed and waiting impatiently for Ben. Her hair was still damp. It would go curly, but who cared.

*   *   *

'Kenny's in the Q Bar under the Opera House across the road,' said Ben. 'I don't want to sound paranoid but the Continental's bar is too quiet. Better to go somewhere more lively, where we can't be overheard too easily. They also do great cocktails.'

Pru didn't care what bar they went to or what drinks it served.

Ben regarded her anxiously. There was a crease across the front of her olive green cotton dress where it had been folded and packed in her bag. Her hair looked thicker, for some reason, making her face seem smaller and more vulnerable. He could see she was making a determined effort to

215

stay calm and collected. A wave of tenderness coursed through him. Once again, he fought an impulse to put his arms around her. He didn't want her to feel she had to reciprocate. She had enough to cope with.

Despite the heat, Pru was grateful for the warm reassurance of Ben's strong arm linked with hers as they crossed the patch of green between the Continental and the Opera House. Already the refreshing effect of her bath and change of clothes was beginning to wear off in the relentless, enervating humidity. He stopped for a moment to point out an imposing ten-storey building which wouldn't have looked out of place in Paris.

'That's the Caravelle Hotel. The bar up top there is where the newsmen used to hang out, comparing notes and stealing each other's stories with their cocktails in their hands, while us boobies were rotting alive in jungle ditches. About as close to the war as most of them ever got. Half the world's TV footage was shot from that roof! After you . . .'

Pru plunged in front of him down some steep concrete steps and into a crowded, candle-lit bar. Pausing a few steps from the bottom, she stopped involuntarily to take it all in. Ben narrowly avoided cannoning into her. Five or six men at the far end of the long, narrow room looked almost identical to the ones they'd seen getting out of the Range Rover earlier on. Real American stereotypes— paunches encased in cheap cotton shirts, ample bottoms in ill-fitting chinos. A baseball cap or two. She looked up at Ben's alert, handsome face. He must be a similar age. How had he turned out so different? He might as well have come from

216

another planet.

Nearer the door, a much younger crowd, seemingly of all nationalities, chattered and babbled. Tanned limbs, toned bodies, expensive designer clothes . . . there to be seen; the centre of their own universe.

As the two of them stood there, one of the cocktail waitresses behind the zinc counter looked up and gave a little shriek of delight. She finished serving one of the check-shirt brigade, almost throwing his change at him, and scampered up to Ben like a delighted puppy.

'Benjie! Where've you been? I haven't seen you for weeks.' She tossed Pru a wary look, dismissed her and resumed her ardent gaze into Ben's eyes, face tilted eagerly towards his, standing just a little too close. 'I thought you didn't love me anymore!' She threw her arms around his neck. He unwound them and kissed her on the forehead.

'I'll always love you to distraction, Tien, you know that.' He took her playfully by the shoulders and turned her round to face the bar. 'Now get us a drink. I'll have a JD on the rocks. What about you, Pru? They do good malts here—very rare for Vietnam. They have some decent wine. Also rare. Or have a cocktail. One of the few positive influences we Americans can claim credit for over here.'

Pru was close to screaming with impatience. Where the hell was Kenny? She picked up a cocktail menu from the bar but couldn't read a thing in the flickering gloom without the indignity of searching for her glasses. She asked for the first cocktail she could think of.

'Margarita, please.'

217

'And a margarita.'

'I bring to you,' cooed the barmaid, fluttering over-made-up lashes.

Ben put a light hand on Pru's waist to steer her in the direction of an archway leading to a muslin-curtained, more cheerfully lit part of the bar.

'Sorry about that. Tien, I mean. She's like that with any half-decent-looking member of the male species.'

'To be honest, Ben, all I'm interested in right now is Molly.'

'Sure, of course.' He took his arm away. 'I think we'll find Kenny through here.'

There was just enough room in the narrow annex for three square tables set against a cream-painted brick wall. At the far end in the corner seat, behind his glass of beer and looking somehow too big for the furniture, sat Kenny, one hand holding a battered and gently smouldering roll-your-own, the other supporting a mobile phone at his ear, half buried in the mass of hair.

He stood to acknowledge their arrival, still talking into the phone.

'I need to know pronto, mate. Like in the next hour . . . Ta, mate. Good on ya.' He sat down again, putting his phone aside on the table.

'Hi, fellas. Lots of news.'

They waited until Tien had brought their drinks and teetered off again before getting down to business. Pru frowned at her cocktail. It looked irritatingly frivolous in its salt-rimmed glass with miniature pink umbrella and wedge of lime.

'So let's go through what we know for sure.' Kenny leaned confidentially across the precarious little table, making the candle flame quiver. 'As I said on the phone, the dispute at Tra Binh is definitely about this Merrilands deal. And I can tell you that they're well down the line with it all. Expecting to sign any day now, my informant tells me.

'I can also tell you there's a substantial allocation in the budget for compensation to the dozen or so farmers who are down to lose their land. A hundred thousand dollars. Enough dough to make up for the loss of this year's crops and help them set up somewhere else. My mate says it's been paid out already. It's gone out of the account. And I'll give you one guess whose greasy pocket it has gone into.'

'They'd pay out a sum like that even before the deal's signed?' asked Pru.

'Sinh will have made it one of his conditions. No dough up front, no deal. It's ten per cent of what the total contract's worth. It sounds a lot but it's peanuts compared with the profits they'll make over the next ten years on a development like this. Tourism is *the* growth industry in Vietnam right now.'

'I thought central government had been trying to stamp out local corruption?' said Ben.

'Yeah, they've started to. And not before time. These little cadres like Sinh have ruled the roost for decades, doing their backyard deals, imposing whatever taxes take their fancy and so on. Some are worse than others. They're not all bad. But there's been too much of it. And Hanoi's trying to attract foreign investors now, so the last thing they want is bribery and corruption stories getting out.'

'But Molly doesn't know about local politics, surely,' chipped in Pru. 'She hasn't been here that

219

long. And I'm sure she won't have heard of the Merrilands Development Corporation.'

'No, but the villagers have been fighting Sinh for a couple of months on this one and we know she's involved herself in that. And she'll know they're not getting any compensation. Apparently Sinh deliberately turned off the irrigation system to the fields he's selling to Merrilands. So, of course, the crops died and now he's telling the farmers the land's not worth compensating them for because it's not productive. He's a full-scale, double-dealing, four-flushing bludger.'

'No wonder they're so angry,' said Pru.

'They rant and rave and chuck stones, but in the end they've just got to put up and shut up and try to rebuild their living somewhere else.'

'I still don't see why Molly should have any bearing on all this.'

'Because she could be the fart at Sinh's tea party. She could cause a humungous stink. No one will listen to the villagers. They haven't got the channels of communication. They're just humble peasants. But Molly . . . she's got access to the outside world, people in the West she can talk to by phone or email. And now Mum's turned up here on the rampage as well.'

'He wouldn't hurt her, would he?' Pru turned to Ben. 'Please say he wouldn't.'

She realised her fingers were trembling on the stem of her cocktail glass. Ben closed his hand over them gently. 'I'm sure he wouldn't. For the same reason. He'd be risking bad publicity.'

'I stick to what I've believed all the way along.' Kenny stubbed out his cigarette and leaned back in his chair, releasing a thin stream of smoke towards

220

the ceiling. 'Sinh just wants to keep her out of the way for a couple of days, just until it's all signed and sealed.'

'She could still blow the whistle when she gets out, couldn't she?'

'Yeah, but the deal will have gone through by then. It'll be a *fait accompli*. There won't be much of a whistle to blow. Maybe the villagers will get to see the advantages of rich tourists coming in to spend their money and it'll all quieten down.'

'We still don't know any of this for certain.'

'Nope. But I'd put money on it now.'

'Where do you think he'd be keeping her?'

'Your guess is as good as mine. What would you do if you were a devious little rat like Sinh? If she's not in Tra Binh, she might be at some other village in the province. She hasn't got a phone. And obviously they won't be giving her a map. She won't know where she is.'

'Oh, God, if that's what's happened she must be so angry. And frightened.'

'She sounds a strong-minded kid, though.' Kenny was trying to be reassuring.

Pru took a deep breath. 'There's something I haven't told you. Molly is strong-minded, yes, but she's not so strong physically. She was born with a heart defect. It's called tricuspid atresia. The worst time was when she was tiny. She went through three major operations before she was three.'

'My God, what a nightmare,' murmured Ben.

'It means her heart will always be vulnerable to any infection that might get into her bloodstream. She has to take a short course of antibiotics just to have a simple filling at the dentist because any bacteria dislodged might settle on the site of the

221

operation.' Pru tried to keep her voice steady. 'This is why the fact that she's disappeared just fills me with dread.'

Neither of the two men seemed to know what to say for a moment. Ben stroked her hand. He turned to Kenny.

'Look, Kenny, if you reckon they'll let her go when the deal is signed and sealed, how long do you think that'll be? It's vital we find that out.'

'It's Friday today,' said Pru. 'Do deals get signed over weekends?'

'I couldn't tell you for sure. I'd guess not,' said Kenny. 'If it's any comfort, I'm sure they won't want the hassle of keeping Molly any longer than they have to.'

'Still,' said Ben, 'even if they sign on Monday and she's freed later that day or Tuesday maybe, we're still talking about an eighteen-year-old kid spending five days as a hostage in who knows what conditions.'

'We've got to find her before that.' Pru's voice was cracking now. 'I can't believe this is happening.'

'We need friends in high places. And that's something we don't have.' Kenny sucked on the end of yet another roll-up.

'I do,' said Ben quietly.

They left Kenny at the bar, causing chaos among half a dozen customers who all seemed to have made the simultaneous decision to go to the toilet at the end of the narrow annex and were, one after the other, falling over his outstretched, booted feet. Pru had made him promise to keep pestering his man at Merrilands and let them know the second there was any indication that the contract was about to be signed.

'And keep your phone switched on and the battery charged,' she'd instructed him. 'We have to know you'll be there if we need you, any time of day or night.'

'Are all the women in the UK as bossy as you? I'm going off the idea of going there now.' Pru drew breath to apologise but he forestalled her. 'Only joking, darl. Good luck.'

*   *   *

Ben hadn't wanted to elaborate on this highly placed friend. All he would say was that it was someone he'd helped out during the war here in 1971 and who was now a member of the communist government's National Assembly in Hanoi.

'That's the equivalent of our Cabinet, isn't it—or your Senate?'

He nodded. 'I never thought I'd have to do this, but I guess now's the time to call in that favour.'

They found an empty sofa in a corner of the Continental's foyer and he dialled a number from his mobile. Pru noticed his hand was shaking. She strained to hear what he was saying but he lowered his voice and turned away from her. She picked up odd words: 'circumstances . . .' and 'unavoidable' and something that was either 'greatest respect' or 'never suspect'.

A minute or two later, he'd ended the call.

'Well, looks like I'm off to Hanoi. I've got a meeting in the morning.'

'So it's not possible to explain things to this guy on the phone without having to go there?'

'No. This needs to be face to face.'

'Did you tell him roughly what it's about?'

'I said nothing at all, Pru. My contact could get into real big trouble if anyone got wind of what I'm asking. It would look like conspiring against another party member.'

'I thought they wanted to stamp out corruption'

'Yeah, but in their own way. In private. Not because of some smart-assed American telling them their business.'

'But you do think he'll be able to find out where Molly is for us?'

'Sure. A real good chance. If there's one thing the communist party is good at, it's the subtle art of keeping tabs on people.'

'This guy must owe you a very big favour then if he's taking such a risk with his career.'

Ben stood up. 'I think so.'

'What did you do?'

'This isn't the right time.' He picked up his satchel.

'I'm sorry. Forgive me.'

'I'm sorry too. I can't. One day, maybe.'

'When's the next flight?'

He looked at his watch. 'There are two tonight—one at eight and one at nine. It's a bit tight for the eight o'clock now.'

'I could come with you,' she found herself suggesting. Did she mean that? Or did she just want to hear him say he wanted her company? It was hard to think logically. There were so many emotions moiling around in her head, vying to be taken account of.

'Sure. I'd like that. But you're nearer to Tra Binh here if there's any news on Molly.'

'I know, but if Kenny is right and she's in another village somewhere, my main chance of finding her now is through you.'

'Well, I don't want to talk you into anything, Pru. It has to be your choice. Just suppose you did hear something during the night—someone finds out where Molly is, maybe, or she's been released— what would you do?'

'Scream with delight, first of all. Then I suppose I'd try and get hold of Giles to take me to her on the bike. Assuming he's got his phone switched on. Or maybe Kenny could take me. Get a car from somewhere. Do you think there's any chance of someone contacting me in the middle of the night?'

'Unlikely. It's dark now. Not at this stage.'

'What time is your appointment tomorrow?'

'Six a.m.'

'Wow. Really early.'

'Yup.'

'And you'll be back when?'

'Mid- to late-morning, I guess.'

Pru made up her mind. 'I'll come with you. If you'll have me. In some ways I feel nearer to Molly here, but realistically any news is going to come through on your mobile, so you're my conduit to keeping track of everything.'

'I don't think I've had a woman see me as a mere conduit before.'

'I don't think I said "mere",' said Pru, smiling in spite of everything.

'It sounds to me like we're both finding reasons for you to come with me.'

'No, it's not that. Well, not really. It's just that I do feel more in touch with Molly with you than

225

without you. I feel disempowered here on my own. And alone.'

'I can't think of anything I'd like more.' Ben smiled down at her.

'As long as you're sure we'll be back in the morning.'

'I'll get reception to book the flights and call Kenny and Giles to tell them what we're doing. Meet you back down here in twenty minutes max. And pack warmer things—it's a lot cooler in Hanoi.'

Before going back to her room, Pru called in at the business centre. She ought to let David know what was happening, without worrying him too much. If she alarmed him now, he might decide to come out and join her. Did she want that? She searched her heart. To her amazement she found she didn't. It might mean risking Ben's support.

It's not just his support you're afraid of losing, is it? It's him. You'd better be careful, my girl.

'There's nothing David could do even if he did come out,' she reasoned. 'Ben is the one with the contacts. Anyway, David made it perfectly clear he thought I was mad to come here. Implied I was neurotic.'

In front of the computer screen, her fingers hovered uncertainly over the keyboard. It was hard to avoid a tone of I told you so! After several deletions and refinements she settled on:

```
Hi David,
Molly    seems    to    have    gone
temporarily missing but don't get
too concerned. I'm in the process
of   tracking   her   down.   As   you
```

226

know, she was up in arms about that family's farmland being sold to some American property developers. I think she became a bit of a thorn in the side of the local village chief who is brokering the deal and making a profit out of it. We reckon he was afraid she'd draw attention to his shady dealings and that he's keeping her out of the way in a nearby village somewhere while the transaction goes through. I've met someone here who can pull a few strings in Hanoi and we're expecting to find out exactly where she is by tomorrow. I'm very glad I decided to come out here! I'll keep you posted. Hope all is well with you. Px

She realised it begged a lot of questions but she didn't have time to write more. Over the years she and David had shared so many anxieties to do with Molly, it seemed strange this time to be handling things without him—especially with the help of another man.

She sent a short email to Roger Griffiths at GapKo, simply telling him she was still 'on the case' and that if he heard from Molly to ring Ben's mobile number immediately. She could almost hear his Welsh lilt; 'See? What did I tell you!'

Chapter Fourteen

They landed at Hanoi amid relentless, lukewarm drizzle. It was too dark to see much of their surroundings on the way to the town centre, but Pru was aware of spending much of the first part of the cab journey on a long, straight, well-made road flanked by acres of paddy fields with occasional enormous advertising hoardings looming out of the darkness ahead, their elaborate support scaffolding straddling the landscape. Of the city centre itself, she had an impression of wider streets, grander houses, and more trees and open spaces. There was a lot less traffic than in Saigon, but then it was getting on for midnight now.

Ben had booked them rooms at the Metropole. As the car drew up outside an elegant, white-stuccoed building, two boys in claret-red uniforms with matching fez-like caps opened the glass doors for them, ushering them through with welcoming smiles. They were allocated rooms on the same floor. Ben made sure Pru was happy with hers before going off down the corridor to his own.

She threw her bag on to the nearest surface and sat down heavily on the bed. The room was clean, comfortable, unremarkable. The silence began to close in on her. On the move, she'd felt she was at least making some kind of progress, however much of an illusion that might have been. Now, in this tidy stillness, the little worm of anxiety she'd grown used to living with over the past few days began to nibble and gnaw at her deep inside, feeding on her fears, growing as it fed, expanding, surging up through her oesophagus until it burst from her throat in an involuntary, sobbing gasp of terror.

The next stage would be madness. Hardly aware of what she was doing, she snatched up her room key and ran down the corridor, following the numbers on the doors until she found Ben's room. She knocked on the door. There was a pause then his muffled voice called out, 'Right with you.'

He opened the door, grappling with the belt of his hotel-issue white towelling robe. 'I thought it might be you.' He took in her condition at a glance and put out a hand, clasping her gently round the waist. 'Come in.'

She collapsed against him. More grateful for human contact than she'd ever been in her life. He felt so good; warm and strong. He held her for a moment, then led her over to a chintz-covered sofa by the narrow French windows and sat her down gently.

'I know what you need.' He found the mini-bar by the wardrobe and knelt to peer inside, taking miniature bottles out and putting them back in. 'Ah, here we are. Cognac. I was about to meditate for half an hour, but this will be just as good.'

He poured the contents into a tooth mug and handed it to her. He then retrieved another little bottle for himself and came back to kneel in front of her.

'I'm sorry,' she mumbled into her glass. 'I've been trying to be so strong and sensible, and suddenly it all hit me.'

'I'm not surprised. I've been amazed at how cool and steady you've been. Drink.'

She took a sip.

'More than that—it'll do you good.'

She took a swig, suppressing a grimace.

'That's my girl.'

Pru smiled weakly.

'See, you're looking better already.'

He took a packet of Winstons out of his robe pocket, put two cigarettes in his mouth, lit them both and passed one over to her.

'We'll find her, Pru,' he said softly. 'I'll make sure we do.'

'I'm so worried. It's this heart weakness she's got. She has to be more careful than other kids. Normally, she's just like anyone else, but if she's ill she's so much more vulnerable. Now she's holed up against her will in some remote jungle village. Just suppose she caught something! My mind runs riot through snake bites, malaria, a tooth abscess maybe, an ear infection—even a tummy bug . . . almost anything could cause real problems for Moll.'

'By this time tomorrow, we might well have found out where she is. We might even have spent the evening together, the three of us, laughing about it all over dinner, telling each other what we've been through.'

'Oh God, I hope so. Do you really think so?'

He got up off his knees and joined her on the sofa, sitting with his back against the arm so that he was facing her.

'The communist party in Vietnam has its flaws, of course it does. But it's like a living being. Tomorrow morning I'll touch the heart of it and from there we'll travel down the main artery and into the veins. Molly is somewhere in that network. The party links are as direct as that. We just need to find the right channel. Once we do, we're as good as there. Tomorrow morning that process will begin. And it really won't take long, I promise you.'

'I can't tell you how fantastic it is to have you . . . to have found you. So unbelievably lucky I met you.'

'Destiny is a wonderful thing.' Ben stood up and went back to the mini-bar. 'We could move on to the whisky or I could call room service for more brandy. Which would you prefer?'

'Is there any wine?'

'I'll get room service to bring some.' He pressed a button on the phone. 'It used to be real hard finding wine in Vietnam,' he remarked as he waited. 'Decent or otherwise. You get better stuff in Hanoi. The French influence maybe. Oh, hi there. A bottle of red wine and two glasses to Room 217,' he said into the mouthpiece. 'Yup, sure . . . Cabernet Sauvignon is just fine.'

Pru drained the last drop of brandy from the toothmug. Ben replaced the phone by the bed and came back over towards her, adjusting his bathrobe which was threatening to fall open.

'I guess this isn't the smoothest way for a gentleman to entertain a lady in his hotel room. I should be wearing a silken smoking jacket, Graham Greene style . . . who did stay *here* incidentally. They've got a suite and a cocktail named after him.'

'That's what you'd normally wear then, is it, to . . . entertain ladies?'

'That depends on the lady.' He smiled. 'So you're a Graham Greene fan, are you?'

'I think he's my all-time favourite author,' she replied. 'I've read almost everything he ever

231

wrote.' Privately, she was wondering how many women he had entertained in hotel rooms. Every woman he met must fall in love with him.

There was a knock on the door. Room service. Ben tipped the waiter, poured two glasses of wine from the already-opened bottle and brought them over to where she sat.

'How are you feeling now?'

'Quite a bit better. Thank you. I'm sorry I went to pieces a bit.'

'It's understandable. Totally.'

'I'm putting all my trust in you and your meeting tomorrow. You've made me feel it's going to be OK.' She sipped her wine. 'This is good. Cheers.'

He smiled into her eyes. 'Here's to finding Molly.'

'You do think she'll be all right, don't you?'

'I wouldn't say so if I didn't believe it.'

'I'm keeping you from your sleep, I know. You've got to be up really early.'

'You don't have to worry about me. I don't seem to need that much sleep. In any case, meditating always recharges my batteries if I start getting low on energy.'

'You're a Buddhist?'

'Yes.'

'Why?'

He looked surprised. 'Why?' he echoed. 'Because it's open and gentle. Because it's non-judgemental. Because it's about a belief in the human spirit and about living in harmony with everything around you. Because it's the answer for me. That's all.'

She had to ask it. 'Are you married now . . . or living with someone?'

'No. I've done that and it's not for me. I used to think what I wanted was the ideal family—a gorgeous, clever wife, a couple of lovely kids. But then I came to realise you can't have the ideal life when you're way off being perfect yourself. The contrast is just too painful. For everyone.'

'Nobody's perfect, though, are they? Everyone has their flaws and faults. It's what makes them lovable. I couldn't bear a man who thought he was perfect.'

'No, of course. Absolutely. And I've gotten to a stage in my life where I accept myself for who I am, faults and all. I just don't expect other people to accept the deal. Why should they?'

'Why shouldn't they? It seems to me you're intelligent, funny, good-looking, kind, sensitive, successful . . . Quite a catch, as my mother used to say.'

'Well, thank you, ma'am.' He topped up their glasses. 'Look, I'm not asking for sweet words. I really am not. It's just that what you see on the outside can be a lot different to what's going on inside. But most people don't take the trouble to look beyond face value.'

'But you did try it. Marriage, I mean.'

'A long time ago. It didn't work out. I changed.'

There was a pause. The silence began to close in again. Thoughts of Molly, alone among strangers in some dark village. She had to stop them.

'What changed you? The war?'

'I don't like to talk about it. I look forward, not back.'

'Isn't it good to talk things through sometimes? Drag the old monsters out of their dark caves and see them for what they are. Or are you still afraid

233

of them?'

'Listen, Pru, they may be old monsters, but they're mighty big and they're mighty powerful. No use you thinking you can do me a favour and reduce them to cute little pussycats. They'll never be that. For the rest of my life, they'll never be that.'

Pru was aware of her heart thumping. This was dangerous ground. If she pushed things too far, he might slam the door shut and never open it again. They may or may not come through it with their trust in each other intact. It was a risk she wanted to take.

'I don't want to force you to talk about anything if you don't want to. And I can't promise to understand everything you've been through. But if it would help, I hope you know you can trust me.'

He looked into her eyes. 'You know something? I think I do trust you.'

He kissed her gently. This time she kissed him back. A stab of desire, like a physical pain, shot through her. She wanted him. She really wanted him. She was shocked at herself. How could her body betray her like this when all she should be thinking about was Molly? He wanted her too. There was no doubting that. Under the towelling dressing gown she could sense his arousal as their kisses became hungrier. It was Ben who broke the spell.

Gently he extricated himself from their embrace and pressed her two hands together, cupping them gently in his own.

'I think we'd better have ourselves some more wine, before we get to the point of no return.' His voice was low and quiet.

'Yes . . . yes. You're right. Of course.'

'I want to make love to you so much. More than anything. But now isn't the right time. You know it and I know it.'

He had learned enough about Pru these last few days to be sure she would feel remorseful in the morning. It was a risk he didn't want to take. It was too soon. This wasn't one of the casual, easy come, easy go relationships he was accustomed to. He and she came from separate continents; a committed relationship had to be almost impossible. And yet all he could think of was that he wanted this woman in his life. He'd never believed he could feel like this. It was important to tread carefully. It mattered.

'Perhaps I should go,' said Pru quietly. And yet, tonight, she dreaded being alone.

'Please don't.' He poured the last of the wine into their glasses. 'I don't think I could sleep now.'

'Talk to me then. Tell me about Ben Coder.'

*   *   *

'When I got back home from Vietnam, after the war, I came out of Port Columbus airport and I realised people were calling abuse at me. I couldn't believe it. Twelve months before, I'd left that same airport as a hero, ready to fight for the honour and glory of my country. I got back to find I seemed to have disgraced it instead. And then I was supposed to forget the whole thing. That was the deal. You forget it and we'll forget it. Let's all pretend it never happened. I was expected to slot right back into the comfortable small-town life I'd been born into. But how could I do that with a

235

head full of gunfire and murder? And I couldn't explain how I felt to anyone—my mom, my old buddies back home . . . specially not to my high school sweetheart Becky. I looked the same to them. How were they to know they were looking at a totally different guy?'

'What about your dad?'

'Dad died a couple of years before. I guess he wouldn't have understood either. Nobody could who hadn't been through it.'

'So did you marry Becky?'

'I thought I could pull it off, you know, the pretending nothing had happened thing. I really tried. We had the family wedding at the United Methodist Church in Mount Vernon, and I got a job in a local attorney's office. But I couldn't keep the monsters down. The memories. Pictures in my head at night. Anger. Betrayal. Fear. Guilt. Most of all guilt, maybe. A whole mess of ugly stuff seething around inside me. I was only twenty-one. I felt like Methuselah, but that's all I was.'

'And when was your daughter born?'

'Kathy May came along a little more than a year after Becky and I got married. She was just the cutest little thing you ever saw. I adored her. But at the same time, all I wanted to do was escape.' He sighed, searching for a way to explain it. 'I think it was the permanent state of pretence. I felt so isolated inside. Becky was commendably patient with me. She did love me. But the problem was, I didn't love myself. And looking back, I guess maybe I came to despise her for loving me. It was almost like a moral high ground kind of thing. I was jealous. She was so good and devoted and blameless while I was all held in and self-obsessed

236

and dried up inside.'

'So how long did you go on, trying to make it work?'

'I gave up on it all quite early on. I just knew I couldn't live like that. It would have destroyed us all. I remember exactly when I left because it was the day after Kathy May's third birthday. I'm sure Becky was relieved to see the back of me by then. I'd been getting more and more unpleasant to live with. It wouldn't have been good for Kathy May. I mean, it must be pretty scary for a kid to see a man punch his hand through the kitchen window in white-hot self-hating fury.

'I never laid a finger on her or Becky, though. I wouldn't have trusted myself if I'd ever gone down that route. What if I'd flipped? What if my mind had suddenly clicked back into war mode? It was like having a time bomb strapped to my own back. I couldn't subject them to that—or me for that matter. I'd look into Becky's eyes and I'd see disappointment looking back at me. With a hint of fear. I couldn't live with that.'

'But you still keep in touch?'

'Oh, sure. We get on real good now. Becky married again, years ago. Nice enough guy. Kath is still adorable. I went to her graduation, and if she gets married one day I'll be at the wedding. But I'm happier on my own. I feel like the real me on my own. Not disappointing anyone.'

'What did you do after you left?'

'I went to New York where nobody knew me. Where I could begin life as the new Ben Coder. The old one was shot to pieces. I got a scholarship to Cornell as a mature student to study law. The rest I've told you.

'You're looking tired. You'll need to be strong tomorrow. It's two-thirty. Now you must sleep.'

They'd talked until the wine was gone, Pru curled up on the sofa next to him, his arm around her. Finally, tiredness took over. She was trying to keep her eyes open but losing the battle. He carried her gently to the big double bed and then lay down beside her, watching her drift off to sleep.

Pru and Molly were walking together in an enormous forest. Molly had arranged to meet someone. Mist was swirling among the trees. The sun was beginning to set.

'I won't be long, Mum,' she called, disappearing already into the mist. 'I'll meet you at the cafeteria. Just follow the path signposted "New Walk".'

Reluctantly, Pru started off in the direction the sign was pointing, but soon came to a fork and another signpost. Though she peered and stared, she couldn't make out the words on it. She made a choice and walked on. She shivered. Figures loomed out of the darkness. She was lost, adrift in this alien place. Where was Molly? She had to find Molly.

She awoke, soaked in sweat, with a strong sense that it was she, not Molly, who needed guidance. Molly had known the terrain and where she was going. Pru was the lost frightened one.

Chapter Fifteen

It was still dark. She was alone on Ben's bed, still fully dressed. The digital clock under the TV read 05.35. She scrambled to her feet. In the light above the bathroom mirror, she looked pale and hollow-eyed. As she splashed some cold water on her face, it occurred to her that if keeping this rendezvous was dangerous for Ben's contact, perhaps it was risky for him too. She remembered how his hand had trembled as he'd made that call. Fear nudged at her guts again. She couldn't just wait here passively. She found her shoes and slipped into the shadowy corridor.

Downstairs, the lobby was surprisingly full of activity considering how early it was. Four smartly uniformed staff were busy at the reception desk, several people were sitting around in armchairs reading newspapers, and a group of grey-haired tourists by a huge stack of luggage were getting in people's way. It was impossible to tell whether they had just arrived or were waiting to check out. '*Ich hab' meine Handtasche verloren,*' one of the women was wailing as Pru went by. She spotted Ben at the far end of the reception counter, wearing jeans and a light blue shirt, sleeves turned up casually just above the wrists. He looked so handsome, it actually made her heart ache. He picked up a newspaper from a pile by the door, looked at his watch and strolled out into the street, acknowledging the boy who opened the door for him with a tense, polite smile. Pru watched to see whether he turned left or right, waited a moment, then left the hotel herself.

The sun was just beginning to rise, but it was a colourless, hazy, damp kind of dawn. Many of Hanoi's residents were already up and beginning their day, but the atmosphere was positively serene compared with the honking madness of Saigon. There were fewer cars and relatively few motorcycles. By far the preferred mode of transport, at this time of the morning at any rate, seemed to be bicycles. She kept as close to Ben as she dared, just near enough to keep him in sight. Once or twice he looked back over his shoulder, but she made sure there was always someone in front of her to hide behind.

He crossed the road and turned into a narrower street. He walked deceptively fast. Not for the first time, Pru found herself admiring the easy athletic way he moved. He could have been a twenty year old. She quickened her step to keep up. Ahead, at the end of the street, veiled in fine, grey mist, she could just make out a long, wide lake, delicately fringed with trees. Pru had read about the famous Hoan Kiem Lake, in whose depths a giant turtle supposedly guards the magic sword that defeated Chinese invaders five hundred years ago.

As she came a little nearer, the mist seemed to be moving; inhabited by shadows that swayed slowly in harmony, like reeds in a gentle underwater current. A few steps further on and she realised what they were: scores of men and women of all ages, in tracksuits or shorts and vests, serenely engaged in synchronised tai chi exercises. Others were simply stretching or jogging round the lake's perimeter. She couldn't stop to watch; she didn't dare lose sight of Ben. He was strolling now alongside the lake, past wooden benches placed every few yards around it. Most of them were in use—as bicycle stands, or props for hamstring stretches, or refuges for student lovers, huddled together, even this early in the morning, lost and oblivious in their own intimate assignations.

Approaching an old weeping willow leaning out across the lake, its delicate green branches trailing in the water, Ben stopped suddenly, putting out a hand to touch the trunk. A woman was walking uncertainly towards him. Pru hastily sat down on the end of the bench nearest her. If he were to look back now, she'd just be another figure gazing out at the misty water, half hidden behind two boys in shorts who were playing badminton using not rackets, but their feet, to send the shuttlecock back and forth to each other.

The tall American and the slender Vietnamese woman stood for a moment beneath the curve of the willow's trunk, close together, like lovers exchanging vows. He put a gentle arm around her waist, guiding her back the way she had come along the lakeside path. They found an unoccupied bench fifty or so yards further on and sat, side by side, deep in conversation.

Immobilised, sitting among the tai chi gyrations and badminton games as the sun worked its way through the mist to start its day, Pru felt sick. No wonder he'd been so cagey. How could she have been so stupid? She'd assumed he was feeling the same magnetic attraction to her as she was to him. Wishful thinking must have clouded her judgement. She'd read things in his eyes that weren't there. He was just being kind, trying to help her out. That was the sort of man he was. But she knew very little about him as a person. Just some stories about his distant past. Almost nothing about his life now. To be fair, he'd not led her on. True, he had kissed her a couple of times, but he'd never let himself be drawn on the subject of any current relationships. Why hadn't she stayed in Saigon?

A shuttlecock hit her on the arm and flopped to the ground. She picked it up and handed it back to the skinny shirtless young man who bounded up to retrieve it. What had made her think she was of any special significance in Ben's life? She'd been naïve.

Pru stood up, turning her back on the couple still locked in conversation together on their bench, and walked back to the hotel.

*   *   *

She was still beautiful. Her glossy hair was shorter now; a businesslike bob framing her face. It made her seem somehow smaller than the last time he'd seen her. That had been thirteen years ago. He had come over with a little group of fellow Americans, war veterans like himself, who had become consumed by the need to confront some of their demons. If they could, in some small way, just try to make amends to the Vietnamese people for the destruction the war had wreaked on their country, they felt perhaps their own healing might begin.

In the spirit of reconciliation, they had been invited to an early-evening reception to meet with representatives of the Vietnamese War Veterans' Association at a province in Central Vietnam. And

242

there, as one of the Provincial People's Committee officials, had been Hong Yen.

He might not have recognised the neatly uniformed party officer at all but as their eyes met, to Ben's amazement, the stern official demeanour dissolved, her face totally transformed by the shy, sweet smile he remembered so well.

*　　　*　　　*

It was the middle of the dry season. 1971. Heavy, humid, ruthless heat. Ben's unit had been detailed to spend six weeks based at the village of Loa Kinh north west of Saigon where, the suspicion was, the Viet Cong were using the inhabitants as spies. Certainly in this sector the VC seemed to be one step ahead of every plan they ever made. The US Army had seen the sense of setting up camp in the villages in an attempt to forestall the spies and defend the inhabitants—most of whom were women, children and old men. Some of the women were so beautiful, he remembered; fragile and slender, yet tough and incredibly resilient. They'd had to be. Little Hong Yen had always cheered him up. She was fourteen, fifteen at most; only five years younger than Ben, although to him then she seemed little more than a child. She had long, shining black hair, darting brown eyes that seemed to speak volumes and a smile that made you melt inside. Hong Yen loved chewing gum. She used to sneak into Ben's hootch when she thought he was out and loot his supplies. She never took anything else. Just the gum. He used to turn a blind eye. He didn't mind. It was one small thing he could do that made him feel he wasn't entirely the devil's lieutenant.

One day the sergeant must have caught her doing the same in his hootch. Lester Caputo was a big man, thick-set and bone-headed to go with it. A bully. Ben avoided his company whenever possible.

That morning, Ben heard a small, stifled cry, which seemed to be coming from the other side of Caputo's hut. Immersed in that oppressive jungle war, day after day, it was the little noises that got you on edge. His first thought was that Charlie had sneaked up on them. He crept up to the side of the hootch and peeped through the loosely woven bamboo wall. As his eyes adjusted from the glare outside to the gloom inside he became aware that a desperate, one-to-one struggle was taking place. A second later, he saw that the two people were Caputo and a young Vietnamese girl. The sergeant had one beefy arm around the girl's neck, crushing her face against his shoulder to smother her screams. With the other hand he was fumbling with his trouser zip. Ben watched, paralysed with revulsion and fear . . . Caputo was a senior officer. He knew if he intervened he'd find himself in very big trouble.

Breathing heavily, spittle glistening at the corners of his mouth, pale eyes wide and staring, the sergeant tore at the terrified girl's loose cotton shirt. She made a desperate effort to wrench herself free, squirming out of his grip and scrambling frantically on all fours towards the door. Growling like an enraged bear, Caputo lunged after her, dragging her back across the hut floor by her hair.

With what felt like a mule kick to the solar

244

plexus, Ben saw the girl's face. It was little Hong Yen. Caputo had her down on her knees now, her face at his groin. She was trying to turn away but he struck her a heavy, swinging blow across the face, forcing her back towards him, squeezing her cheeks with finger and thumb to force her jaws apart.

This couldn't happen. He couldn't let it happen. As he sprinted to the front of the hootch he could hear Hong Yen gagging and choking. He had never been able to forget that sound. It became submerged under a chilling, otherworldly howl, which he realised was coming from his own throat. Caputo must have weighed a solid fifty pounds more than Ben, but livid rage had given the boy superhuman strength. He seized the sergeant's collar and hauled him away as if he were a ten year old, throwing him violently against the wall of the hootch, the bamboo snapping and cracking under his weight.

Still retching, gasping for air and trembling uncontrollably, Hong Yen had half crawled, half stumbled from the hootch, doing her best to gather her torn clothing around her. Bellowing with frustrated lust and fury, Caputo staggered to his feet. Ben had never before or since seen such hatred in a man's eyes. Instinctively he knew he had to keep the thug off balance. He swung at him with every scrap of strength he could muster. All he could remember after that was blood streaming from Caputo's nose, spattering both their uniforms, as Ben hit him again and again and again, until he felt someone pulling them apart.

*   *   *

245

The unit commander, Doug Jacobsen, was a fair enough kind of guy. He knew what Caputo was like. But he hadn't been happy.

'What did ya have to stick your nose in for, boy?' he'd shouted at Ben. 'I've got a war to fight here. I'm not a motherfucking social worker.'

That evening when everyone sat down to eat, Caputo was absent. No one told Ben where he'd gone and he knew better than to ask. He thought maybe the sergeant had been court-martialled, but some weeks later he heard he'd been given a transfer. Been put in charge of a supply depot somewhere near Da Nang. He never knew whether Caputo survived the war. Ben had always hoped he didn't.

Life at Loa Kinh hadn't been the same for him after that. Hong Yen avoided him. Wouldn't talk to him or go anywhere near his hootch—not even for the gum she loved so much. He understood. She felt shamed, humiliated. She was just a kid. She couldn't deal with the situation.

A few weeks later they'd packed up and moved on to a new base and that was the end of that. He had never expected to set eyes on her again.

Yet sixteen years later, in that People's Committee reception room, there she had been, the shy little girl with the penchant for chewing gum, the one whose cheeky smile had meant so much. Ben was pushing forty by now, Hong Yen would have been in her early-thirties. Seeing her so unexpectedly had shocked him to the core; brought back memories he'd thought were long since safely battened down and out of reach.

Softly, in halting English, she'd told him she had

246

thought about him often; that she had been haunted by the fact that she had never expressed her gratitude.

'I didn't know how to. I was so young then,' she'd said. 'I didn't tell anyone what happened. Not even my mother. I've never talked about it, but I have never forgotten. I will never forget.'

They didn't use the word 'rape'.

'Perhaps one day I can do something to say thank you,' she'd said.

'You have nothing to thank me for.' He'd meant it absolutely. 'Seeing you again—your smile, the conversation we have just had—that is thanks enough.'

Now he had to tell her it hadn't been enough after all.

*   *   *

Sitting in the quiet breakfast room at the Metropole, Pru couldn't face eating much. A motherly waitress in an *ao-dai* brought her Vietnamese tea and a basket of rolls and pastries.

You're going to have to pull yourself together.

The Voice was back.

What have I always told you? There's only one person you can depend on in this life and that's yourself.

Pru nibbled dejectedly on a *pain au chocolat.* She felt hollow inside.

You drank too much again last night, for a start. You had just the lightest of snacks on the plane and then you go mixing your drinks—brandy and wine. Fatal! Then you're up half the night talking in this man's bedroom. Really, Prudence! You had four

*hours sleep at the most. You know you need a good
seven or eight hours to function properly. And it's
more important you keep your wits about you now
than it's ever been in your life. You must recognise
that you're highly vulnerable emotionally at the
moment. Think about it for a moment. In the past
four days . . .*

Is that really all it's been?

*. . . you've been through just about every emotion
in the book. Culture shock and general anxiety to
start with, then the humiliation and pain of filial
rejection, then love—or the illusion of it—with this
American who's managed to completely turn your
head. All that followed by the distress of Molly
disappearing and not knowing where she is or what
she's going through. And now, this morning, let's
face it, jealousy—not the most edifying of emotions,
Prudence.*

'Of course I'm not jealous,' muttered Pru to
herself. 'I'm far too long in the tooth to be
knocked sideways by some unrequited schoolgirl
crush.'

'Well, we should hear something useful by late-
morning.'

She jumped violently.

'Sorry. You were miles away.' Putting a soothing
hand on Pru's shoulder, Ben waylaid the waitress
to order coffee. The woman scurried to the
kitchen, her face wreathed in smiles. He managed
to charm everyone.

Why would I think I was the only one? thought
Pru.

Don't be bitter.

He sat down opposite her. Aware that he was
exploring her face with some solicitude, she

248

avoided looking at him directly.

'What's the plan of action?' she heard herself say.

'It seems that they're aware of Sinh and his exploits up here. They just haven't been able to pin anything on him yet. It would be real useful to them to have some solid evidence.'

'Well, that's good. It's Molly I'm interested in, though. Can this person, your contact, help us find her?'

'By the time we're back in Saigon, I'm sure they'll have tracked her down.'

'I hope you're right. I hope it really will be as easy as that.'

Ben's coffee arrived. He poured it and drank it black. He seemed even less interested in eating anything than Pru was. He looked tired. A little strained.

'We were a bit daft last night, we should have had more sleep,' she commented.

'I guess I got talking, didn't I? I don't know why.'

'I shouldn't have come knocking on your door. My fault.'

'But it was great . . .' he began.

She stood up abruptly. 'So we get the first plane out of here.'

'Yup. We'll get the ten o'clock easy. Unless you want to look around Hanoi a bit and get the next one. It's a beautiful city.'

'One day maybe. I can't concentrate on anything until I know Molly is all right.'

'No, of course. I understand that. When we've found her, assuming she's OK, I could bring you back. We could spend a couple of days . . .'

'Let's just take one thing at a time. See you in

249

the lobby. What time?'

He blinked.

'Eight o'clock. You've got half an hour. Are you OK, Pru?'

'A bit tired. It's all beginning to get to me now, I think.'

She turned and walked from the room before he could prolong the conversation any further.

Chapter Sixteen

On the plane, she avoided the need to talk by dropping off to sleep. Yesterday she might have let her head rest on his shoulder. Today, she made sure that she leaned towards the window.

Ben's mobile signalled receipt of a message the minute he switched it on in the arrivals hall at Saigon airport.

He dialled a number and listened. Watching his face intently, Pru noticed his brow furrow. She tried to steady her breathing. Ben pressed a button on his phone and listened again.

'Sinh hasn't got her,' he said finally, putting it back in his shirt pocket. 'It seems he's as anxious to find Molly as we are.'

'You promised me they'd find out where she is! So the last twenty-four hours have been a complete waste of time. Time I could have been spending up at Tra Binh looking for her.' Pru was pacing round in small circles by the exchange bureau near the airport entrance, hardly aware of what she was doing or the odd looks she was getting.

Ben looked pale and stricken himself. He grabbed her shoulders in an attempt to make her stand still for a moment. She shook him off.

'You promised me. I trusted you.'

'Look, let's go somewhere and decide on our next step. You're getting too mad to think straight.'

'It's fine for you. This is just a little adventure for *you*. For me, my daughter's life is at stake. I couldn't live with myself if something has happened to her. I really couldn't.'

'Come on, Pru. Dear, adorable Pru. Please don't get so upset. It isn't the done thing in Vietnam, displaying all this raw emotion in public. Let's go somewhere quiet.'

'I don't care what other people think,' she hissed at him angrily. He was relieved that she had at least lowered her voice and stopped pacing. 'My feelings are my feelings and I'll show them however I want.'

Ben seized her arm and piloted her through the glass doors and into the taxi-rank bedlam outside.

'Where's my level-headed, unshakeable, prudent Pru gone?' he asked as their cab honked and hooted its way towards Saigon's city centre.

'I'm sorry,' said Pru, softening a little now. 'It's just that I'd set so much store by that trip to Hanoi. I'm bitterly disappointed and I'm angry with myself for being so gullible.'

'You sound as though you think I've deceived you.'

'Well, you have, haven't you?'

'How can you say that?'

'You didn't tell me this contact of yours was a woman. And one you seem to have a particularly close relationship with.'

'How do you know it's a woman?'

'Does it matter how I know?'

'You followed me!'

'Yes, I did. I was just . . .'

'Right. That's great. You followed me. I told you how sensitive this meeting was. If anyone finds out she's been liaising with me, in effect spying against the party, it could be the end of her career. I trusted you . . .'

'You did not trust me! You concealed things from me. If you'd been straight with me in the first place, we wouldn't be having this argument now.'

'The truth is, we're having this argument now because my contact is a woman and not a man. Why should it matter that she's female and not male? What relevance does that have?'

'It's relevant when I see that you look like a pair of lovers.' Damn. She hadn't intended to sound jealous. 'Not that I care about that. You can choose whoever you like to have relationships with. It's just that this particular assignation was about *my* daughter. At least, I thought it was. Now I'm not so sure.'

The warmth went out of Ben's deep blue eyes. 'Now you listen up. I've totally done my best to support you in all this. I know how hard it is for you. I can only try to imagine how I'd feel if this had happened to Kathy May. But it's been real hard for me too, asking this favour on your behalf. You need to know that. I've hated having to do it. It's put me and her in a very delicate situation. And if I didn't give you any details about her, has it occurred to you that I might have had a very good reason?'

'Obviously you had a reason.' Pru was beginning

252

to feel she was on shaky ground. 'That's my point. I don't know what that reason is. You kept it from me.'

'Oh, so you feel you have a right to know everything about me, do you? You've known me a couple of days and you think it's OK to chew me up and spit me out.'

'Ben, this conversation is going horribly wrong. Of course I don't. I'm concerned about my daughter, that's all. I feel out of control enough without thinking that you're hiding certain things from me.'

'I have told you absolutely everything that is relevant to finding Molly. Anything I haven't told you has been, to be blunt, because it's not your business.'

There was a tense silence. They'd arrived at the city centre now. Pru recognised the huge neon Pepsi sign by the market. For some reason, the day Fred died came back into her mind. Perhaps because she was feeling the same despairing sense of vertigo, as if she were standing on the brink of a swirling, black, bottomless pit.

For God's sake, don't fall. Turn around. Face the other way. Take a step forward. Back into the light.

'Ben, I'm so sorry. You've been the most amazing support to me in all this. I really can't imagine how I'd have coped if I hadn't met you. I've come to . . . value you enormously—as a person—as well as for everything you've done to help me.'

'I guess we're both under pressure here. We have to cut each other some slack.'

'I feel terrible now. I made too many

253

assumptions.'

'Don't, Pru. You didn't. Maybe I do owe you a bit more explanation. When the time's right.'

'You don't owe me anything. You've done so much. I can't thank you enough. And I'm sure you need to be getting back to your work with the charity and so on. I can manage from now on. Truly. I'll go to the British Consulate.'

She waited, steeling herself against hearing him seize this chance for a graceful exit.

'The Consulate may be able to help, but from what I've heard the wheels of diplomacy grind pretty slow, going through all the proper channels and so on. It could take days. My friend in Hanoi will short circuit all that. What's difficult is having to take it on trust that things are happening behind the scenes. She will come up trumps for us, I know she will.'

'I've made things difficult enough for the two of you already . . .'

'Look, Pru, I'm not about to cut and run—unless you want me to, of course. It's your situation, your daughter. But if you still want my help, you got it.'

They had hardly noticed their cab stopping outside the Continental. The driver was watching them curiously in his mirror.

Pru took Ben's hand in both of hers, then put it to her lips and kissed it. To her own astonishment, she almost found herself saying, I love you. She stopped herself in time, saying instead, 'We'd better get out, I think. And it's about time I paid for something.'

*　　　*　　　*

254

The little wooden hut was damp and gloomy, oppressively hot. The rain pounded down outside, battering the corrugated-iron roof, making her feel even more confined. With a sudden flare of exasperation, Molly closed the novel she'd already read from cover to cover twice and threw it hard against the opposite wall. Her eyes were hurting anyway. Nguyet, the old woman in whose hut she was sitting, looked up in surprise and clicked her tongue against her teeth.

If only she had brought more things to do with her. Apart from that one novel, all her belongings were back at the orphanage. She had tried asking Nguyet if someone could collect them and bring them up to her, but hadn't been able to make herself understood. It wasn't so bad when there were things to do. She'd spent most of yesterday under the shade of some palm trees, breaking open scores of heavy green coconuts, decanting the milk into assorted plastic buckets. The day before that, she'd helped gather honey from a group of bee hives on some rough ground up behind the village. Early this morning, she'd sat in Nguyet's porch shaping chopped pork and chicken into little round balls to be wrapped in moist wafer-thin rice pancakes called *banh uot*. When the time came to cook and eat them, though, her appetite had gone.

Then the rain set in and boredom along with it. She needed someone to talk to. She missed Giles. She missed the children at the orphanage. Actually, more than anything else, she missed home. She lay down on her sleeping mat, suddenly feeling incredibly tired. She'd have a siesta and then apply her mind to getting out of here.

Back in the hotel lobby, Pru and Ben agreed to reconvene after a quick shower and change. It occurred to Pru that, having checked in two nights ago, she hadn't yet slept in her room. Guiltily, she remembered David. She ought to tell him what had been happening. Once in her room, she dialled his number. It went against the grain, using the hotel phone. It would cost way over the odds, but this was more important than saving money. She dialled his home number first. The prim, secretarial voice of Lucy answered.

'I'm sorry, neither of us can take your call at the moment. Please leave a message with your name and number or try us on our mobiles . . .' How cosy. Pru couldn't suppress a sharp pang of jealousy. She hung up and dialled David's mobile. It was switched off. The voicemail service kicked in. God, what message to leave? Too complicated. She'd try again later . . .

He is Molly's father, remember. He loves her just as much as you do. He has a right to be kept informed.

'David, please would you ring me at the Continental Hotel in Ho Chi Minh City? I need to talk to you urgently. Thanks.'

As cooling water streamed over her body in the bathroom, Pru wondered how Sinh could possibly say he didn't know where her daughter was. He had eyes and ears in every village in the district. Perhaps Molly had left the district after all. It wasn't completely beyond the bounds of possibility. She imagined an email waiting for her now.

Hi mum
Hope you got back to England OK
and I hope you've forgiven me for
being so unwelcoming when you
came to see me. I've taken a
break from the orphanage to go to
Cambodia for a couple of weeks.
You know how long I've been
wanting to see the ruined temples
at Angkor Wat. I'm taking loads
of pictures to send you. Love to
everyone back home, Moll

Pru dried herself and rifled impatiently through her half-unpacked suitcase. The last pair of clean trousers she had were white linen, which was offering a bit of a hostage to fortune, but they'd have to do. A pale blue cotton shirt over a white vest top, the faithful navy cardigan round her waist, and she was ready. She'd given up trying to keep her hair sleek and had rubbed it cursorily with a towel and left it to dry naturally. Already it was fluffing out around her face. Ben had said the humidity was above seventy per cent, and it certainly felt it. The perspiration was springing from her pores again already. A minute later she was back in the business centre. Without even sitting down at the screen, she logged quickly on to her email account.

The disappointment was inevitable but none-the-less dispiriting. Nothing at all from Molly. There was one from David, though. She opened it quickly.

```
I'm glad you've found some help
out there. I still have every
confidence that Molly will have
enough common sense to keep
herself out of trouble. I'd offer
to come out myself but it's quite
pressured here at the mo. Keep me
posted. D.
```

It had been sent several hours ago, well before she'd left her phone message. She didn't attempt to reply. Time was of the essence now. There were about five hours of daylight left. It was vital to get to Tra Binh as quickly as possible and do a house-to-house search. Starting with another visit to Le Sinh.

In the lobby Pru called the Nautical Club. Tam answered. She didn't seem to know where Giles was.

'Do you know anything more, Tam, about what's been happening in Tra Binh? Have you heard anything from your family up there?'

'I very sorry. No more news. Very sorry.'

Through the glass doors Pru could see Ben pulling up in the silver Saab outside.

*   *   *

The rain had eased a little, but the atmosphere in the hut was dank and tangibly damp. Molly's whole body was running with perspiration.

'I need some air.' She tried to sit up, but the hammer inside her head began beating so hard against her skull that she had to lie down again. Why did she feel so weak? More sleep. She'd feel better after a bit more sleep.

*   *   *

Ben watched Pru walking towards him and his next breath caught in his throat. She looked so beautiful.

'I've just filled the gas tank,' he said, leaning across and opening her door. 'Do you feel refreshed? You sure look it.'

'So do you.' Pru smiled. His skin was smooth and clean and his hair still damp, brushed back, curling a little over his collar.

'Who were you calling from reception?' he asked when he'd recovered his composure.

'I tried the Nautical Club but Giles isn't there.'

'Try him on his mobile.' He handed her his phone. 'He's under N for Nautical.'

The phone rang several times before Giles's voice answered. He sounded breathless. 'Hi, sweetheart, how was Hanoi?'

'I'm not sure yet. We're hoping to hear something soon. But Sinh says he doesn't know where she is. Do you believe that?'

'It's hard to know what to think, isn't it? I'm up in Tra Binh now. Came up early this morning. No sign of her so far, though.'

'We're on the way there ourselves. Shall we meet you somewhere?'

'OK. Ring me when you get here. I'm not sure where I'll be.'

'Where have you been looking?'

'I've been to all the houses in the village and drawn a blank. Now I'm just riding around the area really.'

'Do you think she could have gone off somewhere without telling you? She was telling me about a stunning place up in the North she wanted to go to—Sapa, is it? Or Cambodia. Maybe she's taken off on an impulse.'

'No! She wouldn't do that. She'd have told me. Definitely. All right, look, I wasn't going to raise your hopes, but I think I have a lead.'

'What? Who from? Where?'

'I was right in the middle of my detective work when you called.' Why hadn't he kept his mouth shut! 'Let me get back to you. I'll call you or see you here at Tra Binh, whichever happens first.'

'But is she all right? Do you know if she's OK?'

'I'm sure she is. Just don't worry, all right? I'm switching my phone off now. I'll be on the bike. 'Bye.'

'Giles? . . . Giles! Oh, for Chrissake!' exploded Pru. 'He says he's got a lead and then he hangs up.'

'What sort of a lead?'

'He didn't bloody say. He just said he'll get back to me and that he's sure Molly's fine.'

'Well, that sounds good, doesn't it?'

'I wish we could wave a magic wand and just be there right now. How far away are we?' They'd left the last of Saigon's sprawling suburbs behind a few minutes ago.

'I'm keeping my foot down.' Ben looked at his watch. 'We're doing good. Should be there by half-three at the latest.'

'Shouldn't we be getting a call from your . . . lady in Hanoi?'

'No. We won't speak again unless there's something real important to say. That's the deal.'

260

Pru wanted to ask more questions about her but she didn't want to risk alienating him again.

'So many people we're having to put our trust in. It's bloody frustrating.'

'Do you trust Giles?'

'I'm not sure. I can't make up my mind. He's not the kind of guy I'd choose for Moll, to be honest. What do you think?'

'I have to admit he's always struck me as a bit of a chancer.'

'So you think so too.'

'Maybe that's not fair. It's just the business he's in, I guess, and the way it is over here ... the contraband liquor, probably contraband other things. Drugs maybe. I've heard he pays the cops a lot of hush money.'

Pru's anxiety level began to rise again. Ben sensed it.

'Real charming with it, though.' He smiled. 'I guess you'd call him a loveable rogue.'

'Which is fine, as long as he doesn't happen to be your daughter's boyfriend.'

'Yes, I guess I can see that.' Ben paused, then added, 'Do you think he loves her?'

'I don't know,' sighed Pru. 'And I don't know whether to hope that he does, for Moll's sake now, or hope that he doesn't, for the sake of her future.'

Seemingly from nowhere, heavy drops of rain began to pepper the windscreen.

'Let's call Kenny.'

She dialled the number and put the phone in its dashboard cradle.

'Hi there, how you going?'

'Hello, Kenny,' called Pru above the measured thump of the Saab's windscreen wipers. 'We're

261

heading back to Tra Binh. All we've got from Hanoi so far is that Sinh says he doesn't know where Molly is and that he wants to find her too. So nothing new really.' Pru cast a sideways glance at Ben. He was staring steadfastly ahead, lips compressed. 'What have you got to report?'

'We thought Merrilands head office back in California ought to know what's going on. I've emailed the CEO warning him his company's reputation could be on the line with this deal. Farmers being swindled and all that. It's a good email, though I say it myself. Should get a reaction.'

'Did you say the local People's Committee chief might be holding my daughter hostage as well?'

'Well, no. We can't make accusations we're not sure of. I reckon if we point the finger at Sinh on the money front, hopefully he'll spit the girl out as well, if you know what I mean.'

'Giles seems to think he's got a lead on where she is. Do you know anything about that?'

'No, but good on 'im. Let's hope, eh?'

'That's all we seem to be doing,' sighed Pru, 'hoping.'

'Thanks, Kenny,' put in Ben. 'Keep hassling for us, won't you. Any other strings you can pull for us, we'd be mighty grateful.'

'Not much joy in Hanoi then, with your Friend in High Places?'

'Things will be happening. It's just that we can't know about it. We just have to have faith that things are moving,' he was looking at Pru now, 'because they will be.'

'I'll get back to you then, mates.'

'Like everyone else,' muttered Pru.

262

'Cheers, Kenny,' said Ben, pressing the hang-up button.

Chapter Seventeen

It was taking all Giles's strength to keep the bike upright. It always surprised him how quickly the rains turned the dusty lanes to a quagmire. Thick, dark orange water formed fast-running shallow streams, coursing along the road, finding the lines of least resistance, joining up with others every so often to form deeper ones.

Several times Giles felt the bike begin to fishtail, the back wheel sliding sideways underneath him, and he had to slow almost to a standstill, putting a foot out to steady himself. Within minutes of the rain starting, his hair was plastered to his face and water had found a way through to just about every part of his body under his hastily donned plastic kagoule. Thankfully, there was very little traffic on these roads. The odd farmer on a bicycle pedalling for the shelter of home. Two cops on a motorbike had passed him earlier. They could have been the same guys who'd flagged him down with Pru a couple of days ago. It was hard to see properly in this rain. Fully expecting the routine flag-down and paper inspection, he'd watched them receding in his side mirror. They had definitely seen him. Must have bigger fish to fry, he thought.

He found a tree to shelter under while he checked his map. He must be nearly there by now. Before he left Tra Binh, the villagers had shown him where the hamlet of Cau Giang was, and he'd

263

drawn a circle round it. It was about twenty kilometres north of Tra Binh, just over the boundary into the next province. And just out of Sinh's jurisdiction.

About twenty minutes' more hard riding, he reckoned, and he'd be there. He couldn't wait to get Molly back to Saigon and see an end to all this drama. It had been hard keeping tabs on business with all this going on. In any case, the girl had done her bit. She could come out now.

Not for the first time, he thanked fate for getting Pru and Ben together. He'd have had to take responsibility for Pru himself otherwise. It would have been tricky trying to keep shtum while she was going through such agonies of anxiety.

*   *   *

'Why has he switched his phone off?' Pru pressed the redial button for the umpteenth time.

'Do you think he's found her yet?'

'If he has, it's unforgivable of him not to have told me.' She slotted the phone back in its cradle with a sigh of frustration.

Ben was swerving the car this way and that around the rain-filled potholes.

'I can't wait to get my hands round that young man's throat and extract this so-called lead out of him.'

'Well, we're here, so you should have the chance to do that any minute now.'

The car sloshed to a halt at their now-familiar parking spot by the grocer's shop. A man talking to the owner inside turned up his collar against the sheeting rain and walked quickly away.

264

'I'm going to buy some bottles of water and some bread—a few supplies in case we need them later.'

Pru hardly heard him. She was looking round for Giles's bike.

'Where is he?' She glared at the phone. 'Call, damn you!'

*   *   *

The rain was easing off as Giles arrived at Cau Giang. At least he assumed that's where he was. It was hardly a village at all. Eight or nine single-storey tin-roofed houses arranged roughly in a row among the banana palms along the right-hand side of the road. A dog barked from somewhere; more of a token gesture than anything. Probably didn't feel like coming out in the wet. One or two villagers who had been squatting in their doorways watching the rain, stood up at the sound of his arrival and disappeared inside their houses.

He switched off his engine and dismounted, returning the landscape to its customary raindrop-punctuated silence. Only one inhabitant remained outside. A woman in a brown tunic and loose navy trousers took a step forward, screwing up her eyes to get a better look at the stranger. Giles tried to marshal in his mind a few basic words of explanation in Vietnamese, but the woman had started to beckon him towards her house. She seemed to have been expecting him. He followed her to the threshold and stood there, dripping, under the overhang of the roof.

In the semi-darkness, Giles had an impression of some mats on the floor, a rickety wooden cabinet,

265

the family shrine and a low table with an electric fan trained on someone sitting with her back against the wall, holding out her arms towards him.

'Giles!'

'Well, hey there. I've been feeling like the guy in that old chocolates advert, riding through hell and high water to get to my loved one. Come and give me a hug, you bad, clever girl!'

'I'm not feeling too good, Giles. Every time I stand up my head hurts and I have to sit down again.'

'Oh, my poor baby,'

'Come in and sit down for a bit. Nguyet won't mind. She's been looking after me. I'll be all right in a while. Now that you're here.'

Giles struggled out of his wet raingear, dropped it beside the doorstep and stepped inside.

Weakly, she held her face towards him to be kissed. 'I'm so glad you're here. I want to go home. It seemed like an adventure at first. I really felt I was doing something useful, you know? Then it got boring. Like playing hide and seek and you find a brilliant place to hide and then nobody comes to find you.' She pulled her knees in to her chest, rocking gently back and forth. 'I threw up this morning.'

'We need to get you back to my place, babe.' He brushed his hand across her forehead and face, kissing her tenderly at the same time. 'You do feel hot.'

'Can you get me some water?'

'So do you want to know what you've achieved?' asked Giles as she swigged gratefully from the bottle of mineral water he'd fetched from the bike.

'I suppose so. I don't think I care any more. I

266

just feel so tired.'

'Your mum is a force to be reckoned with, isn't she?'

'Mum? What's Mum got to do with it?'

'Didn't you know? I told Tam to tell Quang to get a message through to you. She's been on the warpath looking for you. She's been to Hanoi to report Sinh for corruption and kidnapping you.'

'You're joking! So she didn't go to Nha Trang?'

'No. She was getting it together with this American guy she met. Ben. Then the news of the arrests came through.'

'Oh, God. I bet she went nuts.'

'She did a bit. She went straight back up to Tra Binh, of course.'

'Did you take her on the bike again?'

'No. Ben drove her. Anyway, next morning we heard Sinh had let everyone out. But they couldn't find you anywhere. Everyone was back where they belong except you. I was getting frantic calls from your mum. We thought Sinh must be keep-ing you out of the way till his deal was signed. Your mum marched into the People's Committee, confronted Sinh and searched the place. Didn't find you, of course. I was worried sick about you myself until Tam told me the plan. Brilliant idea! "That's my Moll," I thought, "doing what she loves best. Attention seeking."'

'For unselfish reasons, though,' Molly protested faintly.

'Of course, sweetheart. Just teasing. Anyway I thought, Hey, Pru could be really useful here. You were aiming at the local papers and now we'd got Kenny McKinnon going. He totally bought the story that Sinh had you locked up somewhere. But an Englishwoman kicking up a gigantic fuss about her missing daughter could really up the stakes. And it worked. She was brilliant. It was bloody hard keeping my mouth shut sometimes, though.'

'Oh, dear. Poor Mum. She must have been so worried.'

'Yes, I know, but it was only for a couple of days. And all in a good cause.'

'I wish she was here now.'

'I've told her I might know where to find you. She's waiting for me to call.'

'Oh, call her, please. I want to call her now.'

'Let's do better than that. She's down at Tra Binh. She'll be totally blown away when she sees me arriving with you on the back of the bike.'

'Can you help me up? I'm really not feeling so good.'

Giles took both Molly's hands in his and tried to haul her to her feet. She stood shakily for a moment, then buckled and sat back down again.

'Everything's going round and round,' she murmured. 'Horrible headache.'

'Sit there for a minute or two, have some more water, and then we'll get you on the back of the bike and down to Saigon. In a couple of hours from now, you'll be tucked up in bed being spoiled rotten.'

'Can't we take the jeep?'

'I haven't brought the jeep. I sold the jeep weeks ago, remember? I'm on the bike.'

'I'll wait till you come back with the jeep then. I need to stay lying down.'

She wasn't making sense. Giles felt her forehead again. She really did feel very hot and feverish. What if she fell off the bike? Pru and Ben must

268

have reached Tra Binh by now. It shouldn't take them much more than forty minutes to get here. They could take her back in the car. He switched his phone on. The signal wasn't very strong. He dialled Ben's number.

Slowly, still with her knees tucked up against her chest, Molly keeled over sideways on to the floor and closed her eyes. 'I want my mum . . .'

*   *   *

Pru snatched the phone from its rest on the dashboard.

'Giles!'

'Pru.'

'Where are you? Where's Molly?'

'I'm with her now. We're in a village called . . .'

'What? This is really a bad line. Did you say Molly is with you?'

'Yes.'

'Oh, my God. Is she all right?'

'Yes, she's fine. A bit fluey, I think . . .'

'Ben!' Pru yelled from the car window. 'He's found her!' Ben collected his change and ran back towards the car. 'Giles is with Molly now!'

'Oh, boy! That's wonderful news!'

Pru returned to the phone. 'Where are you both?'

'. . . a village called Cau Giang.'

'I can't hear you.'

'. . . about twenty kilometres from Tra Binh.'

'Oh, what a relief!' She leaned across to Ben and kissed him happily on the cheek.

'Are you and Ben at Tra Binh?'

'Yes. We'll wait here for you.'

'Actually could you come up here, Pru?'

'OK. Of course we can.'

'I think that would be better. You can take her back to Saigon in the car.'

'How do we get to you?'

'You'll need a map. It's a bit off the beaten track. Maybe Ben knows it.'

'Wait a minute, I'll put him on.' Excitedly, she thrust the phone at Ben, who winked at her encouragingly.

'OK, Giles. Where is this place?'

'Hi, Ben. I was going to bring her back down on the bike but she'd prefer to go in the car. Not feeling that great.'

'Oh, I see.' Ben cast an uneasy glance at Pru who was pulling the map out of the pocket behind his seat. 'We'll come straight away. Tell me the grid reference.' He smiled at Pru. 'And something to write with, honey.'

She spread the map open on his lap and produced a cheap Continental Hotel biro from her handbag.

'So, north twelve zero . . . say again?' Ben clamped the phone between neck and shoulder, scribbling on the map '. . . uh-huh . . . and . . . sorry, you're breaking up . . . one zero seven what? One zero seven sixty-three. Right. Got you.'

He hung up and examined the map.

'OK, it's only about twelve clicks away. All that area was pretty familiar territory to me a couple of decades ago. I was camped around there for seven months. 1971. It'll be weird . . .'

Shaking off the threat of impending memories, he stretched his arm across Pru to open the glove

270

compartment and took out what looked like a bright yellow mobile phone. He switched it on and peered at it.

'What's that?'

'GPS. Satellite navigator. There's no such thing as signposts up here and I can tell you this little gizmo has been a lifesaver for me on more than one occasion. Right . . . it's got a fix on us. I'll put the co-ordinates in and all you have to do is make sure we follow the direction of the arrow on the screen. There you are. Simple.'

He leaned over and kissed her. She gave herself to it this time. It lasted several warm, velvety seconds.

'I'm so happy.'

Ben started the car.

'You'll be even happier when you're giving Molly a big hug or a smack—or both.' He smiled.

The shopkeeper watched the car out of sight, then dialled a number on his mobile phone.

*　　　*　　　*

The rain had resumed but without its earlier ferocity. Now it was just a steady, indifferent downpour. Pru kept a regular eye on the little yellow navigator, issuing a running commentary on the direction of the arrow on the screen and the constant recalculations it made as to the time and distance left to go before they reached their destination. She put her hand on Ben's thigh.

'We're getting closer. Ten point four minutes away. We'll be there by four.'

He put his hand on top of hers. 'Tomorrow we'll give ourselves the best time,' he said. 'I know just the place I'm going to take you to.'

There was a loud, sickening bang. The car jarred to a halt. Pru and Ben sat pinned by their seat belts for a moment, immobilised in the abrupt stillness.

'Shit!'

'My God, what's happened?'

Ben turned the engine off.

'Fucking pothole.'

He fought free of the safety belt and got out. Pru got out too and they stood in the rain, willing what they were seeing to be a bad dream. The offside front corner of the car was submerged to its wheel arch in a water-filled pothole. The front bumper and wing had been forced inwards, jammed against the tyre. Ben took hold of the metal with both hands and tried with all his strength to pull it away from the wheel. But it was wedged.

They looked at each other, wordless with frustration.

'I'll see if I can move it in reverse. Keep back.' Ben got in and turned the engine over, thrusting it into gear. A plume of soupy orange mud shot out from under the front of the car. There was a juddering sound, a loud crack and a deep sigh as the tyre began to deflate. Ben turned off the engine and got out in time to watch the car sag, then settle, now well and truly entrenched.

'Well, thank God for mobile phones,' said Pru into the ensuing silence.

*   *   *

'Is that you, Ben?'

'We're in trouble here, Giles. The Saab's in a ditch. I'm sorry. We're going to need a winch to get

272

us out. What do you suggest?'

'Where are you?'

'Not that far from you now.' Ben consulted the navigator. 'Less than five clicks. And looking at the map, there's a village called Bu Tanh very close to us. I can get us there on foot. Should take us, I don't know, twenty minutes. Maybe less.'

'I'll come down and meet you there. We'll have to work out what to do.'

'Can't you bring Molly down that short distance?'

'I wish I could. I don't want to worry you, Ben, but Molly isn't too good at all. Since we last spoke she's gone kind of delirious. Can't get any sense out of her. Really high temperature.'

'I see.' Pru was scrutinising his face. He tried to keep his expression neutral. 'We'll meet you at Bu Tanh then. Maybe we can beg or borrow a car there.'

Ben entered the new co-ordinates into the GPS and arm-in-arm, his old army-issue plastic cape draped over their heads, they set off in the direction of the navigator's arrow, leaving the crippled car lolling lopsidedly in the mud behind them.

'May as well take as straight a line as we can and hope we don't get bogged down in something . . . literally,' said Ben. They were trudging round the edge of a field of what seemed to be pak choy.

He decided to wait a while before telling Pru about Molly not being well. They were moving as fast as they could anyway and it was a tonic to see her looking happy at last; so full of excited optimism. He'd have to prepare her at some point.

273

But not yet. The rain petered out again. They extricated themselves from the poncho and Ben folded it loosely over his arm. Pru looked down ruefully at her white trousers, wet and mud-stained almost up to her knees.

'It'll be goodbye to these, I think.'

The field of greens gave way to a gently terraced coffee plantation, and beyond that a dense grove of peppercorn vines intertwined around slender young pine trees. After fifteen minutes of walking, a distant hubbub of male voices reached their ears. The vegetation was thinning out a little and they could see in the distance a cluster of corrugated-iron roofs.

Ben checked the navigator.

'That's the village we're aiming for.'

'Sounds like a boxing match or something going on,' said Pru.

As they drew closer they could see in front of the houses a makeshift arrangement of tarpaulins stretched over poles for shelter and forty or so men and small boys squatting or standing underneath it, babbling excitedly.

'I think it's a cockfight,' murmured Ben.

'Oh, no. Is that legal?'

'I think it may have been outlawed now. Doesn't stop them doing it. It's an ancient tradition, I'm afraid.'

After the afternoon's rain, the humidity was high enough out in the open, but above the crush of bodies under the tarpaulins hung a visible, warm, steamy vapour.

Pru wrinkled her nose. 'You can almost smell the testosterone.'

Ben smiled. 'This is serious, macho stuff. A lot

274

of these guys will bet their whole week's wages on these things. Crazy.'

Two stringy-looking cocks, one black and white, the other black and brown, were alternately circling then flying at each other, clawing and kicking in a confused blur of plumage, the spectators urging them on. Drops of blood spotted the dust among the fallen feathers. Another flurry and somehow the head of the lighter coloured one got caught under the wing of the other bird and the two of them staggered around locked together for a few seconds like a misshapen new species of its own. The men were shouting hysterically, shoving Dong notes into the hand of an old man in a frayed army shirt and homburg hat squatting amid some roughly drawn chalk marks on the ground. The white cock freed itself. There was another frenzied blur of feathers and it was all over. Two men scurried in to retrieve their exhausted birds, checking them over for injuries.

'Looks like they'll both live to fight another day,' Ben commented.

'I think it's disgusting.' Pru turned away as two fresh contestants were set down reverentially in the dust amid a new crescendo of hysteria. 'They should be proud and magnificent creatures, but they just look sad and mangy.'

'It's considered an art form in Vietnam. About honour and spirit and courage.'

'Well, it's exactly the opposite of all those things as far as I'm concerned. Let's get out of here. What do you think the chances are of getting someone to lend us a car?'

'Slim, to be honest. We'll have a tough job even getting anyone's attention here, I think.'

275

A few little boys had come up to stare at them curiously as they arrived but, finding themselves ignored, had quickly lost interest and gone back to watch the sport.

'*Xin loi,*' Ben selected one of the older and quieter spectators, '*toi muon xe?*'

The man turned for a moment and looked them both up and down with a flicker of curiosity that flared for half a second then died, like a struck match. He shook his head and turned back to the scene of the action.

'Classic, isn't it?' exclaimed Pru. 'If we hadn't wanted their attention they'd have been swarming all over us. Here we are, two foreigners who've appeared in their village out of nowhere, and they're not the slightest bit interested. What did you ask him?'

Ben sighed. 'I just said I needed the use of a car. The answer is very obviously no. I'd be surprised if anyone around here owns one anyway.'

'Now Giles will have to bring her down to us. We're stranded here. I'm surprised he didn't get here before us.'

'He probably stayed to look after Molly a bit longer,' suggested Ben.

'Yes, he did say she felt a bit fluey.'

'Actually, Pru, from what he said on the phone, I think she's not feeling so good.'

'What do you mean, not feeling so good?'

'He told me she was feverish.'

Pru stared at him. 'Feverish! My God, Ben, we've got to get to Molly right now.' Her face had turned very pale.

'I know. Where the hell is Giles?'

'How far is it? Where is that navigator thing of

yours?'

She looked quite prepared to run to Cau Giang.

Above the general hullabaloo, to his indescribable relief, Ben discerned the throb of the Honda Shadow. Giles, too, was white-faced and wet with rain and sweat but Pru wasn't going to waste any sympathy on him.

'What the hell have you been playing at? Have you known where she was all along?'

'Not all along. I wanted to tell you . . .'

In her mind's eye, Pru hit him so hard across the face that he fell over backwards in the mud.

'How ill is she?' She articulated each word very slowly through gritted teeth.

'She wasn't too good when I first got up there, but then she got worse.' Seeing that he was trembling, Pru began to tremble too. This was the nightmare scenario she'd always dreaded.

'She's got a fever.' Giles's voice was tired and small. All his dash and confidence gone. 'She was asking for you.'

'These are the symptoms of endocarditis! Heart-valve infection. And she hasn't got her antibiotics with her.'

'How do you know?'

'Because I've got them.' She plunged her hand into her bag and pulled out the little tub of pills. 'She left them behind at the orphanage.'

'It might not be her heart, Pru. We don't know yet. It could be any number of things. Dengue fever, malaria, gastroenteritis, hepatitis maybe . . .'

'Any kind of fever is bad news for Molly. It could be critical for her. We've got to get her to a doctor. I'm trying to keep calm here, but I'm just terrified.'

Ben put a warm, steadying arm round her

277

shoulders. She was grateful, trying to believe in the reassurance.

'How can we get her to hospital without a car?' Giles was distressed too, now. 'She's too ill to go on the back of the bike.'

'Even if we did have a car, we're three or four hours away from Saigon, aren't we?' demanded Pru. 'Molly needs attention sooner than that.'

'I'll call Hong Yen,' said Ben tautly. 'This sure as hell counts as an emergency.'

Moving further away from the clamour of the cockfight, he dialled a number. The ensuing call was so brief, Pru thought he couldn't have got through.

'She's fixing an air ambulance. In the next few minutes I'll receive a text with the co-ordinates of a landing place as near to Cau Giang as possible.'

'Oh, God, please let her be all right.'

'We'll take the bike up there now. Giles will have to stay here.'

'I can get someone to come and pick me up,' said Giles as Ben revved the bike and clicked into first gear. 'Don't worry about me.'

'I certainly won't,' rejoined Pru over her shoulder from the pillion. 'You haven't heard the last of this, Giles.'

*   *   *

Molly moaned softly, turning on to her back and then back on to her side again. 'Get the bears off me . . . They're too hot.'

Nguyet was beside her in an instant, hunkered down, mud-stained toes splayed for balance. Dipping a piece of rag into the pitcher of cool

278

rainwater she had just collected, she squeezed it out and laid it across Molly's forehead, gently stroking the girl's face with the back of her rough, calloused hand.

'Tot hon som, atra tre, som.'
There. There. Gently, my child.

*   *   *

'It's a very good bike this,' Ben called over his shoulder, gaining confidence as he moved up through the gears. Pru was too preoccupied to comment. He was trying to divert his own mind, blocking trains of thought he knew would only lead to pain. The nervous tension combined with the familiarity of the landscape was profoundly disturbing. He could feel the monsters deep inside him shifting in their sleep. He prayed they'd turn over and go back to their slumbers.

As they left Giles and the cockfight far behind them, it occurred to Ben that he hadn't thought how they'd get the sick girl to the helicopter rendezvous. He hoped it wasn't too far. They'd have to carry her somehow. He cursed himself. He couldn't stop and put another call though to Hong Yen now. They'd have to wait till they got to Cau Giang.

It was nearly an hour since the rain had stopped, but the roads were still dangerous; rutted and pitted, muddy and slippery. The bike was capable of speeds close on two hundred kilometres an hour. In decent road conditions, they could have been at Cau Giang in five minutes. He tried pushing it, but almost immediately felt the back wheel beginning to slide from under him and nearly lost control. Behind him, Pru stiffened with a cry of alarm. He changed down and slowed to around fifty, but the slower speed made the bike much heavier to manoeuvre.

'We're just about there, I think,' called Pru, who'd been clutching the GPS.

Ben was surprised to see it was only a quarter to five. The journey seemed to have taken an age. He was acutely aware that in this dense jungle territory, the pilot of the air ambulance would want to land and take off before the light faded. Sunset was about a quarter after six. They had an hour and a quarter at most.

He could see the tyre tracks Giles had left earlier, ending under a twisted old olive tree. A little grey leaf monkey screeched tetchily from the branches and scampered off to observe these new intruders from a more discreet distance amongst some banana palms.

The village seemed deserted. Pru had leapt off the back of the bike even before he'd come to a complete stop and was now running from house to house calling Molly's name, her mud-splashed trousers clinging to her legs. Ben had a strong sense that more eyes than just the monkey's were watching from the jungle. The monsters within him stirred again and grumbled.

He checked his phone. A text had arrived with a grid reference, followed by the words 'Transport On Sight. Good Luck'. 'In sight' or 'on site'? he wondered. Both, with any luck.

God bless you, Hong Yen.

The only vehicle of any description in view was a rusty white pick-up truck, parked beside a washing line strung between two bamboo poles just beyond

280

the line of houses. He ran to investigate.

Pru heard a low moan from the second to last hut. She ran inside. Molly lay shivering, curled up on the floor. The old woman who had been bending over her stood and stepped back for Pru to take her place.

'Girl sick. I cannot . . .' She couldn't find the word she was looking for in English.

'Molly. Darling.'

Weakly, Molly tried to lift her head.

'Mum.'

'I'm here, darling.' Pru stroked her damp hair. She felt so hot.

'I'm so sorry, Mum.'

'How long has she been like this?' But the woman had disappeared.

Pru took Molly's limp hand in hers and felt for her pulse.

Ben came in, breathless, and knelt beside her.

'Is it slow or fast?'

'Fast. Very fast.'

'Take me home . . .'

'Come on then, honey, let's get you out of here.'

'How? *How* can we get her out of here?' yelled Pru. It took every ounce of her self-control to stop herself just screaming in frustration and sheer panic. She had to keep calm.

Gently, Ben shifted the girl on to her back and put his arms under her shoulders and the crooks of her knees. Pru kept hold of Molly's hand as he stood up with her.

'How do we get her to the helicopter?'

'There's a pick-up truck with the keys in it. It has to be for us.'

'Thank God. It's going to be OK now, darling.

281

We're going to get you to a hospital. You'll be fine. It'll all be all right.'

Chapter Eighteen

Pru was holding on to the yellow GPS like a talisman now with Ben set-faced, gripping the wheel of the rackety old truck and Molly propped up between the two of them, her head sagging on to Pru's chest. Sometimes the muddy tracks they had to follow led them away from their designated course and the navigator's arrow would swing wildly off to the side instead of straight ahead. Pru would issue wild instructions.

'We must bear left somewhere, we're going in the wrong direction . . .'

Once the arrow swung through almost a hundred and eighty degrees. Pru was frantic.

'Are you sure this thing works? We need to turn back the other way. Ben! Do a U-turn!' Ben stuck to his guns. He had to switch off every emotion he possessed to do so. Cool, clinical, logical . . . you remember.

'I think she's losing consciousness, Ben!'

'Keep her awake. Keep talking to her.'

He took one hand off the wheel and lifted Molly's head. 'Molly, you got to help us here, kiddo. Hang on in there.'

She made an effort to open her eyes. 'Who are you?'

'Benjamin S. Coder, at your service, miss, all the way from the US of A.'

'Hi.' She closed her eyes again.

'And you've got to talk to me all the way to the hospital. It's orders.'

'Were you in the Vietnam War?' she managed obediently.

'I was indeed.'

'Ben was based around here, weren't you, Ben?' encouraged Pru.

'That's right.'

He didn't tell them that right at this moment his eyes were scanning the rubber plantation on their left for the slightest hint of movement through the trees. Could be an ambush. That patch of elephant grass on the right . . . be careful. The vine tendril on the roadside there . . . unusually straight. Might be disguising a trip wire. It wasn't just being back here, though. He did the same kind of thing just taking a walk in the park back home. 'How are you feeling, kid? Speak to me.'

'Sleepy.'

'Fight it, Moll. You must,' urged Pru. 'You've got to stay awake. Tell us what you were doing up at that village.'

'Long story.'

'Did Sinh take you up there?'

'No.'

'Who did then?'

'People in village.' Molly was slurring her words and her eyes were closed but at least while she was talking, she was fighting.

'The people in the village? But I thought they were your friends. You were trying to help them!'

'Pretending!' Pru recognised the tone of patient exasperation. 'Pretending to be hostage . . .'

'Why on earth . . . ? You *wanted* us to believe that Sinh had got you, is that it?'

283

'Maybe . . .' She was drifting off again

'I still don't see why.'

'Publicity.'

Pru thought about it. 'So the idea was to draw attention to this leisure centre deal and Sinh pocketing the compensation money?'

'He's a crook.'

'You know what?' said Ben. 'Thanks to your mom, you may have got what you wanted.'

Molly managed a weak smile.

'It wasn't just me,' began Pru. 'I'd never have done it without . . .'

'Hey . . .' Ben reached over Molly's head and put a gentle finger against Pru's lips. 'Later. We'll tell her later.' He indicated the navigator. 'How are we doing?'

'It says one kilometre to go.'

In a rice paddy to the right of them a farmer straightened his back and watched them pass. His bike lay on the verge ready for home. Thirty years ago, the guy who waved at you from the fields by day could be the same guy who came looking for you with his gun at night. You just never knew.

'The arrow's going off left.'

Ben turned the truck into a copse of rubber trees. 'Fingers crossed the ground's not too spongy.'

More pictures. Going somewhere. In an APC. Convoy. Four or five of them. No need to keep to the roads. You made your own. Caterpillar tracks rumbling relentlessly on. Churning through a paddy field. A farmer's face. Horror. Hatred. Disbelief. Despair. Throwing his hat to the ground. Stamping it into the mud. Most of his crop, his family's livelihood, wiped out right there.

A broken figure diminishing behind them. So much damage.

Ben shook his head and frowned at his watch.

'I'm real worried about the light going. The pilot's got to be able to see us. We've got forty-five minutes tops before sundown.'

Pru stroked Molly's hair. 'Won't be long now, my darling. We've got a helicopter coming to pick us up. Dramatic or what?'

Once through the rubber trees, all signs of human life disappeared. No more crop fields. No bicycle tracks. Only rampant vegetation on all sides; bamboo, banana palms, elephant grass. Wherever the ground was visible, the rain had left thick, rust-coloured puddles that were almost lakes. It could have been a million years BC.

'Right. We need to go more right.'

With a jolt, Ben realised where Hong Yen had sent them. She must have known. It was his old base camp compound. It had to be. The monsters shook their heads and growled, louder now. This was pushing them too far.

'It's OK.' With any luck Pru would think it was the truck bumping over the rough ground that had caused the slight tremor in his voice. He took a deep breath. 'I know where we're going.'

Pru stopped stroking Molly's head for a moment to reach across and stroke the back of Ben's neck with firm, warm fingers. She didn't say anything. Instinctively, she knew that what he was going through now was far too deep for trite words of sympathy. And empathy was impossible. She glanced at the GPS in her other hand.

'We're back on track now. It says three minutes.'

Their eyes met for a few seconds.

285

'Sounds about right. Keep an eye out for the chopper.'

'I'll never forget seeing you with those children at the orphanage, Moll.' Molly had been drifting off again, mumbling something about being late with her history project. Her temperature had gone up again. Pru began singing, *'Old MacDonald had a farm . . .'* Molly stirred.

'Shut up. You can't sing.' The old Molly was still holding on in there.

'Such a clever way of teaching them English. You've got a real way with children, Moll. They'll be so looking forward to getting you back. Hey!' She looked at Ben. 'The yellow thingy says we've arrived.'

He stopped the truck and turned off the engine. The silence closed in, only mildly defied by the creaking of the truck's suspension, grateful for the respite. He lit a cigarette.

'This is one of my old base camps.' He looked tense. 'I was hoping for some sign of the chopper. I'll take a look around.' He gave her a grimace that was meant to be a reassuring grin. The truck door slammed rustily.

Pru watched him stride towards the enclosure and then stop. Taking it all in. Coping with his memories.

The jungle had done its best to reclaim it. If you hadn't known it was there, from a distance you'd have taken it for a dense patch of rainforest. One of the old watchtowers was still standing. He could see the top of it against the murky sky. The skeleton of it anyway. The ruin of a second one skulked fifty metres or so away; a few planks of rotting wood on brick foundations. The high perimeter fence was overgrown with trees, but it seemed to have stood the test of time surprisingly well. Even the razor wire was still there. He could just see it amid the foliage, wound around between the concrete posts. He pushed through the rainsoaked greenery, peering into the compound itself. There wasn't much of it left. As far as he could see, most of what had been the northern sector had disappeared under saplings and shrubs and waist-high grasses.

More remained of the southern sector, where his regiment had been based, mainly because the ground had been concreted over at this end for the helicopters, but the surface was cracked and crumbling now; weeds and grasses growing up through it, tossing it aside in slow motion.

A few sandbags still lay slumped in soggy heaps, some still intact, others spilling their contents on to the ground. It had been damn hard work filling those sacks. Digging up the heavy red dirt.

Landing here would be no simple matter these days. There was very little room for manoeuvre. It would be a deal easier without all these overhanging branches. He didn't envy the pilot of their rescue chopper. Where was he anyway? Time was running out.

Molly wasn't getting any better, that was for sure. His own diagnosis, for right or wrong, was dengue fever. He'd seen symptoms like this before. His old pal Billy had got it a few years back when they were here setting up a children's day centre in Tay Ninh. Same thing: high fever, making sense one minute and babbling nonsense the next. They had to get out tonight.

Ben jogged over to the old metal gates. Still

there, three metres high, still laced with razor wire, but rusty now. Silent, sulky, almost pathetic. Guarding only memories. But guarding them well. They were locked; secured with a broad iron bar, half a metre long, and a small but solid iron US Army padlock. Ben pictured the last man to leave more than twenty-five years ago, closing the gate behind him, clicking the padlock shut and jumping into the truck to join his buddies and head on out for good. Maybe he had kept the key as a memento, popping it into a pocket in his fatigues. Maybe, in a symbolic gesture, he had hurled it as hard and far as he could. Maybe he just let it fall to the ground. Ben dropped to his knees and groped around in the grass fruitlessly for a minute or two. It would be well and truly buried now anyway. Scrambling back to his feet, he pushed hard on both gates with the palms of his hands. He tried kicking them. He tried running at them and kicking them. They rattled and shook, but old and rusting though they were, neither the lock nor the gates showed any sign of giving way. The only way in would be to climb over them or maybe find a gap in the fencing somewhere. He preferred to hope for the latter. He'd seen the damage razor wire could do to a man.

Watching him, Pru had realised the problem. She settled Molly gently across the passenger seat, with Ben's jacket cushioning her head, then jumped down from the truck. She stood beside him, staring blankly at the padlocked gates. There must be another way. A gap in the fencing somewhere underneath all this vegetation.

'Come on, Ben. We've got to find a way in.' Pru picked up a dead branch and began slashing at the

288

foliage.

'There's no point in wasting time doing that, Pru. Even if we did find a gap, which is unlikely, we wouldn't be able to get Molly through. There's thirty years of growth here.'

'Well, what the hell are we going to do then?' Her determined attempt at composure was slipping away.

'My worry is that the light is going. It'll be too late soon. Landing in a confined space like this is tricky in the best of conditions. Taking off is even trickier.'

'Why?'

'Because it's all so overgrown.'

'You mean the rotor blade might hit a branch?'

'If the tail rotor caught just the smallest of twigs that would be it. We'd be doing a sycamore seed impression. But visibility is a serious problem too. It's going fast.'

'Surely he'll get here before darkness falls?'

'Darkness doesn't fall, you know. It rises. Any pilot will tell you that.'

'What's that supposed to mean?' asked Pru. This wasn't the time for clever wordplay.

'It gets dark on the ground before it gets dark up there. The sun's rays are still up there on the clouds, look, but soon it will have sunk too low below the horizon to reach us down here.'

And darkness was now beginning to rise. He didn't add that on a day as humid as today had been, a dense mist was likely to develop the moment the temperature dropped. Once that happened, taking off would be well-nigh impossible.

'Don't they have night-flying instruments and all

that kind of thing these days?'

'They do, but they won't help here. They don't come into play until you start moving forwards. Not till you've got up to a recordable speed. Taking off here, the pilot will have to climb vertically upwards. It'll be a couple of hundred feet before he can risk starting to move forward. All he'll have to go on is the altimeter. Takes a rock-steady hand on the stick and nerves of steel. I had a similar situation once. It's something I'd never want to repeat.'

Looking back, it always amazed Ben that he'd got away with it. He'd been detailed to pick up a bunch of demolitions guys who'd been debugging one of the US landing zones. It was on a hill top and they'd been marooned there because the weather had turned bad. The guys had gotten desperate, waiting day after day, running out of rations. When, at last, one morning the sun rose in a clear blue sky, Ben headed on out to get them out of there.

As he drew closer, though, he could hardly believe what he saw. He found the hill, but it was completely encircled by dense grey cloud. Everywhere else the sky was a brilliant blue. The fog was only around that particular hill. He made a couple of passes, but he couldn't see the guys down there and they couldn't see him either. They could hear him, of course. He listened to them on his radio going crazy.

Then one of the guys got the bright idea of lighting some night flares and setting them out in a circle for him to land in. What could he do? He couldn't fly off and leave them there. So he'd landed in the ring of flares. That was the easy part.

He'd told them he'd have to wait to take off until the fog cleared, but they'd been there so long, they'd come to the end of their rope. Maybe they'd convinced themselves the fog was there forever. One of the guys was injured quite bad too. They were pleading with him. He'd thought about it and he'd figured if he could lift off vertically and keep on going up dead straight, eventually he must come out the top. He'd need a steady hand and nerve to match, though.

He got everyone on board and lifted off. After one, two, three, four minutes of vertical climbing, he began to lose confidence. The higher he rose, the thicker the fog seemed to get. Maybe he wasn't going upwards at all. The slightest unconscious movement on the stick and he could have blown it. And he couldn't be sure he hadn't moved his hand just slightly . . . Any moment now, another mountain might loom out of nowhere and that would be the end of it. He must have been crazy to think he could pull this off. He was using every bit of his will-power to hold on to his faith in himself.

And then, quite suddenly, he was out! Out into a clear blue sky with the sun glinting on the nose cone. He remembered hearing the cheers from the cargo compartment behind him mingling with those in his radio headset. As he turned and made for base, he'd taken a last look down to see the tip of that hill with its thick grey pointy hat of fog pulled down over its eyes, like a witch on Hallowe'en.

*   *   *

'Listen!' Pru shook Ben's arm. He had that

faraway look about him again. But he had already heard it. The past and the present were so intertwined in his brain, it took him a moment or two to realise the sound was in the here and now: wuppa-wuppa-wuppa-wuppa-wuppa. So many years ago, and still the sound of a Huey seemed as normal as taking his next breath. He realised it had never left him; it had been a low-key but ever-present soundtrack playing at the back of his brain wherever he went and whatever he did. Part of who he was. They stood scanning the lowering grey sky.

'There it is!' Pru pointed wildly.

For a split second he was surprised. There was only the one.

'Dustoff.'

'What?' Pru wasn't sure whether he was talking to her or not. He had a preoccupied look about him.

'Dustoff. It's a Huey. That's what we called them.'

'Why?'

'I guess because of all the dust they kicked up in landing and take-off. They'd come in to pick up the wounded. And the dead. Medevac.'

'We're lucky it's been raining then.'

He looked at her for a moment as if she'd said something in a foreign language.

'Wave! Make sure he sees us. Hey!'

Ben began criss-crossing his arms above his head. Pru did the same. They stood side by side, waving their arms and shouting, staring at the rapidly enlarging insect against the sky, willing the pilot towards them. The chopper passed above them, disappearing above the tree line.

'He's not going to land!' screamed Pru in panic.

The pounding noise increased and the Huey loomed above them. Yawing. Circling.

'He's seen us,' shouted Ben. 'And he's probably cursing us to hell,' he muttered to himself.

The huge machine was directly overhead now. Thumping, roaring, whining. Dominating everything. It felt to Pru as if every organ in her body, every bone, every tooth, was juddering and throbbing along with it. Her mud-stained trousers began to flap around her legs so violently that she felt the seams might just give way and they'd go flying off above the trees. Her hair was lashing her face, stinging her cheeks and her eyeballs. She tried to hold it back with her hands. The onslaught made her want to weep, laugh and scream in fear all at the same time. Molly. This was for Molly. This roaring monster had come to save her daughter's life.

The Huey descended slowly into the compound and settled like a giant bluebottle on the broken concrete surface.

Pru could see the pilot now behind the sloping windscreen in a red baseball cap and a dark blue anorak. The rotor blades still turning, he gestured animatedly for them to come over.

'Why isn't he getting out?'

'He wants to get the hell out of here. That was the deal. The light's almost gone now. It's the worst time.'

'Maybe he'll have a key.'

Ben made key-turning motions at the gate. The pilot shrugged and then held both arms up to make sure they could see him pointing at his watch.

293

The skids were barely touching the ground. 'He looks as if he's about to take off again,' yelled Pru. 'He can't! He mustn't . . .'

She ran frantically at the gates and began to climb them.

'Pru! For Chrissake, you dumb broad.' Ben ran forward and grabbed her around the waist, trying to hold her back.

She struggled free and went back to climbing 'We've got to stop him,' she screeched. The rational side of her knew she was losing control but it let her get on with it.

'There's razor wire on this fence. It's fucking lethal, Pru.'

He pulled her off again holding on to her tight this time, pinning her arms humiliatingly to her sides. She kicked at him but he was far too strong. She could feel the contours of his body pressed hard against hers.

'Well, *you* do something then. You don't know what to do, do you? Why is this such a cock-up!'

As he let her go, she struck him across the face as hard as she could, with all the force of her pent-up fear and frustration.

Just for an instant, his self-control deserted him. He hit her back. It was pure reflex. With the Huey throbbing and pounding on the concrete launch pad, the panic-stricken woman he cared about so much haranguing him, making him feel useless, the urgency of the situation and the sheer desperation of not knowing what to do next. He'd never in his life before hit a woman. Shocked to the core, the two of them stood looking at each other for a second or two. Then held each other tight. He stroked her hair back off her face. 'I'm

294

sorry, Pru.'

'I'm sorry too.'

The pilot had been watching in growing agitation from the cockpit. He was running out of patience. He began gesticulating wildly, pointing to the sky and then tapping his watch.

'OK, Pru, let's get Molly, quick. So he can see we've genuinely got a sick person here.'

He paused a moment to call to the pilot. 'Wait!'

Pru was already running to the truck.

'It's a long time since I picked you up, you big, heavy lump.' She'd always called Molly that when she picked her up, even as a little baby. She'd said it to Jack too. It was just something she always said.

'Is it tea-time?'

'The helicopter is here, darling.' It sounded as off-the-wall as Molly's delirious ramblings.

'Careful, you'll hurt your back. Let me take her.' Ben had arrived beside her. Picking the girl up in his arms like a baby, he carried her out beyond the truck so that the pilot could see her more easily.

Behind him, he heard the truck engine start.

At the wheel, Pru fumbled with the gear stick. Where the hell was first? She let out the clutch. She caught just an impression of Ben's horror-stricken face, frozen in disbelief, as she accelerated past him.

He was mouthing, 'What are you doing?'

She couldn't think of any other way. Thirty yards along the track they'd come in on, she stopped. Should be far enough. There was no safety belt. Have to take her chances. She found reverse gear. Her hand was shaking. So was her foot, hovering over the accelerator.

'Here goes.' She revved the engine twice, let out the clutch, then stamped hard on the accelerator.

She watched the gates in the mirror, getting closer fast. Aim for the middle. Must be the weakest point. For God's sake, stop before you hit the bloody helicopter. Hope the brakes are good on this thing . . .

In the event, the gates were brake enough. The violence of the impact shot Pru's foot off the pedal. The engine stalled and the truck came to rest in a tangle of twisted metal and razor wire.

*   *   *

Ben laid Molly down on a dry patch of ground under a tree and ran to the truck. Pru had jumped down to look at her handiwork, blood pouring down the side of her face from a cut on her forehead.

'Whoohoo!' she yelled above the helicopter's pulsating din. 'We've cracked it!'

He hugged her. 'Nice job, you crazy woman!'

Both gates were buckled. The right-hand one still held stubbornly to its closed position, but the left one was hanging defeatedly on just its top hinge. Ben lifted it and manhandled it open a little wider.

'Quick! Get Molly!'

The Huey's steady pounding changed. Lowered its tone. Pru and Ben looked up in horror.

'He's fucking stopped it.'

'That's good, isn't it? It means he won't go without us.'

'It means he won't go at all.'

The blades were whining to a halt. The pilot

296

jumped down from the cockpit. He pointed again to the sky.

'No fly now,' he called across at them. 'No good.'

He sauntered out from under the slowing rotor, putting a cigarette in his mouth. Ben ran towards him.

'You can't do this. We've got a sick girl here. She could die. We have to get her to hospital. Now!'

'We go morning.' He snapped his petrol lighter open and lifted it towards his cigarette.

Before he could light it, Ben lunged at him and snatched it from his lips, hurling it into the undergrowth.

'You get back in there and you take us to Saigon. You hear me?'

The pilot's eyes grew wide with fright; whether fear of Ben or sheer terror at the idea of having to take off from this gloomy, overgrown place, Ben didn't know. It could have been either. Probably both. Ben grabbed him by his jacket collar, frog-marching him back towards his helicopter. Pru began half carrying, half dragging Molly towards the Huey.

With a sudden, bloodcurdling yell, the pilot wriggled out of his jacket and sprinted out between the mangled gates, down the track and into the forest.

Pru collapsed with Molly on the concrete and howled, completely distraught, 'Now what are we going to do?'

*   *   *

He'd done it once. But that was a long, long time ago. He'd expunged flying from his life. It had

297

been a love affair once, and it had turned to hatred. Just the sight of a helicopter in the distance filled him with revulsion now. Too much destruction. Too much bloodshed.

The last time he'd ever flown was the day before he was due to ship out. A Huey had been shot down. Mortar-fire. A lot of guys were dead. The ones who were wounded were wounded bad. Ben went in as dustoff. He flew in low above the treetops, mortars exploding all around them. He stayed at the controls, barely touching the ground with the skids, ready to get away quick. His mates Donny and Timbo between them were dragging the injured on board. They just stacked them up on top of each other, arms, legs, heads, still hanging out of the cargo-bay door. There was no time for niceties. Since that day Ben had tried to forget the blood, the broken limbs, the sound of sucking chest wounds and, above all, the screams of pain. Never managed it.

As he started lifting off, the Huey had taken a direct hit. How he'd kept it airborne, he never knew. It sure wasn't airworthy when it landed. He did a sharp pedal-turn and flew out low, the tops of the trees slapping against the chopper's steel underside. It wasn't till they were nearly back at base that he realised Donny had taken a hit. He bled to death right there on the floor of the Huey, his liver ruptured. Ben learned later that when he'd been hit, Donny had nearly fallen right out of the aircraft, but Timbo had grabbed on to him and managed to keep him on board. That was an amazing feat in itself as Timbo only had one arm to work with. His left one was still smouldering. Blown off below the elbow.

298

*   *   *

He couldn't do this. Not because he was frightened for himself, but because there was a very real chance of killing the three of them. When he'd done the vertical take-off from the foggy hill that time, flying had been second nature to him. He'd practically lived in his Huey back then, like it was strapped to his back. But all that was the best part of thirty years ago, for Chrissake. The mist he'd dreaded was creeping across the ground like a blanket. Maybe Molly could last till the morning. Surely she would. Maybe they could drive her down in the truck. Except one of the tyres had burst and the impact with the gates wouldn't have done the axle much good. Even if it were instantly driveable, it would take at least four hours to get from here to Saigon.

Pru was rocking back and forth with Molly cradled in her arms. He stooped down beside her and felt the girl's forehead.

'She's hardly breathing,' wept Pru.

Ben made up his mind.

'Help me get her into the chopper,' he said.

The helicopter was kitted out for a medical emergency. Ben set Molly carefully down on to the stretcher bed. Pru scrambled in with her. He slammed the door.

'It's all right, sweetheart,' whispered Pru. 'We'll be at the hospital soon. We'll get you right again in no time.'

Molly moaned softly. She'd given up any effort to take an interest in what was going on around her.

299

Ben was sliding into the cockpit. He closed the door and sat very still for a moment. The sun had dropped below the horizon now and the temperature had reached dewpoint almost immediately. The helicopter was surrounded by swirling, thickening mist. It was now or never.

Pru was watching his back anxiously. Her heart constricted. This was going to take an act of supreme courage, she knew that.

Ben's eyes scanned the instrument panel. Remembering. He took a deep breath.

'Listen, Pru, I've got to focus real hard here. Once I start this baby up, I have to ask you not to talk to me. Whatever happens, however you're feeling, not a sound. Don't speak to me. Don't touch me. I don't want to spook you, but if I fuck up here, we're all dead.'

'OK,' Pru answered obediently from the cargo bay behind him.

'I'm doing this for love. Your love for Molly and my love for you. Nothing else would induce me to fly one of these things again.'

Her stomach was churning.

'I have total faith in you, Ben.'

Chapter Nineteen

He settled the pilot's headset on his ears. There was a map clipped on to a long metal arm between the seats, but he probably wouldn't need it. He'd made this run before. Many times. These memories had been locked away for so long. Now he had to let them out. They would have to do their worst. There

300

was no other way.

Pru watched him unscramble the harness and buckle it across his abdomen. He took one more long, deep breath. He was fingering the *mala* beads on his wrist and mumbling something. It sounded like *'oomtaray tootaray tooray swahar'* repeated over and over under his breath. She guessed it was some kind of Buddhist mantra.

Amen, she thought, to whatever it is.

Slowly he raised his hand to the battery master switch just above his head and flicked it on. A quick pass with the back of his hand over the circuit breakers in the roof. The old routine. Instruments in order. Altimeter set at zero. Most important of all for what he was about to do. He reached for the power lever. The engine began to wind up. Talk to me, baby. He held his hands out at arm's length for a moment. The tremor he'd noticed as he put on the harness had gone. Rock steady. They'd need to stay that way.

The noise was almost deafening now. Even if Pru had wanted to say something, conversation would have been hopeless. Ben's hand hovered over the collective lever that controlled both the rotors. The words of his mantra were substituted by a muttered running commentary. 'OK. Increase the power. Rotor speed set. All temperatures and pressures in the green...' Ease up on the collective beside him. Other hand on the cyclic stick between his knees. Check feet on the pedals. Keep her straight...

The Huey began to lift off the ground. Pru hardly dared breathe.

Now. Concentrate. Keep the cyclic absolutely still. The slightest movement, the least relaxing of

301

his grip, the smallest tremor in his wrist, could send the aircraft off its vital perpendicular course. The mist had closed in, denser now. Ben was flying blind. He reckoned a hundred and fifty feet minimum, before he'd be clear of the compound perimeter and the overhanging trees. Then, he'd have to guess how much more to allow for the fog. Two hundred and fifty feet to be safe. Roaring and juddering, the machine parted company with the ground. He hovered there a second or two.

Concentrate. Concentrate. For God's sake, keep your head still—vital not to interfere with the middle ear's balancing system. He pulled gently on the collective lever again. Steady . . . up she goes. We're climbing now. Hang on to that stick. Keep it still. Keep both controls rock steady. Don't move a millimetre. Can't see anything but fog. Could almost believe we're not moving at all. Nothing to measure anything by. Have faith . . . pray . . . *oomtaray tootaray tooray swahar.* The altimeter's passed the hundred feet mark. Another hundred and fifty to go.

His fingers on the stick began to feel stiff and numb. The seconds went by. The engine roared and whined. Had he moved his hand? Would he have felt it if he had? He glanced down, moving only his eyes. Whitened knuckles. Maybe he was heading back towards the ground. Until the instruments could register forward movement, there was no way of knowing. He began to believe they'd been sucked into a vortex on the edge of the world. No way out. Never get out. Keep cool. Hold on. Only believe. *Oomtaray tootaray tooray swahar.* Upwards, ever upwards.

The altimeter had passed two hundred now. The

302

mist was thinning. They must surely be clear by now. So tempting to ease forward on the collective . . . No, he'd promised himself two hundred and fifty. Two hundred and fifty was what he'd do. Not long now. Nearly there. Nearly . . .

Suddenly the mist was gone. He could see. He'd done it! Beneath him, the thick blanket of grey he'd left behind. Above him and ahead of him, open sky. It was nearly dark, but he could see the loom of Saigon away to the south-east. He eased the cyclic away from him and with a snarl of relief the Huey surged forward. Immediately, the instruments remembered what they were there for. Fifty knots, sixty, seventy, a hundred and twenty . . . already the skulking jungle mist lay far behind them.

'How's she doing?' Ben yelled over his shoulder to Pru.

She knew he couldn't hear her, but she shouted 'OK' anyway. Molly at least seemed peaceful, but the fever was higher than ever. All Pru could do was stroke her brow and pray.

'I'm going to have to contact control,' Ben shouted. 'Get the medics out and ready.'

He turned a switch on the radio in front of him. 'We'll head for Cho Ray and hope my doctor friend is on duty tonight. I should be able to land in the car park this time of the evening.'

The frequency was certain to be set for Saigon.

'Pan-pan. Pan-pan. Pan-pan. This is Red Dawn calling all stations. We have a medical emergency. Young woman with suspected endocarditis. I intend to put down at Cho Ray Hospital, Ho Chi Minh City, District Four. Current position

303

approximately twenty minutes from estimated arrival time. A hundred and twelve knots; eleven hundred feet indicated. Do you copy? Over.' He turned the switch. The radio just hissed in reply.

'A pan-pan call is the international urgency signal,' he called by way of explanation to Pru. 'It's one down from Mayday. Usually signifies a medical emergency.'

He didn't explain the origin of Red Dawn. He hadn't noted the number on the side of the Huey before he got in, so he'd decided to use the same call sign he used last time he'd inhabited the skies over Vietnam, chosen in memory of the flame-haired girl he'd first fallen in love with at the age of sixteen . . . His first trembling, euphoric experience of love-making, before he found out what Ananke, the cold Goddess of Fate and Necessity, had planned for the next few years of his life. He tried the call again.

'Pan-pan, pan-pan, pan-pan. This is Red Dawn. Do you read me? I have a young Englishwoman very seriously ill. Danger of heart failure. I intend to land at Cho Ray Hospital, Ho Chi Minh City. Approximately twenty minutes from now. Request inform Dr Chuong. Over.'

The radio came to life. The voice was high-pitched, staccato.

'Pan-pan Red Dawn. This is Ho Chi Minh City Tower. You must land at Than Son Nhut airport, Ho Chi Minh City. Please await instructions.'

'Red Dawn to Tower. Negative. I must land at the hospital. My passenger is very, very sick.'

'This is stolen helicopter,' spat the radio. 'Very serious consequences. Imperative you land Than Son Nhut. Ambulance will stand by to take

304

passenger to hospital.'

The full enormity of the situation struck him. He hadn't thought of it as stealing, but as desperate necessity. In their book, however, he supposed, theft was what it was. Ben swivelled in his seat to look at Pru sitting behind him, cradling Molly's head in her lap. The girl's face was grey and shining with sweat. He could see she wasn't conscious.

He turned back to the radio.

'Very sorry. Imperative I land at Cho Ray Hospital.'

The owner of the voice sounded almost apoplectic.

'I order you to land at Than Son Nhut! Unless you land at Than Son Nhut you can expect serious consequences . . .'

'There are serious consequences for my passenger unless we get her to hospital in the next few minutes. I intend to land at Cho Ray. Please notify Dr Chuong.'

He turned the radio down to the point where it was just discernible as an angry chirrup against the sound of the engine.

'No point continuing that conversation, I fear.' He smiled ruefully, trying hard to stop his mind wandering on to the price he was going to have to pay for this. He had to keep focused on getting them safely on the ground outside the hospital. He'd cross the next bridge when he came to it. The faint voice continued for two or three minutes more—intermittent angry expletives—and then stopped altogether. He turned the volume up again, but there was no further communication.

The lights of Saigon were twinkling in the

305

distance now, like a diamante brooch on a blue denim jacket.

He twitched the collective lever to adjust his course for District 4. A minute or two later, he could see the incinerator chimney of Cho Ray standing out against the few pale streaks the sun had left behind on its way down behind the globe.

Slowly he began bringing the Huey towards the ground. Towards, God willing, Molly's salvation. And towards whatever fate awaited himself.

There were lights flashing around the site of the hospital car park. Flashlights and vehicle headlamps. And there were more headlamps heading towards it. At three hundred feet, he switched on the Huey's landing light. The whole area below was seething with activity.

'Ben!' Pru leaned forward to shake his shoulder. 'What's going on down there?'

Taking her attention away from Molly for a moment, Pru had glanced out of the window to see, to her consternation, what looked like an army massing beneath them. There was combat green and khaki everywhere. He moved his headset away from one ear to hear what she was saying.

'There must be nearly a hundred soldiers down there!' she exclaimed.

'Quite a reception committee,' he remarked laconically.

Picked out in the landing light beneath them, twenty or so motorcycles and at least a dozen army jeeps and cars were in the process of pouring through the hospital gates, their khaki-clad passengers jumping out and massing round the

306

edges of the car park.

'As long as they leave me enough frigging room to put down . . .' Ben muttered to himself.

Just a hundred feet off the ground now, he could see soldiers waving their arms and running about frantically, chivvying the assembled troops and bystanders to keep clear of the landing area.

'Here we go, Pru.' He could feel his heart thumping in his chest. 'When we land, just concentrate on getting Molly into that hospital. Leave all the explaining to me. Ask for Dr Chuong.'

'Oh, my God, Ben! Why do they think they need a whole bloody army to meet just us? They must think we're dangerous.'

'I guess an American stealing one of their helicopters doesn't go down too well. Even now.'

'They're all armed. Are they really prepared to shoot, do you think?'

'They won't shoot.' He injected as much reassurance into his voice as he could. 'As long as they can see we're not armed ourselves. Don't engage with them at all unless you can help it. Just focus on Molly. And good luck!'

'Oh, Ben. I'm so sorry.'

But he couldn't hear her any more. He'd replaced his headset and was concentrating on putting the Huey down in the midst of the waiting bedlam.

Chapter Twenty

Hardly had the skids settled on the tarmac when all hell broke loose.

The rear door next to Pru's seat slid open with a crash and a large orange plastic container came through the opening, followed by two men in pale green paramedic uniforms and a young female nurse. In seconds, Molly had blood-pressure testing gear wrapped around her arm and an intravenous drip inserted in the back of her hand. A few seconds more, and the stretcher had been manhandled out of the helicopter and on to a trolley alongside it, the paramedics setting off with it at a run towards the hospital entrance under the still-turning rotor blade. Pru jumped down and ran along with them, trying to keep contact with Molly's hand.

Where was Ben? She looked around wildly as she ran. The cockpit was already empty, the door hanging open on its hinges. Then she saw his head, just visible above a score of soldiers shoving and jostling him unceremoniously towards the fleet of waiting jeeps. He was struggling to turn and look at her. With a supreme effort he wrested one hand free to lift to his lips and then hold aloft in salute.

'I love you,' she shrieked in his direction. She meant it with all her being. But he had disappeared, once more submerged in a heaving mass of khaki.

Her last sight of him was a flash of blue denim as he was bundled into the back of one of the vehicles, and immediately the convoy of assorted hardware—jeeps, trucks, a black limousine, a dozen or more motorcycles and too many foot soldiers to count, running behind and alongside, began to roll out through the gates and away.

Pru followed the trolley in through the hospital door. The older of the paramedics made eye contact with her for the first time.

'You are this girl's mother?'

'Yes.' She pulled the neck of Molly's T-shirt down an inch or two, enough to show the start of the scar between her daughter's breasts. 'She has had heart surgery. Look.'

The trolley and its little entourage trundled to a halt just inside the first ward they came to. Pru vaguely registered a stark room with a tiled floor and six iron bedsteads in it, three of which were occupied by children lying listlessly under flimsy sheets.

As soon as he entered the ward, Pru recognised Dr Chuong, the man who had helped Ben load the box of prosthetic limbs into the car the day they first drove up to Tra Binh. He extended a hand and she shook it quickly.

'I think she has endocarditis,' she managed breathlessly. 'You understand endocarditis?'

'I do indeed,' he replied in perfect English. 'Why do you fear endocarditis?'

'Because she had surgery for tricuspid atresia when she was a baby.' She uncovered Molly's scar again for the doctor to see. 'Now she's picked up some infection in a village near the Cambodian border and she didn't have her antibiotics with her.'

Dr Chuong removed the thermometer from under Molly's arm and frowned at it. 'This is very high fever. Forty-one degrees.' He held a short conversation in Vietnamese with the female paramedic, frowned again, then took a miniature torch from the breast pocket of his white coat.

Lifting first one then the other eyelid, he shone it into Molly's eyes. He opened her mouth, flattened her tongue with a wooden spatula and shone the light on to the back of her throat. He felt the glands in her neck, ran expert, probing fingers over her abdomen, and picked up her wrist to check her pulse.

'One hundred forty,' he murmured. 'Not good. Did she complain of headache?'

'Yes.'

'A cough? Aching joints?'

'I don't know. When I got to her she was too ill to say or do anything much.'

He put Molly's hand gently back on the bed. 'I think she may have dengue fever. Maybe dengue haemorrhagic fever, which is a more serious complication. Her liver feels a bit enlarged and there are small red spots on her abdomen.'

'I really don't think so,' protested Pru. 'She has all the symptoms of endocarditis.'

'This is the trouble,' he replied quietly. 'The two diseases have very similar symptoms.'

'I have heard of dengue fever, but what is it exactly?'

'It is mosquito-borne. There has been a big increase in cases here in Vietnam in the past few weeks. We rehydrate with fluids, bring temperature down, and slowly, slowly they recover.'

The doctor pointed to a boy who looked around twelve years old, lying in the bed next to Molly. He

310

looked dully at Pru, then closed his eyes and turned his head away.

'He has it, and so does the young girl over there.' Chuong indicated a girl a little older, perhaps around Molly's age. A woman, presumably her mother, lay curled up asleep on a mat by the bed.

'They are past the worst,' he added. 'Now they need a lot of sleep. Rest.'

The only other patient in the ward was a toddler wearing just a nappy. A young woman was supporting the child's head, trying to persuade him to take some water from a bottle with a drinking straw in it.

'The problem with your daughter,' Dr Chuong continued, 'is what treatment to give her. If she has endocarditis, she must have antibiotics urgently. But if not, then the antibiotics will mask the symptoms of whatever *is* wrong with her and maybe prolong the illness. However, I have no choice. We cannot take chances.' He issued an order to the paramedic nurse who left the ward at a near-run.

'She will bring penicillin,' he said, 'which I will give your daughter immediately. The next twenty-four hours will be crucial. We will find a mattress for you to sleep on.'

*　　　*　　　*

After so much prolonged noise, silence came as a shock; the roar of the helicopter, the frenzied, angry shouting of soldiers; the revving of diesel engines, hooting of horns, footsteps clattering along narrow corridors, a jangling of keys and, finally, the slam of the heavy iron door to the dimly lit cell Ben found

311

himself in now.

He stood stock still for a second or two. Then, without warning, his legs gave way beneath him. He was played out. Utterly drained. He crawled slowly across the concrete floor to a narrow stone bench built into the wall and tried to drag himself up on to it. Fortunately, it was only about six inches off the ground. He wouldn't have had the strength to raise himself any higher than that.

Face down, his legs still trailing on the floor, he passed out.

*   *   *

Once the antibiotics had been administered through a line in the back of Molly's hand, and satisfied that she was stable and comfortable, Pru asked the nurse where she could find a phone.

Following her directions, she retraced her steps towards the hospital's entrance until she came to a small ante-room containing two plain wooden tables with an old-fashioned black telephone on each one and a plywood screen between them. At a smaller table opposite them presided a kindly, middle-aged man in a short-sleeved blue overall. His face wreathed itself in smiles at her approach. Then, taking in her torn, damp, muddy clothing, his expression changed.

'Where you need to call?' He adopted a tone of concerned urgency.

'The UK. London.'

'Take the left one please, Madame.' He checked his watch. 'You pay me on finish.'

Once again, it was Lucy's recorded voice that answered David's flat number. Pru had to leave a

312

message this time.

'Please can David phone me urgently?' She spoke crisply into the mouthpiece. 'It's Pru. I'm at Cho Ray Hospital in Ho Chi Minh City. I don't know the number. You'll have to look it up. Molly is critically ill.'

She dialled his mobile. Please don't let it be switched off . . .

'Hello?' His voice was so quiet, she could hardly hear him.

'David. It's Pru.'

'Pru—I can't talk now.' He had his I'm-in-the-middle-of-a-very-important-meeting voice on. 'This isn't a good time.'

'David. Listen. I'm calling from Saigon. Molly is critically ill. She's in hospital. I'm here with her.'

'What's happened?'

'You need to come out here.'

'Oh, God, Pru, I can't.'

'You don't understand.' She could only get the words out in sobs. It seemed impossible to draw enough breath for more than one syllable at a time. 'I think she's going to die. David, I'm so frightened.'

'Tell me what's happened, for Christ's sake.'

'She got ill up in a hillside village. She didn't have her antibiotics. She had such a fever. She was delirious. And then she just went unconscious.'

'Oh, my God, Pru.' The shock was sinking in. 'What are the doctors doing?'

'She's got drips everywhere. They started antibiotics as soon as we got here. I showed them her scar. And she'd got very dehydrated.'

'But you got her there in time?'

'I don't know. I hope so. It took about two and a

313

half hours to get here after I found her.' Was that really all it had been? 'We had to hijack a helicopter.'

'Fucking hell.' David mumbled something. It sounded as though he'd put his hand over the mouthpiece to speak to someone else.

'What?'

'How soon will they know—you know—how things are going to go?' He was sounding panic-stricken now.

'The doctor said the next twenty-four hours will be crucial.'

'It'll take me a while to get a flight sorted. I'll have to get a visa.'

'This is an emergency. You can get a special visa, I'm sure.'

'Thing is, Pru, I've got an emergency on my hands here too. Oh, my God. What am I going to do?'

'Nothing's as bad as your daughter being critically ill.'

'I have another daughter critically ill. Here.'

'What the hell are you talking about?'

'I'm in a hospital too. Queen Charlotte's. Lucy has . . . God, Pru. This isn't the way I wanted to tell you. Lucy has just had . . . given birth . . . Nine weeks premature. They're in intensive care.'

'They?'

'Twins.'

She tried to speak but her voice wouldn't work.

'A boy and a girl,' continued David quietly.

'And you're . . . the father?'

'Yes.' His voice sounded very small and far away.

'But . . .' wrestling with the maths '. . . she must have been pregnant when we . . . before we . . .'

314

'Yes.'

A swirling, buzzing sensation rose and swelled, filling Pru's head, thundering in her ears, dimming her eyes, turning her stomach to acid. The table began to melt under her elbows, the wall in front of her blurred. Everything that was solid lost its form and shape. Then, as suddenly as it had deserted her, reality returned, crystal clear and sure. She would have to cope with this alone. So be it. An almost mystical feeling of inner strength poured into her, like liquid light.

'Pru? Are you still there?'

'Yes, David. I'm here.'

'Christ, what am I going to do?'

'By the morning, David, we'll know. She'll have turned the corner or she won't. I need to get back to her now. I want her to know I'm with her.'

'She's going to make it, isn't she, Pru?' His voice was cracking. 'She's a toughie, isn't she, our Moll? She'll make it.'

'All we can do now is pray. I don't know who to. But if there is a God up there, maybe he's listening. I'll call you again tomorrow. Sooner if there's anything to report.'

'Will you tell her I love her? I feel so terrible.'

'*You* feel terrible!' She almost laughed. 'David . . .'

'Yes?'

'Never mind.'

She hung up.

The attendant had been gazing at her, enthralled; presumably by the emotional intensity of the conversation rather than its content.

Abruptly remembering what he was there for, he straightened his expression, studied his watch and

315

scribbled a calculation on the memo pad in front of him.

'Twenty-two dollars, Madame, please.'

*   *   *

The nurse looked up with a reassuring smile at Pru's approach.

'How is she?'

'More cool. Forty degrees.'

Pru bent to smooth her daughter's forehead. Molly was still hot, but calmer somehow in her unconsciousness.

'I come back later.' The nurse handed Pru the cloth and jug of water she'd been using to bathe Molly's face and limbs, and withdrew, pausing at the doorway to turn out the light.

A thin, striped mattress had been laid on the floor alongside Molly's bed. Pru lay down on it in the darkness, alone with her thoughts, just the gentle breathing of her two fellow parents and the sleeping children to accompany them.

She reached up to touch her daughter's arm on the bed above her. It was hot and clammy. Please let her get well. Please let us have got here in time.

David would be going through hell now. She had just managed to stop herself saying, 'You're a self-centred shit,' before she hung up. *He* felt terrible! Actually, she did feel a bit sorry for him. Father of twins! And Intensive Care again. All that worry again. And he loved Molly so much. He'd never forgive himself if she were to die while he was holding Lucy's hand in Queen Charlotte's. Had Lucy manipulated him into this situation? Somehow Pru felt that she had. And that David

316

knew it too. He was trapped.

He's made his bed, now he has to lie in it.

She couldn't imagine Ben getting himself into such an emotional tangle. He was far too cautious about relationships. So much stronger. He'd need every ounce of that strength of character now.

She tried to picture him; to tune in to him. Was he sitting alone in a hard, bare cell? Or thrown in, standing room only, with a whole crowd of robbers and murderers? She looked at her watch. It was close on midnight. Was he being interrogated, or were they letting him sleep?

It had been an act of such courage, flying that helicopter after so many years, especially in such perilous conditions. He'd really had to confront those monsters he'd talked about. She remembered how his hands had shaken on the controls at first and then steadied; the supreme effort of will it had taken him. But he'd done it. He'd beaten them. Had he realised the enormity of his victory? she wondered.

Only when she saw all those soldiers and police waiting for them had she realised the seriousness of what they had done. You'd have thought they had been anticipating a *coup d'état.* The conversation she had had with Kenny over breakfast, eons ago, floated back into her mind. His list of crimes that carried the death penalty. 'There's treason, espionage, sabotage, hijacking, banditry—whatever that means . . .'

Hijacking! Taking that helicopter had been their only possible course of action, but that's what they had done. Hijacked a helicopter. She'd used the word herself on the phone to David. Her heart contracted. Ben could be sentenced to death.

317

Surely they wouldn't alienate the American Government by doing that. Something else Kenny said turned her flesh to goose bumps despite the humidity. '. . . a Canadian geezer, back in April. First Westerner they've shot since the war. You don't mess with these guys.'

Molly stirred.

'Mum?'

Pru scrambled hurriedly to her feet. 'Yes, darling. I'm right here with you,'

It was too dark to see Molly's face properly, but her eyes were open. Pru could see them glistening. Taking her daughter's hand in hers, she stroked it lovingly. You're in hospital. You're going to get better. Everything's all right now.'

'I'm sorry, Mum.'

'Shhh. Sleep. Get well. I'm watching over you.'

She renewed the cool, damp cloth on her daughter's forehead. The girl's eyes closed. Her body relaxed and she sank into sleep again.

Pru lay back down on the mattress. She so much needed to sleep herself, and yet each time she drifted off, shadowy monsters with dripping teeth and bloodstained claws patrolled the edges of her dreams, looking for a way in. They were Ben's monsters, lost and angry, searching for him; come to hunt him down in her soul. At all costs, she had to stay alert. Keep them out. They were bent on destruction. She had to preserve herself for Molly. And for Ben.

Chapter Twenty-one

A rough jab in the ribcage woke him. Ben had no idea how long he'd been asleep. It could have been five minutes or five hours. They'd removed the watch from his wrist in the jeep. His *mala* beads had gone too. He looked at his left hand. At least he still had his ring.

'Get up. We go. Now. Fast.' The jab had come from the toe of a soldier's boot. He scrambled groggily to his feet and, with more prodding around the back and ribs, preceded the two soldiers who had come for him back along the long, narrow corridor.

At almost the last doorway, the marching feet stopped abruptly.

'Ngung. Du!' snapped one of the soldiers, rapping on the dark green-painted door.

'Den. Come in.'

The door opened and a hefty push in the small of the back propelled Ben into a windowless room not much bigger than the cell he'd just been in. There were one or two refinements, though. A gun-metal grey desk stood at an angle across one corner, a simple metal chair on his side of it, a vinyl-covered armchair on the other. On the desk itself, an electric fan swung its head slowly back and forth through a hundred and eighty degrees, making little discernible difference to the airlessness of the room. Next to it were a black Bakelite telephone and an old wind-up alarm clock whose steady, hollow ticking took Ben straight back to his tenth birthday and the clock

319

with glow-in-the-dark hands his parents had given him. On its face, a baseball pitcher in blue and white strip had swung at a ball in time with the tick. He had loved that clock. What had happened to it?

The rest of the desk's surface was strewn with Ben's belongings. The battered satchel had been divested of its contents; his laptop computer, notebook, a couple of cheap ballpoint pens, the GPS, two packs of Winstons—one opened, the other still sealed—his cigarette lighter, watch, *mala* beads and mobile phone. His wallet had been emptied too; ID card, passport, a fairly recent picture of his daughter Kathy May and about eighty dollars in various notes were ranged on a plastic tray, like a memory game at a kids' party.

Behind the desk stood two men. Ben felt they'd been interrupted in the middle of an intense conversation. One was tall and thin, in his early-thirties, wearing light camouflage fatigues, sleeves rolled up to his bony elbows. The other was twice his age; plump, bespectacled, white-haired and neatly uniformed, wearing the shoulder bars of a general.

'Mr Coder.' He indicated the metal chair. 'Please sit down.'

Sitting as ordered, Ben took the risk of stretching across the desk and angling the clock towards him for a moment. There was no baseball player. It was 2 a.m.

*　　　*　　　*

Gradually the thick blackness of the ward lightened to granular grey. A new day was

320

beginning. A new day in which Molly had been found and, the gods willing, would continue to recover. And in which Ben was now missing. Half a world away, David would be peering anxiously through the Perspex sides of two cots at his tiny new babies, festooned with tubes and sensors in an Intensive Care unit.

Peeling yesterday's mud-stained clothes away from her body, Pru got quietly to her feet to check her daughter's temperature.

'My instinct was right. She has dengue haemorrhagic fever—DHF.'

She hadn't heard Doctor Chuong slip into the ward. He was standing on the other side of the bed, holding her daughter's wrist. 'It can be fatal if not treated. You got her here just in time. The rehydration is doing its job. When her temperature is back to normal, we can remove the drip.'

'How soon will that be, do you think?'

'Two, maybe three days.'

'And she'll be completely well?'

'She'll be weak. Needing rest for two weeks at least. But fit enough to fly.'

'She probably won't want to go home yet.'

'I don't think she will have a choice,' said the doctor solemnly.

The other occupants of the ward were beginning to stir now. The baby whimpered. His mother picked him up and rocked him, making gentle crooning noises. The two older children were still sleeping. The women smiled at each other. Unspoken kinship. A boy of around nine or ten appeared at the barred window at one end of the ward, jumping up, trying to see into the room.

'*Di! Di,*' Doctor Chuong waved him away good-

321

humouredly and turned back to hang Molly's clinical notes on the end of her bed. 'We continue with the fluids. Keep up with the antibiotics. And we keep watching.'

'Doctor Chuong, you know Ben Coder, don't you?'

'Yes, I do. He is a very good man.' Chuong looked sad. 'He was doing valuable and necessary work here. He will be a great loss to us.'

'What do you mean?'

'After what he has done, stealing Vietnamese aircraft, we will not get him back, I am certain. Very great loss.'

Molly opened her eyes.

'Mum! You *are* here. I wasn't sure what was real and what was my imagination. Am I OK?'

'Ask the doctor.'

'I believe you will make a good recovery. You are a lucky girl. You were on the danger list for a few hours. You have your mother and Mr Coder to thank.'

'I was in a helicopter . . .'

'That's right,' said Dr Chuong gently, 'you were.'

'I've got a headache. Can I have some water?'

Pru went over to the water dispenser and filled a white plastic beaker from the stack underneath it. Molly watched her cross the ward.

'Fuckinell, Mum. What happened to your trousers?'

'I do believe she's feeling a little better.' Pru smiled at the doctor.

'Your mother's been through quite an adventure, my dear.' He smiled too. 'I'll leave her to tell you about it. I have some more patients I must see.'

322

'Dr Chuong. Wait. We were talking about Ben Coder . . . Is he in trouble?'

'I think, big trouble,' he said simply.

'Can you help him?'

'I wish I could. He has been a good friend.'

'Will they let you know what is happening to him?'

'I might hear something in a few days. I don't know. They will be asking him a lot of questions.'

'Who are "they"?'

'Government people.'

'Isn't there something you can do? Tell them what good work he's been doing?'

Shaking his head slowly, the doctor turned towards the door. 'I wish.'

'If you hear something, will you let me know straight away?'

'Yes, of course.' He bowed his head politely and left the room.

*   *   *

Ben sat slowly down on the hard metal chair. Every muscle in his body seemed to be aching. The General spoke to the man in fatigues.

'Wait outside. I'll call you when I need you.'

He marched out, with what Ben sensed was bad grace.

The two men sat facing each other across the desk. It was a few moments before the General spoke again.

'I am General Duc Van Duong.'

Ben inclined his head in acknowledgement.

'You know why you are under arrest.' His voice was a soft growl.

'Yes, I think so.'

'So you tell me why you think you are here.'

'I am here,' he began carefully, 'because my friend had a critically ill daughter who needed urgent medical attention. It was a matter of life or death. I had no alternative but to borrow a helicopter in order to get her to hospital.'

His inquisitor raised an eyebrow.

'Borrow?'

Ben couldn't think what to say next. He was anxious to avoid implicating Hong Yen. He was pretty sure the pilot wouldn't have known who had ordered the rendezvous.

The General took a deep breath.

'Mr Coder, you are charged with assault on a government helicopter pilot, theft of military property, damage to military property,' he counted the charges on his fingers as he spoke, 'unauthorised use of Vietnamese airspace, flying a helicopter without a valid licence, endangering life . . . There is more. Shall I go on?'

'In my defence, I can only repeat that this was a matter of life or death.'

'You had just one sick person to consider. Many more people would be dead now if you had crashed.'

'I am a fully qualified helicopter pilot.'

'I am aware of that. I know exactly who you are. I also know that you have not piloted a helicopter since you left Vietnam in 1972. Now, how do you plead to these charges? Guilty or not guilty?'

'I guess guilty, but with mitigating . . .'

'Guilty or not guilty?'

'Guilty.'

Slowly, the General took Ben's open packet of

324

Winstons off the desk, tapped it twice against his finger and held the carton towards him. Ben took the most prominent cigarette gratefully.

Picking up the lighter, the General walked round to Ben's side of the desk and stood squarely in front of him.

'I know everything, Mr Coder.'

*   *   *

Molly looked curiously at Pru's flushed face. 'Who were you talking to the doctor about just now? Your American friend?'

'Ben. Yes.'

'Why is he in trouble?'

'Because, basically, we hijacked a helicopter and flew it here without authorisation—which apparently is a capital offence. It didn't occur to me at the time. All I could think about was getting you to hospital. You won't have been aware of it, but half the Vietnamese Army was waiting for us when we landed. They grabbed Ben the minute we landed and took him away. I don't know where. I've got to find out.'

Molly tried to sit up. Pru looked around the ward. 'They don't seem to have pillows here.'

'But they'll understand, won't they? It was an emergency. I was ill.'

'Ill? You nearly bloody died! Can you lift your head up?'

Pru folded the mattress she'd spent the night on and arranged it under Molly's head and shoulders.

'And perhaps now,' she continued, 'you can tell me what you were doing up in that village?'

'I thought if I disappeared, I could draw

325

attention to Sinh. People would think I'd been kidnapped by him.'

'Well, it worked. That's just what we did think.'

'Can I have some more of that water?'

Pru handed her the cup. Molly drained it and handed it back, shifting herself higher on the mattress at her back.

'The plan was that Giles would tell the newspapers,' her voice sounded a little stronger now, 'and then they'd start investigating Sinh and people would find out about him stealing Quang and Linh's farm and all the other evil things he's been doing for years in Tra Binh.'

'You put me through hell, Molly.'

'But, Mum, I didn't know you were here! I thought you'd gone away, up to the coast. That's what you said you were going to do.'

'Giles knew what I was going through. So did Tam. Didn't they tell you I was worried to death?'

'No. I didn't have a phone or anything. I'd never have let you go through that if I'd known.'

'I was just beside myself. And that boyfriend of yours knew all along. He could see how desperate I was. It's unforgivable. Ben and I even went to Hanoi and risked someone's whole career in the government there, getting them to pull strings for us.'

'Oh, Mum. You're amazing.'

'And most unforgivable of all, you damn nearly died. How could you take such a risk with your health? You didn't even take your antibiotics with you.'

'Look, Mum, can you stop giving me such a hard time? It was a spur-of-the-moment thing when we got released that morning. Quang took me straight to Cau Giang on his bike. I couldn't collect my things because it had to look as though Sinh was still keeping me prisoner. And it's not my fault you told me you were leaving Saigon and then didn't.'

Pru sat despairingly on the edge of the bed.

'And now a wonderful, brave man is in jail, in God knows what kind of conditions, suffering God knows what kind of treatment.'

Molly was silent for so long Pru assumed she'd dropped off to sleep again. The doctor had warned her it would be a gradual recovery. She went to refill the water jug from the dispenser.

Back at the bedside, she stroked Molly's forehead while images of Ben floated back to her; the way his blue eyes would lock on to hers, flashing with fun and vitality and integrity. His selfless courage and determination. The sharpness of his mind; the strength of his body. Now she wished they had made love in that Hanoi hotel room. It would have been a memory of ultimate intimacy to hold on to in this vacuum of their separation. A vacuum that—she hardly dared think it—might now be permanent.

Suddenly, Molly spoke again, taking her mother by surprise.

'Did Ben actually fly the helicopter here himself?'

'Yes. He was a pilot in the Vietnam War. He hadn't flown for years, though. It was a crazy thing to do. But we had no choice.'

'Wow. I remember talking to him now. In a rattly old van. And I remember kind, strong arms picking me up.'

Pru put her face in her hands. 'I just hope he's all right.'

'Molly!'

A little figure ran across the ward and cannoned into Molly's bed, scraping it several feet across the floor. Composing herself quickly, Pru shot a hand out and caught the drip stand before it toppled.

'Bong!' squealed Molly. 'How did you get here? Give me a hug.'

'I thought it looked like your little face at the window back then.' Pru smiled.

'Giles said I could come in.' They all looked towards the doorway. Giles was standing there, looking none-too-anxious to enter the room.

'You might well look sheepish,' called Pru. 'We've just been talking about you.'

'Giles!' Molly held her arms wide. He approached the bed and, with a quick nervous glance at Pru, returned the embrace.

'How are you, babes? We've all been so worried.'

'Do you know the meaning of the word "worried"?' demanded Pru.

'I bring news.'

'Deflection is the better part of valour, evidently.'

The witticism was wasted.

'They've arrested Sinh,' he continued breathlessly. 'And both his horrible henchmen. Kenny reckons they'll go down for a good five years. That's the sentence a couple of People's Committee chiefs got last month for running some kind of land scam around the Mekong Delta. So that's the end of *his* career in politics. He's history. Isn't that just brilliant?'

'And what about Quang and Linh?' asked Molly. 'Can they keep their farm now?'

'No, but they're giving them another piece of

328

land on the other side of the village. It's on a bit of a slope, but it's bigger. And they're getting the compensation they were supposed to get. About ten thousand dollars.'

'Doesn't sound much,' commented Pru.

'It's a lot to them. Two years' earnings. More, probably. It'll tide them over while they build up their crops again on another piece of land.'

Recovering his old insouciant charm, Giles walked round to Pru's side of the bed and draped an arm round her.

'Forgive me, Pru. I couldn't tell you. You were doing such brilliant work. It would have ruined everything if I had. I wanted to. Really I did. But all's well that . . .' His voice petered out.

Pru removed his arm from her shoulders.

'Giles, if that sentence was going where I think it was, you can think yourself lucky you didn't finish it. I could throttle you. Literally. I'm so angry with you.'

'Can you all just shut up? I'm tired . . .'

Pru removed the extra mattress so that Molly could lie flat again.

'Get some more sleep, darling.' She turned back to Giles. 'It's going to be a while before she gets her strength back. She's had dengue fever, with complications. We're lucky she's alive. Now you're here, you and Bong can keep her company while she sleeps. Have you got your mobile phone?'

'Yes.' He patted his shirt pocket.

Pru reached in and took it out.

'Thank you. I need this for a couple of hours.'

Giles looked horror-stricken.

'I've got some vital phone calls to make. Don't worry, I'll make a note of any messages for you.'

329

'That's what I'm afraid of,' he muttered.

*   *   *

In the taxi back to the Continental, Pru switched Giles's phone on. As she'd hoped, Ben's number was programmed into it. She pressed the button and put the phone to her ear, holding her breath. There was a pause. Then a shrill pre-recorded female voice—a gabble of Vietnamese. Presumably the equivalent of: 'The mobile you have called has not responded.' She waited to see if there'd be a chance to leave a message, but the line went dead.

Controlling her disappointment, she called David to tell him Molly was out of danger. He actually sobbed with relief. She asked him politely about the babies.

'The boy will be fine, we think, but we're worried about the girl. She's so very tiny . . .'

'I hope she'll come through, David. Good luck.'

'You're a special person, Pru. Thank you.'

She found Kenny's number next. Diverted to his voicemail service, she left a long message describing the events of the last twenty-four hours and asking him to meet her later at the Continental, ideally around four o'clock. As she hung up, she realised it had sounded more like a command than a request, but she guessed he'd understand.

*   *   *

Ben kept his eyes on the wavering lighter flame, working to keep his face blank and clear of

330

emotion. Was the General bluffing? Had he and Pru been followed throughout the last four days? He knew it was all too possible. He'd even suspected it. Did they know about Hong Yen's involvement? They probably did. At all costs he must avoid corroborating anything concerning her. He didn't look up to meet the General's eyes until he had taken a long, deep toke and exhaled.

'If you know everything, then you don't need me to tell you any more.'

The General's eyes hardened. 'That is not the co-operative tone I had hoped for.'

Ben had overstepped the mark. It was important not to alienate this man. He had favours to ask. Uppermost in his mind was Molly's condition. She had been so very sick. If the worst had happened and the girl had died, Pru would be utterly devastated. If only he could be there for her. But he knew that was out of the question. His best hope was to be allowed a phone call to Dr Chuong . . . at least then he'd know.

'All right. What else can I tell you?'

'How much do you know about Tra Binh and its People's Committee?'

'Very little. Only hearsay.'

'Which is . . . ?'

'That the chief is bent. And a tyrant. And the place could do with a clean-up. In more ways than one.'

'I think you'll find you are mistaken. We make sure people like that do not survive for long in our political hierarchy.'

'You mean, you've fired him?'

The General's eyes glittered again.

'I mean that you are mistaken. Why did you go

331

to Hanoi?'

Here we go. Crunchtime.

'Because I have friends there. And I wanted to show Mrs Taylor what a beautiful city it is.'

'Arriving at midnight and leaving at nine the following morning? I think she spent more time admiring you than the city of Hanoi.'

Ben said nothing.

'What friends?'

'Oh, just some fellow US Vets. Helping me with my charity.'

'Yes, I know about your charity work.'

Ben couldn't determine from his attitude whether he approved or disapproved.

'It is the children I do it for. And their families.'

'And because it makes you feel good?'

Stung, Ben looked away. This wasn't going well. The General evidently agreed.

'I think we have talked enough for now.' He pushed back his chair and stood up. Ben remained seated. He must appeal to him to be allowed to make that call. The General continued, 'Perhaps we will meet again.'

'May I respectfully ask you, sir, if I could make a phone call?'

'Why?'

'I must find out about the girl. Doctor Chuong at the hospital . . .'

'In due course.'

'If you won't let me call, please would your staff call him for me? I need to know what has happened to her.'

'I will see what can be done.'

'And I should also like to call a lawyer.'

'That will not be necessary.'

332

'You are releasing me?'

'No.'

'Then I shall need a lawyer.'

'When the date is set for your trial, then you shall have your lawyer.'

'When will that be?'

'In due course.'

'Days? Weeks? Months?'

'It depends on many things. A few weeks maybe.'

'In that case, I must contact the US Embassy. It is part of the agreement between your country and mine to be entitled to do that.' Well, he assumed it must be.

'I will arrange it.'

The General growled something in the direction of the door. It opened and the man in fatigues re-entered.

Whether Ben liked it or not, the interview was at an end. The only way of cutting any ice at all in this place, he reckoned, would be by keeping his dignity and remaining polite. He determined not to behave like a cringing, submissive victim.

He stood and put out his hand. Taken by surprise, the General shook it.

'I look forward to our next meeting, General.'

*   *   *

After a short but blissful shower back in her room at the Continental, Pru glanced longingly at the big double bed she still hadn't actually slept in. Half an hour to recharge the battery? She looked at her watch. No. It was nearly eleven. There was too much to do. She could think of nothing but Ben now; what might be happening to him and how to get him released. And how deeply she cared about him.

Finding a laundry bag in the wardrobe, she stuffed all her dirty clothes into it, ticked the right boxes on the list provided and left it in the corridor. Back in the cyclamen dress—the cleanest item of clothing she had left—she went downstairs and asked one of the receptionists to write down the addresses of the British Consulate and the US Embassy.

'You want US Embassy for take photo?' enquired the girl.

'No. For some advice.'

'US Embassy in Saigon is not occupied now. Only for tourist exhibit. Embassies are in Hanoi now. For advice you must visit US Consulate General office. It is the same street as British Consulate General.' She scribbled the addresses on a hotel notepad. 'It is a two-minute walk.'

'Thank you. May I keep this?'

'With pleasure, Madame.' The girl pushed the notepad across the counter towards her with a smile. 'Just turn left from hotel, past the Opera House, and at Notre Dame Cathedral you will see Le Duan Street in front of you.'

*　　　*　　　*

Three hours later Pru was back at the Continental, staring miserably into a cup of Vietnamese tea in the shade of a twisted old frangipani tree in the hotel's courtyard. She switched Giles's phone to silent. She was fed up with fielding the continual calls for him. Most of them—she was hardly

334

surprised—were from women.

'You are looking remarkably cool and elegant considering what you've been through this last couple of days,' was Kenny's cheery greeting.

Pru lifted her sunglasses for a moment. Seeing her hollow, red-rimmed eyes behind them, he grimaced.

'OK, perhaps not.'

He arranged himself clumsily on the chair opposite her, summoned a waitress and ordered a beer.

'So how did you go at the Consulate offices?'

'Not a lot of use. Tell me what you've found out first.'

'Do you want the good news or the bad news?'

'For Christ's sake, Kenny, just tell me what you've got to tell me.'

'Well, the good news,' continued Kenny unperturbed, 'is that as soon as Merrilands found out what was going on, they got their compensation payments out of Sinh's back pocket and into the hands of the farmers they were intended for.'

'Yes, I know about that. Giles told me. He came to the hospital this morning.'

'The power of the press, eh? The whole story— or, to be more accurate, the threat of it getting out—gave Hanoi the perfect excuse to get rid of Sinh and his cronies. Word is, they'd been wanting to do that for a long time.'

'It is good news, but I can't bring myself to care that much, Kenny. I feel so used . . .'

'We were all used, I know. That's true. It's a job well done, though. Thanks to all of us.'

'But in the process Molly could have died. And a

good, brave man is in a Vietnamese jail. I can't begin to imagine what Ben might be suffering. He was just fantastic, Kenny. I'm so worried about him. I remember you said hijacking gets the death penalty.'

'Yeah, it does, but I don't think they'd shoot an American guy.'

'I've been hoping the same thing, but didn't you tell me they shot a Canadian a few months ago?'

'That was for drugs. Worst crime on the planet as far as they're concerned over here. Ben'll get deported most likely.'

'What's the bad news you mentioned?'

'Well, they could keep him rotting in jail for months if they feel like it. Just keep postponing the court hearing. They do that here.'

'Can we visit him? The guy I saw at the American Consulate General's office said he's probably at a jail called . . . hang on a minute . . .' She foraged in her shoulder bag for the hotel's notepad and leafed through the several pages of notes she'd taken. 'Chi Hoa. Have you heard of it?'

'Yes, I have. The pre-detention centre. Frigging huge place. Full of people waiting for trials that never happen. Political prisoners, a lot of them. And persecuted Christians. Appalling. You don't want to hear about it.'

'Oh, Ben. All he's done is save Molly's life. He doesn't deserve this. How will they be treating him?'

'It's hardly the Continental Hotel, put it that way.'

'Will you take me there? I can try to talk my way in to see him.'

336

'No chance. Nobody's allowed to visit that place.'

'Can you at least let me try? It's only because of me and Molly that he's in this terrible situation. Please?'

'Look, Pru. Not even the United Nations Commission on Human Rights managed to get in there when they tried a couple of years ago.'

She thought for a moment or two, fighting a growing sense of despair.

'Ben's best hope must be for the US Embassy to take up his case then? Make it a matter of diplomacy.'

'They are entitled, I think, to send a lawyer in, to make sure he's being treated reasonably and all that. Check for signs of, shall we say, over-zealous interrogation techniques. But they'd have to make a formal application first.'

'How can we get them to do that? They won't do it at my behest, that's for sure. They gave me pretty short shrift this afternoon.'

'Because you're not a US citizen?'

'Exactly. The man I finally got to talk to, after keeping me waiting nearly an hour, said there was nothing they could do to help because I'm not married to Ben, I'm not American, and that in any case he was doing me a big favour by seeing me, because I hadn't made an appointment.'

'Did he take any details from you at all?'

'I told him the basics. I said my daughter had been taken seriously ill in a remote village and the only way we could get her to hospital was for Ben to commandeer the helicopter that had been sent for her. And I described the terrifying reception we got when we landed—Ben being dragged off,

337

literally, by scores of Vietnamese soldiers.'

'And what did he say to that?'

'He looked shocked. Then he said something along the lines of, when you visit a foreign country there is no excuse for breaking their laws and if you do, you have to accept their punishment. More or less what I remember telling Molly once.'

'He took a note of Ben's name and what you told him, though, did he?'

'Yes, he did. And he said he'd notify his superiors. Then he told me to go to the British Consulate. Which I'd already done.'

Kenny opened his little tobacco tin.

Pru looked round anxiously to see if anyone was watching.

'You're not . . . ?'

He anticipated her. 'I'm just making a rollie . . . chill, girl.'

'The last thing I need is another brush with the authorities.'

'They might actually do more than they let on, you know,' he said. 'Behind-the-scenes diplomacy or whatever you call it. An American citizen carted off by half the army is serious shit.'

He ran the tip of his tongue along the edge of the cigarette paper with practised precision.

'I'll tell you what I'll do. I'll get my good old pal at the *Review* on to it. Get him to give the Consulate General a call. That way they'll know the press is taking an interest as well.'

'Can you do that straight away?'

'Sure.' He unhooked the phone from his belt and put it on the table. 'And what reception did you get from the British Consulate?'

'Tea and sympathy, but nothing practical to help

338

Ben. I was expecting to see an Englishman in a crumpled linen suit. Like *The Honorary Consul.* But all the staff there seemed to be Vietnamese. Spoke perfect English, though. The woman I talked to said I should think myself lucky Molly and I weren't arrested as well.'

'Most likely they wouldn't want to risk word getting out. Arresting an Englishwoman with her daughter at death's door wouldn't be the best advert for tourism.'

'I asked if I could extend my visa. It runs out the day after tomorrow. I need to be here for Ben. But she said that was out of the question and that I should leave the country straight away, taking Molly with me. She seemed to think we were both liable to be deported.'

Kenny pursed his lips around the tiny cigarette, which had almost burned away already. 'So have you booked your flights?'

'I'm scheduled to go the day after tomorrow. But I can't just go home and leave Ben in that prison.'

'If they say you should go, you should go. Believe me. I'll keep on the case on your behalf here.'

'Will you? You promise?'

'I promise. Cross my heart and hope to die.'

'And if he gets in touch with you, you'll tell him how to get hold of me?' Pru scribbled her address, email and phone number on her pad.

'Of course. Absolutely.'

'Are you sure there's no one I can talk to, to ask if I can stay on a while?'

'Pru. Read my lips. Your visa has run out. They said you must go. So go. And book Molly on the flight with you.'

'I'm sure Molly won't want to leave. She might not be well enough, in any case.'

'She can recover at home. Dengue fever just needs lots of rest.'

'And if she won't go?'

'She'll be deported. With maybe a little sojourn in police custody somewhere first. It won't be pleasant and she won't be allowed back. They'll have all the details of her escapades at Tra Binh. No question. I advise you to be persuasive, Pru.'

'I'll try,' she said despondently.

'You'll have to do better than just try.'

It all seemed like a bizarre dream. She and Molly faced with deportation. Ben in a Vietnamese jail. Pru finished the last of her tea and got to her feet.

'I'll do my best then. I must get back to the hospital now anyway. See how she's doing.'

'Good luck.'

'Thanks.' She got to her feet. 'Oh, and Kenny?'

'Yes?'

'You were calling your friend on the *Review.*'

'I hadn't forgotten.'

Pru left him dialling the number.

*　　　*　　　*

In the hollow isolation of his cell, Ben couldn't help reflecting on the bitter irony that in the throes of the American War, several of his rrrrrrrrrrrrfriends and colleagues had ended up either here at Chi Hoa or at the Hanoi Hilton in the North, while he himself had managed to evade capture on more than one occasion. Now, thirty years on, just when he'd found a way of doing good

340

instead of harm, trying to heal the damage, here he was, kicking his heels in South Vietnam's most notorious jail.

What would happen now to his charity? To the families whose trust he'd worked so tirelessly to earn and to whom he'd promised so much? To the hard-won deal with General Motors? He hoped Doctor Chuong would be able to carry it forward somehow. He was a good man and the charity had become as close to his heart as it was to Ben's. If only he could contact him.

At least Pru and Molly were in capable hands. He imagined Pru at her daughter's bedside, desperately praying for her recovery. Would that husband of hers come out to support her? For Pru's sake, he hoped he would. For selfish reasons, he hoped he wouldn't. He lay down on the stone bench that served as a bed and tried to sleep.

Chapter Twenty-two

Giles had brought Molly's belongings down from the orphanage and he and Kenny rode with them to the airport in the ambulance Dr Chuong had organised to take them there.

To Pru's surprise, Molly had given in almost without a fight to the idea of going home. She seemed too weak and tired to argue. Kenny's point had clinched the argument: that if she didn't leave now, she was likely to be banned from Vietnam for the foreseeable future. And Giles had added his enthusiastic support.

'We don't want them banning you forever, do

we, babes?'

Pru had tried not to look as he and her daughter engaged in a lingering and oblivious series of succulent farewell kisses.

She turned to Kenny.

'You will tell me the moment there's any news about Ben, won't you. And you've got my phone number to give him.'

'For crying out loud, Pru. I may have my faults but I do keep my promises. That's why I don't usually make any.'

'Thanks for everything, Kenny. Maybe we'll meet again.'

'That'd be good. I hope so. Take care now.'

Pru had secured seats by the emergency exit, for more leg room and manoeuvrability in case her daughter needed any medical attention during the flight. Molly sat now, head against the window, looking pale, thinner, but remarkably chipper for someone whose life, only three days ago, had been hanging in the balance. Doctor Chuong had provided Pru with several sachets of oral rehydration salts, instructing her to dilute them in mineral water and to make sure Molly drank as much as possible during the flight.

'It's nice to be allowed to mother you again for a while.'

'It's nice to be looked after again for a while, too,' agreed Molly.

'Good. Well, we can indulge ourselves in a bit of co-dependence for the next couple of weeks,' said Pru.

They buckled their seat belts.

'How do you feel about leaving Giles?' ventured Pru. 'You'll miss him.'

342

'Yes, I will, a bit.'

'But you'll see him again?'

'He said he might come over around Christmas time. I'll believe it when it happens, though.'

A week ago, Molly would have told her to mind her own business. Pru continued. 'You think he didn't mean it?'

'Oh, no, he meant it, probably. But . . . there's a lot going on in Giles's life.'

'Yes. I noticed. He seemed pretty keen on you, though.'

'I think I'll look back and be glad I had that time with him. These last few weeks in Vietnam have been amazing and a lot of that was because of Giles. But he isn't my destiny, you know, Mum. He's too . . .'

'Unreliable?' supplied Pru.

'He's a party animal. He always will be. We had some amazing fun times and I'll never forget him. But I'll miss Vietnam more. I loved my kids, Bong and poor Nhung. Who's going to play with them now? Who's going to teach them things? Now they've got nobody again.'

'At least they had you for a while.'

'It's not good enough, though, is it?'

They fell silent. The plane taxied to the beginning of the runway and waited, gathering its resources, its engines beginning to whine.

'And what's the latest with your friend Ben?' asked Molly.

'I don't know. I just hope and pray he's all right. It's tearing me apart inside, flying out of Vietnam, leaving him in prison. I can only begin to guess the treatment and conditions he has to endure. It's so wrong that he should be suffering such punishment

343

for what was not a crime at all but an act of incredible heroism.'

'You seem very . . . fond of him,' said Molly.

'Yes, I am.' Pru fumbled in her bag for a tissue.

Molly peered down from the window as the plane transformed itself from lumbering beast to graceful bird, parting company with Vietnamese soil and beginning its steep trajectory into the stratosphere. It was a minute before she could bring herself to turn and look at the pain she knew was etched on her mother's face.

'I've put you through so much, Mum. I didn't mean to but I'm so, so sorry.' She took her mother's hot, clenched fist from her lap and brought it across the seat-arm to her own, gently uncurling the fingers and entwining them with hers.

'Ben will be all right, Mum. You'll see. We'll get him out of there. When we get home I'll help you. We'll tell the whole world.'

Pru couldn't help laughing. 'Don't ever change, Moll!'

*   *   *

Ben lay on his back in the meadow behind his parents' house. It was summer. The insects buzzing purposefully past him was almost the only sound. Occasionally the trees rustled when a passing gentle breeze made them move their limbs. The birds were too lazy in their afternoon contentment to be bothered to sing. He squinted through his eyelashes, making shapes with little shafts of sunlight. Suddenly, something flickered across his face. Puzzled, he opened his eyes wide.

Standing above him he saw Pru, smiling, the sun behind her turning her mass of tawny hair into a glowing halo around her head. He held out his arms to her and she knelt over him, stroking his bare chest with gentle fingers. She leaned forward to kiss him; full round breasts, pale hard nipples, pressing against his chest. As slowly, gently, he entered her, the trees bent to give their blessing and the sun wrapped them in a timeless cocoon of warmth. In that sublime moment, he knew what heaven was, what goodness was, what perfection was, what the very essence of life was.

Iron jangled against iron. Harsh voices. Getting closer. Rough hands seized his hair, dragging him to his feet. Turned him round. Slammed him against the wall, crushing his face into the crumbling stucco. Something hit him across the back. And again behind the knees. Heaven turned to hell.

* * *

It was mid-morning when they arrived home: 11 Blakeway Drive, Wandsworth, London, looked somehow diminished since Pru had last seen it; complacent in its comfortable, predictable, English normality.

Pru got Molly into bed with a cup of tea and went straight to her office to switch on the computer. Without even checking her emails, she typed 'Ben Coder' into the Google search box and, within a second, a page of references appeared on the screen. There was even a picture of him receiving an award from something called the Feinberg Foundation. *'This prize has been awarded*

345

annually since 1982 to individual lawyers, law firms or corporations who put their resources and legal skills to work for the public good. Ben Coder, of Coder and Silverman, has rendered an extraordinary public service in representing so many claimants, with his vigorous advocacy and professionalism.'

There was Ben, smiling on her screen, half proud, half embarrassed, receiving what seemed to be an engraved glass goblet from a distinguished-looking judge with white hair and tinted spectacles.

Pulling herself together, Pru found his firm's contact details in Manhattan and scribbled down the phone number. If she could talk to a colleague of his, she could ask their advice. They were lawyers after all. They'd know what to do. There was no point in calling now, though. New York was asleep. She had six hours to wait.

*   *   *

'That's enough!'

The onslaught stopped. Footsteps retreated.

Ben sank down on the bench and shook his head, trying to clear it. Everything had happened so fast, he could almost have thought it part of his dreams had it not been for the taste of blood in his mouth where he had bitten his own tongue, and now the beginning of a dull ache across his shoulders, legs and arms.

His saviour sat down beside him.

'They will be punished for that,' he said. 'Way out of order.'

'Who are you?'

'Donald Halligan, Ambassador's office. You

OK?'

'Grateful you stopped by. Ben Coder.'

They shook hands.

'That wasn't fun.'

'Retribution apparently. Something you did to a colleague of theirs. A pilot.'

'A bit over the top. I only decked him.'

'And humiliated him. You took his helicopter.'

Ben rubbed the back of his ribcage. His kidneys hurt. Bastards. He studied his new ally. Early-thirties at most. Round-eyed, open face; the kind of face that nobody had really lived in yet. Pale brown hair, parted at the side; lightweight, stone-coloured business suit; neat brown slip-on shoes. Company man.

'I need the use of a phone.'

'I can do better than that.'

'How?'

'You're out of here.'

'What?'

'Seems you've built up a few brownie points.'

'What's going on? Who's arranged this?'

'Sorry, pal. Not authorised to answer questions. Let's just say a deal has been done. Your jacket and bag are in my car outside. We'll swing by the Continental for the rest of your gear on the way to the airport.'

'I'm leaving town, am I?'

'One-way ticket home, buddy. You got off lightly.'

'I have to make a couple of calls.'

'You want to know about your friend and her daughter.' It was a statement, not a question.

'Yes.'

'They've gone back to the UK.'

347

'Really?' His sprits rose and fell at the same time. 'The daughter's OK?'

'Yup. Dengue fever. On the mend.'

'Thank Christ. Her mother had me convinced it was heart failure.'

'That's women for you. Always overreacting. Let's go.'

'She wasn't . . .' he stopped. There was no point trying to explain. It didn't matter what this greenhorn thought anyway. 'Lead on, Donald.'

*   *   *

In front of the departure board at Ho Chi Minh airport, Halligan dropped Ben's holdall and held out a formal hand in farewell.

'It's about a four-hour wait for the New York flight. Strictly speaking, I should wait with you. See you off the premises. But you don't want that and neither do I.'

'Don't worry, Donald. I'm not going to go AWOL.'

Halligan looked at him earnestly. 'We're both in the shit if you do. You're probably being watched in any case.'

'Yes. I assume that. Goodbye, and thank you for liberating me.'

'No problem. Anything I can get you before you go through?'

'No, thanks. I'm fine.'

'I'll get going then. What more can I say? Have a good trip.'

He loped off. Just before the exit, he stopped and looked back.

Ben lifted a reassuring hand, picked up his

348

holdall and began to walk in the direction of the international departures sign. Satisfied, Halligan disappeared through the automatic glass doors and into the crowd outside.

So this was it. For so long, Vietnam and its destiny had been woven into Ben's life and now it was goodbye. Thirty years ago he'd arrived to fight for what had seemed a simple enough cause—to save a country from a malign and dangerous regime. A matter of weeks later it had become a personal struggle to work out what was right and what was wrong. He'd seen so much blood spilled into this country's warm red earth. Was any cause worth such destruction? Such moral degeneration? Whatever the answer, he had decided, just asking the question involved too high a price. A price that was paid then—and was still being paid now—by the Vietnamese, and by the thousands of young Americans who were sent to fight alongside them and against them, and who would carry their own private, unshareable memories, their own private scars, guilt, justifications and denials, with them to the grave. The destiny of a whole generation either stopped dead in its tracks or permanently blighted.

Ben had found comfort and redemption in coming back, in trying to mitigate just some of the damage done. But now it was over. Ended. He ought to feel bereft. Why didn't he? Instead, his heart felt light and free. It struck him like a thunderbolt. He had served his time and paid his price. There was nothing he needed to prove to himself any more. He could still keep tabs on the charity from back home in New York. He'd done all the spadework. For perhaps the first time in his life he was master of his own destiny instead of just

349

pretending to be. He almost laughed out loud. And it was all due to Pru.

He wondered what emotions she had been going through, walking across this very concourse with her daughter. Had they left of their own accord or had they been expelled? Had she thought about him? Had she tried to find out what had happened to him? Or had concern for her daughter eclipsed all thoughts of the profound rapport they'd experienced in their few short days together?

He ran his eye down the list of destinations on the departure board. He didn't have to go straight back to New York. He'd always wanted to go to Australia. Sydney was such a beautiful city. Or some R & R in somewhere like Taipei could be just what he needed. Then again, he'd always promised himself a good long visit to Europe. Paris, Berlin, Vienna, London . . . There'd be a special reason to visit London now. Choices, choices . . .

*   *   *

Molly put the phone down, eased herself off the sofa and shuffled to the foot of the stairs in her dressing gown. 'Mum?'

'Yes?' Pru stepped out of the bath and wrapped herself in a towel. 'What is it?'

'That was Dad. He's coming over.'

'Now?'

'Yes. He said he's been so worried about me and he wants to come and give me a hug. To see for himself that I'm really OK.'

'Good old Dad.' Pru winced. That had sounded sarcastic, but Molly didn't seem to have noticed.

350

'I'll put the kettle on for some coffee, shall I, Mum? Have we got any biscuits?'

'If we have, they'll be stale ones. I'll have to hit the supermarket later.'

Revelling in the luxury of clean, fresh clothes and tamed, shampooed hair, Pru entered the living room ten minutes later to find David had already arrived and was perched next to Molly on the sofa, holding both her hands in his.

'I can't describe the sheer agony of knowing my Princess, the light of my life, was so ill on the other side of the world and being totally powerless to do anything. I couldn't even get on a plane. It was almost worse than the time you had your heart surgery.' Hearing the door open, he looked up. 'Oh, Pru. Hi.'

'Hello, David. Coffee?'

'Please. So, where's my present from Vietnam then?'

'I think getting your daughter back in one piece is probably as good as it gets.'

'Oh, absolutely, of course. Just joking.'

'And how are the twins?' asked Pru.

'Little Jessica . . . she's such a little fighter. She's like you were, Moll. She's really hanging on in there.'

'You must be so relieved,' Pru said sympathetically.

'We're not out of the woods yet, though. We're tied to Intensive Care for another four weeks at least. But, yes, the doctors are really optimistic.'

'Can I come and see them soon?' Molly chipped in.

'As soon as you've got your strength back! I can't wait for you to see them, Moll.'

'So the girl is Jessica. What's my new little brother called?'

'Well, Lucy and I are still arguing. She wants Ethan because it's unusual and because no one can abbreviate it. I think it sounds like a tranquilliser. I want something more traditional. Like Christopher James.'

'People will abbreviate anything. He'll be called Eeth,' laughed Molly. 'I hope you win the argument, Dad!'

'There is one thing I need to tell you both.'

Whatever it was, it was going to be hard to swallow. It was in the tone of his voice.

'Don't tell me,' Pru put his mug of coffee on the table in front of him, 'you want to sell this house.'

'Exactly. I wanted to give you a bit more time. Wait for Molly to get off to Uni and all that. But now with the twins to take into consideration, Lucy's flat just isn't big enough.'

'OK, well, we'll have to get it valued and put it on the market then. We'll get Christmas over with, and then I'll get myself on a few estate agents' lists.'

'I'll help you, Mum. We're staying in London, though, right?'

'It's a choice, I suppose. A smaller place around here, or somewhere about the same size as this but quite a bit further out. Thames Ditton maybe. Or Kingston-on-Thames. We'll have to think about it.'

'One bit of luck, though,' David interjected, then paused, presumably hoping for some encouragement, 'we can save ourselves a lot of hassle. This guy I took on at Fraser's last year— Pete Buckley—he's got a real flair for marketing, I'm grooming him for great things. Anyway, he's

352

just had his third child and Wandsworth is really handy for . . .'

'. . . and he wants to buy our house.'

'He does, yes. He just loves it. He's so enthusiastic. You'll really like him.'

'You showed him round while I was away?'

'I had to. I knew you wouldn't mind, Pru. He wants to move in as soon as possible. Before Christmas. He says it's just ideal for his purposes.'

'Well, that's terrific, David. And now I'll tell you what's ideal for *my* purposes. And that is that your mate Pete can bloody well wait until after Christmas! After New Year in fact. I cannot and I will not be pushed out of here in four weeks flat. I want one last Christmas at Blakeway Drive with Jack and Molly. After that, as I said, I shall put myself on some estate agents' books and I shall look around. And when I find somewhere I like the look of, for the right price, then—and only then—I shall arrange to move out of this house. I do hope that is clear, David.'

Good speech. You're learning.

'That's all right, isn't it, Dad?' Molly had always hated even the mildest of disagreements between her parents.

'Well, it would be for me, but it's Lucy, you see. She'll need more space, being at home all day with twins. And we'll probably need a nanny. Perhaps you could rent somewhere. You know, *pro tem*. I would help you with the rent, of course.'

'David, it is out of the question. End of subject. Now I'll leave you two to chat. I've got some urgent calls to make. I'll be in my office, Moll, if you need me.'

The screensaver gave way to Ben's face; still there, smiling his quiet, private-joke kind of smile. Pru caught herself smiling back. She kept his picture on the screen while her emails downloaded. There were at least sixty of them, so it took a minute or two. Finally she opened the list. One name jumped out at her. Kenny McKinnon. Ignoring the rest, she opened it. He hadn't wasted any words.

```
Ben    out    of    jail.    Deported.
Apparently   none   the   worse   for
wear.
   Thought you'd want to know.
Kenny
```

Trying to keep calm, she dialled Ben's mobile number. Surely he'd answer now. The recorded voice answered again. She hung up. He must have left the phone behind in Vietnam, already on a plane back to New York.

*   *   *

'Hello, Coder and Silverman. Can I help you?'

'Could I speak to . . .' her voice wobbled. She cleared her throat '. . . to Ben Coder please?'

'I'm afraid he isn't here right now. Can I put you through to his partner, Robert Silverman?'

'Oh. Yes, please. Thank you.'

'Rob Silverman. What can I do for you?'

'My name is Prudence Taylor. I'm calling from London, looking for Ben Coder. Do you know where he is?'

'Ben is semi-retired now, Ms Taylor. Is this a professional or a private enquiry?'

'It's private. I met him in Vietnam and then lost track of him.'

'Well, Vietnam is Ben's spiritual home now. That's where he'll be if he's not in New York.'

She wanted to wail, No, he isn't. He's been deported. And it's my fault. But it wasn't her story to tell. Instead she asked, 'If he arrived back in New York, would he contact you?'

'Not necessarily. He doesn't come into the office so often now. Shame, I miss him. As do a lot of people.'

Pru liked his voice. It sounded kind; intelligent.

'Would he contact his daughter?' she enquired.

'I really can't say. I don't know so much about his private life this last couple of years.'

'Do you have a number for Kathy?'

'I'm sorry, I don't.'

'All right. Well, thank you, Mr Silverman. Oh, one favour, please? Ben doesn't know my London address. Can I leave it with you in case he contacts you before me?'

'By all means, Ms Taylor. And if you do find him, give him my very best, won't you?'

*   *   *

Pru called his picture up on the screen again. She couldn't bring herself to shut down her computer yet.

'Where are you, Ben?'

If he cares for you, he'll find you. You shouldn't be running after him. Where's your pride?

Don't be so ridiculous. He went to jail because

355

of me. He's lost the charity he cared about because of me. And his whole lifestyle. Most of his life revolved around Vietnam, and now that's gone. I should at least let him know how sorry I am. And how deeply grateful. He saved Molly's life.

He's probably far too busy recovering from it all to want to start tracking you down.

You're wrong. He cared. We had feelings for each other that neither of us had experienced before. I'm sure of that.

Lucky you didn't sleep with him, that's all I can say. Just put it all down to experience and move on.

I can't move on without him. I can stay in the same place. Frozen. Paralysed. But I can't move on. I don't want to either.

What romantic nonsense!

'Are you talking to yourself?' Molly's head appeared round the door. 'Dad's gone. Said to say goodbye to you.' As she so often used to do, she came up behind Pru's chair and started plaiting her hair. 'Hey, is that Ben?'

'I'm trying to find an address or a number for him. He's been deported.'

'Really? So he's out of jail. Brilliant!' Molly studied his picture on the screen. 'He's quite sexy, isn't he? For an older guy.'

'Well, I think so.' Pru smiled up at her daughter.

Molly looked thoughtful. 'We owe him big-time, don't we? Quang and the other families getting their compensation, and Sinh getting his comeuppance . . . And saving my life, of course.'

'He's amazing,' agreed Pru. 'He's not like anyone I've ever met before. It took such courage to fly that helicopter. I could see the enormous effort it cost him. Then to be arrested as a criminal

356

and thrown out of the country when in fact he's been so ... heroic. It's crazy.'

'So you are trying to find him, to thank him?'

'Yes, of course.'

'And?'

'What do you mean, "and"?'

'Well, there's more to it than that, isn't there?'

'Well, I did get very fond of him. I'd hate to lose touch.'

'How fond of him?'

Pru fidgeted.

'I'm just very glad I got to know him. And I wouldn't have, if it hadn't been for that mad one-girl crusade of yours. As nerve-racking as those few days in Vietnam were, I can't regret any of it.'

'So are you in love with him?'

'Oh, I don't know. I think about him all the time. I have dreams about him at night ...'

'Sounds like you are then. Why don't you just admit it?.'

'Because I might not see him again.'

'Does he feel the same way about you?'

'I'm pretty sure he does. Or did, anyway.'

'What about Dad? You loved him once.'

'Yes, I loved your dad, of course I did. In some ways I always will. He's been part of my life for more than twenty years. We went through so much together. And yet, this—Ben and me—it's a feeling I didn't know existed. It's as if we both vibrate at exactly the same frequency. As if we were formed from the same clay.' She laughed. 'I sound like a love-struck teenager, don't I?'

'I don't know how you can be made from the same clay when you're from Europe and he's from America, thousands of miles away.'

357

'I just feel I've found the perfect person for me. That's all. It's hard to describe.'

'And what's he like in bed?'

'Molly!'

'You're going pink.'

Really! Is this a suitable conversation to be having with your teenage daughter?

'We didn't get that far.'

'It can't be really serious then.'

'It felt very serious. To both of us, I know that.' Pru gazed at his face on the screen. 'I don't know what to do.'

'What if you never saw him again?'

'I think the rest of my life would be a bit . . . numb.'

'We'd better find him then.'

'I think I'll have to wait a while. Get Christmas over with, and moving house. And then I'll go to New York to see if I can find him.'

'New York's a big city though, Mum.'

'I know. But at least I'll know I tried. I'll never forgive myself if I don't give it my best shot.'

*　　*　　*

Christmas was coming; the first Christmas Pru could ever remember not looking forward to. A family Christmas had always been symbolic in a way, an affirmation that whatever problems there were with the world in general, at least the family was together; they loved each other, would look after each other, and that was what mattered more than anything else.

This year, though, with David gone and Jack and Molly well and truly setting off in their own

358

directions in life, it seemed so much less significant. She felt almost paralysed. It was hard to muster any enthusiasm for it. This time last year she had been hectically busy masterminding the festivities as she had done for nearly twenty years: pinning up decorations, stringing up Christmas cards all over the kitchen units, planning Christmas dinner.

And you used to feel put upon because they all just let you do it; took it for granted that the turkey would be on the table with six choices of vegetable, the candles, the crackers, the holly, the presents you took hours wrapping, the stockings you stayed up until 2 or 3 a.m. to fill on Christmas Eve. Sometimes they forgot to buy you a present at all—or didn't think you'd mind waiting until the New Year. Now you say you're going to miss all that? Nothing's right for you, is it!

'I just can't face it somehow this year. All the fun and spontaneity has gone out of it.'

You're still pining for that American, aren't you?

'Yes, I suppose I am. I'm trying not to.'

It wouldn't work anyway. What about the practicalities. Where would you live?

'We could alternate between London and New York. And we could go off on long trips together. We've both come to a stage in our lives where we're fairly unencumbered by responsibilities. We'd be great travelling companions—we've found that out already.'

Well, no use wasting energy yearning for what might have been. You've got Christmas to think about. Jack comes home tomorrow. And you've got to start looking for somewhere else to live as well.

She had at least bought all her Christmas

359

presents now: some aromatherapy soaps for her mother—not that she'd have a clue who had given them to her, poor dear; hair straighteners for Molly, who had been dropping heavy hints for days; a digital camera for Jack, and some little bits and pieces for stocking fillers. They still gave each other stockings at Christmas, although this was likely to be the last time. The natural cut-off point for that would come when they all moved out of Blakeway Drive and she found herself a flat.

On Christmas Eve, Pru and Stella hit the Kings Road and finished their last minute shopping in one hour flat before repairing to a restaurant for a goat's cheese salad and three glasses of champagne each. They giggled together like old times and, admittedly due in large part to the champagne, Pru felt her spirits rise for the first time since her return from Vietnam. Back at home, one look at the living room and they took a sobering nose-dive again.

Since her convalescence. Molly had staked a permanent claim to the sofa. Jack was sprawled in the armchair. There were mugs and sticky glasses on every available surface; two large plates contained half-eaten slices of cold pizza and take-away sandwiches.

'Molly—you may have been ill, but there's no excuse to turn into a slob. You're a lot better now. You might at least put things in the dishwasher and put the dirty pans in soak. Same goes for you, Jack. Show some bloody consideration, both of you.'

'Sorry, Mum,' they mumbled in chorus, their eyes not leaving the television screen. Pru stalked across the room, switched it off and stood in front of it.

'You can both go and get yourselves a bit of fresh air and exercise and collect the Christmas tree I ordered from the greengrocer. Then you can help me decorate it. Jack, I'll need you to fetch me down the box of decorations from the cupboard in your room.'

She watched the two of them walking down the front path to the gate; two tall, self-possessed young adults—to the outside eye at any rate.

A commotion at the front door half an hour later brought her out of the kitchen. Jack and Molly were manhandling an enormous Christmas tree through into the hall.

'That's not the tree I chose!'

'No. Yours was too small,' replied Molly.

'We thought because this is our last Christmas in this house we should make it something to remember,' enthused Jack.

'So we've got a lovely great big one,' continued Molly. 'The man said we could have it half-price, seeing as it is Christmas Eve and most people have bought theirs now.'

'No one's got a living room big enough, more like it,' laughed Pru. 'It wouldn't be out of place in Trafalgar Square. It's got to be twelve foot at least.'

They did have to cut a few inches off the top with secateurs, but after a bit of manoeuvring it stood proudly dominating the room from the corner near the television.

'All we've got to do now is decorate it,' said Pru as the three of them stood back to admire it.

'Leave that to us, Mum,' said Jack. 'Molly and I are going to do it. I'll make you a cup of tea and you can get on with the cooking and stuff.'

361

'I think we should open a bottle of wine,' said Pru. 'Christmas starts here.'

There was the usual palaver disentangling the Christmas lights that had been wound up so carefully last January but had been tied into knots by some malevolent gremlin when no one was looking, breaking some of the bulbs in the process. Then Pru left them to unpack the tinsel and baubles while she took her glass of wine into the kitchen to get to grips with tomorrow's vegetables. This last five years she'd missed her mother on Christmas Eve. Mum was too ill to leave the home now, but it wasn't the same without her, despite her constant criticisms. And this year, no David either. She'd bought a chicken. A turkey would be too big for the three of them, even taking Jack's appetite into account. How flat it all seemed. But the children were doing their best. She must keep her end up for them. It would be strange for them too.

There was a ring on the doorbell. Molly got to the door first.

'Hi, Dad. Happy Christmas!' She flung her arms round his neck, lifting both feet off the ground and nearly overbalancing him.

'Hey. Steady. I'm not as young as I was and you're a lot bigger!'

She smacked him playfully on the arm.

'Come and see the amazing tree me and Jack bought.' She pulled David into the living room by the hand. Jack turned to face him, a length of purple tinsel draped round his head.

'Hello, Dad.'

Pru realised this was the first time Jack and his father had actually seen each other since the

362

break-up.

'Hello, Jack. Great tree. Literally.' They hugged each other stiffly. 'University OK?'

'Yep. Great, thanks.' Remembering the tinsel, Jack unwound it from round his ears and put it back in the box.

'Got a girlfriend yet?'

'*A* girlfriend?' chipped in Molly 'He's got three. He told me.'

'Hello, Pru. Happy Christmas.' They kissed each other chastely on the cheek.

'Do you want a glass of wine?'

'Better not, thanks, I've got to get back to Lucy and the babies. Two of them are a bit of a handful. And we've only just got Jessica back from the hospital.'

'Christmas dinner at home tomorrow, is it?'

'No, we're going over to her parents' in Reigate. Christmas with the in-laws.'

'Great,' said Pru weakly.

'So I was wondering,' David turned to Molly. He could relax more when talking to her. 'Molly and Jack, do you fancy popping over for a drink at ours? I've got your presents to give you both, and you could see the twins.'

Jack glanced anxiously at Pru. 'We'd better not, Dad. We've got to finish the tree.'

'Listen, you go,' said Pru lightly. 'I'll finish it. I haven't got much else to do, to be honest.'

'Are you sure you don't mind, Mum?' asked Molly.

'Absolutely not. I'll enjoy the peace. See you later.'

They kissed her, the door closed behind them, she heard David's car doors slam outside and then there was silence. She put a Christmas Carol CD on. Usually she enjoyed singing along to 'Once in Royal David's City', 'O, Come All Ye Faithful' and 'Most Highly Favoured Lady'. Now, she couldn't quite get herself in the mood.

She poured herself another glass of wine and looked at the tree. Where was the fairy? For the last fifteen years at least, the same fairy had graced the top of the tree each year. Going back to her own childhood, it had always been a special moment when the fairy came out of her cardboard box where she'd been cushioned reverently in tissue paper for eleven and a half months, waiting to take her rightful short-lived place of honour again. Pru picked up the old shoe box, still bearing Molly's childish writing on the side in red felt pen: 'chritmas fiary'.

She went to get the step ladder from behind the kitchen door. Then, reverently, she opened the box and took out the fairy. She still looked almost as good as new with her china face, white feather wings and stiffened gossamer dress. Her wand had been broken a few years ago and Pru and Molly had constructed a new one, cutting out a cardboard star, covering it with tin foil and gluing it on to a drinking straw. Pru tweaked her dress back into shape, teased the long golden hair and blew gently on the feathers of her wings to smooth out the gaps.

'Looks like it's just you and me tonight, kid,' she told her. 'Happy Christmas.'

Holding her gently, she climbed the ladder.

The doorbell rang again.

Great piece of timing. Probably carol singers. Patiently, she climbed back down, set the fairy on

364

the coffee table and went to the door.

The figure on the doorstep looked familiar. She peered at the visitor, her eyes adjusting to the dark. She was imagining things now.

'Hello Pru.'

No, the voice was unmistakable.

'Ben!'

'Aren't you going to invite me in?'

'Ben. Oh, Ben.'

And then they were in each other's arms.

*   *   *

'Have you made some coffee?'

Jack looked up as his sister slouched into the kitchen.

'And Happy Christmas to you too, dear sis.'

'Happy Christmas, Jack.' She sat down at the table. 'Was your Christmas stocking on the end of your bed last night?'

'No, it wasn't. They're still by the Christmas tree with our presents.'

'Unlike Mum. She must have forgotten.'

'She didn't finish doing the tree either. In fact, it doesn't look as though she did anything at all last night after we went out.'

'Maybe she got drunk. She must have finished all that wine. And she'd been drinking at lunchtime too.'

'Have you seen her yet this morning?'

'Nope.'

'Maybe she's gone out. Maybe she forgot something she needed for Christmas dinner.'

'No, the chain's still on the door.'

'She's usually up by now. 'Specially on Christmas

Day. I think I'd better go and see if she's all right.'

'Happy Christmas, kids.' Pru had appeared in the doorway, in her lilac silk dressing gown, her hair tousled round her face.

'Oh, there you are,' said Molly. 'We were worried about you. You've overslept.'

'Have I?' She glanced at the digital clock on the cooker. 'Oh, yes, I suppose I have.'

She looked flushed. And ten years younger. Aware of her children's eyes fixed curiously on her, she crossed to the fridge, took out a bottle of milk and decanted some into the little floral jug she hardly ever used. Opening a new carton of orange juice, she poured some into two large glasses. Behind her back, Jack and Molly exchanged quizzical glances.

'Is this coffee fresh?'

'Yes, just made it,' said Jack.

'Great.' She took two china mugs from the cupboard and poured some coffee into each one. Then, choosing a lacy cloth from the linen drawer, she arranged everything on a tray, picked it up and walked back towards the kitchen door.

At the doorway she turned and beamed at them radiantly.

'See you later.'

'Erm . . . Mum?' Jack called after her.

'Yes?' Holding the laden tray carefully, Pru reversed a couple of steps and looked back at them enquiringly.

'Have we got a visitor?'

'Yes, we have. A friend of mine called unexpectedly last night while you were out.'

'Someone we know?'

'*I* know who it is,' shouted Molly. 'I know exactly

366

who it is. I can tell by your face. It's . . .'

'How do you do?' said a deep, warm American voice.

Pru was joined in the doorway by a tall, handsome man in a white towelling robe.

Jack and Molly gaped, stumped for anything to say.

Smiling at them both, the man put his arm round their mother; a picture of easy, effortless happiness.

Recovering from her astonishment, Molly got to her feet, ran across to Ben and hugged him violently.

She turned back to her brother excitedly. 'Jack, this is the man who saved my life!'

'Mine too,' said Pru.